THEY WERE IN the middle of the lunch rush—Carlin behind the counter and Kat making the rounds with a pitcher of tea in one hand and a carafe of coffee in the other, because she could handle pouring on the go better than Carlin could—when the cowboy walked in. Carlin couldn't help but notice him. What warm-blooded woman wouldn't? He was tall and muscular, and he moved with an iron confidence that said he knew his strength and hadn't met much that could stop him. She had to call him handsome, though he wasn't, not really. His face wasn't perfect and sculpted, it was on the rough and hard side, but she was going on her reaction to him rather than what her eyes saw. She went warm and breathless, and looked away because staring at him was abruptly too much, too dangerous in a way she sensed but couldn't quite grasp, at least not consciously. He was every inch the heartbreaker cowboy Kat had warned her away from—and damn if he didn't charge the air when he walked into the place.

The Men from Battle Ridge

Running Wild

A Novel

LINDA HOWARD
and
LINDA JONES

BALLANTINE BOOKS • NEW YORK

Running Wild is a work of fiction. Names, characters, places, and incidents are the products of the authors' imagination or are used fictitiously. Any resemblance to actual events, locales, or persons, living or dead, is entirely coincidental.

A Ballantine Books Mass Market Original

Published in the United States by Ballantine Books, an imprint of The Random House Publishing Group, a division of Random House, Inc., New York.

BALLANTINE and colophon are registered trademarks of Random House, Inc.

This book contains an excerpt from the forthcoming book *Shadow Woman* by Linda Howard. This excerpt has been set for this edition only and may not reflect the final content of the forthcoming edition.

ISBN 978-0-345-52078-4
eBook ISBN 978-0-345-52079-1

Cover design: Lynn Andreozzi
Cover photographs: © Audrey Hall (man), © George Kerrigan (face)

Printed in the United States of America

www.ballantinebooks.com

9 8 7 6 5

Ballantine mass market edition: December 2012

On Thursday, April 21, 2011,
we lost our best friend Beverly Beaver,
who wrote as Beverly Barton.
There hasn't been a day since
that we haven't thought about her,
heard her voice, her laughter,
and realized anew that,
though we have so many memories,
there will never be enough of them.
So this one's for you, Beverly.
Love you, miss you.
Make them all behave, up there in Heaven,
and mind their manners.

Running Wild

Prologue

LIBBY THOMPSON CROSSED her plump arms and tried to look stern, which wasn't easy considering the undeniable sadness she felt. "Don't give me that look, A.Z. Decker. Those puppy-dog eyes haven't worked on me since you were nine years old." Not that he'd had puppy-dog eyes even back then, and he certainly didn't now, but she'd learned a long time ago that the trick to handling him was to never let it show how blasted intimidating he was when he looked pissed and flinty-eyed, the way he did now.

Zeke glanced down and to the side, where Libby's bags sat. They were a hodgepodge of hand-me-downs, three different makers, three different colors: red, brown, and black. The bags were all stuffed so full they bulged and threatened to split their zippers wide open. Everything she owned was in those bags.

"I gave you two weeks' notice," she said in her best no-nonsense tone, because if she gave an inch, in no time flat he'd have her talked into staying. She couldn't let her guard down, not even for a minute. The trick was to remember that he looked at problems as things he could solve if he just didn't give up, which was great if he was working on your behalf, and not so great if

you were on the other side of all that bullheaded determination.

"I tried to find a replacement," Zeke growled, glaring
at her accusingly, as if his failure was her fault.

"Really?" She snorted. "You put an ad in the *Battle
Ridge Weekly*." That was when she'd realized he hadn't
taken her seriously when she'd told him she was leaving,
otherwise he'd have placed multiple ads in the news-
papers in larger towns. As much as she loved him, that
had really ticked her off. If he thought he could bulldoze
her the way he did everyone else, then he was about to
get his perception of the world rearranged.

"Two more weeks," he bargained.

She blew out a breath of frustration. In her fifty-seven
years, she'd faced down a lot, and never let life get her
down even when she was widowed at a young age and
left with a baby she needed to support. But from the time
she'd first come to work here at the Decker ranch, she'd
needed every bit of ability she possessed to stay ahead of
Zeke. As a toddler he'd been a chubby, charming hellion;
as a gap-toothed little boy he'd been a skinny, charming
hellion; and since his teenage years he'd been a heartbreaker, with a whole lot of hard-ass thrown into the
mix. He always got his way, but this time she simply
couldn't let that happen.

She'd been working at this ranch house for thirty-odd
years, at first part-time and later, after Zeke's mother re-
married and moved to Arizona, full-time. She and Jenny
had had their own rooms here, just off the kitchen. She
knew this house as if it were her own, knew Zeke as if
she'd given birth to him. His sisters had become a big
part of her life, too, but they were both older, and Libby
hadn't played as large a part in their lives as she had in
Zeke's. For more than thirty years she'd cooked, she'd
cleaned, and she'd blessed him out when he needed it.

She'd mothered him, mothered the ranch hands, and spoiled him rotten. And she was on her way out the door.

She sighed, and her gaze softened a little. "Zeke, I hate to leave you in the lurch, you know I do, but I promised Jenny I'd be there this coming weekend. She's at her wit's end, with Tim out of town on business more often than not and those three kids running her ragged, and another one on the way. She's my daughter, and she needs me."

"I need you," he growled, then his jaw hardened as he finally faced the reality, once and for all, that she was leaving. "Okay. Damn it—okay. I'll get by."

"I know you will." Libby stepped toward him, patted him on one cheek while she went up on her toes and kissed him on the other. She backed away, and was all business once again. "I think Spencer knows his way around the kitchen; he'll do until you find a replacement. I left a couple of cookbooks on the kitchen table. The recipe for my beef stew is in the one with the green cover." He loved her beef stew, always had. She felt more than a little sad that she might never make it for him again, but at least the recipe was there so *someone* could.

"Thanks."

He didn't sound very grateful; he still sounded pissed as hell. Well, he could just stay pissed, because she'd made up her mind. Ignoring his sour mood, she continued, "I filled the freezer with stew, a pan of lasagna, and corn bread. There's a big pot of chicken and dumplings in the refrigerator for tonight. Once that's all gone, you can either find another housekeeper or you can get your ass busy finding another wife. That's what you really need."

That was a safe gambit, because if there was one subject Zeke avoided, it was marriage. He'd tried it once, it hadn't worked. By his way of thinking, he'd have to be nuts to put himself through the torture of trying again. He wasn't a monk, by any means, and if he put himself

out to find another wife he'd find himself standing in
front of a preacher in no time; he definitely wasn't hard
on the eyes, with those broad shoulders, green eyes, and
that thick, light brown hair. The right woman would rise
to the challenge of meeting him halfway—if he were
looking for a wife, which he wasn't. Why would he,
when he'd been able to find sex whenever he wanted and
Libby was here on the home front taking care of all
things domestic? All he wanted now was a cook and a
housekeeper, and that was a horse of a different color.

Not many women would be happy on a ranch in the
Middle Of Nowhere, Wyoming. The nearest town, Battle Ridge, was an hour's drive away and was damn near
a ghost town these days, anyway. Well, not really; there
were still stores, but ten years ago over two thousand
people had lived there, and now there was only about
half that many.

And the bus only came through twice a week. Libby
was about to get on it.

"Well come on, damn it," he said, reaching for the
bulging red bag. "It's time to get you to town. You're
right, we'll find a way to get by until I hire someone to
replace you. No one's going to starve, and I can damn
well do my own laundry." He snatched up the brown
bag, too, leaving the black one, the smallest, for Libby.

She couldn't help it. Her voice softened some when
she said, "You know, you could call your mother . . ."

"No," Zeke said sharply. Well, she'd known that was
a nonstarter. He'd love a visit from his mother, but if she
came her husband—Larry—would tag along. Zeke
didn't begrudge his mother happiness, but he and Larry
had never seen eye to eye. A few days were about all he
could stomach; no way would he ask them to move in
for a stay that could turn into weeks.

"One of your sisters, then."

"No." This particular *no* wasn't as harsh as the first one

had been. "They've both got families, kids, jobs. Neither of them could take that much time away to stay here."

"Kat might—"

Zeke snorted. "She's got a business of her own to run. Why would she leave it to work here?"

"She could still cook some stuff for you to freeze, for emergencies. All you have to do is unbend enough to ask her." Kat was a damn good cook, which was why she did so well with her little restaurant in Battle Ridge; she and Zeke were first cousins, so she'd help if she could, though her schedule was so crowded there was no way he could rely on her help to keep the hands fed full-time.

Libby opened the front door for Zeke, since his hands were full, and he stepped onto the porch. Half a dozen hands were waiting by the truck, waiting to say good-bye to the woman who had become a second mother to many of them. For a couple, she was the first real caring mother they'd ever known. There wasn't a smile to be seen on any of those weather-beaten faces.

"Like I said, we'll get by." He shot a narrow-eyed look at Spencer, who shifted his feet and looked both guilty and confused, because he didn't know what he'd done to earn the boss's scowl. "Though we'll be lucky if Spencer doesn't give us all food poisoning."

"Things will work out. They always do," Libby said optimistically. She patted her hair, making sure all was in place, then rose on tiptoe to kiss his cheek again. "I'll be back for a visit every now and then," she said, going down the steps to say good-bye to the ranch hands.

ZEKE WASN'T AS optimistic as Libby. As he drove her into town he tried not to growl his answers to her conversational chatter, tried to be happy for her, but—*hell!*

He'd miss her. He couldn't remember a time when she hadn't been here. She was a spark plug of a woman, short and wide, with the kind of spirit that drew other people to her. When other women were settling into their senior years, Libby was dyeing her hair a different color every other week—it was flaming red right now—and bossing everyone around, making plans to take her grandchildren on a hot-air balloon ride, and generally steamrolling through life. At the same time, she had the kindest heart he'd ever seen.

Damn it. He couldn't replace Libby. Someone else might do her job, but no one could replace her.

You'd think with the economy as tough as it was, hiring someone would be easy, but folks were leaving instead of digging in their heels and fighting to keep their lives intact. Battle Ridge was full of empty houses, most of them with "For Rent" or "For Sale" signs on them, and not a sign of any renters, much less actual buyers. Businesses were closing, families were pulling up stakes and heading south, where the brutal winters didn't hammer at you, where you might still be unemployed, but at least you wouldn't be freezing.

He'd try. So far he hadn't really put his mind to it, because up until the last minute he'd thought Libby would back out of her plans and stay. It galled him to think he might not succeed, but he was enough of a realist to know that right now, the deck was stacked against him.

Getting a woman to come out to the middle of nowhere for a lot of hard work and nominal pay—he wasn't a miser, but no one was going to get rich working at the Decker ranch—wasn't as easy as she seemed to think it would be. Things didn't always work out. When God closed a door He didn't necessarily open a convenient window. No, Zeke figured he was pretty much fucked.

CARLIN WALKED QUICKLY to her desk, a frown on her face, her heart beating too hard. *Be rational.* She told herself that over and over, trying to reassure herself. She was just being paranoid; her imagination working overtime. There were thousands, maybe hundreds of thousands, of Toyotas that particular shade of blue in the state of Texas. Just because one had *appeared* to follow her from her apartment to work, and just because the driver—who she'd barely been able to see when she'd checked her rearview mirror—had dark hair, that didn't mean Brad had tracked her down. No way.

The frighteningly familiar vehicle had kept going when she'd turned into the building's parking garage. No one had followed her. She was perfectly safe here. Damn it, she had to stop letting that psycho get into her head! Hadn't he already done enough?

She'd completely uprooted her life because of him. She'd quit her job, moved to Dallas—which was more than a four-hour drive from the Houston suburb where she'd lived for almost a year—and left her worries behind . . . she hoped. She'd been working here for three months, and Brad hadn't so much as called. He sure as hell hadn't shown up at her apartment time and again without warning, the way he had before she'd moved.

No way did he know where she lived or where she worked. She kept telling herself that. *No way.*

She'd taken precautions when she'd moved, paying all her outstanding bills before leaving town and not telling anyone where she was going, not even her coworkers at the kitchen supply company where she'd been in charge of billing. Her mail was being forwarded to a post office box on the other side of Dallas, rather than to her new apartment. She'd left in the middle of the night—literally—taking only what she could fit in her car. She wouldn't say that Brad couldn't possibly find her, but she'd been very careful and she'd hoped—and prayed—that once she was gone he'd turn his attention elsewhere. She felt a little guilty about that, because what woman deserved Brad?

She wouldn't wish him on her worst enemy . . . well, maybe she would, if she had a worst enemy, but right off the bat she couldn't think of anyone she disliked that much.

If anyone had listened to her, if even one cop had been on her side, she might still be working in Houston. She had been so naive! She'd been sure that once she filed a complaint, the authorities would take care of Brad. But when a cop decides to stalk a woman and he knows how to cover his tracks, when everyone is so quick to take his word over hers, there's not much to be done except start over, which was what she'd done.

From the window she saw a line of clouds on the horizon; it hadn't started raining yet, but according to the weatherman rain was coming. Carlin slipped off her red raincoat and hung it on a hook at the edge of her cubicle. She loved that raincoat so much she almost looked forward to the occasional fall shower just so she could wear it. Now her nerves were so unsettled she didn't want to deal with rain, or traffic, or even a phone call. If her phone rang now . . . what if it was Brad? What if he'd not only found— No, she needed to stop thinking about him. She'd seen someone who reminded her of him, but that was all. Nothing had happened.

Jina Matthews, who worked at the cubicle directly beside Carlin's, wasn't having a good day, either. She was on her phone, her expression tense. She and her boyfriend had been fighting a lot lately, and it looked as if Jina was at the end of her rope. She said a few choice words, then thumbed a button on her phone. Looking across the aisle at Carlin, she made a wry face.

"It was *so* much more satisfying when you could slam a phone down. Pushing a button just doesn't have the same gratification factor." Her phone, set to vibrate, buzzed around on the desk as another call came in. Jina picked it up, looked at the caller ID, and jabbed the button again.

"Unless it's the *off* button." She leaned forward and spoke to the silent phone. "Call all you want, jackass. I can't *hear* you," she said in a singsong falsetto.

In spite of herself, Carlin laughed. Jina smiled, though the anger and sadness and frustration remained clear on her face.

Jina was gorgeous. She was blond, like Carlin, and about the same height, but that was where the similarity ended. Carlin knew she was acceptable, even above average, but she'd never be a knockout. Jina was. Men literally turned around in the street to stare at her. Unfortunately she had terrible taste in men, a strange and self-destructive attraction to the bad boy. She'd probably have a new boyfriend by the end of the week, and maybe this time she'd choose more wisely. God knows she had her pick of men, so why she went for the jerk instead of the straight-up guy was anyone's guess.

Jina's phone buzzed a couple more times, and each time she rejected the call in favor of work. For a couple of hours they each handled billing for the insurance company that owned this building in downtown Dallas. It was a boring job, most of the time—all right, *all* of the time—but the pay was decent. Carlin figured she was lucky to have the job, considering the general state of the economy. She wasn't in charge, like she'd been in Houston, but this was a much larger company than the one she'd left behind and there were opportunities for advancement, if she stayed for a while, kept her nose clean, and didn't screw up. When she put her mind to doing something, sheer stubbornness made her keep at it until she could do a good job. Working in billing wasn't glamorous, but so what? It paid the bills. Now and then she'd think about going back to school, but until her mind settled on one career path, what was the point? She needed a job; she didn't have a calling, and that was okay with her because that made her more flexible, instead of being focused on one thing.

Jina was antsy, up and down from her desk, bringing Carlin—and herself—coffee a couple of times. Just before lunchtime, she jumped out of her chair and crossed into Carlin's cubicle. "Did you bring your lunch?"

"Yeah. A sandwich and a bag of chips." Cooking wasn't her thing. Some of the women who worked in the office brought in little individual containers of homemade soup, or lasagna, or casserole, which they heated up in the break room microwave. Carlin preferred a sandwich any day over going to all that trouble.

The "yuck" face Jina made was almost comical, but then she was into gourmet stuff. "That doesn't sound very good. I'm going down the street to pick up a veggie pizza. Split one with me?"

Pizza sounded good, and Jina obviously needed company, so Carlin agreed. She pushed away from her computer, stretched out the kinks in her shoulders, and reached for her raincoat. "I'll walk with you."

Jina cocked her head and pursed her lips. "I was kinda hoping to borrow your raincoat. I left mine at home, along with my umbrella. And I really do need to walk off some of this . . . let's call it excess energy."

"If you're sure." It didn't seem fair that Jina should brave the rain alone for the pizza, but on the other hand Carlin definitely understood needing to work off some temper.

"Positive." Jina snagged the raincoat and slipped it on, then rubbed an appreciative hand over the sleeve. "Nice. I wish I could find a raincoat this color! If you ever decide to get rid of it . . ."

"I'll hang on to that raincoat until the day I die—but I'll look online this weekend and try to find one for you."

"Oooh, shopping. I'm in serious need of some retail

therapy, though a mall is more my style than a computer. It's more interactive. Plus there are restaurants. We should do that this weekend."

"Sounds like a plan." Carlin smiled, glad enough that she didn't have to go out in the rain. Spending part of the coming weekend shopping with Jina didn't sound like a bad idea; she could use some retail therapy herself. "I have a couple of Diet Cokes in the fridge, if that suits you."

"Yep. I'll be right back!" Jina hurried toward the elevator, dialing the pizza place as she walked. Carlin went on into the break room to get the drinks, paper plates, and napkins. Over pizza Jina could tell her all about this latest boyfriend issue, if she wanted to talk. Maybe she needed a place to stay until she could get the live-in cleared out, if this was a serious breakup and not just an argument. It wouldn't hurt to offer, Carlin thought.

They could make plans for shopping. She sat down and stretched her legs out, relaxing. She felt better, and ready to laugh at herself. Okay, not laugh, but at least she wasn't about to come unglued. That hadn't been Brad's Toyota; Brad was in south Texas, and had no idea where she was. She had a new life here, was making friends, and not even Brad Henderson was going to ruin it for her.

BRAD STOOD ACROSS the street from the skyscraper and watched the front entrance from the shelter of a green coffee shop awning. He sipped on his second cup of coffee, a tall, hot latte, and wondered which floor Carlin was on. If he knew exactly where she was, he might be able to corner her somewhere inside the building, in a restroom or an empty office, but that was relying too much on coincidence and happenstance. A lot could go wrong; he didn't know the routine of anyone in the building, didn't know the layout or how stringent the security was. He was content to watch and wait—for now.

This was his second trip to Dallas since Carlin had run away from him. Normally he wasn't a patient man, but being impatient would be a mistake. These things took time, and careful planning. The bitch would pay for what she'd done. She thought she could file a complaint against him and just waltz away? It hadn't taken him more than five minutes to find her. He'd told her he was good with a computer; she should've believed him.

Who did she think she was, blowing him off the way she had? He'd thought they had something special. Instead she'd suddenly started turning him down when he asked her out, and when he tried to talk her around she'd freaked, filed a harassment complaint against him. Thanks to his buddies on the force no one had taken the complaint seriously, but it was on file; if anything happened to her, he'd be at the top of the list of possible suspects.

So he'd planned carefully. Yeah, this was one of his days off, but there wasn't anything he could do about that. Instead he'd looked at the situation from every angle, and he was certain there weren't any holes in his alibi.

It was laughable that the stupid bitch thought she could outsmart him and get away from him. She hadn't even moved out of the fucking state. How easy was this? If the opportunity didn't present itself this time, eventually it would. He just had to be prepared to act, and act immediately. She was going to die. Too bad he couldn't grab her and take her off somewhere, have some fun with her first, but he couldn't be out of town that long without setting off some alarms. What fun would it be if he got caught?

The weapon he carried couldn't be traced back to

him; he'd taken it off a low-life drug dealer who had subsequently been dumped in the bay, and filed the serial numbers off. He'd also programmed his computer to show intermittent activity during the day: chat rooms, Facebook posts, instant messages . . . it would look as if he'd been on the computer off and on with no eight-hour-plus break to drive to Dallas and back.

Security in the parking garage was too tight for him to try to catch Carlin there. Eventually she'd leave, though. Maybe she'd walk to one of the nearby restaurants for lunch, or she might even head his way for a cup of coffee. Wouldn't that be a fucking kick? He'd love to see the expression on her face when she recognized him, right before he put a bullet in her head.

All he had to do was wait, and watch. He was good at waiting.

Just before noon, he saw her. She'd been wearing a red raincoat that morning when she'd left her apartment, and she was wearing it now; he actually spotted her before she stepped through the glass front doors and onto the sidewalk, even though the rain was falling hard enough to blur visibility. The hood was up, a silky hank of blond hair peeking out, as she lowered her head against the driving rain and started down the street.

She didn't cross the street toward him. Well, that had been asking a lot. The possibility had been fun to think about, but he'd known it was a long shot. Instead she turned right, walking fast through the rain.

Brad thought about setting what remained of his coffee on a nearby outdoor table, but thought better of it. DNA was a bitch. He poured it out, and stuffed the paper cup in his jacket pocket.

He pulled his own dark hood up and forward, hiding his face. Thanks to the rain, no one would think anything about it; almost everyone else was doing the same.

He mirrored her movements on the opposite side of the street, and crossed at the corner, his eyes focused on that red raincoat the entire time. He didn't want to lose her, but he'd have to be piss-poor at trailing someone if he did. The circumstances were perfect; everything was falling into place, as if this opportunity was a gift. Rain kept a lot of people off the streets, and those who were out kept their heads down and their focus on their feet. It wasn't a day for a leisurely stroll, for checking out the other pedestrians. And with the rain falling as it was and his hood up, even if someone did look his way they wouldn't be able to see him well. No one would be able to give a description. Eyewitnesses were notoriously unreliable. And even if they did manage a vague description, he had his alibi.

His stride was longer than hers, and while Carlin walked with purpose, so did he. He was right behind her, so close—closer than he'd been in months. A part of him wanted to look her in the eye as he pulled the trigger, wanted to make sure she knew that he had been the one to kill her, but the situation was what it was. He'd take what he'd been given. He'd offered Carlin Reed his devotion, and all he'd gotten in return had been insults and rejection. She deserved to die.

Ah. She turned down a side street, and they had a long section of the sidewalk to themselves. Yes, a *gift,* that's what this was. It was a near perfect opportunity that might never come again.

He reached into his pocket and gripped the automatic. His pace fast and smooth, he closed the distance between them, his rubber-soled shoes silent on the wet sidewalk. When he was just a few feet from her, Brad pulled out the weapon, aimed, and fired, then immediately tucked the weapon back into his pocket.

It was a good shot, but he'd known it would be. He

was the best shot on the force. The bullet entered Carlin's brain just an inch or two above the nape of her neck. Her body jerked and she dropped, facedown, onto the sidewalk. By his calculations, she'd been dead before she landed. The hole in the back of her red hood was neat; the view from the front would not be so clean, but he couldn't stick around to turn her over to survey the damage. The gunshot had drawn attention from those few who were walking in the pouring rain, and at least one man was looking directly at him, but Brad didn't think he'd seen the pistol. People—from the sidewalk, from the businesses along the way—ran between him and the man. He lost sight of the witness as he calmly walked away, confident that the rain and the hood and the excitement would make the eyewitness less than useful.

The rain began to fall harder, steadier. Head down, Brad took long strides toward his car. It was his car, but the license plate on it wasn't his; he'd taken the precaution of stealing one that morning off a junker that looked as if it hadn't been cranked in years. He'd covered all the possibilities. He kept his hands in his pockets, his right hand on the pistol grip in case the man who'd seen him at the crime scene decided to do something stupid, like follow him. But no one came after him, and he got lost in the confusion. Sirens sounded in the distance—he needed to get in his car and on the road before streets were blocked. He had time. Not much, but he had time. Already his mind was working ahead. He'd dump both the coffee cup and the gun somewhere between Dallas and Houston. He'd also dispose of the stolen tag and reattach the right one. No one would ever be the wiser.

He felt good. Lighter. Vindicated. Carlin was dead, and he was happy. *Dead*. It was her own fault. She was his, he'd laid claim to her, and she'd tried to run away. He'd missed her at first, but not now. What choice had he had? None. None at all.

There was no reason to second guess himself. Carlin had gotten what she deserved. It was done.

Chapter One

10 MONTHS LATER

BATTLE RIDGE, WYOMING, didn't look like much. Carlin Reed pulled her faded red Subaru into a parking space in front of an empty store and looked around. There probably wouldn't be any jobs here, but she'd ask around anyway. She'd found work in some of the damnedest places, doing things that she'd never before have considered. Work was work, money was money, and she'd learned not to be picky. She wasn't above doing yard work, washing dishes, or just about anything else as long as it didn't involve prostituting herself. Her first attempt at mowing a lawn on a riding mower had been something worthy of a clip on YouTube, but she'd learned.

From what she could see, Battle Ridge had fallen on hard times. Her atlas gave the population as 2,387, but the atlas was six years old, and from what she had seen driving in, she doubted Battle Ridge supported that many residents now. She'd passed empty houses, some with "For Sale" signs that had been up so long they'd become dingy and weather-beaten, and empty stores with "For Sale or Lease" notices in the windows. Here in the West it would still be considered a fair-sized town, especially in a state the size of Wyoming, with a grand total population of half a million people. Nevertheless, the reality was that half the buildings around her were standing empty, which meant she'd likely be moving on.

Not right this minute, though. Right now, she was hungry.

Not surprisingly, traffic was light. Hungry or not, Carlin sat in the dusty four-wheel-drive SUV and through her dark sunglasses carefully studied everything around her, every vehicle, every person. Caution had become second nature to her. She hated losing the unconscious freedom and spontaneity she'd once known, but looking back she could only marvel at how unaware she'd been, how *vulnerable*.

The level of her vulnerability might change depending on circumstances, but she was damned if she'd add in the factor of not being aware. She'd already noted that the license plates of the cars and trucks parked on each side of the street were all from Wyoming. There was little chance her movements could have been anticipated, since she hadn't known she'd be stopping here, but she still checked.

Two buildings down on the right was a café, The Pie Hole; three pickups were parked in front even though two o'clock in the afternoon wasn't exactly a prime mealtime. The name of the café amused her, and she wondered about the person who had come up with it, whether a quirky sense of humor or a don't-give-a-damn attitude was behind the choice. Her amusement was momentary, though, and she returned to studying her surroundings.

Directly behind her was a hardware store, another small cluster of vehicles was parked in front of it. To the left was a general store, a Laundromat, and a feed store. A block back she'd passed a small bank, and beside it had been a post office. Down the street she could see a gas station sign. There would probably be a school, and maybe people from fifty miles around drove their kids here. Was the town big enough to support a doctor or a dentist? To her, it seemed like a good deal: a thousand or more patients, and no competition. A person could do worse.

After she'd watched for a few minutes, she settled back and watched some more, waiting for that inner sense to tell her when she'd been patient long enough. She'd learned to listen to her own instincts.

The normalcy seeped into her bones. There was nothing frightening here, nothing unusual going on. She got her baseball cap from the passenger seat, pulled it on, and grabbed her road atlas and hooded TEC jacket before getting out of the Subaru. Though it was summer, the air was cool. The TEC was very lightweight, just a couple layers of nylon, but it had so many pockets that it had actually taken her days to locate all of them. If she had to run, everything she needed was in those pockets: ID, money, a throwaway cellphone—with the battery removed and stored in yet another pouch, a pocket knife, a small LED flashlight, even a couple of ibuprofen and some protein bars. Just in case. Seemed as if these days she surrounded herself with "just in case" items and scenarios; she was aware *and* prepared.

She hit the lock button on the remote, and slipped the key and remote into her right front jean pocket, then headed toward the little café; her leggy stride covered the distance at a fast clip, just one more detail about her that had changed during the past year. Once, she'd never gone anywhere in a hurry; now her instinct was to *move*, to get from A to B, get her business accomplished, then move on. While it was true that a rolling stone gathered no moss, she wasn't worried about getting mossy; more to the point, a moving target was harder to hit.

Still, when she reached the café door, her own reflection startled her. Baseball cap, long blond hair in a ponytail, sunglasses—when had she acquired the whole Sarah Connor–Terminator vibe? When had she become someone she barely recognized?

The answer to that was easy: the moment she'd realized Brad was trying to kill her.

She opened the door of The Pie Hole; a bell over the door sang as she walked in. Stepping to the side, she took a moment to do a fast assessment, looking for another exit—just in case—evaluating the three men currently riding the stools at the bar counter, their legs spread and boot heels hooked on the railings as if they were on horseback—again, just in case. There was no clearly marked rear door she could see from her vantage point, though there was one door with a plain "Keep Out" sign. Could be a storage closet, or an exit. She could also assume there was a back door off the kitchen, though, and maybe a window in the bathroom. Not that she'd need either, during this short stop.

The three men at the counter evaluated her right back, and she found herself tensing. She didn't like attracting notice. The more she stayed under the radar, the less likely it was that Brad would be able to track her. It was reassuring that there was nothing remotely familiar about any of the men, and that their clothing proclaimed them local. She'd gotten good at judging what was local—wherever "local" happened to be—and what wasn't. These men fit right in, from their creased hats down to the worn heels of their boots.

She shouldn't have come in here. Too late she realized that *any* stranger would stand out in a place this small, where the locals might not all personally know one another, but they'd certainly recognize who belonged and who didn't. She didn't.

She thought about leaving, but that would attract

even more attention. Besides, she was hungry. The best thing to do was the normal thing: sit down and order. She'd eat, pay the bill, then move on down the road.

The café itself was a smallish, pleasant-looking place, gray linoleum floor, white walls, an honest-to-God jukebox against the back wall, red booths along the street-front windows, and a smattering of small round tables in the center of the place. The counter, complete with a couple of clear pie cases and an old-fashioned cash register, ran the length of the right side of the room. A pretty brunette in a pink waitress uniform stood behind the counter, talking to the three men with the ease of long acquaintance; like the men, she'd glanced up at Carlin's entrance, and even through her sunglasses Carlin caught the brilliant glint of strikingly pale eyes, making her alter her grade of the waitress's looks from pretty to something more. Maybe those eyes were why the three cowboys were camping on those stools, rather than the lure of food. Good. If they were flirting with the waitress, they were less likely to pay a lot of attention to anyone else.

The last booth was positioned against a solid wall; Carlin chose that one and instinctively slid in so she was facing the doorway . . . just in case. The plastic menu was inserted between the napkin holder and the salt and pepper shakers; she removed her cap and sunglasses and grabbed the menu, more from curiosity than anything else, because all she wanted was coffee and pie. She'd get something to eat, and use the break to study her map of Wyoming, figure out exactly where this little country road went, and pick a place to stop for a while.

She'd been so sure Brad wouldn't bother to follow her to Dallas. She'd been wrong, disastrously wrong. Now when she stopped she took extra precautions. No one got her social security number. There could be no bank account, no W-2, damn it; somehow she had to fall off the radar, something that was increasingly hard to do with everything computerized. He'd bragged about his computer skills and she'd hoped that was all it was—bragging—but evidently not. She didn't know how he'd found her in Dallas, but he had, and she'd barely made it out alive. Jina hadn't.

If she let herself think about what had happened her stomach would knot in panic, and she'd feel as if she were strangling on her own breath, so she'd pushed the memory away and focused on simply moving, doing what was necessary to stay alive. He'd try again, but she was damned if she'd make it easy for him. Somehow she'd figure out what to do, a way to outsmart him, set a trap—something. She couldn't live like this forever.

But for now, she couldn't stay in any one place too long. Unfortunately, she didn't have enough cash to just keep driving around the country on a permanent road trip, so she'd work her way around the country. Ideally, she'd find someplace to stay through the winter, which was why she'd ventured this far north. People on the run tended to head toward warmer climes, bigger cities. She'd done the opposite.

She'd told Brad once that she hated the cold, and joked about one day retiring to Florida. Maybe, if he remembered that detail, he wouldn't think to look for her in Wyoming.

She studied the menu. The offerings were simple: eggs, burgers, and a mysterious "daily special"—along with, of course, the "pie of the day." Today was Thursday. Maybe Thursday's pie was apple.

"What can I get you?" The brunette in pink arrived at the booth. She didn't carry an order pad, but with such a limited menu, there probably wasn't much need for one.

Carlin glanced up. "Kat" was embroidered on the breast pocket of the pink uniform, and the waitress's eyes were even more striking close up, a kind of electric gray that tended toward blue, as clear as a mountain lake.

"What's the pie of the day?"

"We have cherry and lemon meringue."

"I was kind of hoping for apple," Carlin said, "but cherry will be fine. And coffee, black."

"Coming right up."

After Kat walked away, Carlin placed her atlas on the table and opened it to Wyoming. Her finger traced the road that had led her to Battle Ridge. She followed it on beyond, to other names of other towns and other roads and miles and miles of nothing, on into Montana. In the periphery of her vision she saw Kat approaching with her order and she moved the atlas to the side to make room.

A silverware set wrapped in a napkin and a small plate bearing a huge slice of cherry pie were slid in front of her, followed by a saucer and an empty cup. Lifting the coffeepot from her tray, Kat expertly filled the cup. "Are you lost?" she asked, nodding toward the atlas.

"Not really."

"Where are you headed?"

That was the sixty-four-thousand-dollar question. "I haven't decided yet."

"That sounds like freedom," observed the waitress, and walked away without saying anything else.

Picking up her fork, Carlin took her first bite. The not-apple pie was amazingly good. For a minute, maybe two, she forgot all her troubles and simply indulged her taste buds. The crust was flaky and buttery, and the filling was perfectly sweetened. The coffee was good, too. She took a deep breath, and realized that it was the first time in weeks that she could honestly say she was relaxed. It wouldn't last, but for now she'd take it.

While she was eating, a man came in for a slice of pie

to go. Seemed as if she wasn't the only one who thought the pie was outstanding. Idly she listened as he and Kat chatted, about neighbors, about the weather. Yes, beyond a doubt the waitress was as much of a pull as the pie, at least as far as the male populace was concerned.

Carlin looked out the window. Battle Ridge wasn't much to look at, that was a fact, but it had everything a small town needed, at least as far as she was concerned: a place to eat, a Laundromat, a general store. The people who passed by The Pie Hole all glanced in and waved, even though they didn't stop.

Pulling her jacket close, she unzipped one of the pockets to get money for her food, instinctively counting the bills. Oh, there was plenty for the pie and coffee, but not enough, not nearly enough. Living on the road was eating through her savings faster than she'd expected.

She gathered her things and walked toward the cash register with money in hand. The man who'd come in for lemon meringue left, his gaze lingering on Carlin for a moment too long. There it was again; the look was curious, not malicious—she knew the difference—but one more person had noticed her.

Kat took her money, rang up the sale, and passed back the change. Carlin laid down a dollar tip. It wasn't much, but percentagewise it was generous, and no matter how poor she was she wasn't going to stiff a nice person who'd earned a tip.

Carlin knew she should take her atlas and go, but she didn't. There might be a job opportunity in town, but if she just drove away without asking, she'd never know. She slid her butt half onto a stool and asked, "How long have you worked here?"

A slow smile curled Kat's mouth. "Seems like forever. It's my place. I'm cook, waitress, manager, and chief bottle-washer all rolled into one."

Out of all that, one thing registered uppermost. "You made the pie? It was great."

"I did. Thanks." The grin widened. "Apple tomorrow, if you're still around."

"Depends on whether or not anyone around here is looking for help." Carlin figured there were two places in a town where pretty much everything would be common knowledge: the beauty salon, and the café. She'd planned to eat, fill the Subaru's gas tank, and head on down the road, but her plans were fluid, and she'd take advantage of whatever break came her way.

For a long moment, Kat was silent, her gaze still clear but not giving anything away as she did her own assessment. "Maybe. Can you cook?"

"I can learn." She could cook enough to get by, for herself, but she for certain wasn't on Kat's level. If anyone had ever asked her what her life's ambitions were, cooking would have been way down close to the bottom of the list. Okay, it probably wouldn't even have *made* the list. Her life had changed though, and she was willing to do any kind of work.

"You got anything against doing dishes and mopping floors?"

"Nope." She wasn't proud; she'd scrub floors on her knees, if that was what it took to earn some money.

"Ever done any waitressing?"

"A little. It's been a while."

"Some things never change." Kat pursed her lips. "I can only afford to hire you part-time, and the pay isn't exactly great."

One thing she hadn't expected when she asked about available jobs was to find one here in this little café. She wasn't about to turn it down, but now came the tough part. "That's okay. The thing is . . ." She paused, looking at the three other customers to make certain they couldn't hear, then glancing out the window to take a quick study of the street before taking a deep breath and turning back to Kat. "I need to be paid in cash. No record, no taxes, no paperwork."

Kat's easy smile died, and something flashed in those clear eyes. "Are you in trouble? More specifically, are *you* trouble?"

Carlin tilted her head, considering that, then shrugged. "I guess you could look at it both ways, but I'd say *in* trouble."

"What kind of trouble? Legal, or man? It has to be one or the other."

"Isn't that the truth," Carlin muttered, then said, "Man. Stalker, to be specific."

Small-town didn't mean stupid. "Why didn't you go to the cops?"

"Because he is one," she said flatly.

"Well, that complicates matters, doesn't it?" Kat's eyes narrowed. "There are bound to be good cops, too, wherever you're from. I really hate the thought that one bad apple can force you to take to the road. Maybe you should try again."

"Twice was enough to suit me."

"Well, shit." Kat stared at her, hard, her gaze as sharp as a knife's edge. Carlin had no idea what she saw, but whatever it was, her next words were brisk and decisive. "You're hired. Just part-time, like I said. Some cooking, the easy stuff, but mostly cleaning, waiting tables. I do all the baking. Business is okay, but I'm hardly raking in the dough, if you'll pardon the pun. I'll make it worth your while, though. Still interested?"

"Yes." She said it without an instant's hesitation.

"Do you have somewhere to stay?"

Since Carlin had just now—as in the very second Kat had made her offer—decided to stick around, the answer to that was a big *no*. She shook her head. "Do you know where there's a room I can rent? Nothing too expensive, just a room with a bed." She hadn't seen a motel driving in, but surely there was someone in town who would rent her a room.

Kat tilted her head toward the single restroom door at the back of the café; beside it was that closed door that was decorated with a "Keep Out" sign. "I have a place upstairs. You can stay there. No charge for employees," she added. "It's really more of an attic, but in the winter I stay up there when the weather's so bad I don't want to drive back and forth from the house. Might as well have someone living up there," she said, as if the offer wasn't a big deal. It was, at least to Carlin. She wasn't so proud that she'd argue about paying rent. Every dollar she saved gave her more of a chance of not getting killed.

Besides, it wouldn't be for long. She'd make a few dollars, catch her breath, maybe come up with a more permanent plan. "Thank you." She managed a smile. Having the near future settled took away some of her anxiety. "I can start right now; just tell me what to do."

"Good deal." Kat offered a hand across the counter. "Since we're going to be working together, I should introduce myself. Kat Bailey."

Carlin hesitated a moment, thinking hard, then took the offered hand. She wasn't ready to give her real name to anyone, not until she knew exactly how Brad had found her the last time. Not that she didn't trust Kat; she'd simply learned that she really couldn't be too careful. Her gaze scanned the counter. A few feet away was a full bottle of ketchup, and inspiration struck. "Hunt," she said swiftly. "Carlin Hunt."

Kat snorted as she ended the handshake. "Well, at least you didn't look at the floor and tell me your last name was Linoleum."

Caught. She wasn't a very good liar, and that had to end. Like it or not, she had to get better at spinning tales. Wrinkling her nose and not bothering to deny the fib, Carlin waited for the offer of a job and a place to stay to be rescinded.

But Kat merely gave her a brisk nod, and that was that. "Get your stuff; you can at least get unpacked before you start work." Evidently a fake surname wasn't something that upset Kat Bailey's apple cart.

As Carlin went out to the Subaru to fetch her backpack, she blew out a huge breath of relief. She had a place to stay and a way to make a few dollars, a way that didn't require a lawn mower or a weed eater. And tomorrow there would even be apple pie.

It was the first time in a long while that she'd been able to think of a "tomorrow" that wasn't full of anxiety and uncertainty.

Chapter Two

"It isn't much," Kat said briskly as she led the way up the dark, narrow stairs. A single lightbulb with an industrial shade lit the head of the stairs; it was needed because the staircase was an interior one, without any other source of light. The wooden steps were sturdy, the sound of their footsteps ringing in the tight space. Carlin felt a little uneasy. Was this the only access?

As they reached the top step, Kat unlocked the door and pushed it open. Carlin followed her inside and looked around. She hadn't lied, Carlin thought; it *wasn't* much. She gave it a swift, encompassing look. One room, sparsely furnished, and a bathroom. There was one window, overlooking the street, which relieved her concern about being trapped up there. She dropped her backpack to the floor and crossed to the window, looking down and assessing how far down it was to the ground.

"The view's pretty good," Kat said, and only then did Carlin think to look farther out, lifting her gaze to the gorgeous mountains that loomed over the small town.

"Oh," she said, her tone faintly surprised.

There was a pause. "You hadn't noticed." It was a statement, not a question. Kat crossed the room to stand beside her, crossing her arms as she looked down at the street the same way Carlin had done, then across at the mountains, as if measuring one view against the other. No doubt about it, the street view didn't compete. "Looking for someone?"

"No. Just checking the height."

"Thinking about jumping?"

"Only if I have to," Carlin said blandly. She never knew if it would come to that—and that was the problem: she never knew.

Kat gave her a long, steady look, which Carlin met without flinching. She could have wasted the effort layering on some blarney about being the careful type who always checked for the location of any and all exits in a hotel, but given that she'd already told the bare basics of why she was there, why bother? She hadn't yet made up her mind whether or not she'd tell the rest of it, but regardless of that, she had no one other than herself on whom to rely. She had to trust her instincts, and after Brad had found her the last time, her instincts told her to never go to sleep before she located an exit and planned how she would get to it, and out.

But there was something about Kat that made Carlin trust her, even on such short acquaintance. She couldn't put her finger on it, couldn't have articulated any particular detail that warranted trust, but there it was. Instinct, again. Instinct might keep her alive. God knows listening to others' opinions of "Oh, he wouldn't do that" hadn't worked out, and she was guilty of that herself. She simply hadn't wanted to believe Brad would go to such lengths, and now an innocent person was dead.

Turning from the window, she studied the other details of the room. A futon served as both couch and bed, with a single end table and a small reading lamp on the left. Against one wall was a clothes rack on wheels, as well as a single kitchen cabinet unit with a small microwave and a hot plate sitting on top: closet and kitchen taken care of in a six-foot expanse of wall space. Other than that, there was a round bistro table maybe two feet in diameter and a single chair. She could see into the bathroom: it consisted of a toilet, a not-very-roomy shower unit, and a single sink, above which hung an old-fashioned medicine cabinet.

She could tell a lot about Kat simply by looking at this room, primarily that she didn't entertain men up here, she wasn't a fussy woman who required a lot of creature comforts around her, and she took care of the necessities first.

"It'll do," she said, her tone definite. Luxurious? No. But the spare quarters met all of her needs, and even without the private bath it was far superior to sleeping in the Subaru, which she'd done more than once, and didn't like.

"No TV up here," Kat said, "but there's one downstairs in the kitchen. And there's a toaster oven down there, too, if you want to bring it up. You get two meals a day, which will be whatever I'm serving that day. I do breakfast and lunch, open at five o'clock April through September, six o'clock the rest of the year, and I close at three—which means you stopped by at a good time, because after you've unpacked you can help me close and we'll have time to talk."

"I can unpack later. Put me to work," Carlin replied, barely able to believe her good luck. A place to stay, plus food? That more than made up for the low pay. With two meals a day, if she timed it right, she wouldn't need to eat dinner at all. She could get by with a late breakfast and then a mid-afternoon meal, maybe right before closing. Or she could eat half of her lunch and take the other half up for dinner. Either way, that was a big money-saver.

"All right then, let's get started," Kat said, handing the door key over, then heading back down the stairs. Carlin slipped the key into her pocket, but didn't lock the door behind her. If she had to move fast, she didn't want a locked door in her way. She started to drop her jacket on the futon, but at the last second caution made her keep it in her hand. No matter how tiny the chance that she might have to run, she wanted the jacket close by.

The three stool-riders were still in place at the counter, but as soon as Kat reappeared they grabbed their tickets, slid from the stools, fished tip money out of their pockets, then ambled toward the cash register situated at the end of the counter closest to the door. A quick glance at the clock on the wall told Carlin they were leaving with ten minutes to spare. Kat efficiently rang up the tickets, ignored one customer's attempt to flirt, and as soon as the last one left she flipped the sign on the door so it said "Closed," then turned the lock.

"I hate it when someone comes in at the last minute," she explained with a slight grumble in her tone. "Throws off my whole schedule."

Carlin figured closing a little early had more to do with the "talking" Kat wanted to do, but because she was interested she asked, as she hung her jacket on a coatrack not far from the door, "When do you do your baking?"

"If I have any special orders I usually stick around after closing to bake, so I don't get overloaded during business hours. If I'm here late anyway, I'll go ahead and bake for the next day, too. Otherwise I head home shortly after closing; baking usually starts as soon as the breakfast rush is over."

Carlin made herself handy removing the dirty crockery from the counter and, after a nod from Kat, took it through to the kitchen area. From her few brief stints as a waitress she knew there were all sorts of health department rules that had to be followed, and each state had different laws, so obviously things had to be done a certain way. Still, cooking was cooking and eating was eating, and some chores were the same except for the volume of what needed to be done.

Kat didn't strike her as a naively trusting person, despite the speed with which she'd offered the job, so Carlin waited for the questions to begin. Kat had acted on her own reasons, and she might or might not divulge them. That was fair enough, considering Carlin had already decided to keep some things to herself, too, such as her real last name.

While the huge commercial dishwasher was running, they tackled the public area. Carlin did the mopping while Kat did the refilling and putting away stuff, though she kept an eye on her employer to see how things were done. Starting at the far wall, she mopped toward the kitchen area, scrubbing the floor with a solution that smelled like pure bleach and burned her sinuses. She wrinkled her nose. "Any germ that still lives after being drowned in this stuff deserves a nice cushy home on Easy Street."

"Any germ that lives could get my doors closed until it's been hunted down and killed," Kat returned.

"Got it." Carlin swabbed more bleach into a corner, unwilling to risk losing this job for a few germs, and in a vengeful tone said, "*Die*, you little bastards." As soon as the words were out she mentally smacked herself in the head and darted a glance at Kat. "Sorry. I got carried away."

Kat shrugged. "That's okay. I've called them worse."

"I try to watch my mouth," Carlin confessed, giving another swipe at the corner, just in case. "The problem is I come from a long line of smart-asses, and things just . . . pop out."

"DNA's a bitch." Looking over at her, Kat suddenly

grinned, her eyes lighting up. "I guess that explains your name, huh?"

"Carlin? Yeah. At least they didn't name me 'George.'"

They both snickered. Carlin relaxed more now that she knew she didn't have to tamp down her more irreverent observations—everyone remembered a smart-ass, and not drawing attention to herself had been tough. On the other hand, staying alive was really good motivation, so she'd been working on being as anonymous as possible.

"My mom loves George Carlin," Kat said. "She's always said any man who can make her laugh . . ." the sentence trailed away, as if some unexpected remembrance had derailed her thoughts.

They worked in silence for a few minutes, but the quiet didn't help. Carlin was getting antsier by the second. Why wait until Kat decided to start the questions? Why not begin with some of her own?

"So, what made you decide to hire me? That was a fast decision, especially after I told you I needed to be paid under the table."

Kat looked a little startled, as if she hadn't expected her new employee to take charge. She paused, her head tilting a bit to the side, her pale, clear eyes sharp as she gave Carlin a considering look. "I know what it's like to be afraid of a man," she finally said, her tone completely level. "Never again."

That simple explanation was good enough for Carlin. If she ever got out of this mess, if she was ever free and clear . . . she'd gladly help another woman who found herself in a similar situation. Call it karma, call it gratitude . . . call it one woman who had survived helping another to make it through another day. For now, Carlin decided just to call it good luck.

As her employer, Kat could've asked for details, could've demanded them, but she didn't. Instead she went to the jukebox, carefully avoiding the segment of the floor Carlin had already mopped while digging change out of her large apron pocket. She didn't study the selections, just dropped in some quarters and started punching buttons, lining up a few songs for them to work by. As Kat turned around, the first song she'd chosen began to play. An instrumental Carlin didn't recognize began, the notes filling the quiet café; Kat half-closed her eyes, her body moving in a gentle shimmy and sway. A moment later, Michael Bublé began to sing an upbeat version of "Cry Me a River."

Why that song? Carlin was suddenly tempted to tell Kat more. She wanted to tell her new boss that she had never cried over Brad, that it hadn't been that kind of relationship, not ever. She had cried over some of the things he'd done, but mostly she'd been angry and frustrated—until Jina died, and after that things had changed. She didn't cry now. Now, she worked hard at surviving.

But Kat simply put on the music and got back to work. She didn't speak, and Carlin pushed away the temptation to talk. Was this Kat's normal way of doing things, or had she fired the jukebox up so it would be possible for them to work without speaking? Questions would inevitably come, but obviously not right this minute. Good enough.

When "Cry Me a River" ended it was followed by Trace Adkins, with a kickin' country song about bars and nice butts. Kat had an eclectic taste in music. Carlin was interested, but not surprised.

Music filled the background, set the pace for their work, made it impossible for either of them to take notice of uncomfortable silences, because there were none.

When she'd driven into Battle Ridge, Carlin had looked around and pretty much written the town off. She'd asked about a job out of habit, but hadn't expected anything. She hadn't expected she'd find herself here, mopping The Pie Hole, taking on a new job in the blink of an eye. And now she had a place to sleep, two meals a day, and she'd take in a little bit of cash along the way. Perfect. She wouldn't stay here long. She *couldn't* stay anywhere for very long. But she was safe for now, and that was enough.

When the café was spotless and put to rights, they moved into the kitchen. The music came to an end, and there it was . . . silence. Everything unspoken seemed to hang in the air. Kat stopped working and turned to Carlin, looking at her with those arresting eyes.

Okay, here it was. Carlin didn't exactly hold her breath, but she went still, waiting. This was the moment, and it could go either way. If Kat didn't ask, she wasn't going to volunteer information. But if Kat did ask, she'd have to either lie or simply refuse to answer. Much as she would love to spill her guts, unload on a kindred spirit . . . The less Kat knew, the better off she'd be.

But when Kat started talking, she went straight into a territory Carlin hadn't expected. "If you're going to be here awhile, there are a few things you should know."

Depends on how long "awhile" is.

"There's a drugstore and a grocery store at the edge of town. Neither of them is much to look at, but they sell the basics: mascara, tampons, cookies, milk. If you want anything fancy you're going to have to drive into Cheyenne."

"Good to know." Amusement at what Kat considered the basics made her lips twitch. But she wouldn't be driving into Cheyenne, barring some kind of crisis. The bigger the town, the less comfortable she was. It was impossible to spot a stranger, but larger towns tended to have more security cameras, more curious cops, just . . . *more.* Besides, she didn't have any exotic needs; it sounded as if she could get everything she wanted right here in Battle Ridge, Wyoming.

"There's a library just down from the hardware store,"

Kat continued. "They don't have a great selection of books, but they do have a decent fiction section and a couple of public computers, if you have need for that sort of thing."

"Thanks." *Public computers*. Her cup runneth over. "I could stand to do a little reading while I'm here." She saw no need to share the news that her heart had gone pitter-pat at the mention of a public computer.

"And a warning," Kat said ominously. "Stay away from the cowboys."

"Cowboys?"

"Battle Ridge is lousy with them, I'm afraid."

"You don't like cowboys." The tone of Kat's voice when she said the word made that a fact, not a question.

"They'll break your heart and leave you in a trail of dust," Kat said dramatically, widening her eyes, but then she ruined her own show by laughing.

"Did a cowboy break *your* heart?" Carlin asked, her tone as irreverent as her boss's.

"Oh, hell no. I grew up around here. I've known from birth that cowboys are to be avoided at all costs."

She could relate to that; since meeting Brad, Carlin hadn't wanted a relationship with *any* man, for reasons both emotional and practical. The emotional part was kind of like the time she'd eaten a slice of bad pizza, and spent the night and next day throwing up; she hadn't wanted pizza at all for the next several months. The practical part was, she couldn't have a relationship when not only did she fully intend to keep moving around, but if Brad did find her and she was involved with someone else, that person's life was then in danger. But instead of going there, she said, in her best John Wayne voice, "I'm sorry to hear you say that, little lady."

Kat laughed again, finished wiping down a stainless-steel counter beside the large stove, and directed Carlin and her mop to an area by the oversized freezer. Carlin smiled as she continued to clean. How long had it been since she'd relaxed enough to laugh?

Too long. But at the same time, getting too comfortable in Battle Ridge would be a Bad Idea.

They finished up at about the same time, and Kat said, "I officially call this finished, and in half the time it usually takes me. Good deal. How about a decaf, or a cup of tea?"

Carlin glanced at the clock on the wall, a little startled to see how much time had passed. They'd been working for a couple of hours. Hard work deserved a treat. "Tea would be great."

"Something else to eat? There's pie left. Or I could throw together some sandwiches."

"No, that's too much—"

"No trouble at all. I have to eat, too. I can either eat here, or I can drive home and eat, but it'll be a sandwich, regardless. After cooking all day I never cook dinner for myself."

Her tone was wry, and completely honest. Carlin wasn't hungry, but she knew she would be later if she didn't eat something now. Besides, she couldn't assume this little town was as safe a haven as it appeared to be, that Brad couldn't find her here. She didn't see how he *could*, but she'd underestimated him too often. She might well be running again tomorrow.

"Okay, thanks. That would be great. I'm not picky, and I don't have any strong likes or dislikes. Except for cabbage. I hate cabbage. And caviar. *Blech*. Whoever thought eating fish eggs was a good idea? And rutabaga. I don't like rutabaga."

Kat waited a moment, then said, "Is that all?"

"Pretty much."

"Good. I can firmly promise you that I won't make a cabbage, caviar, and rutabaga sandwich."

"Good God, that's a repulsive idea," Carlin said, shuddering.

The sandwiches Kat slapped together were regular ham and cheese, and the two women sat on stools in the kitchen, eating and sipping hot tea. In between bites Kat shared tidbits about Battle Ridge. This was home for her, and while she loved the place, she recognized its faults. And yet she stayed. Carlin started to ask why, and stopped herself. She didn't need to know; didn't need to like Kat Bailey any more than she already did. Maybe the fact that this was home was reason enough for Kat to stay.

Carlin didn't want to get personal, but she did ask questions, about shopping and parking and business, about her new job, and the clientele—lots of cowboys, apparently. They even talked about pie, which was evidently a subject near and dear to both of them. Kat had learned the art of pie-baking from her mother, and Carlin loved to eat pie, so there was an instant connection. She'd seen some of her girlfriends get married with less in common with their new husbands than that.

The shared meal and the conversation were nice. Comfortable. Carlin felt herself relaxing even more, almost as if something inside her was uncoiling. She shook it off, gave herself a good, hard mental poke in the ribs.

Getting comfortable was not an option. Relaxing could get her killed.

Chapter Three

ZEKE HAD BEEN up for two hours, and the sun had been up for one. He was already frustrated, irritated, and so hungry he was ready to gnaw on anything that resembled food—even Spencer's earliest attempts at cooking.

The morning had started out at five a.m. with the discovery that part of the fence was down and all of the horses were out. He and all of the hands should have been heading out to the hay fields; instead they'd been cussing and chasing horses. The good news was that the horses hadn't gone far and they'd stayed together. The bad news was that they evidently weren't of a mind to go back into the fenced pasture, so rounding them up had taken longer than it should have. Spencer was the best on the ranch with animals of any kind, so Zeke had had to enlist the kid in helping with the horses, which suited Spencer just fine because he hated his cooking duties and made no bones about it. Unfortunately that meant the rest of the men either had to start the day without hot food, or be delayed. It was Zeke's ranch, his men, and his call. First and foremost, he took care of his men, so his only remaining option was a late start.

Spencer had tried to get by with serving muffins and cereal for the first meal of the day, he'd even tried doughnuts once. But without a hearty breakfast the men were all hungry before mid-morning rolled around, and hungry men were not efficient workers. They needed a hot, filling meal, and for now it was Spencer's job to provide that meal, as well as two others.

As soon as the horses were back in the pasture, Zeke told Spencer, "Throw together something hot and fast while we fix this fence." They'd be working late tonight, thanks to the damn fence and the damn horses.

"Sure, boss." Spencer bobbed his head and headed for the bunkhouse kitchen at a fast trot. Zeke spared a brief moment of appreciation for the kid. The other hands rode him hard, teased him about all the shit chores that got thrown his way, but the way Zeke saw it, Spencer was showing his mettle by doing what was asked of him, instead of quitting. Give the kid another ten years or so, and he figured Spencer would be foreman here, bossing some of the same men who were giving him such a hard time now. Not all of the crew would still be here, of course; some would move on to other ranches, some to different jobs, but a few would hang in there. He had a good crew now, so he hoped they'd hang together for at least a few more years.

"Hope he doesn't cook that oatmeal shit again," Darby grumbled as he nailed a heavy board into place.

"We'd still be chasing horses if it wasn't for him," Zeke said, no temper in his tone but enough grit to tell the men to lay off Spencer no matter what he served up for them to eat—not that *he'd* be real thrilled to get oatmeal. It wasn't that he didn't like oatmeal . . . normally . . . but Spencer's oatmeal tended toward a gluelike consistency.

They needed something more substantial for the long day ahead of them. Ranch work didn't pay any attention to the clock; summer was short, and they had only a set amount of time to get enough hay cut and baled to last through the long winter.

His ex-wife, Rachel, had called the winter weather "inhuman" and "brutal" and insisted no one with any sense would live here. If he wanted to be strictly fair, he had to admit she had some truth on her side, but "strictly fair" had gone out the window with the divorce, and as far as he was concerned she was a spoiled bitch who wouldn't know what real work was if it bit her on the ass. He was a Wyoming native, he loved where he lived and what he did, and he figured everything else more than made up for the winters.

The hard truth was that he hadn't missed Rachel after she left. By then all he'd felt was a sense of relief at having some peace and quiet again. Hell, with Libby there taking care of the cooking and cleaning and his laundry, life had rocked on exactly as it had before Rachel had come along. She hadn't made a place for herself, hadn't put her stamp on the household, hadn't taken over any of the decisions. Instead she'd left all of that to Libby, and spent her time sulking because there was no place to shop, no coffee bar, no friends nearby. She could have had friends; it wasn't as if there weren't women in town. But Rachel hadn't wanted Wyoming friends. She'd wanted her friends—or others just like them—from Denver.

Yeah, like people flocked to Denver for its great winter weather.

Rachel hadn't liked summer in Wyoming, either. Summers meant unrelenting work, from before sunrise until sometimes long after sunset, getting ready for winter. Hay became the most important thing in his life, and a bad growing season could spell disaster for the ranch. The ranch hands traded horses and four-wheelers for tractors. Every night he'd pray for good weather, because any rain caused a delay he couldn't afford. His hay fields weren't counted in acres, but in square miles; that was a lot of hay that had to be cut, dried, and baled. When he'd come dragging in at ten o'clock at night, after an eighteen-hour day, Rachel had wanted attention and he'd wanted a shower and then sleep, another thing that had made his wife very unhappy.

Another truth: he missed Libby way the hell more than he'd ever missed Rachel. This morning he'd discovered—again—that he was out of clean socks. Maybe he'd have noticed beforehand if he'd folded his laundry and put it away in the dresser drawers the way Libby had always done, but this was summer and all he had time for was taking the clean clothes out of the dryer and dumping them in a laundry basket. That was his system: dirty clothes on the floor, clean clothes in the laundry baskets. Unfortunately, in the tangle of underwear, he hadn't noticed that there were no more clean socks. He'd taken the time to throw a bunch of clothes in the washer and turn it on, and he just hoped to hell he remembered to transfer them to the dryer when he dragged himself back to the house tonight.

Come to that, he hoped he'd put detergent in the washer, but he couldn't remember if he had or not. Shit. Maybe he'd be able to tell by smelling the wet clothes whether or not they'd been really washed, or just rinsed. If not, he guessed he'd have to run the washer again, just to be sure. He sucked at this housekeeping stuff.

He swung the hammer and it glanced off the heavy nail, catching him on the side of the thumb. "Fuck!" He said several more swear words, shaking his hand. That was what happened when you let your mind wander while you were trying to hammer something. Good thing he hadn't been on a horse, or he might have ended up sitting on his ass on the ground.

But thinking about his domestic arrangements—or lack of them—wasn't exactly letting his mind wander. Since Libby's departure, all of that crap had been an ongoing problem. He and the men worked hard; they needed meals prepared for them, he needed clean clothes, by now it would probably take a pitchfork to clean out the house, and all of that made running the ranch harder than it needed to be.

But damned if he knew what the solution was. In the months since Libby had left he'd hired three different women to take her place. Well, no one could take her place; all he wanted was someone to cook, clean, and do laundry. Was that too much to ask of a decently paid employee? Apparently so, because none of the three had stayed. One had sat on her ass watching TV most of the time instead of getting things done. Another had said it was driving her nuts to be so far away from everything. In Zeke's opinion, that particular drive hadn't been a very long one. And the third one had caused trouble between the men, which had taught him a lesson about hiring a young single woman who was even remotely attractive.

So they were back to eating Spencer's cooking again, and Zeke had been doing his own laundry, when he happened to remember it. As for cleaning the house . . . well, it would get done, eventually.

Aggravations aside, Zeke was a man who knew his place in the world and was happy in it—as happy as a man who didn't have any clean socks could be, anyway. While other ranches were losing money, being sold, even turned into— God forbid—dude ranches or summer homes for movie stars with more money than sense, he worked hard to keep his corner of the world the way he liked it. Maybe the cash didn't flow in nonstop, but he always found a way to get by, to keep his accounts in the black. It didn't hurt matters that he'd been a big saver back when things had been great. Those savings had come in handy over the years.

His gaze went beyond the men to the mountains in the

distance. He wasn't a sentimental sap, but this was home. He didn't want to be anywhere else.

Just about the time they finished repairing the fence, Zeke saw Spencer step out onto the bunkhouse porch. "Come and get it!" the kid yelled before ducking back inside.

Zeke pulled off his gloves and tucked them into his belt. After putting away their tools, everyone trooped toward the bunkhouse. As ranch accommodations went, the bunkhouse wasn't too bad. Only five of the men actually lived there; two were married and had their own houses, and the foreman, Walt, who was both the oldest and had been with Zeke the longest, had his own very small private house beside the bunkhouse. The larger building had six small bedrooms and three full baths, as well as a sizable common area that was furnished with battered recliners and a big-screen TV, and a full, if not very modern, kitchen. The bunkhouse was solidly built, had a wood-burning stove to back up the heating system just in case, and essentially served its purpose. The long trestle table would comfortably fit all of them; sometimes Zeke ate with them, though most of the time he opted for a sandwich, eaten alone, while he slogged through paperwork.

As soon as he stepped into the bunkhouse, his heart sank. It was oatmeal, all right, but then all he'd specified was that the food be "hot and fast." Spencer had also added some cheese toast to the mix. The consistency of Spencer's oatmeal aside, cheese toast wasn't something Zeke would ever have picked to go with it. He felt like gagging. Judging from the expressions on the other men's faces, he wasn't the only one. Jesus. When he had time to do something about it, he seriously needed to look for a cook.

But not a woman. After the last fiasco, never again would he hire a woman unless she met the triple criteria of being at least middle-aged, married, and completely uninterested in horny cowboys. What he really wanted, now that he thought about it, was a male cook. Men could cook as well as women. Weren't all the great chefs men? The fact of it was, nine dicks and one vagina together on one large slice of land just didn't work, unless the woman was married to one of the men.

With a noticeable lack of enthusiasm, some of the men sat down to shovel in a bowl of the gluelike oatmeal. Others opted for the cheese toast. None of them ate both. Patrick mentioned, in an almost offhand way, that he'd had instant oatmeal before and it wasn't too bad. Figuring the cheese would stick with him longer than the oatmeal, Zeke grabbed a couple slices of toast before the others beat him to it.

Hell, he couldn't fault Spencer. The kid hadn't hired on to be a cook, didn't want to be a cook, but did whatever Zeke asked of him. He did a marginally decent job in the kitchen, but he wanted to be a cowboy. God knew he'd never be a brain surgeon.

"Where do you need me, boss?" Spencer asked eagerly, around the toast he'd stuffed in his own mouth. His gaze went to the window, scanning the land before him and the mountains in the distance with the same kind of reverence Zeke himself felt. It would be cruel and unusual to put him to housework full-time. "Won't take but a minute to do the dishes."

"All hands in the hay fields," Zeke answered briefly. Until the hay was in, everything else was on hold, including collecting semen from his prize bull, Santos. Selling bull semen had turned into a profitable business aspect of the Decker ranch, and no one was better with animals than Spencer. Whatever it was about him, he had a calming influence on them: horses, dogs, cattle—even bulls. When you were collecting semen from a two-thousand-pound bull, keeping him calm was important—or at least as calm as could be expected, under the circumstances. Therefore it only made sense that even though he was the youngest of the hands, and the one who had been here the shortest time, Spencer was the one in charge of this job.

Sperm collector and cook. Wouldn't that look impressive on a résumé?

Walt cleared his throat. "Any answers to your latest want ad?"

Spencer looked up, hope in his eyes.

"None that'll do." He'd had one query, but the "no housework" stipulation had stopped that one cold. He'd rewrite his ads. He didn't think he could get away with "elderly battle-ax preferred," but he could sure add that a man was preferred. "Someone will turn up, though. Let's get going, boys. This hay won't get cut and baled by itself."

SUMMERTIME, AND IT was barely seventy degrees in the middle of the day. After the broiling heat of Texas, Carlin enjoyed the mild temperatures, but she couldn't help but wonder what winter would be like here—not that she'd be around to find out. Winter was months away, and there was no telling where she'd be by then, but it almost certainly wouldn't be here.

The thought of moving on was surprisingly tough; the regular customers already treated her like she was one of their own, and always had been. She'd have been suspicious of a stranger showing up out of nowhere, but Kat simply told everyone she was a friend, and that was good enough for her customers.

Had *she* ever been that trusting? Yeah, she had—once upon a time. But not now, and maybe not ever again. Before waiting on her first customer, she'd decided to tell them all to call her Carly. It was nice that Kat called her by her real name, that she hadn't disappeared completely into a false identity, but to have an entire town—no matter how small—knowing her name wasn't a good idea. One post on a social site about Carlin at The Pie Hole might be enough to bring Brad here; it simply wasn't worth the risk. Besides, Carly was close enough so that she didn't stumble when someone called her by that name.

Not for the first time in her life, she wished her parents had given her a normal name, like Mary, or Maggie, or any one of a hundred well-used names that didn't stick out like a sore thumb. Her brother and sister hadn't been spared the family curse, but Robin was a relatively normal name for a woman, and Kinison could be shortened to Kin. Her parents had loved to laugh so much they'd named all three of their kids after their favorite comedians. God, she missed them. They'd died too soon.

Today's lunch crowd was a good one: mostly men, as usual, but there were a couple of women chatting away in a corner. One of the regulars was a skinny cowboy named Sam who tipped his hat and winked as he walked in the door. Carlin had already learned to dismiss the flirts, taking her cue from Kat. Usually all she had to do was simply ignore any overtures. If that failed, a cool look would do the trick. Maybe single women were a hot commodity in these parts, because a new one certainly did stir up a lot of interest.

Kat said business was up some since Carlin had started working there. Two single women, serving pie and burgers and endless cups of coffee, were apparently an irresistible draw for many of the cowboys Kat had warned her about.

That kind of attention made her a little nervous, but the flirting was good-natured, and most of the men—once rejected—seemed resigned to satisfying themselves with baked goods, caffeine, and a little harmless staring. She hadn't had any real trouble with any of them, so she stayed.

She was settling into a comfortable routine. In the back of her mind she knew comfortable meant dangerous, but it felt good to just relax a little, let her guard down a notch and pretend she had a halfway normal life. She liked what she was doing, liked her employer, liked the lack of drama. She wanted to hang on here for just a while longer.

Routine was nice. Once lunch was done and the doors were locked, she and Kat would clean to whatever music Kat was in the mood for that day, which could be anything. Kat might get some baking done while Carlin cleaned, depending on whether or not she had any special orders. Then they'd share a quick, early supper, and Kat would head home, while Carlin went upstairs to quiet and solitude, which went a long way toward healing her tattered nerves. The next day they'd start all over again, except for Sunday, which was two days away. The café was closed then.

Carlin wasn't sure what she'd do with herself, with an entire day and nothing to do. Well, nothing except her laundry, and cleaning her room, but that wouldn't take long. It seemed forever since she'd had the luxury of time.

Maybe she'd read, or watch a baseball game in the kitchen.

Then again, maybe she'd have too much time to think, get antsy about this too-good-to-be-true situation, and run.

Chapter Four

ZEKE DROVE INTO Battle Ridge, taking care of a Monday-morning run he could've assigned to any of his ranch hands. He had to hit the hardware store, the feed store, and pick up a couple of pies from Kat's place. Spencer had already bought groceries for the week, so he was saved from that chore. He had a thousand things on his mind, and driving alone gave him time to think. Ranch business was at the top of his list—hell, ranch business was his only list—including his inability to find a suitable cook and housekeeper. Over the weekend he'd tried again; he'd talked to a couple of applicants by phone, hoping to find someone who would do for now. If he could just find a cook to get them through the winter . . .

But not one applicant had been acceptable. Yes, he'd significantly narrowed the field when he'd decided not to bring another woman into the mix, but you'd think with the economy the way it was he'd have a good crop of men to choose from, honest men whose background checks panned out, and it would sure as hell be nice to get an application from someone without a violent criminal background.

Damn it, it was beginning to look as if Spencer might be doing all the cooking at the ranch from now on, which didn't make anyone happy, Spencer least of all. Zeke knew he was running the risk of losing the young hand if he didn't get his domestic situation straightened out, but for now they were making it work. Zeke hated doing his own laundry, and despised housework—not because of the work itself, but because it was added on to his already long hours. But, hell, what choice did he have? Spencer couldn't cook three meals a day, handle his usual ranch duties, collect bull sperm, and be a full-time housekeeper, too. It was bad enough that the hand who was collecting the sperm was also doing the cooking; seemed like someone asked, before every meal, "Spencer, did you wash your hands?"

Spencer was a good kid, and he didn't let the teasing get to him—for now, anyway. The situation was stable. Zeke wasn't looking for perfection—that had been Libby—but right now he wasn't desperate, either. He'd eventually find an older guy who liked ranch living, could cook, and didn't mind doing laundry and all the other household crap. He didn't have to settle for just anyone.

Traffic was light in Battle Ridge, as usual these days. Not for the first time, Zeke wondered what he'd do if many more of the businesses in town went under. The necessities were still available, but if the hardware store or the feed store closed, he'd be in a world of hurt. It would mean more hours on the road, driving into Cheyenne for those supplies he chose not to order from an online store. Besides, he liked having a hometown. Maybe he wasn't the most sociable man in the world, but that didn't mean he wanted to be a hermit.

He spotted a parking space in front of the hardware store, and was headed for it when a woman jogged across the street just ahead of him. He slowed to let her cross, and automatically gave her a swift, assessing look: blond ponytail, baseball cap, sunglasses . . . great ass, in a pair of nice-fitting jeans. She lifted a hand and waved, fast and casual, not even slowing down. He couldn't see her face well, because of the baseball cap, but he was sure he'd never met her. It wasn't like he knew everyone who lived near or shopped in Battle Ridge, but he'd damn sure have remembered that ass.

I'd look good on that, he thought, his eyes following the fine ass all the way to the library.

The instant thought was accompanied by a burst of heat in his groin, reminding him that it had been way the hell too long since he'd had sex, even with his fist. He'd been too damn tired after they got in from cutting hay, but thank God that was done now and he felt better about having enough hay to see the herd through the winter. Now he could think about other things, first and foremost being how it would feel to have a woman under him—maybe even that sassy blond, whoever she was. He couldn't remember ever seeing her before, but the town was small enough he could probably find out who she was by asking one or two people.

Maybe he should check out a book . . .

After he parked Zeke headed for the hardware store, not the library. Nice ass aside, he had errands to do, and the blonde probably had a husband or a boyfriend. Or a face that could stop traffic—and not in a good way. A nice ass did not mean the rest of her was as appealing. Maybe he should just enjoy the memory of the unexpected sight and continue with his day.

Still, it was amazing what the mere sight of a heart-shaped butt in a pair of tight jeans could do to improve his mood.

CARLIN HAD BEEN in Battle Ridge for eleven days, long enough to have learned the rhythm of the town. The breakfast rush was over, Kat was working on the day's pies, and a fifteen-minute break was just long enough for her to cut catty-corner across the street to the small library, which was tucked in just a couple of doors down from the hardware store. A pickup truck coming down the street slowed, allowing her plenty of time to cross. She couldn't see the driver well enough to tell if she recognized him, but she threw him a quick "thank you" wave as she picked up her pace. She was getting used to doing stuff like that. Already some people—regulars in The Pie Hole—smiled and waved when they saw her, as if they'd known her all their lives, as if she was one of them.

It was a little disconcerting. Until Brad had forced her out of her comfortable life, she'd been accustomed to the anonymity of cities, where she could come and go without being acknowledged by anyone outside of her circle of friends and acquaintances. She'd always felt safer, being anonymous. Yeah, that had worked out well, hadn't it? Regardless of that, being noticed still made her feel exposed.

She also felt guilty, being the recipient of such unguarded friendliness. She wasn't one of them, and she didn't plan to stay around very long. But because it was the proper thing to do, and the move that would attract the least amount of attention, she always smiled and waved back.

The cool quietness of the library enveloped her, and she went directly to the public-access computers. She wouldn't put her family in danger by contacting them directly, but that didn't mean she was willing to completely lose track of Kinison, or Robin and her family. A fake Facebook profile connected to a free online email account and an old friend who served as intermediary made it possible for Carlin to touch base, now and then. She could let her family know she was okay, and see the occasional photo of her nieces and nephew. They were growing so fast, changing every day. It wasn't as if she'd seen them all that often before her life had fallen apart, but they'd talked regularly. And she'd always known she could go see them at any time, if she wanted to. Now she couldn't, and that loss cut deep. It was when she was in front of the computer, reaching out for a snippet of news about her family, that she felt most angry. Brad had taken her family from her, and she didn't know when she'd ever get them back.

She logged on to Facebook under her fake name, Zoey Harris. Her sister had suggested the name Zoey because it was unusual enough that someone looking for a bland, unnoticeable name would never think of it. It was a little like the "hide in plain sight" theory.

The fictional Zoey Harris lived in Florida, and was ostensibly no more than a casual friend to her sister. Carlin never posted a private message on her sister's page, because Facebook accounts could be hacked, which she assumed meant that private messages could be read. She didn't know for sure, but she wasn't willing to take the chance. Whenever she did post something on her sister's wall, she did it right out in the open, where it wouldn't look important.

She read all of Robin's posts; nothing out of the ordinary was going on, just the usual family activities. Then she went to her brother's page, and found the same thing, only Kin's comments tended more toward sports. Back again to her sister's page, where she posted a brief message about wishing for summer vacation to end so the kids would be back in school. That kind of innocuous message signaled her family that she was all right.

It was tempting, while she was in front of a computer, to run a check on Brad's name to see if he'd been arrested. He'd gotten away with Jina's murder, but maybe he'd moved on to someone else and run into trouble. No matter how tempting it might be, though, she didn't type his name into the search bar. She didn't dare. There were programs you could use to find out who'd searched your name. If Brad had one of those set up, he'd know instantly where the search had originated. Maybe right before she left town, she'd run a search and see if anything popped up.

No. She couldn't do that.

A shudder walked down her spine. She'd never purposely draw Brad here, to a place where people she liked lived and worked, to a place small enough that he could gather bits of information about her. Maybe on her next stop in a big city, wherever that might be, she'd do a search on him. Maybe she'd go to Chicago. Yeah, let him spend a few weeks trying to find her *there,* long after she'd moved on.

Carlin was back in The Pie Hole in plenty of time to change into her uniform—pink like Kat's, with a curly "C" embroidered over the pocket—and get the main room set for lunch. The pies and cakes were baking, so the place smelled wonderful. It smelled like . . . home. Not a home Carlin had ever known, because the domestic arts hadn't figured prominently in her life, but she didn't know any other way to describe the scent.

Time passed fast when the place was busy, and as usual she and Kat fell into a kind of rhythm as the pace of business picked up. It was almost like a dance: serving food, talking to the customers, laughing at jokes that were sometimes funny and sometimes not, making sure no one's drink glass or mug was ever empty, cooking up orders whenever someone didn't choose the daily special. Maybe it could be classified as menial labor, but Carlin was enjoying herself. She liked the people here, and Kat was gradually becoming a real friend.

They were in the middle of the lunch rush—Carlin behind the counter and Kat making the rounds with a pitcher of tea in one hand and a carafe of coffee in the other, because she could handle pouring on the go better than Carlin could—when the cowboy walked in.

Carlin couldn't help but notice him. What warm-blooded woman wouldn't? He was tall and muscular, and he moved with an iron confidence that said he knew his strength and hadn't met much that could stop him. She had to call him handsome, though he wasn't, not really. His face wasn't perfect and sculpted, it was on the rough and hard side, but she was going on her reaction to him rather than what her eyes saw. She went warm and breathless, and looked away because staring at him was abruptly too much, too dangerous in a way she sensed but couldn't quite grasp, at least not consciously. He was every inch the heartbreaker cowboy Kat had warned her away from—and damn if he didn't charge the air when he walked into the place.

He was bad news all the way around, she recognized that much right away. She ignored her racing heartbeat as she refilled a cup of coffee, smiling at the older man sitting on the other side of the counter while she concentrated on not looking at the new customer.

The cowboy nodded to Kat, who gave him a bright smile. She couldn't wave, considering she was carrying both a pitcher of tea and a coffeepot, but her pleasure at seeing him was obvious. He took a booth, the same one Carlin had chosen her first day here, sliding into the seat that put his back to the wall and gave him a clear view of the door. So, who was *he* running from?

No damn body, that was who. She didn't know him, but Carlin doubted he'd ever backed down from much in his entire life. He just had that look, which meant he was probably a pain in the ass to deal with, but at least the physical scenery was fine.

A couple of the cowboys at the counter said hello, greeted the newcomer like an old acquaintance. *Hey, Zeke.* He returned their greetings, but that was it. From his slightly grim expression he seemed to be in a bad mood, though that could be his default setting.

Out of the corner of her eye, Carlin saw Kat head in Zeke's direction. They spoke like old friends, she took his order—without writing it down, as usual—and then she came back to the counter. "A daily special and a coffee, black, for my wayward cousin."

"Wayward?" And her cousin?

"He doesn't come to see me nearly often enough. If not for my pies I'd be lucky to see him twice a year."

The Pie Hole was small, and of course Zeke heard every word Kat said. "I'm busy," he explained, his voice raised slightly so Kat could hear. "Give me a break."

Then his gaze moved to Carlin, held, focused, and she gave a quick, involuntary shiver. He might be in a bad mood, but he wasn't shy. He didn't look away, the way most of Kat's male customers did if they were caught looking too long or too hard. No, he just kept staring, steady and still and . . . lethal. The shiver walked down her spine, a tickle of instinct. Zeke looked at her the way a hungry man might look at a slice of Kat's apple pie.

Oh, crap. That was a comparison she didn't need to have in her head, even if she hadn't voiced it aloud. She felt her face turning red.

"I'll get his order," she said, turning on her heel and all but bolting for the kitchen. She felt a little like she was making an escape.

Heaven save her from macho men who thought they ruled the world just because they had a penis. Well, penises. Plural, right? And, yes, she was assigning him to that category because the last thing she needed was to let herself get involved. The strength of her reaction to him was warning enough.

She put the order together on his plate: meatloaf; mashed potatoes and gravy; green beans that were too underdone for her tastes, but then again she liked her green beans cooked to the point where they no longer actually resembled a bean of any kind, the way her mom had made them; a soft roll—homemade, which kind of blew Carlin's mind. Who made homemade rolls when the prebaked ones were fine? Okay, these were extra-special good, but still. Kat didn't make homemade rolls every day, but at least once a week the entire place was filled with the scent of baking bread; therefore, if Carlin was never again completely satisfied with a ready-made dinner roll, it was all Kat's fault. The customers liked them, too; word seemed to spread whenever there were fresh rolls on the menu.

The order was ready; Carlin left the kitchen with the plate on a tray, prepared to hand it over to Kat, who'd waited on Zeke the cowboy-cousin. But Kat was talking to a customer at the counter, and waved Carlin over to her cousin's table.

Great.

While Carlin had been preparing the order, Kat had placed a steaming mug of coffee and silverware wrapped in a napkin in front of Zeke. All Carlin had to do was set the food before him, ask if he needed anything else, and skedaddle. She didn't have to look at him, didn't have to notice whether or not he was looking at her.

But of course he was looking at her. Hard. And it was impossible not to notice.

She couldn't say the cowboy and Kat shared any strong family resemblance, but there was something about their eyes. Not in color—his were green, and Kat's were that arresting blue-gray. It wasn't the shape, either. But when it came to intensity, there was a definite similarity. Those eyes could look right through her. She approached him feeling as if she were Superman getting closer and closer to Kryptonite.

As she set the food in front of him his gaze never wavered. It wasn't a particularly friendly look, but it was definitely male and assessing. He didn't make even a token attempt to disguise what he was thinking; mentally he already had her stripped. If she hadn't had such a visceral reaction to him she'd have been able to ignore the look, but having to deal with herself as well as him had her nerves on edge.

"Thanks," he said, but he didn't even glance at the plate.

With an effort, she kept her expression bland and unresponsive, and her tone the same way. "Can I get you anything else?" That was good; she sounded just like any of a million other waitresses who just wanted to get through their shifts without any trouble.

"No, I'm set."

Okay. Easy enough. She blew out a mental breath of relief. She was about to make a quick getaway when he said, "You're new."

Damn! So close . . . Annoyance seeped in; she didn't like feeling as if she wasn't in complete control of herself, and she resented him for being such a testosterone carrier, resented herself for being susceptible. She didn't like his interest, didn't welcome his questions. In another time, another place—but this wasn't that other time or place, this was here and now, and she had enough of a load already without throwing a hard-ass cowboy into the mix.

"Not really," she said, her tone just a little curt. "I'm older than I look."

Zeke's eyebrows barely lifted. His gaze flickered, got even more intense. Instead of being put off by her response, it seemed to push him further.

He glanced down at her breast. "What's the C for?"

"Cautious," she fired back. Whose idea was it to put the monogram on the breast, anyway? Why wasn't it on the sleeve? Or the collar?

He made a low sound in his throat, a kind of acknowledgment that he'd received the hands-off signal she was sending. He acknowledged it, but that didn't mean he was giving up just yet. "Where are you from, Cautious? Not from around here, I know that much."

"Do you know everyone who lives in a hundred-mile radius of Battle Ridge?"

"Nope, but the accent is all wrong, and you've got a bit of a tan. It's fading, but it's still there. It's not a fake tan, either, like you'd get from a tanning bed. I saw you on the street earlier and you were wearing a jacket. Lightweight, but more than a local would need, so I'd say you're used to warmer weather. From the accent, I'm guessing . . . Texas."

His accuracy sent a chill down her spine. She didn't need anyone guessing anything about her, especially not where she was from. This was a heads-up to start work on altering her accent. "You're a regular Sherlock Holmes," she said, and managed a tone of supreme disinterest. Then she ruined it by pointing out, "You have a tan."

"I work outside. You don't."

"I don't live my entire life inside. You need to eat before your food gets cold," she added, stepping away to make a quick escape before she slipped up again and showed more interest than she wanted.

Finally he looked down at his plate, and he heaved a big sigh. It was so unexpected, so . . . *human,* that it stopped her. "Stone cold, this would be the best meal I've had in weeks." Then the laser beam gaze came back to her. "You didn't answer my question."

Carlin gave him a fake smile. "Not gonna." She turned away from him then, went back to the counter where she grabbed a carafe of coffee and refilled a few mugs even though Kat had made the rounds just a few minutes ago. She looked at everyone in the place *except* Zeke. She smiled at those men she already knew as regulars, but her thoughts were churning. Was Zeke with the hard green eyes and way too much interest going to force her to leave a good situation before she was ready? Possible. Maybe even probable.

She'd always known Battle Ridge, Kat, and The Pie Hole wouldn't last; she'd never had any intention of staying. Even though she'd stumbled onto room and board and nice people, Carlin had been poised to leave, possibly in the middle of the night, without saying goodbye, without offering explanations. It was as if she'd been standing on the edge of a canyon, knowing that sooner or later she'd have to jump.

But she didn't want to jump, not yet, and it made her angry to think that she might have to leave because some cowboy started asking too many questions. What business was it of his where she came from, anyway? None, that's what.

Stubbornness was a character flaw, but in that moment she mentally dug in her heels. Maybe she couldn't stay here forever; maybe she couldn't entirely let down her guard, but she was damned if one nosy cowboy was going to run her out of town before she was ready to go.

Chapter Five

ZEKE ATE TOO fast, his gaze staying on the new waitress—
"Cautious," my ass—as he shoveled in the hot meal.
Something about her didn't ring true, but he couldn't
quite put his finger on the problem. Maybe there was no
problem. Maybe his dick was getting in the way.

When she finished waiting on the men at the counter,
Kat headed his way with two boxed pies in her hands.
After eating Spencer's cooking for a while, the guys were
going to inhale those pies tonight.

She placed the boxes on the other side of the table,
then slid onto the opposite bench. "How've you been?"

"Busy."

"I know summer is a tough time on the ranch." She
sounded almost . . . sympathetic. That wasn't like her.
Kat was a no nonsense "buck up and do what you have
to do" kinda girl. "Have you had any luck finding a new
housekeeper?"

The sparkle in her eyes, the unusual attempt at
sympathy—why did he think this wasn't just a casual
question from a caring cousin who was merely concerned
about his home life?

"Nope."

Kat's mother, Aunt Ellie, had moved away from Battle

Ridge years ago, after remarrying—to a decent man, this time around, one who didn't need to have his ass kicked as he was being run out of town. Kat looked a lot like her mother, and she had also inherited Aunt Ellie's touch in the kitchen.

"You can always leave this behind and come work for me." It wasn't the first time he'd made the suggestion, or the first time she'd laughed at the very idea. He wasn't serious, anyway. She had her own business, her own life, and while blood might be thicker than water that didn't mean she was going to throw away everything she'd worked for just because he couldn't find a combination cook/housekeeper.

"In your dreams. But I *did* have a thought . . ." There was that sparkle again, the one that made him wary. For as long as he could remember, that particular twinkle in her eyes had always meant trouble. "The new girl, Carly . . ."

"No," Zeke said decisively.

"You didn't even let me finish the sentence!"

"Not necessary. You've picked up a stray and you can't afford to keep her on through the winter, so you want to pawn her off on me. How close is that to the truth?"

Kat frowned. "Carly's not a stray," she snapped, then lowered her voice. "She can cook well enough to cover the basics, she needs the work, and you're desperate."

"Not *that* desperate." He knew better. Cautious Carly would be trouble on the ranch. He'd already been through that once, with three of the hands going after the young-ish, unattached woman he'd hired, and he'd almost had to fire all three of them just when he needed them most. Being shorthanded in the middle of haying would have been disastrous. He wanted a male cook; failing that, a woman who was at least middle-aged was his second choice. One of Kat's strays, and an attractive one with a sassy mouth to boot, was dead last on his list; he could only imagine the trouble she'd cause.

Besides, if she worked for him that would complicate things. Even a moderately pretty woman on the ranch was a bad idea, he knew that now. A young, pretty woman who made his dick stand up and salute? Disaster.

As it was, he couldn't get that extra-fine ass out of his mind; when he had more time he might do something about it.

Kat slid out of the booth, and keeping her hand low so no one but him could see, she shot him a quick but decisive middle finger. He laughed and returned to what was left of his meal, which wasn't much; he'd eaten most of it on autopilot. It was no wonder the male customers lingered after their lunches were long gone, drinking coffee, talking to one another and eating dessert, watching the two women who all but danced around the place. This place was like a male fantasy: Kat and Carly—one brunette, one blond; both good-looking. Good food. Hell, the only thing missing was a stripper pole—okay, forget the stripper pole, because Kat was his cousin. Or reserve the stripper pole for Carly. Yeah, that worked for him.

Kat disappeared into the kitchen, leaving Carly working the counter. Zeke caught her eye and said, in a voice just loud enough to carry, "Hey, Cautious, how about a piece of pie and a refill on my coffee?" He lifted his half-empty mug. The Pie Hole was a casual kind of place where customers thought nothing of calling out comments to each other or to Kat, and now Carly was part of it.

"Sure thing, Sherlock," she shot back. "Blueberry or caramel?"

Either one would be good, though he'd been kind of hoping for apple. "Surprise me," he answered, then settled back to see what she brought. As long as it wasn't a cow pie, he was good.

*   *   *

"THAT COUSIN OF yours is . . ." Carlin searched for the right word, as she and Kat sat on stools in the kitchen and ate fat sandwiches. Their work was done for the day; the shared supper had become a ritual, one Carlin enjoyed.

"Hot?" Kat supplied with a grin. "Having part of the same DNA doesn't make me blind. Immune, but not blind."

Carlin waited until she'd swallowed the bite of chicken salad on whole wheat that was in her mouth, then she gave a decided *pfft*. "I was thinking of a word more like annoying."

Kat shrugged. "That, too. He's a lot of things, but the one thing he isn't, is boring."

"He's a cowboy, right?" The worn, scarred boots, the hard hands, the sun-browned skin made that a foregone conclusion.

"Pretty much. He owns a good-sized ranch about an hour away."

"Are you first cousins?"

"Yep. His dad and my mom were brother and sister. We grew up here together—well, almost together. He's a few years older than I am."

"Zeke—is that short for Ezekiel, or something?" It was kind of an unusual name, but somehow very fitting for the area, and for the man himself.

"Zeke's a nickname. His real name is A.Z. Just the initials, they don't stand for anything. But on his first day of school the teacher called him A.Z. and some of the other kids thought she was saying 'Hey, Zeke.' They called him Zeke and it stuck. He's been Zeke ever since." Kat shifted on her stool. "I don't know what Aunt Helen was thinking when she named him. It was some family name on her side—a great uncle, I think. Maybe her grandfather, or her mother's first cousin's godfather. You know how it goes with families."

"Uh, yeah," Carlin muttered wryly, thinking of her own name.

Kat slanted a knowing glance at her, a look that carried more impact because of those witchy eyes. "So, you're interested, huh?"

"What? No!" Except she'd asked too many questions—not a lot, but about two too many. The last thing she needed in her life right now was a man, especially one who asked so many questions. So what did it matter to her if his name was short for anything? It didn't. It couldn't. She should keep her mouth shut, starting now.

She shifted on her stool, put on an air of indifference. "Maybe he is a little hot, *if* you like the type," Carlin conceded. Tall, hard, good-looking . . . yeah, *that* type. *Woo hoo!* She tamped down her reaction and blithely lied. "But he's also a cowboy, and since you know the area and the people so well I feel honor-bound to follow your wise advice about avoiding the John Wayne wannabes." Plus she wasn't looking for any complications, but that went without saying.

"You are so full of shit," Kat said, grinning. Then her smile faded. "Okay, to be honest, I was kind of hoping that Zeke might hire you on as his cook and housekeeper. Since Libby left last year he hasn't had much luck finding a replacement, and he's getting desperate."

What? Carlin felt the floor fall out from beneath her. Kat was letting her go? Why else would she be trying to find someone else to hire her? Talk about being blind-sided—one minute she's relaxed, happy, joking with a friend, and the next she was mentally thumbing through the atlas wondering where she'd be headed next. She'd thought she had more time to grow her savings, plus she really liked Kat and this place, damn it. But life was what it was, and she'd deal. "You don't have to find me another job. If this isn't working out for you—"

"No!" Kat said vehemently. "That isn't it at all. I love having your help, and we get along great. It's just that I know that business slows down every winter, and when that happens I won't have the money to pay you. We're good for a couple more months, but I was just trying to think ahead."

Crap. Carlin hated to think of leaving, but she'd known all along this was temporary. "When you can't afford me any more I'll move on," she said sensibly. She'd keep an eye out for a decline in business, and if Kat didn't let her go when that happened, she'd take care of it herself. It wouldn't be the first job she'd quit since she'd started running. Usually she just left, without a word of warning and especially without any hint where she might be heading, but then the kind of jobs she'd had generally didn't require notice. She wouldn't leave Kat in the lurch like that. "I don't want to be your cousin's nanny, anyway. He struck me as a hard man to please, and life's too short." Besides, he was too curious, asked too many questions, and would probably balk at the idea of paying her under the table.

"Just as well." Kat's eyes gleamed. "He wasn't keen on the idea, either."

Carlin's heart thudded hard. "You already asked him?" Her tone was just short of a squeal. Embarrassed, she cleared her throat.

"I was just feeling him out. Don't worry, he shot the idea down pretty quick, so I didn't even get to the details about the way you need to be paid. He's none the wiser."

Out of all that, what stuck with Carlin the most was that Zeke didn't want her on his ranch. It was perfectly all right that she didn't want to go, but the fact that he'd dismissed her out of hand stung a bit.

Then a memory surfaced, and she felt herself turn red

with anger. She hadn't thought anything about it at the time, but—"I came out of the kitchen for a minute while y'all were talking, and I heard him mention something about a *stray*. I thought maybe he was talking about a dog or a cat, but he wasn't, was he? He was talking about *me*." Brad had called her a lot of things, none of them complimentary, and hadn't dented her at all because after just two dates she'd known something was way off about him, but knowing Zeke Decker had called her a stray roused every fighting instinct she had.

"He didn't mean anything by it," Kat soothed, then she paused. "Hell, I'm not going to lie to cover his ass, but he *is* under a lot of stress, so try to cut him some slack."

Carlin wasn't about to argue with Kat about her cousin, but she was boiling inside. Stray! He could kiss her ass.

Jerk.

SPENCER HAD FINALLY gotten the message about oatmeal. This morning's breakfast had been somewhat better, though a mess of toaster waffles was no one's idea of a great meal. Zeke had spread peanut butter on two warm, round waffles and slapped them together. The others had done the same, knowing they'd need some protein before lunchtime rolled around. At least they weren't being served cold cereal, which held them for about two hours before they were all starving again. Thank God there had been a huge pot of hot coffee to wash the sticky mess down.

With the hay baling behind them, the pace of his days on the ranch had eased a little. He'd managed to do some laundry, so he had clean socks *and* underwear. Would wonders never cease. He'd never thought he'd be so grateful to have a laundry basket full of clean underwear. The hands were at work and Zeke was just about to settle down with another cup of coffee and bank records to compare and reconcile, when he heard the bang of the kitchen door being thrown open and a frantic voice calling, "Boss!"

Sounded like Bo, which was bad news because Bo never panicked. Boots clumped hard and fast on the floor, and Bo appeared in the open doorway to Zeke's office, his expression urgent. Zeke was already up and on his way to the door. "What's happened?"

"Spencer," Bo said simply. "Santos got him."

Shit! A big bull could do a lot of damage to a man; Santos didn't have horns, but a swing of that big head could send someone flying, or a well-placed kick could break bones. Had Santos gone for Spencer after he was down? Normally the bull was calm, and like most animals behaved well for Spencer, but a bull was still a bull and not a house pet.

Zeke pushed his way past Bo, running through the house and out the open kitchen door, toward the barn. *Fuck!* Spencer had been set to collect semen from Santos this morning. He'd never had any trouble before; Spencer was a much better cowboy than he was a cook.

"How bad?" he asked, as they ran.

"His arm's hurt, but I can't tell how bad it is until I can get close enough to check it out. No blow to the head, he's conscious and talking, but the bull is between Spencer and the rest of us and won't move. I suppose if anybody tried to jack me off and sell my sperm I'd get pissy, too."

Inside the barn, the scene was pretty much as Bo had described. Three hands—Walt, Eli, and Patrick—stood between Santos and the door. Santos was agitated, pawing the ground and swinging that big head, facing the men and looking as if he might charge at any second. Spencer was on the ground, sitting propped against a stall, cradling his left arm. There wasn't a lick of color in his face.

"You okay?" Zeke asked, his eyes on the bull.

"Yes sir," Spencer said and swallowed "It's my fault. I was getting ready to move Santos into the head catch and I got distracted. I think I moved too fast and spooked him. He started bucking and I was in the wrong place at the wrong time. Don't blame him, boss, he's just being a bull."

Another reason why Spencer would be here for a very long time. The kid was hurt, but his first words had been in defense of the bull. "We'll worry about that later. Everyone else out." Too many people standing too close were part of the reason Santos was still spooked. And with all the others out of the way, the number of Santos's targets had decreased.

When it was just the three of them—Spencer, Santos, and Zeke—Zeke eased toward the bull. Already the animal seemed to be calmer. Zeke made low, soothing sounds as he moved forward. He'd actually petted the bull a few times, and Spencer had more than just a few, so this wasn't a mean animal. He was just big, and he was a bull. Enough said. His plan was to get Santos into the stall and locked up, and then get Spencer to the doctor—simple enough in thought, more difficult in execution, but not as difficult as it could have been. After some initial contrariness, Santos seemed to get bored, and simply turned and walked into the stall.

Zeke closed the gate and latched it, then called the rest of the men in as he went down on one knee beside Spencer. "Where do you hurt?"

Spencer's white features showed the stress of pain. "Just the shoulder. Hurts like a son of a bitch."

Thank God it was nothing more than a shoulder, which was bad enough. A kick to the head, and he and Spencer wouldn't be having this conversation. "I'm going to get you to town, let the doctor have a look at you." If they were lucky it was just a strain, and the doc in the local clinic would be able to take care of everything. If the injury was more complicated, they'd be headed to Cheyenne before the end of the day.

"I'm sorry, boss," Spencer said as Zeke helped him to his feet. "I know this is a bad time for me to be down even for a few hours. Maybe Darby can cook, or Eli. They said they can't cook a lick, but everybody's got to eat tonight."

"Don't worry about any of that right now," Zeke said. "We're grown men; we can take care of ourselves for a while." Never mind that with Spencer hurt they were now short a hand and they'd been working long hours anyway. How in hell could he spare anyone else to do any cooking? One night they could handle, but if the injury required surgery, if Spencer was going to be one-armed for a long period of time . . . If worse came to worst, Zeke would figure out how to throw a meal together himself. He'd tried that a time or two, trying to give Spencer a break, and each time it had been a disaster. Not only did he have a tendency to burn everything he cooked, he always managed to use every damn dish in the kitchen in the process.

Kenneth and Micah were married. Maybe one of their wives, or both of them, would agree to prepare a meal or two, since this was a real emergency. They'd refused before, not wanting to be pulled into a full-time job they wouldn't be able to escape from. They each had small children, so it wasn't exactly an ideal situation. One way or another, though, everyone would get fed.

Libby had spoiled them all, with three hot meals a day—not just hot meals, but hearty, good food that was filling and provided the fuel they needed to work a long, hard day. Maybe they could get by with sandwiches and cereal for a while, but it wouldn't be good enough, not when they needed four or five thousand calories a day just to break even. They'd work it out, somehow.

But as he drove toward Battle Ridge, a silent Spencer sitting in the passenger seat beside him cradling his left arm, Zeke wasn't feeling hopeful about the situation.

Chapter Six

CARLIN HATED THE new nip in the air, the cooler mornings, the shorter days, the undeniable signals that winter was coming. Business at The Pie Hole hadn't taken a hit yet, but it soon would, if Kat's previous years were anything to go by. The past couple of days she'd taken out her atlas at night, opened it to Wyoming, and run her finger along the road that would take her away from Battle Ridge, much as she had on that first day here, when she'd thought she was stopping for a bite to eat and not really hoping for anything more.

Things had changed during the past weeks. Now she didn't want to leave. But what she wanted, and reality, were two different things. It was almost time to move on.

She no longer automatically checked the exits when she walked into a place, maybe because everywhere she went was so familiar that the details were burned into her brain. Her routine took her to a handful of places where she recognized the employees and sometimes the regular customers on sight: the grocery store; the small pharmacy; the library. Those were the only places she went when she ventured out of The Pie Hole. She no longer cringed inside whenever anyone took notice of her. It wasn't that she recognized every face she saw on the street or in the café, but someone in the vicinity always did. A stranger would stand out like a sore thumb here, the way she'd stood out a few weeks ago.

Leaving would mean starting all over again, not trusting anyone, never sleeping deeply, never laughing, never dancing as she mopped. Kat would be a problem. They'd become friends; she'd want to know where Carlin was headed and how they could stay in touch.

The idea was tempting, so tempting that she didn't dare. No, Brad had no idea she'd landed in Battle Ridge, but how could she stay in contact when she didn't know how he'd found her in Dallas? Had it been her cellphone, her utility bill, her social security number—*what?* There were so many ways it could have been, and she wasn't an expert at living underground. She was learning, she was smarter now than she'd been, but she wasn't in the same class with Brad. Not only was he a wizard with the computer, as he'd told her several times during their two dates, but he was a cop and presumably had access to resources she had no idea even existed. She couldn't tell Kat where she was going; it was too dangerous. The safest course would be if they didn't stay in touch—safest for her, and definitely safest for Kat. Carlin would never let herself forget what had happened to Jina, never put Kat in that kind of jeopardy.

The best thing for her to do was just pack up her Subaru in the middle of the night and go. Kat would be pissed. Maybe that was for the best.

If she waited until the dead of winter to leave, snow and ice would hamper her. She needed to be settled somewhere before the worst of it arrived. But when her finger traced the road leading from Battle Ridge, it never landed anywhere. It just slid along the page and then drifted up.

She wasn't ready to leave.

* * *

ZEKE OPENED THE Pie Hole door and went in; it was early yet for the lunch crowd, but a couple of tables were occupied. Kat was wiping down the counter. A fresh pot of coffee was working, gurgling and competing with the scent of recently baked pies. He was dog tired, worried, but the comforting smells soothed him.

Kat gave him a sympathetic look. "I heard about Spencer. How's he doing?"

Zeke slid onto a stool at the counter. She put a coffee cup before him and expertly filled it almost to the brim. Carefully Zeke lifted the cup, took that first sip, sighed at both the taste and the situation. "He'll be fine. It could've been a lot worse."

"You look frazzled."

He *was* frazzled. It had been a week since Spencer had had his run-in with Santos, and Zeke was at the end of his rope. The moderate tear of the rotator cuff had required day surgery, which had meant a trip to Cheyenne. Spencer's physical therapy started next week, but thank goodness a physical therapist visited the clinic in Battle Ridge once a week so weekly trips to Cheyenne would not be necessary. But someone would have to drive Spencer to town for his session, which would mean on those afternoons Zeke would be two men short instead of one. He'd been trying to handle the cooking himself, what little he could do in the time he had to do it in, which wasn't much. The results had been stomach-turning. "It's been a long week." And that was the understatement of the year. Of course, the year wasn't over yet. There was still a lot of shit that could happen. "Spencer's going to be in a sling for at least six weeks."

"Have you found a cook yet?" Kat asked, and if not for the almost imperceptible lilt in her voice he'd think it was a perfectly innocent question.

He scowled at her. "You know damn well I haven't. A couple of the men tried, but, hell, they aren't cooks. I even brought in Kenneth's wife. Once." Then she'd told him flat out she had too much to do at her own home to take on his mess, too. She'd left the bunkhouse with a promise that she wouldn't be back. Micah's wife had turned him down flat. "I've been doing it myself, mostly."

Kat gave him a cheerful smile. "Well, it sounds like you've got everything well in hand," she said. "Do you want lunch or just pie? I have apple today."

Well in hand, my ass. Zeke sipped at the coffee, ignoring the smugness she wasn't even trying to disguise. The coffee was great; it was hot and strong, just the way he liked it. "Both," he said, relieved at the thought of a hot, well-prepared meal, but too damn irritated to work up a smile.

Kat started to turn away, to go into the kitchen where apparently Carly was preparing today's lunch special. Zeke sighed, faced what he had to do, and bit the bullet. He stopped her with a word. "But . . ."

She spun back around, and the expression on her face was almost evil, it was so smug. "Yes?" She tilted her head, waiting.

She knew, damn it. She *knew* why he was here and she was going to make him beg. The bad thing was, he *would* beg, if that's what it took. That's what he'd been reduced to, but he couldn't keep on the way he was going. All the hands would quit, and he couldn't blame them. Hell, he might even quit himself. "The new girl—Carly. If she's interested, I could use her at the ranch," he said grudgingly, and added, "Temporarily, of course."

One of the customers stood and headed for the cash register. Kat held up a finger to silently tell Zeke to wait while she rang up the ticket. She even engaged in a little light conversation, almost as if she were purposely making Zeke wait. "Almost?" There was no "almost" to it. She downright enjoyed torturing him.

But within a few minutes she was back. She leaned against the counter, smug smile still in place. "You were saying?"

"Damn it, Kat," he growled under his breath. "I'm desperate. I've got to get someone to fill in until Spencer is able to take on the cooking duties again, even if it is a *blonde* who . . ."

"Who what?" Kat prodded when he stopped himself before he said too much.

He needed to have his head examined. No, he *needed* someone like Libby, or a man who could cook. What he didn't need was a sassy blonde living in the same house, one who made him hard and pissed him off at the same time. Kat thought *she* was torturing him? She was nothing compared to what having Cautious Carly in his house would be like, but he wasn't about to tell her that. "What do you know about her? I'll run her references when I get a chance, but until then—"

Kat's smile vanished. She gave him a long, level stare. "We have to talk about that."

Oh, fuck. He'd known *something* was up with Miss Cautious, and Kat had just confirmed it.

She disappeared into the kitchen, and was soon back with a plate of some chicken and gravy and rice dish that had his mouth watering on sight.

"Eat first," she said. "Then we'll talk."

It didn't bode well that she was trying to make sure he was in a good mood before they continued the conversation.

She left him to eat in peace while she checked on her other customers, refilled cups and glasses. Then she waited until they left before she came back, which told him she wanted privacy for this conversation.

What the hell was he getting himself into?

What choice did he have?

*   *   *

CARLIN KNEW ZEKE Decker was in the restaurant. She'd heard his voice, distant but distinct, as soon as he'd come in. His tone was low, but deep and kind of raspy, probably from barking orders all day long. Or maybe it was like the voice of doom. Yeah, that was a great comparison. She was glad today she was the one cooking the daily special—Kat's recipe, but an easy one for her to get in some practice—instead of working the counter. The last thing she wanted to do was wait on that ass who'd callously called her a "stray," and wouldn't consider hiring her even though, according to Kat, he desperately needed someone out at his ranch. Not that she *wanted* to work for him, but it was the principle of the thing.

Then Kat stuck her head into the kitchen. "Hey, turn the heat off under everything and come on out here for a minute, okay?" Carlin's heart jumped, which was a stupid thing for it to do, but evidently cardiac muscles just had impulses, not brains.

She took a deep breath and turned everything off, then washed her hands and thoroughly dried them—twice—before she left the kitchen.

The first thing she saw was that Zeke was the only customer there. It was a little early for the regular lunch customers, and the last of the breakfast crowd had left. Zeke had cleaned his plate and had a half-eaten piece of apple pie sitting in front of him.

He looked at her as if he was very unhappy with what he saw. He did everything but growl. Yeah, well, let him try to look nice wearing a gravy-stained apron and a hairnet; she gave him back as good as she got, all but snarling at him.

Kat glared at him, and rapped her knuckles on the counter to emphasize her point. "Before I start, you have to promise me that everything we say to you will remain confidential."

His scowl got even darker, and he groaned as he rubbed his face. "Shit. This can't be good."

"Promise," Kat insisted. "Or this won't go an inch further and you can go look somewhere else for a cook."

What? Carlin shook her head in protest. She didn't want to go cook for Grumpy and his not-so-merry band of cowboys. This was *so* not a good idea. She glared at him. And exactly what was Kat going to tell him? Surely not about—

He glared back, but said, "Fine. I promise." He didn't sound happy about it, but Kat seemed to be satisfied.

She got straight to the point. "Carlin has some trouble of the stalker variety. She needs to stay completely off the grid for a while."

"Kat!" Appalled, Carlin stared at her. So much for keeping her name a secret. Maybe he hadn't picked up on it, because Carly and Carlin sounded so much alike, but she glanced at him to find him staring at her with an intensity that told her he'd noticed, all right.

Kat raised her hand to forestall any more protests. "Trust me," she said. "He can help."

"Yeah? How?"

"His situation has gotten worse, and now you're in the driver's seat because he needs you more than you need him," Kat said, gloating even though Zeke was sitting right there listening to everything she said. She smiled. He made a sound in his throat that might be a growl.

Zeke was already shaking his head. "I can't believe this. The last thing I need is to take on another problem—"

Kat snorted. "Yeah, because you're doing so well on your own. Carlin can cook and clean, and the ranch would be the perfect place for her to lay low for a few months." Her hands went out and up. "Win-win."

"I just need someone for a few weeks, until Spencer's

out of his sling. And I sure as hell don't need anyone
who has to *lay low*."

"And why would I be *laying low* at the ranch anyway?"
Carlin asked. "Why couldn't I stay here and drive out to
the ranch every day? Assuming I wanted to work for him
anyway, which I don't, me being a stray and all. We strays
don't like to work hard." She curled her lip at him to let
him know exactly how much she appreciated his choice
of words, which was zero, zip, nada.

But Kat shook her head. "It's a long drive, at least an
hour, that you don't want to be making twice a day, especially at night. You'd have to get up at three-something
in the morning to get to the ranch in time to have breakfast ready, and wouldn't get home until ten, eleven at
night, sometimes. It just wouldn't work, not even when
the weather's good. The days are getting short now, and
once winter rolls around the roads can get pretty icy.
This is definitely a live-in job." She shrugged her shoulders. "And besides, I stay upstairs in the winter when
the roads are bad."

Yeah, she'd mentioned that before, but Carlin had settled into the attic room and gotten so used to it she'd forgotten. "Oh." So it was all or nothing. She had to choose
Grumpy, or she had to hit the road.

"From what I hear, Spencer wasn't doing such a great
job before his accident, anyway," Kat continued, turning her attention back to Zeke, determined to force this
situation in the direction she wanted.

"Maybe he wasn't, but no one has gone hungry." An
unspoken "yet" hung in the air. Then he admitted defeat, his scowl deepening. "Damn it, if I had any other
choice, I wouldn't even consider—"

Carlin lifted a hand to cut him off. She'd heard enough.
Maybe—probably—she should have her head examined,
but instead of deterring her his reluctance had the opposite effect. She *wanted* to work for him, but on her

terms, not his. She wanted to make him eat his words—
which, honestly, might taste better than her cooking. She
was learning, but *learning* was the operative word. And
Kat was right. This was a near-perfect, short-term solution. "It sounds to me like you could use some help. I'm
willing to take on the job, but only if you agree to some
things. I don't need to be fired in the middle of the winter
in Wyoming," she said, taking control of the situation
and warming to it, because his gaze was getting more
narrow and hostile by the moment. She was doing good.
"I either move on within the next couple of weeks, or I
stay until spring."

Zeke studied her for a moment with those piercing
green eyes that held no sympathy. "If I don't hire you,
where are you going?"

"That's none of your business. And even if it was, I
wouldn't tell you."

Kat stepped back and crossed her arms, apparently
satisfied to set this conversation into motion and then let
the two involved parties fight it out.

The idea of a place to stay for the winter, food and
lodging, a ranch that was literally in the middle of nowhere . . . it was the perfect solution, except for one
irate, stubborn ranch owner. She was so tired of running, she'd enjoyed her weeks here in Battle Ridge, and
no way was she going to let him ruin this for her. He
needed her more than she needed him. Still, she might as
well throw him a bone.

"I'll work hard, and I'll stay out of your way," she told
him briskly. "All I ask is that you pay me in cash, keep the
name 'Carlin' to yourself, and stay out of *my* way. And
keep me on until spring. In the spring I'll move on." By
then she'd have a good bit of cash in her pocket, and—if
she was lucky—a plan of some sort that would free her
from this prison Brad had created for her.

Zeke still looked unconvinced and suspicious. "How

do I know this stalker story isn't a bunch of bull and you're wanted by the police? For all I know you're a con artist, or wanted for murdering your last employer."

"Hey!" Kat yelped, outraged on Carlin's behalf. "*I'm* her last employer."

Carlin thought that maybe she should be outraged herself, but she wasn't. She knew how this had to look to Zeke, but she couldn't tell him the details. She couldn't plead her case. And she would *not* beg. Zeke Decker would take her for the winter, or he wouldn't.

"All I have to offer is my word, I suppose. I'm guilty of being naive. Nothing more."

He took a few minutes to think it over. It was obvious he wasn't pleased by the development, but he hadn't dismissed the idea of hiring her out of hand, either. He must really be in a tight spot to even consider it.

"You can cook, can't you?" he finally asked.

"I can," Carlin said confidently. Maybe she wasn't on Kat's level, but she had learned a lot working at The Pie Hole and she could follow a recipe. She could learn more.

"You got anything against doing laundry?"

"Nope." She thought about telling her prospective employer that she was willing to do anything, but she didn't. She didn't want to give him the wrong idea with a vague and possibly suggestive *anything*. "I also do windows."

Zeke took his last bite of pie, chewing it and the situation over at the same time. She could tell he was sorting through his options, which, from what she'd heard, weren't good. He either hired her, or he did without a cook. He was obviously unhappy when he growled, "Fine, you're hired. Fair warning, though: the windows haven't been cleaned in about a year."

Carlin caught herself smiling, and she doused it immediately. She didn't want him getting the wrong idea, that maybe she was *grateful*. She was, but not the way he'd think. She didn't want him to assume he had all the power in this new professional relationship. He needed her as much as she needed him. No, he needed her *more*. She wouldn't allow him to forget that.

There was still the matter of her salary to negotiate. And she had to figure out what she was going to do about the way her heart kept beating faster every time he was close by.

Suddenly she felt very uneasy. For months, she hadn't found any man attractive, because Brad had left such a terrible imprint on her psyche. Now, all of a sudden, her wayward insides were taking notice of a man she knew for sure she was going to leave. What the *hell* was wrong with her?

Okay, it was official: she'd gone nuts.

Chapter Seven

CARLIN'S HEART WAS pounding at a ridiculous rate the next day as she followed Zeke Decker's dark green pickup truck down one narrow road after another. Kat had been right—it was a damn long drive through a lot of nothing to get from Battle Ridge to the ranch. She tried to calm down by calling herself silly for being so excited, she tried to distract herself by first one thing then another, but the fact was: she was going to be working at Zeke Decker's house!

And if that wasn't silly, she didn't know what was, to be as giddy as a teenager at the idea of being close to a man. Not dating him, not doing anything except probably working her butt off, but—being close to him! Seeing him every day! Handling his dirty underwear!

She was mentally unbalanced. Had to be. She couldn't feel this way about him. It wasn't just silly, it was impossible. And dangerous. Considering her situation, nothing could—

Oh, wow!

Her mouth fell open at the grandeur around her. She hadn't been able to distract herself, but God and Mother Earth had done the job, and how.

They'd long since left the asphalt highway, turned right

onto a graveled road, then left onto another one that was less well graveled, then sort of veered onto a dirt road that seemed to meander all over creation and back. It was noon, the sun was directly overhead, so she didn't even have any idea what direction they were traveling in. All she knew for certain was that they were climbing higher in altitude, because her ears kept popping.

And the scenery was beautiful. No, the word "beautiful" was too mild; the scenery was absolutely breathtaking. She almost gave herself whiplash trying to see all the gorgeous valleys and the awe-inspiring mountains. The view from Battle Ridge of the mountains had been beautiful, but now she was much closer, and she felt almost as if she could barely breathe this close to something that words couldn't really describe. All the head-swiveling didn't do anything to help her keep her sense of direction, but what the hell, that was already blown, so she might as well enjoy the drive.

On a more practical note, this job on the Decker ranch had better work out, because there was no way in hell she could find her way back to Battle Ridge; she'd effectively be stranded out here, at least for a while. Her short and not-very-sweet acquaintance with Decker made her less than optimistic that he'd take pity on her and lead her back to civilization, especially since he was in such dire straits. He evidently needed a cook and housekeeper bad enough to hire a "stray."

"Stray," she muttered. "I'll show you stray."

Just thinking about that made her get pissed off all over again. No, there was no again to it, because she hadn't stopped being pissed off to begin with, and that was good. She wasn't certain exactly what she meant by showing him, or what she could do, but she'd think of something to get back at him. She needed the money, she needed the job, but right now he needed her even more and that gave her the upper hand. She liked being pissed.

Pissed off was the best mood for her to be in. Otherwise, Decker was too much of a temptation.

Hell, he was a temptation even when she was pissed off.

Damn it. Damn him, for being so blasted sexy—and he didn't even try! Please God, she though frantically, don't let him ever try. She didn't know if she could resist him. Once upon a time, before Brad, she'd have been dancing on the ceiling at the way Decker made her feel: the thumping heartbeat, the nervousness and excitement in the pit of her stomach, the restlessness, the sensation of her skin being too hot and tight. Was it coincidence or a warning that the symptoms of strong attraction were pretty much the same as those for a dread disease? She could imagine that if she went to an ER with those symptoms she'd be slapped into a cardiac unit, or isolation, or both.

But there was no dancing on the ceiling now. He'd made it clear that she was just a fill-in until he could find someone permanent, preferably a man, and that suited her fine. For now the Decker ranch—the wonderfully isolated Decker ranch—was a very good place to hide. If Decker found a permanent cook before the winter was over, she expected he'd fire her even though he'd promised not to, but considering her circumstances she was really okay with that. After all, she'd forced him to make that promise only to piss him off, the way he'd pissed her off. Fair was fair, right?

All she had to do was keep him at a distance, and far away from her overactive hormones. I can do that, she thought, and smirked to herself. She might even have fun doing it. And if she indulged her hormones by eyeing the eye-candy from time to time, that was okay, because washing his dirty underwear would even things out and keep her head out of the clouds. As long as she didn't catch herself sniffing his shirts, she was fine.

He turned his pickup onto a graveled road that was marked by two posts so big and rough it looked as if someone had simply cut down two trees—two really big trees—and hacked the limbs off, then stuck the trees in the ground. The twenty-foot-tall posts supported a cross member that could be yet another tree, a rough-hewn slab of wood easily twice as thick as her body, into which the words "Rocking D Ranch" had been carved. Carlin steered the Subaru in the truck's dusty path, feeling as if she were crossing an armed and barricaded border into a foreign country. Okay, so she hadn't seen any machine-gun nests . . . yet. They might just be well hidden.

"Wow," she muttered. As far as entrances went, she found this one pretty impressive: primitive, but impressive. Someone had really wanted that top tree slab up there, because the process couldn't have been easy. She'd felt the same way about the Hoover Dam the first time she'd seen it: someone had to have been desperate to dam that river, to have gone to that much effort. Not that this compared to the Hoover Dam, but still.

Finally they reached civilization . . . kind of. The first sign was fencing, and she saw some horses grazing peacefully in the pasture. She wasn't sure how she felt about horses. They were pretty, but big, and she thought they might be unpredictable. Didn't matter; she was here to cook and clean, not ride a horse.

There looked to be a couple of storage-type buildings, and a huge barn. As soon as they drove past the barn, she saw the house. It was a pretty house, obviously remodeled and added on to: two-story, white, with a wide porch running across the entire front. There was a one-story addition, with a single step leading up to an inset rectangular concrete porch. Even farther to the right was a long, low building that she assumed was the bunkhouse. Between the two houses, and set back by itself, was a cabin that could be no more than two rooms, and both of them small.

Decker stopped his truck at an angle in front of the small porch. Dollars to doughnuts one of those doors opened into the kitchen, or more likely a mudroom leading into the kitchen. No one else was in sight. From the way Kat had described the ranch, Carlin had expected it to be bustling with activity, but except for the grazing horses she hadn't seen any other living creature. Well, and Decker. She supposed he counted as a "living creature."

She got out of the car and stood in the open doorway, abruptly suspicious as she looked around. Alarm sent tingles skittering up her spine. Okay, she knew it was irrational; Kat wouldn't have steered her wrong, wouldn't have sent her into a dangerous situation. Still . . . she was out here all alone with a man she didn't know, regardless of how he made her hormones all jittery and happy. Common sense told her everything was okay, but common sense had been wrong about Brad. Keeping her right foot on the floor mat, poised to jump back in the car and hit the door lock, she gave Decker a flinty, narrow-eyed look. Her tone was flat as she asked, "Where is everyone?"

"Working," he said shortly. "The cattle don't live in the house."

She didn't want that to make sense, but it did. She slid her keys into her pocket, eased her foot out of the car and onto the ground. "Lead on."

He reached for her car door, evidently to get her scant luggage from the vehicle, but some knee-jerk reaction made Carlin quickly thumb the remote and all the locks clicked down. Decker straightened and scowled at her. "What the hell are you doing?"

"I'll carry my own bags," she said curtly. It was a small hill and she didn't intend to die on it, but for now it was just the right size for needling him.

His green eyes went cold and narrow as he hooked his

thumbs in his belt. His grim mouth set in a hard line so thin she could barely see his lips. "I don't give a damn if I carry them, you carry them, or they walk in on their own, just stop wasting time so you can get started doing your damn job, and I can get back to mine," he barked.

Jeez, what a grouch. She turned her head in case she couldn't control the satisfied smile that threatened to break loose as she unlocked the car and hauled her bags out; he muttered something she was glad she couldn't understand, then wheeled around and stalked up onto the porch.

He opened the door, and she noticed that he didn't have to unlock it first. He might not like it, but unlocked doors were now something in his past, at least while she was in the house alone. And that reminded her . . . "I'll need a house key," she said as she followed him into the house.

"Why?"

The question so stupefied her that she stopped in her tracks and stared at him. "So I can get in when you aren't here," she explained as slowly and carefully as if he were just now learning English.

In response he said, "Let me show you something," in almost exactly the same tone she'd used. He pulled the door shut with a bang. "See that round thing? We call it a doorknob, and we use it to open the door. Pay attention, now. See how I put my hand on the doorknob? Turn it to the right, and—" Slowly he demonstrated, and triumphantly thrust the door open. "I'll be damned if the door doesn't open! That's how you get in when I'm not here."

Ohhh, bonus points for both the demonstration and the sarcasm; she knew great smart-ass-ness when she saw it, and this was championship.

"Correction," she cooed. "That's how it used to work. From now on you'll need a key, because I will be locking the door while I'm here alone during the day, and if I go to Battle Ridge for supplies I'll lock the door when I leave. I hope you have two keys, otherwise you'll be knocking on the door to be let into your own house." Then, because she couldn't help herself, she smirked at him.

He crossed his arms and leaned a broad shoulder against the doorframe. His expression hadn't lightened, but a glint in those green eyes suddenly gave her the impression he was almost enjoying himself. "Suppose I can't find a key?"

"Suppose I call a locksmith out and have the locks rekeyed?"

"Suppose you can afford that?"

"If I have to, I suppose I can." Oh, yeah, she could play up-the-ante all day long.

"Will you give me a key if you do?"

She opened her mouth to shoot back that he could have a key only if he paid for it, but abruptly she realized the reason for his enjoyment. "Oh my God! You really don't know where your house key is, do you?"

He shrugged. "It's around somewhere."

He was blocking most of the doorframe but one side of it was free, so she banged her head three times against the wood. Looking up at him with a scowl, she said, "I'm a woman. Wo-man. You might feel safe living way out here and not locking the house, but I don't. I've been taught from the time I was in kindergarten to be cautious of strangers, to lock my doors, to park under a streetlight if I have to be out at night, and how to use my keys to jab out a man's eyes. I need a house key. I can't sleep in an unlocked house."

"Can't jab out anyone's eyes, either."

"I'd use my car key for that."

His lips relaxed a little and he cocked his head to the side as he studied her for a long minute. She'd spent long months trying to avoid just that kind of attention, and it didn't escape her notice that, with Decker, she was breaking her own rules about staying under the radar. She was smart-mouthing him when an employee in desperate need of a job, as she was, should be tripping over all the yes sirs and no sirs coming out of her mouth.

What the hell. Given the fierceness of her attraction to him, the only way to balance it out was to fight fire with fire, and keep needling him. He'd pretty much disliked her on sight—and never mind that, if she thought about it, the idea always gave her a little pang of hurt—so she'd do everything she could to keep that dislike bright and alive.

"Fine. You're right," he finally said. "I'll look for the key tonight. If I find it, I'll have it duplicated for you."

"Tomorrow," she insisted. "No longer. If you don't take care of it, I'll call a locksmith tomorrow." She studied the lock on the door. "Come to think of it, I'll call the locksmith anyway. Don't bother looking for the key. You don't even have a deadbolt. I'll have one installed on all the outside doors."

He rolled his eyes up. "You're paranoid, you know. People out here all tend to have rifles and such, and anyone breaking in would have to assume—"

"I want to borrow one of your rifles, and a butcher knife, to keep in my bedroom until I can get some decent locks installed on these doors."

He paused, eyeing her, and after a moment said cautiously, "A butcher knife?"

"For close-contact battle. Just in case." She wasn't kidding. She might be exaggerating a bit, but she wasn't kidding. Since Brad, she'd done a lot of improbable, just-in-case things, arming herself with whatever she thought might work and cause some harm, or gain her enough time to get away, or both. She hadn't slept with a chain saw beside her bed yet, but she didn't rule it out, either.

"Paranoid, homicidal, and delusional—as in, if you

think you couldn't stop someone with a rifle, you'd have a chance with a knife."

"Knives are more scary than guns. Most gunshots miss, you know."

He gave a dismissive snort. "Mine don't."

No, his shots probably didn't miss. He'd probably been hunting since he could walk. Okay, another exaggeration, but probably not by much. "Well, considering I've never fired any kind of gun, I'm betting I'd miss. Maybe I should go for a shotgun."

"I vote for a straitjacket."

"Hah," she replied, wrinkling her nose just enough to imply a sneer, to show him what she thought of his opinion. She gave a swift tilt of her head. "Are you going to show me the house, or keep me standing out here holding these bags until sundown?"

Having insisted on carrying the bags herself, she was fully prepared for him to snap something insulting at her, but instead he just rolled his eyes and gave her a mocking bow, sweeping his hand toward the door. "After you."

She stepped inside a combination mudroom and laundry. There was a bench to the right, against the outside wall, and in front of the bench was an assortment of boots—regular boots, insulated boots, cowboy boots, even a lone set of sneakers. The congregation of boots wasn't neat and orderly; it was a jumble, some standing like sentinels, some on their sides like fallen soldiers. One sneaker had sneaked in among the military contingent, while the other lay forlornly half behind the bench. The wall beneath the high window was lined with hooks, which looked to be three-deep in coats and jackets. The man was serious about his outerwear.

To the left were a modern front-loading clothes washer and dryer, mounted on pedestals . . . she thought. Either that or they were perched atop a truly astounding pile of clothes; she couldn't tell for certain because the mounds completely covered the bases of the machines. She could see parts of two laundry baskets, but they, too, were mostly buried.

Carlin didn't say anything. She couldn't; she was too busy mentally calculating exactly how many loads of laundry those piles represented, and how long it would take her to get everything washed, dried, and put away. The laundry alone had to afford months of job security.

At the other end of the small room was another door, the top half of which was glass panes. She could see into the room on the other side, which was the kitchen, and she actually skidded to a stop, took a reflexive step back. She wasn't Catholic, but—Holy Mary Mother of God!

He opened the door into the kitchen and stepped inside, threw an impatient look over his shoulder. "Are you coming, or not?"

"Not," she replied, her eyes wide as she surveyed the wreckage behind him. "Holy crap! You lied. You lied like a yellow dog, with apologies to the dog."

Dark brows drew together, eyes narrowed. "Lied?" he repeated softly.

She pointed into the kitchen. "The cows do live in the house!"

He turned his head to give the kitchen a slow, considering look. Then, damn him, a very pleased smile curved his lips. "Should keep you busy for a while," he said cheerfully. "Come on, I'll show you where you'll bunk."

In silence, her eyes wide, she followed him through the kitchen piled high with dirty dishes, pots and pans, empty grocery bags, spilled flour . . . or salt . . . or sugar . . . or all three—and yet more dirty clothes. Ye gods, this man owned enough clothes to fill a department store, as long as the department store dealt in not much else besides denim, cotton, and flannel.

From the kitchen they went down a short hallway to the left; she could tell they were still in the added-on part of the house. "These were Libby's rooms," he said, opening a door. "It used to be two bedrooms, when her daughter lived here, too, but after Jen grew up and left I remodeled it so Libby had her own living space and privacy. You have your own bathroom, too, of course. It isn't fancy, but it's private."

Under other circumstances she'd have been ecstatic, but she was still shell-shocked by the condition of the laundry and kitchen.

The first room they entered was the sitting room, definitely on the cozy side, but nice. Well, once she got rid of the boxes he'd stored in the room it would be nice. Empty boxes, half-empty boxes, unopened boxes. Compared to the mess she faced in the kitchen, though, this was nothing. She'd have it set to rights in no time.

The walls were painted a neutral beige, just dark enough to edge into the warm tones. There was enough space for a small sofa and a chair, two end tables that each held a lamp, a coffee table, and a surprisingly up-to-date flatscreen TV mounted on the wall, which she supposed was almost necessary given the size of the room. An entertainment center, even a small one, would have eaten up most of the remaining floor space. There was even a small gas fireplace, which she imagined would be extremely welcome during the winter.

"The bedroom's back there," he said, pointing to a door. "And the bathroom attaches to the bedroom. That's it." He adjusted his hat on his head, his expression so satisfied she wanted to slap him. "I'll leave you to it. There are nine of us. You'll be feeding nine for breakfast and lunch. There will just be seven for supper. Two of the hands are married, and they go home at the end of the day."

"As they should," Carlin said, dropping her bags on the floor. Her bedroom could use a dusting, but at least there were no boxes stored here.

"You can cook and serve everyone here or in the bunkhouse," Zeke said. "Your choice. Spencer always felt more comfortable in the bunkhouse, but when I cooked I did it here, in the house."

She shot him a dirty look. "So that mess in the kitchen is yours."

He grinned. "It's yours, now."

She thought about the mess seven or nine men would make, a mess she would have to clean up no matter where it was made. And then she thought about making the short trip between the house and the bunkhouse three times a day. Not so hard now, but when winter arrived it would be a different story. "House," she said simply.

Zeke nodded once. "We'll be back at dark, so have supper ready." His tone mirrored his expression, which meant she now wanted to slap him twice.

Nine. Nine. She could do this. She'd just pretend she was cooking for a crowd at Kat's. But tonight for supper, there would be seven hungry men, and she had so much to do before then! Somehow she was supposed to get that wreck of a kitchen organized enough to actually cook something, not just slap sandwiches together.

Daunting as that seemed at the moment, it was far from the toughest job she'd ever had.

On the way out of the room Zeke paused and looked back. "Oh, yeah—don't forget to cook enough for yourself, too."

Chapter Eight

A GRIN SPREAD over Zeke's face as he drove away from the house. A huge sense of relief spread through him, one so strong he had the urge to stop, throw his hat in the air, and run around the truck whooping with joy. Thank you, Jesus! He didn't have to cook supper tonight!

It didn't matter if Carlin could or couldn't cook even half as well as Libby. All she had to do was put edible food on the table, and she'd pretty much beat both his own and Spencer's efforts. Now he didn't have to try to remember to put a load of clothes in the washer before he rushed out to put in a long day on the ranch, or after he dragged himself in from the same long day. Now he didn't have to figure out what he'd done wrong with the dishwasher, why suds were running every fucking where, because as far as he could remember *that* had never happened before. Dishwashing detergent, dishwasher, dishes; what about that equation would cause a Vesuvian-type eruption? Damned if he knew, and now it was Carlin's problem.

Food he hadn't cooked, clothes that were clean, not having to fight his way through the house because he hadn't had time to even halfway pick stuff up since Spencer had gotten hurt—if that wasn't the definition of heaven, he didn't know what was.

If he hadn't enjoyed so much the look of horror on Carlin's face when she'd first seen the kitchen, he might have been embarrassed—but he had, and he wasn't. In fact, he'd gotten a great deal of pleasure out of leaving the mess for her to handle. *That* had stopped her smart mouth.

He had to admit, though, he'd kind of enjoyed all the sass. Despite her stalker troubles—assuming her tale was true, and Zeke didn't ordinarily take everything he was told at face value, so he was withholding judgment on that—she didn't show the least bit of fear. Some women might have turned timid, but not Carlin. She wasn't afraid of him at all, and he liked that. He liked it almost as much as he liked that heart-shaped ass of hers.

Nope, on second thought, it was no contest: her ass won by a landslide.

Half an hour later he reached the site where Darby and Eli were repairing a water pump station that had been damaged by one of the tractors while they were cutting hay. Eli was the best on the ranch with mechanical stuff; Darby was a good all-around hand, which was why Zeke kept him on despite the man's nonending litany of complaints about any- and everything; when tempers got short it was hard listening to him, but some people were never satisfied no matter what, and Darby was one of them.

As he got out of the truck, both men straightened from where they were bent over the pump. Eli swiped a greasy hand across his forehead, wiping away sweat but leaving a black smear in its place.

"How's it going?" Zeke asked, pulling on his gloves to help, if needed.

"We've about got it done," Eli replied. "Another half hour, maybe."

"Good."

Darby arched his back to relieve the strain in his muscles. "Got the new cook settled in?"

"She's there. I don't know if she's settled in or not." Thinking of the expression on her face when he'd left her to it made him want to smile again.

"I hope to God she can cook better than Spencer," Darby grouched. "But then, almost anybody could cook better than Spencer—except for you, boss."

That was the literal truth, so Zeke didn't take umbrage. Then Darby continued, "How old is she?"

Just four words, but they were enough to set off Zeke's alarms. Darby had been involved in the situation that caused him to lose the last cook. "She's young enough," he said sharply, "and you stay the hell away from her."

"Oh ho!" Darby grinned at him, though there was precious little humor in the expression. "Got the hots for her yourself, huh?"

Whether he did or not—and he admitted to himself there was a definite physical spark, at least on his part— had nothing to do with the situation, and he didn't want the men thinking he looked at Carlin as his private sexual preserve. She deserved to be treated with respect, and he'd make damn sure she was. On the other hand, anything going on with Darby was something he wanted to nip in the bud, right now.

"No, what I have is a cook and a housekeeper, and I'll be damned if I let you cause me to lose this one."

"That wasn't my fault—" Darby began, a whiny note entering his tone.

"I never said it was," Zeke interrupted. "What I'm saying is, I don't give a shit. Evidently I can find another ranch hand a hell of a lot easier than I can find a cook, so stay the hell away from her or it's your ass that'll be put on the road, not hers. That goes for every hand working here, not just you, so you might want to spread the word."

He'd have to stay on his toes, he thought. Carlin was pretty. Not beautiful, not overtly sexy, but her features were finely drawn and delicate enough to make a man take notice, without even factoring in the pertness of those small, high breasts and the roundness of her ass. Men would always react to her. He'd have to make it plain to the horny single men on his place that she was completely off-limits.

For that matter, he'd have to remind himself. His dick had stood up and taken notice of her the very first time he'd seen her, and under different circumstances—well, the circumstances weren't different. She was in a difficult situation, and her thorny disposition made it plain she wasn't looking for any kind of romance, even the temporary kind, which was all he wanted anyway. Too bad. He'd live, though; a lack of sex was damned annoying, but it wasn't fatal.

It was also too damn bad that he didn't like walking away from something he wanted. He hadn't had a lot of practice at it, and he wasn't a good loser. What was good about losing? Not a damn thing.

What the hell had he been thinking, hiring her and bringing her out here?

Well, that part was easy. He'd been thinking that he wanted a clean house, clean clothes, and food that was worth eating. He'd been desperate enough that he'd deliberately ignored the physical attraction he felt for her. And, face it, he really wanted some long, hot rolls in the hay with Carlin and her sassy mouth, not to mention that fine ass. His good mood abruptly faded a bit, thinking of the months—maybe—ahead when he'd have to deny himself. There was no telling how long she'd stay, but one thing was for damn certain: she wasn't here forever. The minute she didn't feel safe, she'd be in the wind.

"What's her name?" Eli asked. He was single, too, but not a horndog like Darby. Eli was in his forties, had been married once a long time ago when he was rodeoing. He'd go to some of the bars, do some dancing, but seldom actually dated. That didn't mean he wouldn't like to date, though. Zeke added Eli to his mental list of men to closely watch.

"Carly Hunt." Thank God "Carly" was close enough to "Carlin" that if he slipped and said her real name the odds were no one would catch it. "What I just told Darby goes for you, too, Eli. Hell, it goes for everybody." *Even himself. Damn it.*

"You don't have to worry about me, boss," Eli said evenly. "I reckon I'm as sick of what's been passing for food around here as everyone else is." His lips twitched a little, but he knew better than to smirk.

Darby didn't.

CARLIN PAUSED TO take a breather—a very short one, because she felt as if she'd be crushed under an avalanche of laundry if she rested for too long. The washer and dryer were both running, as they had been almost constantly for the past three hours. The dishwasher was running, too, and she'd washed the worst of the pots and pans by hand. No dishwasher in the world would've gotten those burned pots clean. She was beginning to feel better about her job. Not only was she making progress, she hadn't seen Zeke at all during those three hours. And she knew job security when she saw it; he obviously needed help way more than he'd let on.

Maybe if she didn't have to see him, she wouldn't have to worry about her out-of-control hormones misbehaving. Besides, by the end of the day she'd be so tired, even the most insistent hormone would be too exhausted to quiver.

Her first order of the day had been to take stock of the pantry and fridge, see what was available, and make a plan for dinner. Both were well stocked, for which she was deeply grateful. She supposed she should also be grateful that her boss hadn't expected her to prepare lunch for nine—ten, if she counted herself—the minute she'd set foot in the house. Maybe the men were eating sandwiches in the bunkhouse, or else they'd had an early lunch. The "why" didn't matter. The end result was she had some time to set things straight before she had to cook.

She threw together a huge but simple tuna casserole; it was ready to go in the oven. The casserole was one of the few things she didn't need a recipe for, because she'd done it so often, but never before on this scale. It was easy: rice, cream of mushroom soup, lots of tuna, mixed vegetables, some seasoning, and enough cheese to constipate an elephant. Belatedly she wondered if any of the men were lactose intolerant. If so, too bad. Someone should've told her if there were any special dietary needs.

She had made a huge casserole, so there would be more than enough left over for lunch tomorrow. She'd decided to make corn bread, because the directions on the side of the box of corn bread mix seemed simple enough, but if that was going to be any good it would have to be prepared at the last minute. There was also brownie mix and ice cream. Would they expect dessert every day? She hadn't asked, but it would get her off to a good start if she provided something sweet her first day here.

A roast for tomorrow night was thawing in the refrigerator. Planning ahead would be the trick to surviving here. And she *would* survive, green eyes, mounds of laundry, nice butt, and nasty kitchen aside. Survival was what she did these days.

Carlin heard the insistent knocking on the back door, and wondered how many times whoever was out there had tried to get her attention. *Whoever*—ha! It had to be Zeke, checking up on her. She dried her hands on a kitchen towel, put a hand to her hair to rearrange a couple of wayward strands, then surveyed the kitchen and assessed her progress. Let him wait. Of course, the longer he waited the more pissed he'd be, and she was the one who had to face him down while he was in that apparently semipermanent state.

But the man on the other side of the double-paned window set in the door was young, blond, and fresh-faced. A combination of shame and disappointment washed over her. It wasn't Zeke, after all. She'd made someone else wait. Phooey.

She unlocked and opened the door. One good look, and she knew who this man was. "You must be Spencer."

"The gizmo on my arm gave me away, huh?" He grinned, the wide, unfettered grin of a man-child who had no enemies, no emotional pain, no worries at all, beyond a bum arm in an impressively complicated sling. "What's wrong with the door? I couldn't get it to open, and then I knocked and knocked. It must be broken. I'll tell Zeke."

Yet another man who was unfamiliar with locked doors. "The door isn't broken, it was locked."

He looked shocked. "Why?"

She needed an explanation, something besides the out-and-out truth. "New place, out in the boonies, I guess you could say I'm a little spooked. I'm Carly," she said before he had a chance to pursue the subject, sticking to the nickname that wouldn't stand out the way Carlin would. "Sorry I didn't get to the door right away. With the washer and dryer and dishwasher running, I just didn't hear you knocking."

"Nice to meet you, Carly." As Spencer walked in, he glanced around the mudroom, and his eyes widened. "Wow! You've been busy, that's for sure. That pile of dirty clothes was at least two feet higher last time I was here. The boss doesn't much care for washing clothes."

"Or anything else, apparently," Carlin muttered. "What can I do for you, Spencer?" There had to be a reason he was dropping by, and she didn't have time to visit and chat, not today.

"I thought maybe you could use some help. The doctor told me to rest, and Zeke won't let me do a darn thing, so I'm kinda going stir-crazy. Did you know there is absolutely *nothing* good on television during the daytime?"

"I did, yes," she said with admirable seriousness, while she was wondering what she was going to do with him.

His intentions were good, but Carlin had no idea how a one-armed man would be able to help her. He'd only be underfoot, and the last thing she needed was a man to trip over as she attempted to clean and cook. Spencer was so earnest and friendly, though, she couldn't very well tell him that. Sighing inwardly, she decided she'd just have to bear with him, because no way was she going to hurt his feelings.

"Why don't you have a seat and tell me all about this ranch and the men I'll be cooking for?" She pulled a chair away from the kitchen table, and placed it in the corner where her visitor would be out of the way. "You can tell me what you all like to eat, if there's anything I shouldn't cook, if there's anything I particularly need to know . . ." Like, why isn't a man like Zeke Decker married? Why isn't there a girlfriend, at least, washing his underwear? Nope, no way was she asking that. She might wonder, but she wasn't asking.

"We're not picky eaters. Except Darby, but he's just a complainer, you know? Never happy with anything." Spencer pursed his lips as he considered his answer. "Truth is, no matter what you make it's bound to be better than what I cooked when I was doing it, and don't tell him I said so, but the boss is even worse as a cook than I am. He pretty much burned everything. At the end of a long day we're usually so hungry it doesn't much matter what you put in front of us as long as there's plenty of it, but eating his cooking . . . *gaah*. It was bad. So don't worry; we'll eat whatever. Just try not to burn everything."

"I'll remember that."

The dryer buzzed, indicating that yet another load was finished. Carlin excused herself, unloaded the clothes from the dryer into a laundry basket, and carried it through to the connecting dining room. It was there that the crew would eat. The long, plain wooden table would easily seat twelve—and it made the perfect place to fold clothes.

She emptied the laundry basket onto the middle of the dining room table and began to fold. In the name of efficiency, she'd folded here and then stacked the clean clothes on the sofa in the next room. When she had a couple of minutes she'd run the folded clothes upstairs to Zeke's room.

She had no doubt she could identify his room when that time came. It would be the room with the unmade bed and piles of dirty clothes on the floor.

Spencer stood in the doorway between the kitchen and the dining room. "Please tell me you didn't fold the boss's drawers on the table where we eat our food."

"Of course not." It was a small lie, one meant to soothe the boy who watched her fold a load of flannel and cotton shirts. "Why don't you tell me about the other hands?" she said, shaking out one of many work shirts.

He settled down and did as she asked, telling her a bit about each and every one of the men he worked with. Her heart softened a bit; Spencer saw only the good in everyone. He still trusted those around him completely. He trusted her, even though he didn't know her at all. She listened, wondering if her impressions of the men she'd be cooking for would be half as rosy as his were.

AS USUAL, IT was dark when they all straggled back to the house. Zeke had to admit to a sense of . . . gratification, maybe? . . . when he saw the lights on in the house. The kitchen was brightly lit, the curtains pulled open so he caught sight of Carlin as she moved back and forth. The lamps were turned on in the living room, too, an oddly welcoming touch. The bunkhouse was lit up, as well, though that could be Spencer's doing.

Then Spencer came out the back door, a big grin on his face as he stood on the porch watching them. Oh, shit, Zeke thought tiredly. If impressionable had a face, it would be Spencer's. In this case, he couldn't even tell the kid to stay away from her, because he needed Spencer to show her around and give her a hand—singular— whenever possible. Warning the kid would be like telling the wind not to blow; in this case, the warning would have to go to Carlin, which would probably piss her off. Tough.

"Shit," Walt grumbled to Spencer as he slid out of one of the ranch pickups. "I had my hopes up we'd have some real food tonight, but instead here you are coming out of the kitchen."

Spencer grinned, not the least bit offended. He was probably happier than all the rest of them put together that he wasn't doing the cooking. "I haven't touched a thing, I swear. I've just been showing Miss Carly where things are, keeping her company while she works."

"You mean there's real food? Hot?" Micah put in.

"But not burned black?" Patrick asked with real hope in his voice.

The back door opened again and Carlin stepped outside. The porch light gleamed on her blond hair. Her ponytail was looking ragged, dangling off to the side with tendrils of hair hanging loose around her face. She wore an apron that covered her from neck to knees, and the apron was stained with a multitude of colors, though the sixty-watt yellow bulb made it difficult to say exactly what those colors were. If she'd had on any makeup that morning—Zeke couldn't remember—it was long since gone. All in all, she looked like a woman who'd gone a round or two with the can opener, and the can opener had won. Or maybe not, considering she was still standing.

"I'm the new cook," she announced to the men. "My name is Carly. I've spent most of the day raking out the kitchen and hosing it down, but there's food. Tomorrow I'll have more time. Tonight there's tuna casserole and corn bread, with brownies and ice cream for dessert."

"Tuna casserole?" Bo muttered.

"There was plenty of tuna in the pantry. I figured it wouldn't have been there if someone hadn't liked it."

Her logic was unassailable. Zeke liked it okay; he made the occasional tuna sandwich and Libby had sometimes made some stuff that had tuna in it, but Zeke suspected Spencer had simply bought a bunch of it on sale. He manned up and said, "I like it," because he was damned if he'd let the men mutiny and run his cook off just when he thought he could see daylight—and clean underwear, as well.

But having said that he liked it, now he had to eat it. He hoped like hell it was good. He'd settle for okay. Or even edible. As long as he didn't gag, he'd eat it or die. Or eat it *and* die.

"Cheer up," Carlin said, evidently having caught on that tuna casserole wasn't a raving hit. "The ratio of cheese to tuna is two to one."

Okay, that was more like it.

The men trooped into the bunkhouse to wash up, and Walt went into his own little cabin to do the same. Carlin zipped back into the house, followed by Spencer. Zeke figured he'd better get started on his own quick shower, or he'd be sitting down to dinner smelling like cow shit. Stepping into the mudroom, he toed off his dirty boots and set them aside, then opened the door into the kitchen. The warm aroma assailed him, and he stopped in his tracks. He couldn't say exactly what it was, but the smell was homey and welcoming. Chocolate—yeah, he could smell the brownies. A napkin-covered bowl on the kitchen counter held a huge pile of corn bread muffins. He could just see the edge of one golden brown muffin peeking out beyond the napkin. The corn bread wasn't burned black. Hallelujah.

The second thing he noticed was the lack of dirty dishes stacked everywhere. There were cooking utensils and other things in the sink, but nothing like the god-awful mess that had been there before.

Carlin opened the oven door and peeked inside. Her back was to him but she must have heard him come in. "It'll be ready in seven minutes," she said crisply. "You'd better hurry."

He ran upstairs in his sock feet, taking the stairs two at a time. His shirt was off by the time he cleared his bedroom door, and he sort of tossed it toward a chair. His jeans hit the floor in front of the dresser. His underwear and socks came off right in front of the bathroom. Fewer than thirty seconds later, he was standing under the spray of water. It was barely lukewarm, the hot water not having had enough time to reach him yet, but the shower got warmer by the second.

He had four minutes left when he turned off the water and gave himself a fast, rough toweling. He raked his hand through his thick wet hair, threw on some clothes, and was heading back down the stairs with almost two minutes to spare. He couldn't remember the last time he'd been this anxious to eat something that might make him gag. What the hell; even if he didn't like the casserole, there were brownies for dessert!

The men must have been following the same rough logic, because they came filing in almost at the same time.

When she saw him, Carlin said tersely, "I need help."

God almighty, what had happened? Had she burned supper, after all? His heart sank. "What's wrong?"

"The casserole. I managed to get it into the oven, but it's too heavy for me to handle while it's hot. I should have made two smaller ones, but I didn't think about it until it was too late."

This was a manageable crisis—and no crisis at all, from his point of view. The oven mitts never had fit his big hands every well, so Zeke got two kitchen towels and folded them, then opened the oven door and pulled out the huge casserole pan. Golden cheese bubbled on the top, crisping brown around the edges. The smell was . . . God, if it only tasted half as good as it smelled, he was happy.

She hurried to put two big pads on the dining room table, and he set the casserole down on them. The table was already set with plates, silverware, and tall glasses filled with ice. She darted back to the kitchen, came back with a tray loaded with a big pitcher of tea and the bowl of corn bread muffins. "I didn't know what any of you wanted to drink, so I made tea," she said. The tray held two more items: two big, long-handled spoons, which she buried in the tuna casserole like arrows in a target.

Spencer moved to relieve her of the corn bread muffins, but Zeke forestalled him; the bowl was too big and heavy for the kid to handle with just one hand. Carlin said, "Thanks," without looking at him.

"No problem."

She handled the pitcher of tea with the practiced ease of a seasoned waitress, which she was. Working at The Pie Hole would have broken her in, fast. If only she'd picked up some of Kat's cooking skills, too, then he'd really lucked out.

Because he'd said he liked tuna casserole, and because he was the boss, he nutted up and dipped himself a big helping.

There was rice. Rice was okay; he was neutral on it. There were some mixed vegetables. He liked vegetables, so that was a plus. There was tuna. And, as she'd promised, there was a lot of cheese. He dipped his fork into the steaming hot mixture and, trying not to show how wary he felt, carried it to his mouth.

He should have let it cool a little beforehand, but he felt such massive relief he was barely aware of the heat.

"Damn," he said in surprise. "It's *good*!"

Chapter Nine

CARLIN WAS SO exhausted, she expected to fall asleep the minute her head hit the pillow, but that didn't happen. Her mind was spinning, and she couldn't get comfortable, even though the bed in her room—her *rooms,* she had her own little mini-suite—was the most comfortable she'd been able to call her own in so long she couldn't even remember. It was a vast improvement over the futon at Kat's place, though she was definitely fond of both Kat and the attic room.

The doors were locked, but, damn it, this house would be too easy to break into. A broken or cut window, and anyone could reach in and unlock a door. Not easily, unless they had freakishly long arms, but with a tool of some kind it was definitely possible. She calmed herself by making plans to talk to a locksmith in the morning, and by reminding herself that there was no way Brad could find her here. Even if he did, there were *two* locked doors between her and the outside world—either of the doors to the outside world and the crappy lock on her bedroom door—and the locks on her windows were a lot more reassuring than the ones on the doors. She'd also placed a chair under the doorknob to her room. Someone might be able to get in, but by God they wouldn't sneak up on her.

And there really was a butcher knife tucked into the top drawer of the bedside table. Just in case.

She'd learned to sleep through fear; learned that sleep was necessary for survival and she only hampered herself if she went too long without it. In truth she was as safe here—safer—than she'd been anywhere else for a very long time.

Nice, soft bed; butcher knife; isolated from the outside world.

Carlin stared up at the ceiling. It was Zeke Decker who was keeping her awake, damn him—Zeke Decker and her damn hormones. As she lay there in the dark, she tried to reason with herself. He was good-looking, in a rough-hewn, totally masculine way, and she'd been forced to spend several hours in his company. Add to that the fact that she'd been without any male attention for, well, years.

The thought made her pause. Had it been that long? Even before Brad had come along and screwed everything up, she hadn't exactly had an active love life. Her friends had always said she was too picky, but she really didn't think it was out of bounds to have *standards* when it came to allowing a man into one's bed and body.

Maybe her current state was the simple matter of her biological clock kicking into gear, and Zeke just happened to be the closest appropriate male. She'd read about the biology of attraction, analyzed it. Men liked women with big breasts because that meant they could feed all the babies. Women, on a cellular level, went for a man who could take care of the saber-tooth tiger that was trying to get into their cave. When it came to simple genetics, Zeke *was* rather caveman like. He hadn't yet grunted at her, but she was certain he would, sooner or later.

Logic was her friend. So why didn't it help? When she closed her eyes, a part of her wished like hell that she wasn't alone in this comfortable bed. After months of running, of separating herself from others, of not being touched *at all,* she craved the weight of a man, the pleasure of his mouth on her body, the release that would come . . .

Yeah, this was going to help her sleep.

Carlin closed her eyes, rolled onto her side, and took a long, deep breath. Maybe she should just stop fighting it and arguing with herself, and deal with reality. So, she had the hots for her boss. It wasn't as if she could act on the attraction. The tingles and the butterfly stomach and the twitches in a place she'd thought would be twitch-free forever should serve as a reminder that her life wasn't over. He'd tried, but Brad hadn't taken everything from her. On the other hand, because of him she couldn't act on the attraction, and she hoped he burned in hell.

She burrowed under the covers and imagined Zeke lying in the bed with her, that tall, hard-muscled body stretched out beside hers. She imagined until she could almost feel the heat of the body that wasn't there, until she could almost feel the dip of the bed where he didn't lie.

And finally, gently, she imagined herself into a deep, dream-filled sleep.

SHE HAD NEVER realized that men who engaged in physical labor all day had such hearty appetites. It made sense, but Carlin felt as if it would be impossible to prepare too much food for this bunch. If people working regular jobs ate this much, they'd be humongous, but Zeke and the other hands regularly put away twice as much food as she'd initially expected.

Leftovers would *not* be an option.

Nine men had plowed their way through a mountain of scrambled eggs, pounds of bacon, and an entire loaf of bread, toasted, in a matter of minutes. Carlin had stood back and watched them eat as they talked about the morning chores. It was rather like watching a swarm of locusts descend.

But, dang. As she'd watched them eat, an unexpected feeling had come over her. She was needed. In the most basic of ways, of course, and it wasn't as if she were doing a job no one else could do, but it was nice to be needed for a change.

After they'd had breakfast and tromped out to go to work, she had the house to herself for a few hours. All the men—Zeke included—had literally eaten and run. Even Spencer had declared he needed a pain pill and a nap in the recliner where he'd been sleeping since getting hurt. She could take a breather now. The dishwasher was running, the washer and dryer were both working hard—she wondered if it would be possible to catch up on the laundry in a month or so—and the locksmith was scheduled to arrive between one and three in the afternoon. Carlin made herself a cup of coffee and sat at the kitchen table with a selection of cookbooks she'd found on a shelf in the dining room. There were quite a few, but she'd chosen the three that looked the most well used. Then she leafed through, looking for pages that were marked by breaks in the spine or splatters of food on the pages. Those would be the favorite recipes, the dishes that had been prepared in this house again and again, right? It made sense to her.

Chili; beef stew; stroganoff; corn bread dressed up with corn and onions; biscuits; chocolate cake; apple pie.

Like she'd attempt to compete with Kat in the pie department. She might tackle a cobbler, but an actual lattice-top pie? No way. If Zeke wanted a pie, she'd order one from Kat.

Over the hum of the appliances, she heard the knocking on the back door. The pain pill must not have knocked Spencer out for very long! This time she wouldn't make him stand there and wait. She jumped up, and rushed to unlock the door.

Just her luck. It wasn't Spencer who stood there, but Zeke, scowling at her through the glass. She supposed it was too late to turn around, take a sip of coffee, and head this way again, taking her time.

"Didn't find your key, I see," she said as she opened the door.

"Found it," he said through clenched teeth. "Left it in my room this morning."

"Early-onset Alzheimer's?"

He glared down at her. "I happen to think I shouldn't need a key to get into my own damn house in the middle of the damn day."

Carlin turned her back on him and stalked toward the kitchen. "We'll just have to agree to disagree, but the door *will* be locked again when you leave the house."

"I won't be leaving for a while," he said.

Great! The last thing she needed was Zeke Decker underfoot. Frowning at him, she demanded, "Why not?"

"It's my house, I don't have to make excuses to you. I've got . . ." He stopped mid-sentence, inhaled deeply, then looked at her. "What's that smell?"

"There's a Mexican shepherd's pie in the oven for lunch and a roast in the Crock-pot for dinner."

"I have a Crock-pot?" He couldn't have sounded more astonished if she'd told him he had a unicorn's horn sprouting out of his head.

She held back a smile. "I found it in the back of the pantry."

He made a grunting noise, deep in his throat, and headed for the coffeepot. "Libby must've bought it."

Carlin tried not to acknowledge the surge of jealousy, but unexpectedly, there it was. Kat had mentioned Libby and so had Zeke, as he'd shown her to her rooms. But no one had shared any real details about the woman and her place here. Girlfriend? Wife? Kat said Zeke had been married once. Unable to help herself, wondering why she'd chosen this moment to become not only curious but a little peeved, she asked, "Who's Libby?"

Zeke poured coffee and turned to face her. "She had this job, *your* job, for years. Libby was cook, housekeeper, and surrogate mother to the men. She cooked, cleaned, and lent an ear to anyone who wanted to cry on her shoulder. During calving season we could count on her to help out, if we needed her." He took a long sip of coffee. "Until her knees started giving her fits."

"She sounds perfect."

"Damn near," he said baldly.

Perfect was something Carlin would never be, or try to be, so she might as well make it plain what her boundaries were. "Well, I don't plan to help out during calving season"—not that she had any idea what or when that was or what would be involved in helping—"and I will *not* be your surrogate mother."

Zeke started to smile then caught himself. "Noted." He pushed away from the counter and headed toward his office. "I've got some paperwork to take care of." The *damn it* was unspoken, but there.

"Before you go," Carlin said, stopping his exit just as he reached the door between the kitchen and the dining room. He turned to face her, a suspicious expression on his hard face. "We never did discuss my day off."

He looked almost horrified. "You want a day *off*? You haven't even been here twenty-four hours, and you're already talking about taking time off?"

"Yes! Half a day, anyway," she conceded. "Aren't there labor laws in Wyoming? Aren't you required to give me some time off? I'll make sure there's food, no one's going to starve, but I'd like to see Kat, check out a book at the library, just . . . chill." And check in with her family on one of those public computers in the library, though she wouldn't tell Zeke, or anyone else, that detail.

Now he just looked annoyed.

"Libby never took a day off?" she asked.

"Not really."

"No wonder you can't keep a housekeeper," she muttered. From the way he talked, it was clear no one would ever be able to replace the perfect Libby. Did she dare to attempt the recipes she'd been reading? They were probably Libby's, and no matter how she tried her efforts were unlikely to measure up.

Zeke leaned almost casually—his body was wound so tight she wondered if he was ever truly casual—against the doorframe. He took a sip of coffee and maybe, just maybe, unwound a tiny bit. "You can visit Kat and the library when you go to town to do the grocery shopping."

"That would hardly make it a day off, then, would it?" She hadn't thought much about buying groceries, though of course that would be part of the job. She tried to wrap her mind around shopping for nine hungry men. If she didn't plan well, she be in Battle Ridge four days a week! "And besides, I couldn't find my way back to town on a bet."

"I'll take you tomorrow. Until you're sure of the way, either Spencer or I will go with you."

He had an answer for everything! "Why can't Spencer go with me tomorrow?" Spencer didn't make her jumpy, didn't make her mouth go dry, and didn't invade her dreams at night. She'd much rather be with him, because then she wouldn't do anything stupid.

"I want him to rest awhile longer, and besides, I need to stop by the hardware store and the bank."

Arguing with him would be silly. At the moment, she just wanted him out of her kitchen and out of her sight. "Fine. We'll talk about my day off then, I suppose."

"Half day," he said, and then he turned to walk away,

headed for his office and paperwork. The man *did* look good walking away. Tight cowboy ass, in tight cowboy jeans, equaled *yum*. And she needed to get that thought out of her head.

Carlin opened her mouth to shout something after him, but changed her mind. She'd take a half day, for now.

SHE WOULDN'T LAST.

He couldn't decide if that was good or bad.

Zeke tried to concentrate on the payroll before him, but his attention kept drifting off the numbers. His mind kept wandering to the woman who had taken over his house and, evidently, his wits. Desperate as he'd been, it had been a mistake to hire Carlin. She could cook well enough—more than well enough, so far—and she was making progress in the house, but still, it had been a mistake.

He remembered to call her Carly in front of the other guys, but Carlin suited her better. It was different. He'd never known anyone named Carlin; he'd never met anyone like her. And that was where the mistake came into play.

This was Kat's fault. If she hadn't suggested Carlin for the job he never would've thought of it on his own, because he knew trouble when he saw it, and right now trouble was living in his house. How in the hell had he been talked into this? Here he was now, stuck in the position of employer, when the missionary position was what he really wanted. Carlin, naked, under him, her legs wrapped around his waist—oh, hell yeah. His eyes half-closed, because he could almost feel the wet heat of her body closing tight around his dick.

But he'd screwed up by hiring her. Hell, this whole situation was screwed up. He'd have asked her out the first time he'd met her if she hadn't hung such a huge "leave me alone, you jerk" sign around her neck. Now he knew why, but in the meantime their relationship, such as it was, had disintegrated from wariness on her part to something that wasn't quite downright hostility, but close. It was as if she wanted them to be at odds, as if she used that smart mouth of hers to keep him skating on the edge of his temper. If the stalker story was accurate, he could even understand why she'd have that attitude. His divorce from Rachel had been "amicable," which meant they were both glad to see the last of each other, but even so it had been a while before he'd wanted anything to do with women. He hadn't sworn off them or anything stupid like that, but he'd definitely needed some woman-free time.

Was that what she was doing? Had she picked up on how often he mentally stripped her and tossed her into his bed, and was throwing up the attitude to keep him at a distance?

Except Carlin was nothing if not mouthy; if she didn't want anything to do with him as a man, all she had to do was say so, and he figured she wouldn't be shy about it, either. The fact that he was her boss wouldn't stop her. She struck him as perverse enough that she might even get a kick from figuratively telling him to fuck off.

And he was perverse enough to enjoy the push he got back from her. Libby hadn't taken any shit off him, and Carlin didn't seem inclined to, either. That was good. He didn't have the time to mollycoddle anyone's feelings, and while he was very definitely the boss when it came to ranch matters, as far as he was concerned, it was with great relief that he'd turned over the kitchen and everything pertaining to the house to Carlin. As far as he was concerned, she was now in charge, and she seemed to be on the same page with that.

So in a way they were equals here. No boss, no employee, and never mind that he paid her salary. She was still in charge. He'd agreed not to fire her, but she hadn't said she wouldn't quit if the notion moved her.

He leaned back in his chair and thought that last part over, because it hadn't occurred to him before now. That little shit! She'd got the upper hand on him, and he'd just now realized it!

What he'd realized from the beginning was how damn tempting she was.

When she'd said she wasn't going to be his surrogate mother, he'd almost responded, "I'm one baby you'd never wean." For once, his common sense had jumped in front of his big mouth and won the battle for dominance. Maybe he'd get used to walking into the house and seeing her here; maybe the sight of her would stop hitting him low and hard, once he got used to having her here. Maybe she'd stop glaring at him as if he were a plague carrier. Yeah, *maybe*.

So, what was he going to do? Push her away, or keep her? Try to find a less-stressful solution to his problem, or enjoy the hell out of her while she was here?

In six weeks or so, Spencer would be out of his sling and able to take on the cooking again. All the laundry would be done by then, he imagined, and the house would be set to rights. He'd told Carlin that he wouldn't fire her until spring, but if she *quit* that would be another matter. She was already annoyed with him over the day-off thing. If she stayed annoyed, would she walk away?

A part of him—the part in his pants—wanted her to stay until spring. By then he should be able to find a man or an older woman to take the job, and Carlin would be more than ready to move on. Until then everyone on the ranch would be well fed, he'd come home every day to hot food, a clean house, and no laundry waiting for him. Spencer would be available when calving season began, when every able hand would be needed. It made perfect sense to attempt to make it work.

Too bad that same part made him wonder if he'd really be able to share a house with Carlin for months without trying to get her into bed with him, or going crazy because he knew damn well he couldn't. Shouldn't. Except why shouldn't he? As to whether or not he *could* . . . that was yet to be determined.

All he knew for sure was that he wanted to get his hands on her worse than he'd ever wanted any other woman, and that she was beyond a doubt going to be a lot of trouble either way, in bed with him or not.

He took a long sip of the cooling coffee. Damn it, even her coffee was better than his.

Chapter Ten

THE MEN, ALL seven of them, dug into the huge roast and devoured it. There were potatoes and green beans, too, and like the roast those were all gone. Tonight's bread had been simple—frozen rolls. Maybe it was cheating, and maybe they weren't as good as Kat's homemade rolls, but they were obviously okay with the men because not one of them whined about the rolls while they were grabbing them from the basket.

And using the time she'd saved by using the Crock-pot and frozen bread, Carlin had rummaged through the pantry and come up with the ingredients for a dessert recipe she'd found in one of the cookbooks. The page itself was clean, uncreased, so this was probably *not* one of Libby's recipes: Never Fail White Cake. The recipe seemed to be tailor-made for her.

She didn't eat at the table with the guys. Instead she made herself a small plate and ate in the kitchen. A couple of the men—Zeke included—had asked her to join them, but she'd declined. She was more comfortable in the kitchen, by herself, and besides, while the table was long enough to seat a dozen there were only nine chairs there. She would've had a choice of sitting next to Zeke or Darby, and she really wasn't in the mood to be too close to either. Zeke made her jumpy. Darby had wandering eyes.

Sitting alone in the kitchen was just more peaceful.

But when it came time to serve dessert, she proudly carried the white cake into the dining room. It was a layer cake, homemade top to bottom. And it was *pretty*. The white frosting was fluffy and sweet; she hadn't been able to taste the cake, but she'd sneaked a bit of the frosting onto the tip of her finger and tested it. *Yum.* She'd never thought herself much of a cook, but the training at Kat's had been superb, and the men she'd been feeding seemed to like her cooking. She could do this, and do it well.

The men *ooh*ed and *ahh*ed when she placed the cake on the table. While they admired her work, she hurried back into the kitchen for dessert plates, coffee cups, and clean forks. A pot of coffee—decaf, since she didn't want to be accused of robbing any of the men of their sleep—was ready.

Walt took a clean knife and began to cut the cake while Carlin poured coffee for everyone who wanted it. Plates were filled with big slices of cake and passed around, until everyone, including her, had one. It was Walt who insisted that she sit with them for dessert, and because it would be rude to refuse—and because she wanted to watch them enjoy the cake—she agreed. She took the chair next to Zeke because he seemed to be the lesser of two evils. Maybe he was annoying, but he didn't stare at her unimpressive cleavage, and not once had he winked at her. She probably would have fallen out of her chair if he had.

Almost simultaneously, all the men cut into their wedges of cake. Carlin watched them before doing the same.

One by one, expressions of delight turned to confusion and then dismay. The men all chewed, and chewed, and chewed. And chewed.

Carlin put a piece of cake into her own mouth. The

taste on her tongue was great. What was their problem? And then she chewed. Once.

The cake had the consistency of a sponge. Not just any sponge, but an old, tough sponge. "Never Fail," my ass! She glanced around the table in horror. To a man, the guys who'd wolfed down the meal and began eating their dessert with relish wore expressions of surprise and dismay. Six of them continued to chew. Only Darby grabbed a paper napkin and spit the cake into it. He opened his mouth to say something—she could only imagine what— but Zeke interrupted him.

"You know, I'm just stuffed. I can't possibly finish this cake."

"Yeah," Walt said. "It's . . . good, really, but I just can't . . ."

Eli and Bo both swallowed long swigs of decaf behind an inedible chunk of cake before they nodded their heads in agreement.

Patrick and Spencer each scraped off a forkful of icing and downed it with relish.

Darby looked at the men around him and shook his head. "If it was anybody else but a pretty girl who made this cake you all would be raising the roof."

"Darby," Zeke said simply, and in a low, almost threatening voice.

"It's okay," Carlin said. All eyes turned to her. "I'm so sorry. This cake sucks."

"It's not that bad," Spencer said. "It's just a little . . ."

"Rubbery," one cowboy supplied when Spencer faltered.

"Chewy," another chimed in.

"Tough as old saddle leather." Everyone laughed at that one.

Carlin was embarrassed, and angry that she'd wasted so much time on the blasted cake, but at the same time . . . With one notable exception, the men had all been concerned about hurting her feelings. Six out of seven had swallowed a piece of that awful cake, and if she hadn't acknowledged its suckiness, they wouldn't have said anything.

It was very possible that she found herself surrounded by gentlemen, of a sort. Rough and tumble, yes, but still . . . gentlemen.

If she'd learned nothing else in the past few months, she'd learned how to roll with the punches. This was a culinary setback, but it wasn't a disaster.

"For your information," she said as she lifted some icing onto the tines of her fork, "the name of this luscious dessert is Never Fail White Cake."

They laughed at that, as she'd known they would. "Feel free to pick off the icing, if it suits you. It's actually pretty good. And believe me, the next time I make this cake it *will* be better."

The laughter died. A couple of them stared at her. It was Spencer who said, kindly, "There doesn't have to be a next time, Miss Carly. I think Libby used those cake mixes. She just added eggs and water and viola, she ended up with a cake that was pretty darn good."

Carlin bit her lip to keep from laughing. *Viola?* Surely he meant to say *voilà,* but she wouldn't embarrass Spencer by correcting him at the table. After all, he'd gone out of his way not to embarrass her. Maybe sometime when they were alone she'd use the word correctly and maybe, just maybe, he'd take the hint. "We'll see," she said. "I'd hate to let some flour and shortening and eggs get the best of me. I just need to figure out what I did wrong."

"The brownies you made last night were good," Walt said.

"And you know," Eli added, "you can always buy some pies from Kat." He looked at Zeke. "Before you came to work here, those pies were the only decent food we'd had for . . ."

"Hey!" Spencer interrupted. "I did the best I could. I didn't see your sorry ass in the kitchen trying to help out." The words might've been harsh, but there was no real animosity there. Then he looked at Carlin and his face turned red. Sheepishly he said, "Pardon my French."

It struck her that these men had formed a family, of sorts. From what Zeke had said earlier, Libby had been a big part of that family. Carlin didn't think she'd ever be accepted that way, not into the heart and soul of this place. Maybe if she stayed for years instead of months, but . . . she was temporary; welcomed and needed, at the moment, but temporary.

She stood and started gathering dirty dishes. "Well, you'll be happy to hear that I called Kat this afternoon and ordered a couple of pies for tomorrow night."

The announcement was followed by several wide grins and at least two hoots.

As Carlin walked into the kitchen she added, "But I *will* make that Never Fail White Cake again, and it *will* turn out the way it's supposed to." By golly, by the time she left this ranch she and her Never Fail White Cake would be as famous as the perfect Libby. After months of doing her best to be invisible, she was determined to make her mark.

ZEKE LOCKED UP after Walt, who'd been the last to leave since they'd spent some time in the office discussing the next day's chores. He shook his head at the *two* new locks Carlin had had installed that afternoon. One replaced his apparently unacceptable doorknob and lock, and the other was a heavy-duty deadbolt, set up high—he supposed so no one would be able to reach it from a broken window. The front door had gotten the same treatment.

He started to grumble as he headed for the kitchen, but stopped when he noted that the piles of laundry were significantly smaller, and that his boots and shoes had been lined up neatly and, he was pretty sure, cleaned.

Carlin had her back to him as she unloaded the dishwasher. Another load would need to be run before she called it a day, and he was happy to leave that job to her capable—if paranoid—hands.

"This isn't exactly New York City, you know," he said, sounding more than a little grumpy.

"My bad. And here I was all set on going to a Broadway show on my half-day off," she responded calmly, without turning to look at him. "I guess I'll just have to use my opera glasses to spy on cows."

Zeke started to grin, caught himself, and growled, just a little. He didn't want or need to be entertained by her, but damn, it was hard to resist. The thing was, unless he was wrong about her, she *wanted* him to get grumpy at her verbal jabs. "They don't dance much, and they never sing. I hope you didn't have your heart set on a musical."

Instead of giving as good as she got, as usual, she laughed. It was a nice laugh.

He needed to change the subject. Standing in the kitchen and sparring with Carlin was just too damn much fun. "The locks are a little much, in my opinion, but I suppose if it makes you feel better . . ."

"It does. I put a set of keys on your bedroom dresser," she added, "and a spare set is hanging on a hook in your office. I have keys of my own, of course, but when I leave I'll hand them over."

She finally turned to face him. A few strands of hair were falling from her once-neat ponytail, and her face was flushed. There were a number of stains on her oversized apron. And damn, she was beautiful—not because of the food, not even because of her face, but because of the fire he could see in her spirit.

"You know," she continued, a definite hint of reprimand in her voice, "you really should tell Spencer that

the proper word is '*voilà*,' not '*viola*.' He's going to embarrass himself one day."

Zeke grinned. "I tried to tell him once. He said in his
family they pronounce it '*viola*.' As far as he's concerned,
that's the final answer."

He leaned against the cabinets and watched her move
back and forth, putting the dishes away, trying to think
what he should do now. He had time to catch a little
television, if anything worthwhile was on, but he'd had
so little down time since Libby left that he didn't know
what came on, or when. Or, hell, he could just go to bed
early. Either way, he really needed to get out of the way
and leave Carlin to finish up in the kitchen. But, *damn,*
he liked watching her. She didn't seem so thorny tonight.
Maybe, even though she'd just been here a day and a
half, she was already settling in, feeling at home.

She straightened, gave him what he could only classify
as a modified death stare. "I guess I'll see you in the morning, then." It was a dismissal. A nice one, he'd give her
that—she hadn't asked him what the hell he was doing in
her kitchen or ordered him to get out—but it was a dismissal nonetheless.

"We'll head to town after breakfast," he said. If she
could be all business, so could he—for now. The bank
opened at nine and so did the library, but she'd already
know that.

She stuck with the all-business theme. "I wasn't sure
how long the trip would take, so I planned sandwiches
for tomorrow's lunch. If I'm back in time to put things
together, fine. If not, I figure the guys can fend for themselves."

"They can." He needed to say good night and leave,
but instead he settled in, still watching. He liked watching
her, so why *should* he leave? He wasn't in the way. He
wasn't harassing her. He wasn't coming on to her. He was
just watching—and she knew he was watching. He could

tell by the tension that was slowly building in her body. She ignored him and continued to work, but some of the ease he'd noted earlier was gone, and he both hated that he'd been the cause of it and was gratified that she wasn't oblivious to him. But maybe now was the time for some strategy.

"Do you mind if I grab a cup of decaf?" There was enough left in the pot for a cup, or two. "I don't want to get in your way, but you do make good coffee, and I hate for it to go to waste."

It wasn't his imagination that she relaxed a bit, thinking he was hanging around for decaf, not her.

"Of course." She grabbed a mug, filled it. Zeke moved up behind her and reached around to take the mug from her hand. For the moment they were close, so close that he could dip his head a little and smell her hair, which he did, and lean in and touch the length of her body with his, which he *didn't* do.

The last thing she needed was to think she had another stalker, though she might classify him more as a predatory employer.

"You're doing good," he said, keeping his voice low because they were so close. "With the exception of the cake, that is." He grinned, and Carlin gave in to a smile herself.

"I need to ask Kat what I might've done wrong," she said, moving around him and resuming her chores. She grabbed a broom and started vigorously sweeping. He didn't think it was an accident that she now held a makeshift weapon, or that there was a broom between them.

She hadn't been kidding when she'd told him the C on her uniform stood for Cautious.

He lifted the coffee cup in a small salute, and headed for the door. "See you in the morning."

"Yeah," she said, sweeping hard. "Good night."

Zeke didn't look back, but he thought, as he headed for the den and the television he might stare at for a while, that he could get accustomed to having Carlin Hunt in the house.

CARLIN FINISHED UP in the kitchen and headed for her rooms. A shower and bed were the next items on her agenda. If she turned on the television and sat down in front of it, she'd be out like a light in no time.

Behind closed doors she stripped off her clothes, threw them into her dirty clothes hamper, and headed for the bathroom. She was exhausted; curiously content, but exhausted. Feeding Zeke and the hands and catching up on what appeared to be months of neglected housework and laundry had her hopping, but she liked being busy, liked feeling that she'd accomplished something. She could see the light at the end of the tunnel, though; once she was caught up on the housework, she'd be able to take some time for herself in the afternoons—not a lot, but she could catch a nap, or watch TV, or read. Zeke would question her trips to the library if she didn't read *something*.

The spray of hot water felt good, really good. For a while she just stood there and let the spray pound her tired muscles. She didn't think she'd have any trouble getting to sleep tonight.

This job was almost perfect. She was definitely off the grid, there were now decent locks on the outer doors, and most of the men she'd been feeding were perfectly nice. Darby was a jerk, but wasn't there always one in every group? Patrick was very quiet, and you never really knew what a quiet man was thinking. Spencer was a sweetheart, though, and Walt was almost like a father-figure to them all.

But damned if she could figure out Zeke Decker! One minute he was annoying as hell, and the next he was being nice to her. How dare he? He should pick one and stay with it, because she hated trying to predict what he would do and how she should react. Being physically attracted to the man was enough of a problem, even when he was being a shithead; if he made a habit of being pleasant, how would she push the attraction away?

Scrubbed clean, Carlin stepped out of the shower and briskly dried herself. She'd deal with him somehow. One thing was for sure: the first time he came home and she instinctively greeted him with a sweet "How was your day?" she'd know it was time to move on.

Chapter Eleven

CARLIN ENTERED WHARTON'S grocery store with Zeke on her heels. She didn't like that he was there, didn't like the way he was right behind her, didn't like the way he made her feel as if she were under guard. She wanted to take her time shopping, not feel as if he had a stopwatch in one hand and a whip in the other, in case he thought she was taking too long. Slave driver? Oh, yeah. The only thing that kept her from braining him with something was that he pushed himself as hard—or harder—as he did everyone else.

She had a list; if she went strictly by it, she could gather the items and be out of the store within half an hour, maybe even twenty minutes. But she'd been reading a lot of cookbooks and she had a gajillion recipes dancing in her head—two or three, anyway. She wanted to look at stuff, think about what she could do that both sounded interesting and that a bunch of unadventurous men would eat. She might see ingredients that weren't on the list, and be inspired. She might—

Who was she kidding? And what in God's name had she been thinking? Cooking had never been her thing, yet here she was, devoting most of each and every day to thinking about cooking, getting ready to cook, cooking, then cleaning up after cooking. Something was wrong with this picture.

Working on an isolated ranch, getting paid in cash, going under an assumed name—it had all seemed like such a perfect situation, a perfect plan for staying under the radar, making some money and saving it, catching a breather from the stress of constantly running and being on guard. Working her butt off was okay, but she was being taken over by cooking. She was fairly certain there was some DNA-altering going on, because otherwise wouldn't she be able to just say "Oh, well" about that damn lying-ass no-fail white cake and move on, instead of obsessing about tackling it again until she got it right?

Maybe it wasn't altered DNA. Maybe it wasn't a form of mental illness. Maybe she was just being competitive. She was okay with being competitive. If she looked at it that way, trying the damn cake again was more admirable than alien.

But she couldn't shop effectively with Zeke-the-dragon breathing fire over her shoulder, telling her to hurry. And he would; she could feel the first "hurry it up" coming her way, probably within . . . say, five minutes, if she wanted to bet with herself.

Well, he could just breathe fire all he wanted, she thought grimly. *She* was in charge of this expedition, and if he didn't like doing it her way then he could just find somewhere to sit and wait until she was finished—

Uh-oh. Reality abruptly punched her between the eyes. She looked at her list again and almost groaned aloud. The list itself wasn't extraordinarily long, but she needed a *lot* of the items on it. She didn't need five pounds of flour, she needed at least twenty. Ditto for the sugar. She was buying multiples of literally everything, which meant there was no way it would all go into one cart; she'd need at least two, maybe three—and that meant she needed Zeke.

But along the silver-lining-in-every-cloud line of thought, at least he could do the grunt work.

She jerked and tugged a cart out of the line, shoved it toward him, then freed another one. "Ground rules," she said tersely. "Don't try to hurry me up, or I'll forget something. Don't mess with me while I'm thinking, or I'll forget something—"

"How can you forget anything? You have a damn list. Just check off each thing as you get it."

"And don't interrupt," she added. "Any idiot can get what's on a list. It's what *isn't* on the list that requires creativity."

"It's a shopping list, not a work of art."

"But it isn't a *complete* list. That's why I need to think, and why you need to just follow along and be quiet."

A thin, elderly white-haired woman wearing jeans, boots, and a denim shirt pushed a cart past them and said, "You tell him, honey."

Zeke gave his head a little shake as he watched the elderly woman walk away and, raising his voice, said wryly, "Thanks, Mrs. G."

"You're welcome, darling." Mrs. G. never looked back, just trundled on into the produce section where she stopped and began examining every offering of lettuce.

Carlin pursed her lips thoughtfully, then cut her gaze up at him. "Ex-girlfriend?"

"First-grade teacher."

For some reason, imagining him as a gap-toothed six-year-old made her stomach squeeze. As she'd cleaned the house she'd seen a couple of pictures of him—not many, which made her think he'd probably packed most of them away—so she had a good idea of how his adolescent face had morphed into the hard-edged features of the man, but she hadn't seen any of him as a child. It kind of made sense. What man wanted his baby pictures sitting around? Pictures of his own babies, yeah, but not of himself. Okay, that was another stomach-squeezing moment, thinking of Zeke as a father. No, actually, it was the baby-making part that affected her stomach. Oh, God, instead of getting used to him and building up immunity, she was actually getting worse.

"You look like you're about to puke," he observed, pushing his cart forward.

With a quick, inner shake she gathered herself and cut him off to take her rightful position as lead cart. "I was trying to imagine you as a kid. It was horrifying."

He grunted. "You're on the right track." Then he grinned. "But Mrs. G. had my number. She could back me down with a look."

"I gotta go talk to her." Just to get a rise out of him, she actually steered her cart in Mrs. G.'s direction, but he reached out and locked a hand over the cart handle, stopping her in her tracks.

"I don't have all day. Let's get these groceries bought and get out of here."

Too bad she hadn't made that bet with herself on how soon he'd say "hurry up"—or words to that effect—because she'd have just won the jackpot.

"All right, but—" She shook her finger at him. "Remember the rules: follow me, pick up what I tell you needs picking up, and don't talk."

"Oh, so now I'm supposed to do your manual labor for you?"

"A smart worker uses whatever tools are available to her," she said, leaving it to him to decide exactly what she meant by that.

"A smart worker stops wasting time, and starts working."

The only reason she didn't bother with a comeback was that he was right. She had a ton of groceries to gather, and they wouldn't hop in the carts by themselves.

The produce department was easy: none of the men,

present company included, were big on things like romaine or celery. Onions, potatoes, some squash, and that was about it. But still, she needed a *lot* of potatoes, a *lot* of onions.

Her brain was humming with the recipes she'd read as she wandered down the aisles, pondering the different types of diced tomatoes, dried soup packages, and whether mac and cheese was still mac and cheese if you used some other kind of noodle. She also pondered on whether or not she could manage mac and cheese; it had always struck her as the type of thing that *looked* simple, but was in reality a cesspool of culinary disasters just waiting to strike. For God's sake, it was noodles and cheese; what could go wrong?

"I don't know what that Kraft box did to you, but you've been scowling at it for five minutes," Zeke growled. "Either pick it up, or move along."

"I'm deciding."

"Decide faster."

"Do you like mac and cheese?"

"I'm a man. I pretty much like anything with cheese on it."

"I didn't see any of these in the pantry."

"Then I guess Libby didn't use the boxed kind. Spencer never made mac and cheese, and God knows I never tried. Buy it or don't, but let's get moving." Impatience was beginning to put an edge into his tone. Figuring she could at least give it a shot, Carling grabbed the family-sized box and tossed into her cart.

"Just one?" he asked. "If you're going on a mac and cheese binge, you'd better stock up, because it's too far to drive to town to pick up one or two items."

"I've never made mac and cheese before," she replied, a little humiliated by the admission. What kind of cook did that make her, other than an inadequate one? "If it turns out okay, I'll get some more next time."

"I guess we're all in for an adventure, then," he muttered.

Thank God for ungrateful, unsympathetic employers, because annoyance promptly rescued her from humiliation. Humiliation was embarrassing; she could work with annoyance. She curled a lip at him. "You remember the 'be quiet' part of the rules? Embrace it."

"I'm just a little curious: did you ever have any kind of professional training? Were you absent the day they went over the part about not being a smart-ass to the boss?"

"I'll have you know I'm an exemplary employee. This situation is a little different."

"Yeah? How?"

"We both know it's temporary. Therefore I'm under no constraints to kiss your butt—metaphorically speaking, of course. It may be more temporary for me than it is for you, so I'm in the driver's seat. In fact, given your housekeeping skills and how the house looked the first time I saw it, you should probably be the one watching your mouth, because you don't want to piss me off. I might leave. And come spring, they'd find your body buried in that house under a pile of your own stinking laundry."

They'd been walking along as they shot words at each other; she consulted her list as they walked, and she'd pointed at a couple of items for him to put in his cart—multiples, of course. In his household, there was no such thing as buying *one* can of diced tomatoes; she needed *ten,* and she hoped that would be enough to get her through at least a week.

She turned her cart and headed up the baking aisle, where all good things resided—well, except for the other good things, like ice cream and candy and cookies. She could already spot several rows of cake mixes, which only reminded her of her ignominious failure. There wasn't a thing wrong with cake mixes; if they were good

enough for Betty and Duncan, they were good enough
for her—

A dark-haired man walked across the front of the
aisle, his face turned away from her.

Brad. She was swamped by terror so sharp and over-
whelming that the brightly lit store went black for a moment, and the floor seemed to fall away from her. Carlin
felt her heartbeat literally stutter, and she stopped so
abruptly she might as well have slammed into an invisible wall. Zeke, following behind, had to swing his cart
hard to the left to keep from running into her.

"Damn it, watch what—" he began, but Carlin whirled,
her face paper white, operating on sheer instinct as she
abandoned her cart in the middle of the aisle and darted
past him, heading for the back of the store where there
was always a delivery dock and therefore an escape.

But quick as she was, Zeke was faster. His long arm
snagged the back of her shirt, hauling her to a standstill.
She struck at him, rattler-quick, using her fist like a hammer on his forearm to stun the muscle and loosen his grip.
"Shit!" he said between clenched teeth, because she'd hit
hard and right on target, but before she could tear herself
free he grabbed her arm with his other hand. "What the
hell are you doing?"

Chapter Twelve

"LET ME GO!" Carlin's eyes were wild with fear, but she fought him with a fierce determination that made him feel as if he were trying to hold a ninja worm, attacking and wiggling all at the same time.

God almighty, what kind of attention were they attracting? People would think he was attacking his housekeeper right there in the middle of the grocery store. But by some quirk of luck at the moment they were the only ones in this particular aisle, and no one had passed by since she'd freaked out.

"He's *here*!" she hissed, lashing out with her foot and catching him on the shin.

"*Ow!* Shit! Damn it, stop fighting!" Catching her from behind, he wrapped both arms around her and lifted her off her feet, because that was the simplest way to control her. But as he spoke his head was swiveling as he looked for the man who had thrown her into a panic, his expression settling into a hard, grim look that some people had had the misfortune to see before, right before he took care of business. A few times that business had left the other person bleeding, and this might be one of those times.

Her heels hammered against his shins; damn it, he'd

have bruises for the next month, because she kicked like a small mule. "Stop it," he commanded in a low, hard voice. "Where is he? Point him out to me."

Wildly she shook her head. "He'll *kill*—you, me, anyone!"

"No, he won't. I guarantee you half the people in this place are armed." He put his mouth close to her ear, so he wouldn't have to use a normal voice. Part of him registered the smell of her skin, the silkiness of her blond hair, but the rest of him was focused on handling the situation, and number one was getting her calm enough that she could point out the stalker—though that might be as simple as locating the only stranger in the store. "I know for a fact the store manager is. We'll protect you, and we'll protect ourselves. That's a promise. Just calm down. I won't let anything happen to you. Where did you see him? Can you point him out?"

"He—walked by—end of aisle." She was panting so hard she could barely talk, and her delicate features were so white he was surprised she was still conscious. She sucked in air, held it for a moment as she fought for control. "Dark hair. Green shirt."

"Good enough." He plunked her down, spun her around so she was facing him. "Stay here. Do *not* run. Do you understand me? I need to know where you are." He grasped her shoulders, gave her a little shake as his sharp green gaze bored into her. "Promise."

She was trembling from head to foot. He could feel tension running through every fiber of her body, like electricity through a fine wire. The blue of her eyes were the only color in her face; even her lips were white. No one could fake this kind of physical response, and any doubt he'd had about the truth of her stalker tale vanished as if it had never been. Some son of a bitch was terrorizing her, and if he got his hands on the bastard—

"*Promise,*" he said again.

Her eyes walled around as if looking for some escape, the way all captured or frightened animals did, infuriating him even more that she'd been reduced to this.

Promising was beyond her. She stared up at him and Zeke had to choose between maybe letting the bastard get away, or continuing to hold Carlin so she didn't bolt.

Well, if she bolted, it would be on foot, because he had the truck keys in his pocket.

"Stay," he said in harsh command, then released her and moved swiftly toward the front of the aisle, rounded it, looking for his target—

—who was astonishingly easy to find, standing just two aisles down, looking over a selection of snacks. Zeke was already gathering himself for a bone-crushing tackle when what he was seeing clicked with his brain and he skidded to a halt.

He backed up a couple of steps, so he could look down the aisle where he'd left Carlin. He more than halfway expected the aisle to be empty except for two abandoned carts, but she still stood there, frozen and white, her wide gaze locked on the front of the aisle for all the world as if she expected a monster to appear there.

Zeke lifted his hand and beckoned her forward.

Violently she shook her head.

He gestured more emphatically. "It's okay," he said. "Come on."

Gingerly she eased forward. When she was within touching distance, he put his hand on her arm and pulled her closer, so she could see around the edge. "Is that him?" he asked, pointing toward the man in the green shirt.

She was terrified, but she had grit, and she looked. He felt the jerk in her body as she instinctively recoiled, then she stopped, looked again.

"That's him," she said in a thready tone. "But it isn't *him.*"

"No. It's okay. That's Carson Lyons. He owns a little ranch just south of here, works it with his wife and two kids."

She sucked in air, then doubled over and braced her hands on her knees. "Oh my God. I didn't see his face, just . . . his hair, the shape of his head. I—I couldn't think. I panicked. I'm so sorry, I made a complete fool of myself—"

"Easy." Using his body, Zeke herded her backward into the narrow confines of the aisle. "You didn't make a fool of yourself. You perceived danger, and you reacted. It's okay. That's what you *should* do. But if there's a next time, just point him out to me, and I'll take care of the problem. Now let's get the rest of the groceries rounded up so we can get out of here. I've got a lot to do today, and we're wasting time."

The ruthlessly logical approach was just what she needed. He pretended to ignore her as he shoved the cart down the aisle, but instead he surreptitiously watched as she gathered herself, focused, forced herself to the task at hand. She was still trembling, but she didn't let herself falter.

He felt a mixture of admiration and a grim sense of protectiveness. She was dealing with something that was evidently a lot more serious than he'd thought, and she was hanging in there. Yeah, grit was a good word for her.

She was under his protection now, and he'd be damned if he let anything happen to her.

BRAD HENDERSON STARED at the computer screen, his full attention on the information before him. More accurately, the *lack* of information before him.

Carlin had dropped off the map this time, damn her. If she was working, then she wasn't using her social security number. She hadn't gotten a speeding ticket, hadn't participated in any social media, hadn't opened a bank account. He'd hacked into her sister's Facebook account, but that had been a waste of time. He knew Carlin wasn't all that close to her brother and sister, but you'd think they were keeping in touch *somehow*. He just hadn't figured out how, yet.

His eyes narrowed as he glared at the screen. Maybe she wasn't all that tight with her siblings, but if he cut their throats she'd care. If he killed every member of her family and made sure they knew it was Carlin's fault before they died, then she'd be sorry she'd run from him.

Brad took a deep breath. Murdering the family would only satisfy him if Carlin was there to watch. It would be a waste of time, and a danger to his own safety and freedom, to do the deed otherwise.

In the comfort of his own house, in the home office he'd set up for himself, Brad searched and cursed and imagined what he'd do to Carlin when he finally found her. It would be risky to use one of the computers at the station, using police resources to get information he couldn't find on his own, but if he didn't have better luck soon he might have no choice but to take that risk.

Stupid bitch, what did she think she'd accomplish by running? Sooner or later, she'd make a mistake; all the idiots who tried to run from the law did. She should have listened to him; he'd tried so hard to explain it to her. Didn't she know that she was his? She belonged to him, and had since the moment he'd first seen her. She'd smiled at him, and he'd known in that instant.

She was *his*. When he'd thought he was taking her life, he'd felt no remorse; because she was his, he could dispose of her however he wanted, like any other piece of trash. When he'd found out he'd killed the wrong woman—that damn red raincoat had fooled him—he'd suffered a few moments of guilt, but the feeling had passed. If the woman hadn't interfered, she'd be alive today. Not his fault.

His search at an end, for now, Brad opened up another file. Pictures of Carlin filled the screen, one and then another popping up. In one of the photos she smiled. In the others, she hadn't even known her picture was being taken. He reached out, placed the tip of his finger against her cheek in one particularly sexy photo.

He whispered, "Mine."

CARLIN WAS STILL shaking a little as she put away the groceries. The ranch hands had made a mess in the kitchen, putting together their sandwiches, opening bags of chips, drinking tea and soda and milk and leaving glasses and plates everywhere. Compared to what she'd found here when she'd arrived, the job ahead of her was certainly manageable. She was even glad to have something extra to do, to keep herself occupied. She tried to concentrate on the mess, to plan the cleanup that would follow the task of putting away the groceries.

Then there was tonight's dinner to cook: spaghetti with meat sauce and garlic bread, and dessert would be the pies she'd picked up from Kat's place. She'd purposely chosen something that wasn't time-consuming or complicated, given that she hadn't been certain what time she and Zeke would get home.

She tried to think of mundane things, but she still shook. Her own reaction pissed her off, and that didn't help matters at all.

She'd let herself relax, had let her guard down, and that had been a mistake. Seeing the man she'd thought was Brad, however briefly, had come as a shock because she hadn't been prepared. She'd let herself feel safe, become content in Battle Ridge, and she'd been thinking of other

things: meal planning and recipes and that damn misbehaving white cake, and Zeke Decker. She couldn't forget
him, because he was her biggest distraction and the biggest danger to her safety, at the moment. She'd kept her
distance, she had no illusions about her place here, but
damn, she liked him. He was sexy and aggravating and
all-man and unbearably distracting.

She'd have to be Superwoman to be immune to him,
and "super" didn't in any way figure into her reaction to
him. The "woman" part . . . now, that was different.
Damn, again.

She was so distracted, she didn't hear him come up behind her. When he reached a hand around and laid it over
hers—she still held a can of peas in that hand, and it was
halfway in and halfway out of the pantry—she froze.
Zeke didn't touch her. He *never* touched her. Oh, damn.
He was *touching* her. Come to think of it, he'd touched
her a lot today, but a bear hug from behind to keep her
from running in the grocery store didn't count . . . much.

His hand was hot and hard and big. His body, so close
to hers, put out heat like a wood-burning stove. She
hadn't given a lot of thought to how much bigger he was
than her, but standing so close how could she not be
reminded?

"You're safe here, you know," he said in a low voice,
his tone calm and definitely softer than usual.

Carlin shook her head, willing herself not to look at
him. "I'm not safe anywhere, not really."

He didn't move, didn't drop his hand. "You can't let a
man, any man, do this to you."

She reached into the pantry and put the peas on a shelf.
That broke the contact, but Zeke was still close, too
close. She dipped down and skirted around him, a kind
of evasive do-si-do.

Not that he would just let the subject drop.

"Let me help you."

She tried to laugh at that, but the sound was short and choked. She didn't want to put Zeke or any of the others in Brad's path. "What are you going to do?" she asked, her voice sharp. "Hunt him down and kill him for me?"

"I was thinking maybe I could have him arrested," Zeke said wryly. "It's true that I have a horse and some guns here, but I'm a rancher, not a gunslinger."

Despite herself her lips curved in a small smile at his sally, but then the smile twisted. "I've tried having him arrested. It didn't work."

She didn't want to talk about Brad, didn't want to relive the nightmare she'd managed to put out of her mind for a while. Was she careless, or was that a survival mechanism to look forward instead of staying mired in the awful circumstances of Jina's murder?

"Are you going to run forever?"

"That's a million-dollar question." It was one she'd asked herself many times, every day, and the answer was always no. But what could she do? She couldn't think of any way to end the nightmare. So for Zeke, she was honest. "I don't know."

"Give me his name and I'll . . ."

"No!" she snapped, whirling on him. Her heart had jumped into her throat at just the idea of him doing something that might bring Brad here. She poked him in the chest with a finger. "The son of a bitch is a computer hacker. A friend died in my place, because he thought she was me, do you understand? *Do you fucking understand?*" She didn't often swear like that, but when it came to Brad there were no words bad enough.

For a long moment, Zeke stared at her, his eyebrows raised slightly. What, did he think she was a sweet young thing who didn't know how to curse when it was appropriate? Right now was appropriate. She stared back, not giving an inch.

"Fine," he said, his voice tight but calm. "We'll do this your way. Promise me one thing, though."

She started to tell him she owed him nothing, least of all a promise, but he seemed to be trying so she decided to play along, for now. "Maybe. What kind of promise?"

"When you decide it's time to leave, talk to me first."

"Why should I?" And how the hell had he looked at her and known she was thinking about running? Oh, right—it might have been the way she panicked in the grocery store and was going to bail out through the unloading dock in back.

"So I can help you. When you do move on, as I'm sure you will, you need to have a plan. A *plan,* Carlin, something besides getting on the road and stopping when you run out of gas." He sounded a little angry, now. "Don't let one asshole ruin your life. You're as safe here as you'd be anywhere else—safer than most places, because of where we are, and because you're surrounded by people with guns who'll fight for you."

Before she could respond, he headed for the back door. "I'll lock the door behind me," he called without looking back. "Don't worry. I have my key."

ZEKE COVERTLY WATCHED Carlin as she served dinner. She'd recovered enough by the time dinner was served that no one else would ever guess that she'd had such a scare at the grocery store. She even smiled and joked with the men as she got everyone settled in, made sure they had what they needed. And again, she ate alone in the kitchen.

The spaghetti was good and filling, the garlic bread crisp and tasty. The men ate like they were starved, and after a long day's work, maybe they were. Spencer had a tough time eating one handed, but he managed well enough. They were all enjoying the recent upgrade in the cooking at the Rocking D. They'd be sorry when Carlin left.

And damn it, she *would* leave, eventually. He'd hired her wanting her to leave as soon as Spencer was able to resume his duties in the kitchen. At least that had been the plan when he'd grudgingly hired her, and just as grudgingly agreed to keep her on until spring. But in just a couple of days she'd made her mark here, and he'd found he didn't like the idea of her not being here. It was nice to come home to a decent hot meal and clean clothes, even if those assets did come with a sharp tongue and a nice ass that drove him to distraction.

She'd even washed the sheets on his bed and neatly made it up, the first time his bed had been completely made since Libby had left. Carlin was a more than competent housekeeper and cook. That was the only reason he'd interfered that afternoon when she'd looked like she was on the verge of bolting.

Yeah, right.

It was probably a good thing he'd be so busy for the next couple of weeks, moving the cattle from free range into the pastures near the house, getting ready for the October market. Carlin would have the house to herself all day, and the next time she went to town Spencer could ride along to navigate—and to keep an eye on her, too. She didn't want anyone else knowing about her stalker, but he could tell Spencer to make sure no one hassled her. He wouldn't deny to himself that her safety was a big consideration.

Spencer wasn't going to like missing the cattle drive; it was one of his favorite times of the year. It was hard work, that was true, but it was also classic cowboy work. Some of the ranches used four-wheelers—and even helicopters, he'd heard—during roundup, but at the Rocking D they did things the old-fashioned way, on horseback.

If all Spencer had was a simple broken arm, they might find a way to make it work. But the shoulder needed to be good and healed before he sat a saddle again. Not that the kid had ever fallen or been bucked, but there was a first time for everything, as the incident with Santos had proved. A torn rotator cuff was nothing to fuck around with.

So Spencer would stay with Carlin, and Zeke wouldn't feel anxious about leaving her out here on her own so much. He couldn't remember ever feeling anxious about Libby being on her own, but then he'd never been so sharply aware of Libby's presence, either. He loved her like a mother, but she'd been part and parcel of his everyday experience, simply *there*.

It was different with Carlin. Having her in the house, cooking and cleaning and doing *some* of the things a man might expect from a wife, was a constant tickle on his subconscious. If she took a shower, he imagined her naked. When she was in bed, he imagined her naked and in bed with him. When she was bent over unloading the dishwasher, he imagined her doing it naked. He'd never once thought of Libby naked—God forbid! He shuddered at the idea.

But Carlin . . . yeah. Naked. All she had to do was breathe and he thought about her being naked and breathing.

With a start, he realized he'd been sitting at the table, not eating, fantasizing about Carlin being naked, while the food steadily disappeared from the bowls and he was about to lose out. He grabbed the last piece of garlic bread before anyone else could get it, and set about filling his stomach.

Their appetites satisfied, the men settled back to talk of the upcoming cattle drive. Spencer looked sulky because he was going to miss all the fun, but his expression soon cleared; he wasn't the type to stay unhappy for long. Zeke concentrated on the subject, because a lot of his yearly income depended on it, going over what they'd do even though all of them had done October market before. He thought he was doing a good job of keeping his mind on work until Carlin brought two pies into the dining room, one apple and one key lime. He looked at her, he saw the pies, and he thought about her bringing them in naked, except of course he'd be the only one here to appreciate the sight.

He was so fucking horny he thought he'd probably come if a fly landed on him.

"All *right*!" Spencer said, grinning. A couple of the hands actually clapped, and Eli whooped. Zeke and Walt both stood to take the pies and put them on the table for her.

Looking at her, he thought, you'd never guess how terrified she'd been just a few hours ago. She was smiling at them, joking. "One day I'll bring a pie into the dining room and y'all will say, *Oh, Carly, I'm so disappointed. I really wanted Never Fail White Cake for dessert*." She said the last in a falsetto, making fun of herself.

"Yeah, *that'll* happen," Darby said sourly as he reached for the pie server. Carlin had left a stack of dessert plates and forks on the table when she'd set it for dinner. "Hey! There's a piece of apple pie missing."

"It's not *missing*," Carlin said sweetly. "I know exactly where it is. It's on a plate in the kitchen, and it has my name on it."

"I don't see why you get first dibs," Darby grumbled.

Behind Darby's back, Carlin stuck out her tongue. The men who could see laughed, then covered their laughter with coughs and exclamations about the pie.

When she went back into the kitchen, Zeke briefly thought about getting up and helping her, grabbing some coffee mugs and helping with the fresh decaf he could smell from where he sat, but he stayed put. She didn't need to be crowded right now, and if he hovered over her she wouldn't like it.

Besides, she'd made it plain she didn't want any kind of physical or emotional connection to anyone around her. He understood that; he didn't necessarily agree, but he understood. She was in a difficult position. What made it more difficult was that it was obvious to him such enforced solitude wasn't in her nature. Look how she got on with the men, shooting jibes back at them, blending in as if she'd been here for years.

Huh. She didn't treat any of *them* with that veiled hostility—just him. And yet he didn't get the feeling that she disliked him. Following that thread, then he was the only one she had to work to keep at a distance, which must mean—

Like a wolf on the hunt, he knew exactly what it meant. He sensed her weakness where he was concerned. He was a threat to that distance she wanted to keep around herself, and the other men weren't. And because he was a threat, if he pushed too hard—hell, if he pushed at *all* right now—she might bolt.

His instinct was to go after what he wanted. A lot of times, with nothing more than bone-breaking work and sheer determination, he'd twisted and molded events and things to the outcome he wanted, and he'd learned to not give up. It went against his gut feeling now to pull back, but his brain insisted he had to. That didn't mean he was giving up; he was making a strategic move. He had to get past that wall of hers, get her to trust him, rely on him, and pray that chemistry or sex or whatever else he could call the black magic of attraction, did the rest.

As a strategist, he knew that if he had a prayer of making this work, he needed to treat Carlin like any other employee—for now. Let her think the situation was unchanged, that she would be working for him for a few months and then she'd be gone. It was up to him to make sure that she was happy, and that she'd by God be safe while she was here.

He'd never before thought of a deadbolt as a seduction strategy, but she could have all the locks she wanted, if that made her feel better.

Chapter Thirteen

"HEY THERE, MISS Carly," Spencer called as he stepped into the kitchen. "What time do you want to head to town?"

Zeke had just left, and since they'd known Spencer would be coming to the house he hadn't locked the mudroom door. He'd checked with Carlin first, of course, to make sure she knew the door was unlocked and didn't mind. It was one of the rare communications she and her boss indulged in these days. She did her job, he left her alone. When it came time for her to be paid, he handed over an envelope of cash. If he was having second thoughts about paying her that way, he never said so.

She was both relieved and resentful. She was glad he was leaving her alone, but she resented that she disliked her own boundaries so much. Sometimes life just sucked.

Spencer was smiling, but then he almost always was. He was one of the sunniest people she'd ever met. He'd be out of his sling in a couple of weeks, and he couldn't wait; she'd never been so physically bound and restricted herself, but it looked downright miserable. She imagined he was making the best of the situation and it bothered him more than he let on.

She had just finished cleaning up the breakfast dishes;

she was still astonished at the amount of bacon and eggs nine men could eat. One of these days she was going to try the biscuit recipe she'd found, but right now getting eggs, bacon, and toast on the table was still enough of a challenge that she didn't want to add anything else to the difficulty level. She was out of bed at four-thirty, had food on the table at five-thirty, and the men were usually out the door at six. If the coffeemaker hadn't had a timer and taken care of itself, she didn't know that she'd have been able to meet the schedule—and if she couldn't handle making coffee along with everything else she had going on in the mornings, then she knew for damn sure she couldn't handle making biscuits. Maybe she'd make them for supper, instead, when she wasn't as pushed for time.

"Give me a few minutes to finish putting the dishes away and I'll be good to go," she told Spencer.

Shopping was her least favorite part of the job, not because she didn't like to buy groceries, but because it took her out of this safe, controlled element. Going into Battle Ridge on a regular basis was the only drawback to an almost perfect job. Of course, it wasn't like she was headed into Cheyenne.

She hadn't had any kind of a scare since that first day she'd gone shopping with Zeke, but she hadn't forgotten, either. Before the horrifying moment when she thought she'd seen Brad in the grocery store, she'd allowed herself to get comfortable in Battle Ridge. She'd relaxed, she'd felt at ease. The incident—the terror—had made her throw up her guard all over again. She hated that she didn't feel the same, but she'd hate it a whole lot more if something actually happened and she wasn't emotionally prepared. So she was always hyperalert whenever they went to town, which meant she was always exhausted from the effort when they got back to the ranch.

Since that day, Zeke had assigned Spencer to ride to

town with her. They often timed the trips so he could go to physical therapy while she ran errands, went to the library, and visited with Kat. Spencer said he could steer one-handed, but Carlin insisted on driving. She didn't need directions to town and back anymore, but it was nice to have an extra hand to steer one grocery cart while she managed the other. And even with the heavy items Spencer could help, using his one hand to aid Carlin's two.

Seeing Kat and checking in with Robin and Kin via computer made the trips worthwhile. She hated leaving the safety of the ranch, but that contact was a lifesaver. She missed seeing Kat every day, and sometimes she just needed a woman's company after being around so many men. Could being exposed to too much testosterone poison her brain? She'd wondered that aloud in front of Kat one day, and had to wait a full five minutes for Kat to stop howling with laughter.

But even with the overload of testosterone, the stinky socks, and the long hours, she was enjoying herself. As long as the ranch hands were well fed and happy and the house was clean, and she stayed out of Zeke's way, the job was a good one. True, being secluded at the ranch had its trials, but it also had its benefits. She saw the same handful of people day in and day out. Some of them she liked better than others, but that had been true at every job she'd had. There hadn't been any problems. There were no surprises, no fear that she'd turn around and find Brad standing in a crowd. Here at the ranch there *was* no crowd.

And here at the ranch, she was relaxed, and every day she could feel herself settling in more. Never mind that Zeke was a never-ending irritant, an itch she refused to let herself scratch—she liked the job, she liked most of the men, she liked having her own little suite to herself. There was nothing extra special about the two rooms, but they were downright luxurious compared to some of the places she'd lived in while she was on the run. And come to think of it, there *was* something a little special about them, because they'd been remodeled out of love. Sure, it was love for the perfect Libby, but Carlin was still benefiting from that care and consideration.

"The list is on the table," she said as she placed the last stack of clean, white dishes in the cupboard. "Look it over and see if I've forgotten anything."

Carlin immediately headed down the hallway, toward her rooms, and after a couple of beats Spencer called after her. "Broccoli? Do we really have to have *broccoli*?"

She laughed easily, something she could do these days. "Yes!"

Observation—and the recently discovered Food Network, which she'd been watching regularly lately—had taught her that when it came to food and men, keeping it simple was the best strategy. Zeke and his ranch hands would gladly live on meat and potatoes, so she made sure to provide plenty of both. However, she also felt it was her duty as cook—and as the lone woman in the group—to sneak a vegetable onto the menu now and then. If she covered the veggies in cheese or disguised them in some other sort of sauce, she could usually slip something green past the guys a couple of days a week.

In her room she grabbed her jacket, cap, and sunglasses, in preparation for the trip. She'd stop by The Pie Hole while she was in town, say hello to Kat, and pick up the pies she'd ordered. Pie sometimes improved Zeke's mood . . . temporarily. There probably wasn't enough pie in the state of Wyoming to turn him into a bearable human being. He seemed to be in a perpetual state of disgruntlement. She didn't know why, and she didn't care. Having him that way was easier on her own state of well-being.

If he spoke to her, it was usually to growl something that she might or might not bother to interpret. He was pretty much leaving her alone these days, but when he came home at night he was, well, grumpy. Spencer said getting ready for the October market was stressful, and once that was done everyone would be in a better mood. A few of the hands would leave the ranch soon, and come back when calving season arrived. Some would go home; a couple of them rodeoed. Walt, Kenneth, and Micah—the foreman and the two married hands—were year-round employees. Even Spencer went home for a week or two, though he came back before the others, he said. He liked it here. This ranch felt more like home to him than his family home.

Carlin wondered what Spencer's family was like, if it was an entire enclave of Pollyannas. Spencer was Zeke's opposite in personality. He smiled, made jokes, and dealt with the handicap of an out-of-commission arm as if it were truly no big deal. Maybe he wasn't the sharpest knife in the drawer, but he was the kind of man who would go out of his way to help a friend, something she deeply appreciated. He had certainly gone out of his way to make her feel welcome here.

They'd spent a lot of time together since she'd arrived here on the ranch. He couldn't do much in the way of physical labor since his accident, but he'd been great about helping her learn her way around the house and answering the gajillion questions she had about the way things were done. Because he'd cooked for the crowd himself, before his injury, he knew where the spices were stored, what the guys liked to drink, and what foods they hated (vegetable lasagna topped the list). He also shared Zeke's view that the previous housekeeper—the apparently perfect and angelic Libby—had made the best chocolate cake ever. Damn, sometimes she thought she could really get a hate on for this Libby person. Well, not really, because she didn't know her. But she could definitely feel jealous of Libby's prowess in the kitchen.

What with Libby and her chocolate cake, and Kat's gift with pies, and the disaster with the white cake, Carlin knew it was a waste of time to try anything fancy in the dessert department. She picked up pies from The Pie Hole when she went to town to buy groceries, and she bought lots of ice cream. Who didn't like ice cream? Brownies made from a mix were also popular, and easy. One of these days she was going to try the white cake again, but she kept finding reasons not to. Failure was never pleasant, and abject failure was humiliating. Kat had told her she'd probably just overmixed the batter, but Carlin didn't see how that could turn what should've been cake into an inedible spongelike substance. She did find a recipe for corn bread cake that—surprise—didn't have a lick of cornmeal in it, and it had turned out really well, but it was a sheet cake and somehow that didn't count. Layer cakes, the bastards, were what counted.

Spencer had adapted to the sling that immobilized his left arm well, and probably could've continued to work as a ranch hand in some capacity, but Zeke had insisted that he help her until he was healed. She wondered: was it a job meant to make things easy on the young hand, or did Zeke trust her so little that he wanted someone he did trust to keep an eye on her? There had been a time when she would've been insulted, but she now understood lack of trust all too well.

As they drove down the long and winding road—no joke—that eventually led to the road that led to the road that led to Battle Ridge, Carlin glanced at Spencer and asked—not for the first time in the past couple of weeks—"When are you going to tell me exactly how you hurt your shoulder?"

His cheeks went red. He was barely twenty-one, all but a baby. "That's not something a man wants to tell a woman, Miss Carly. It was bad. That's all you need to know."

"I know it has something to do with collecting bull semen," she said. "I just can't quite get the picture in my head . . ."

"Ma'am, you don't want that picture in your head," he said earnestly. "I don't either, but since I was there I don't have a choice. I'm just glad it's my left shoulder and not the right one. I'd have a heck of a time doing anything if I couldn't use my right arm."

She didn't think the nine-year difference in their ages made her a ma'am, but it was a habit she hadn't been able to break him of. She was either ma'am or Miss Carly, not just to him but to every man on the ranch . . . except Zeke.

She'd even done some research on the library computer, and knew there were several ways to collect bull semen. Some of the methods seemed almost cruel to her, but apparently the bull didn't usually mind being electrically jacked off.

"Usually" being the operative word here, since obviously with Spencer's last attempt *something* had gone wrong.

"I have a question for you," Spencer said. He pointed at her hat and sunglasses, which were sitting on the seat between them. "Why is it that every time you go into town you put on a disguise? It's almost like you're a movie star or a singer going inflagrante."

Carlin bit back a laugh. It would be rude, and she didn't want to make Spencer feel stupid. He did have a habit of using the wrong word, now and then. "Incognito," she said.

"What?"

"Not inflagrante. Incognito."

"Well, whatever the right word is, why?"

Kat and Zeke were the only two who knew part of her story; as far as she was concerned, no one else needed to know a single detail, and they knew only because she had to be paid in cash. The more people who were in on her secret, the less safe she'd feel. For a while she'd let her guard down in Battle Ridge, and not taken the precaution of sunglasses and hat, though she'd always made sure her TEC jacket was with her. But since that heart-stopping moment in the grocery store . . . damn it, she was going to have to let that go, sooner rather than later. Learn from it, and let it go. But maybe not right now. Maybe the next trip.

But Spencer had asked, and he'd keep asking, so she tried to come up with a girly-girl answer that would throw him off track. "I can never get my hair to behave like I want it to, you know? The ball cap hides all the flyaways."

"I like your hair," he said with complete seriousness. "I think it's real pretty and soft. And blond," he added, as if that made up for any flaws she saw in her own hair. He seemed to have a weakness for blondes, though she suspected he had a soft spot for all women, period.

"And flyaway, on occasion," she said.

"What about the sunglasses?"

"My eyes are sensitive." That made sense.

"But you're not wearing them now, while you're driving," he argued.

"The sun isn't in my eyes." It wasn't, but the excuse was a weak one and she knew it.

He shook his head and said, "All right, all right. You don't have to tell me, if you don't want to. You know, if you're a pop singer hiding out, or if you were the star of some reality show, you're safe from me. I only listen to country music, and I don't watch much TV. Don't have time to. You didn't kill anyone, did you?"

"Of course not."

"I never watch the news. It's just too depressing." For someone of his disposition, she could see why the news would be a downer. "You could've killed your whole family and everyone in the country could be looking for you, and I wouldn't know it." The thought didn't seem to bother him much. "You don't seem like the type, though. And besides, Zeke watches the news and he never would've hired you if you were wanted by the cops. Well, if he knew about it."

"I'm not wanted by the cops," Carlin assured him. *One* cop, yeah, but as far as she knew Brad hadn't gone so far as to come up with a fake charge and set the whole country to looking for her.

No, he didn't want anyone else around when he found her the next time. She shuddered, remembered Jina, and reminded herself of all the reasons why she couldn't share the details of her life with a nice, simple guy like Spencer.

"I didn't figure you were," he said. "But I swear, your hair is just fine."

Before they hit the grocery store Spencer had a physical therapy session. Carlin took the opportunity to run into the library first, then visited Kat to pick up the pies she'd ordered. The breakfast crowd had left and the lunch crowd hadn't started arriving yet, and her baking had been done for the day, so Kat wasn't busy. She smiled when Carlin came through the door, her pleasure evident.

It struck Carlin hard, realizing how long it had been since someone had genuinely smiled just because she'd walked in a door.

"Hey, girl. How's it going?" Kat asked.

"Good."

"How's Zeke been treating you?"

Carlin sat at the counter. "Like a chief cook and bottle washer he tolerates because he has no other choice." That wasn't completely true, but close enough.

"So, like a wife without the benefits."

"Benefits?" Carlin kept her tone deadpan. She didn't want even Kat to see where her mind had taken her. Zeke was a pain in her ass; he was grouchy and evidently didn't trust her as far as he could throw her. But he was a real man, tough and hard, and if her mind occasionally— several times a day, maybe—went where it shouldn't, well, no one needed to know about it.

But Kat's witch-eyes saw too much, as usual. "Honey, do not—I repeat, do *not*—get suckered in by the way Zeke Decker looks. He's the kind of man some women dream of taking on and fixing, but he is who he is and he can't be fixed."

"Fixed, how?" Carlin asked, because he sure didn't seem broken. Bullheaded, stubborn, and a lot of other things—sexy as hell among them—but not broken. "He's your cousin. Shouldn't you be singing his praises, or something?"

"He's my cousin, so I know him too well."

"Well, the last thing I need or want right now is a man, fixable or not." She needed to be free, free to run, free to start over at any moment. She kept telling herself the same thing over and over: any kind of relationship— even the one she'd developed with Kat—might tempt her to stay in one place too long. She had to be willing to run, to leave everything behind and not look back. The fact that she had to keep reminding herself was down-right scary.

"Too bad Spencer is so young and addle-brained," Kat said. "Well, not addled, but you know what I mean. He has a couple of plusses. He's cute, and he's got that hard, young body."

"Kat!"

"But he's a cowboy," Kat blithely continued, "and you know how I feel about cowboys. Besides, I think he's a virgin who'll probably feel he has to marry the first woman he sleeps with. It's a real chore to take on a lover who needs instruction, and I don't know about you, but I don't want a man I sleep with to be that grateful. Blown away and ecstatically happy, yes, but not 'I can't live without you' grateful. That's such a burden. Even if he does have a nice ass."

Carlin laughed. "Stop it! I have to work with Spencer every day. I don't want to know if he's a virgin or not, and I do not want to hear about his ass. He's like . . . a puppy."

"Sorry, but there's a dearth of suitable men around here, and a girl's mind does wander." Tapping her hand on the counter, Kat stood up. "Your pies are ready. Do you want to go ahead and order for next week?"

Carlin placed her order for the following week, throwing in a request for a piece of apple pie right now simply because it was apple pie day and she wanted one. As Kat poured a cup of coffee to go with that pie it crossed Carlin's mind that if Spencer was a puppy, Zeke Decker was a wolf. Given a chance he'd eat her alive.

No, thanks.

Wait. *Rewind*. She thought about those words and felt her heartbeat pick up, felt a tingle deep inside. Crap, she needed to concentrate on her pie and stop speculating about Zeke's oral skills.

"So." Kat leaned on the counter and watched Carlin dig into her dessert. "You're going to stay, right?"

"Until spring." Unless something went wrong.

"In that case, you're going to need a warmer coat." Kat grimaced at the TEC jacket. "And boots."

"I know." It had been getting colder with every passing day, and Carlin had given some thought to those things she'd need before winter arrived. Zeke had a ton of heavy coats; she could borrow one of them when she needed it. All she'd have to do was roll up the sleeves. She'd look like a homeless woman, but she didn't see the sense in spending good money on a coat when she didn't know if she'd need it next year.

Next winter she might be in Florida, or some other

warm place, and she wanted to save every dime she could. She had the money, she'd been squirreling away every dime she was paid, but she was hoarding it like a miser.

The coat situation she could handle, but she couldn't very well borrow Zeke's boots. "Where's the best place around here to find what I'll need?"

"Tillman's, right down the street. They'll have everything you need to get through the winter."

That taken care of, Kat asked Carlin if she'd tried to make the accursed Never Fail White Cake. Carlin told her no, and again Kat listed all the things she might've done wrong. The wrong kind of flour, old ingredients, and her favorite—overmixing. Carlin wasn't a big fan of "might've." She wanted to know exactly what had gone wrong so she wouldn't make the same mistakes over and over.

Maybe it was time to try again, though. She'd add cake flour to her grocery list and pick up one bag. Just one. She didn't see what the difference could be. Flour was flour, right? But she didn't share that thought with Kat, because as a baker she assumed Kat would think differently.

A couple of customers came in. Kat tried to refuse Carlin's payment, but she insisted. She said good-bye, took the pies, and headed for the truck, where she put the pies on the narrow floorboard of the tiny backseat.

Spencer wasn't back yet, so Carlin walked down the sidewalk to Tillman's. Her TEC jacket was sufficient for weather that was simply chilly, but the nip in the air was a warning. If it was this cold in October, what would December and January be like in Wyoming?

When she entered Tillman's store, a bell overhead rang, announcing her presence to the older woman behind the counter. There were no other customers, not at that moment, and Carlin wondered how a business like this one survived in a shrinking town. She smiled, said she was just looking, and then a coat caught her eye. Oh, that would look so much better than an oversized throwaway! She picked up the coat, checked the price . . . and immediately returned it to the rack.

So *that's* how this place stayed in business. One sale, and they'd be set for the month! There were other, less expensive coats on the rack, but none of them were what she'd call cheap. Good thing she'd decided to make do with Zeke's old coats, because no way was she paying that much for a coat, no matter how luxurious the shearling felt. She headed for the shoe section, wondering if she should even bother to look. Maybe the general store would have something. Or Goodwill. Did Battle Ridge have a Goodwill?

There was a small "sale" section, and in it she found a pair of boots in her size. They weren't all that expensive to begin with, and they were marked down to half price. It didn't matter than she didn't like the color—who'd thought it was a good idea to manufacture boots in that particular shade of green?—or that the material didn't look all that sturdy. She just needed a pair of boots to get her through one winter. They'd be okay, as long as she had nice, thick socks.

She paid for the boots, but as she left the store, she eyed the overpriced coat. Man, it was gorgeous. And it looked so wonderfully warm.

But if she had to run, the price of that coat would cover a month in a cheap hotel. Make that two months. She wanted the money in her pocket, not in a coat.

Her stomach turned at the thought. She didn't want to run again; didn't want to face the uncertainty of another off-the-books job. Maybe something would happen and she could stay—

No. She didn't dare let herself hope, not for that. She had to stay aware, stay ready, and go on the assumption that in a few months she'd be on the road again.

When she got back to the truck with her new boots, Spencer was there, waiting, with a smile and a small brown paper bag from the hardware store. The only errand remaining was the grocery store and a honking huge list.

"What did you buy?" Spencer asked as he stepped into the passenger seat.

"Boots." Carlin placed the green boots in the backseat, making sure they were secure so they wouldn't migrate onto the pies.

"Oh yeah, you'll need plenty of warm clothes before the end of the month." He started to list all the things she'd need. In addition to the boots, a heavy coat—or two; hats, gloves, scarves to cover her nose and mouth because otherwise her lungs could freeze. Carlin didn't tell him that she planned to glom onto Zeke's leftover coats; if she did, he might wonder why she was being so chintzy with her money—or, even worse, he might feel sorry for her and start taking up a collection to buy her clothes. She could so see Spencer doing that.

And she could see people giving, out of the goodness of their hearts.

She was so lucky to have found Battle Ridge, Kat . . . even Zeke. By the time spring arrived she'd have a good amount of cash to get her to wherever—a good amount of cash, some warm memories, and an ugly-ass pair of cheap green boots.

Chapter Fourteen

ZEKE AND SOME of the men were just pulling up to the house for lunch when the back door crashed open with a force that sent it slamming against the wall, and Carlin burst out at a dead run, carrying a flaming pan and screaming, *"Gaaaaa!"* at the top of her lungs. Zeke slammed on the brakes and shoved the gear into park as he leaped out of the truck. He rounded the hood and raced toward her, his heart in his mouth. Those flames could blow back into her face—

"Drop it!" he roared.

Startled, she did, right there at her feet. It was sheer luck, but the pan landed upside down. A few little flames licked out from under the edges, then died away.

She stood there staring down at the pan, breathing hard. Warily, the men were climbing out of the other trucks, wondering if it was their lunch they had watched crash and burn—well, burn and die. Zeke reached her and whirled her around. "Are you okay?"

"Yeah," she said, still breathing hard. She glared down at the pan. And then she kicked it. The first kick sent it tumbling a couple of feet; something black and gooey came out. The second kick got better distance, maybe because it wasn't as heavy now. Evidently unsatisfied, she advanced on one of the pickups and grabbed a hammer from the back. Going down on one knee, she swung the hammer for all she was worth and beat the hell out of that pan, then she got up and kicked it one more time for good measure.

"Damn," Walt muttered. "I'm not ever going to say a single bad thing about her cooking."

"Yeah," Eli muttered in return. "No matter what it is, I'll eat it or die. Even that cake."

"More like, eat it *and* die," Patrick put in.

Zeke would have laughed, if his heart wasn't still pounding with fear. "Damn it," he yelled at her, "you don't run with a flaming pan—"

"You do when you can't get the damn fire extinguisher to work," she snapped back. She was evidently finished taking out her frustration on the pan, because she returned the hammer to the truck and grimly surveyed the men standing around eyeing her with more than a little trepidation.

Spencer knew her better, so he gathered his courage first. "Uh . . . what was that, Miss Carly?"

"An experiment," she said, and her tone told them all not to ask another question. "Don't worry, it wasn't lunch. Y'all get inside and eat. Now."

One and all, even Zeke, they turned and filed into the house.

Lunch was sometimes served in shifts; the men came in and ate when they could. It wasn't ideal, but Carlin could see the reasoning behind it so she'd learned to go with the flow. After the incident with the flaming pan, she was glad she had to deal with men coming and going today, because it gave her time to settle down. Damn biscuits. Not that they'd looked like biscuits; they'd resembled flaming hockey pucks more than anything, but she'd figure out what she'd done wrong. She was fairly sure biscuits weren't supposed to flame up like that.

Finally the last two hands, Darby and Patrick, were finishing up while she took a break in the kitchen, sipping on a glass of tea. Once they were out of the way she'd clean up and get to the laundry that never seemed to get completely finished. At least there was no longer a quarter mile of dirty clothes piled in front of the washer and dryer; the chore was much more manageable these days. She had a laundry basket devoted to her clothes, and so did Zeke, as well as a separate one for towels. None of the baskets ever overflowed. There were times when it might've made sense for her to wash his clothes and hers together, but she never did; shared laundry would indicate an intimacy they didn't have.

Patrick made his way through the kitchen, thanking her for lunch—he was always so polite—and heading out and back to work. That left only Darby, finishing up in the dining room. Great. She wondered what he'd find to complain about when he left. With him, there was always something. If he'd been one of Snow White's dwarfs, his name would have been "Bitcher."

A few minutes later Darby came out and said, "That casserole was damn good."

Carlin almost dropped her glass of tea. A compliment? From Darby? He was the one who'd complained that he wanted to know exactly what he was eating, and in a casserole he couldn't always be sure. Something was up. The hairs on the back of her neck stood up in warning when he stopped by the small kitchen table and just looked at her for a long, uncomfortable moment.

"I won't be here much longer, you know," he said.

How was she supposed to respond to that? It would be an out and out lie to say she'd be sorry to see him go, and rude to say "good riddance." So she managed a noncommittal hum, and got up from the table to put a little more space between them, just in case. She didn't like him, and she didn't trust him.

He didn't take the hint and move on. Instead he said with a hint of cockiness, "After October market, I'm going down to Texas to rodeo. I'm a bull rider in the winter rodeo, and I've done some bronc riding as well. Want to see the buckles I've won?"

God, was this his version of "want to see my etchings"? If she'd been sipping her tea right then, she'd have snorted it out her nose.

"No, thanks," Carlin responded, wishing he'd just move on. "But, uh, good luck." She could hardly say she hoped he'd get gored in the 'nads, now could she? For a split second she felt bad that she'd even had the mean thought.

"Are you sure?" He drawled the words, gave her what he might have thought was a sexy look but struck her more as a smirk. "I keep 'em in the bunkhouse. You ever been to a rodeo? A lot of women are turned on when they see a man control an animal the way I can."

He made that statement sound more suggestive than it should've, and that was saying something. Her bad feelings about having mean thoughts evaporated in an instant. There was no way he could interpret her carefully bland responses as intense interest, or even casual interest, in anything he said or did.

It wasn't her. She couldn't let doubt undermine her. When Brad had first started stalking her, after just two dates, she'd felt guilty and gone over and over those two dates, looking for anything she could have said or done that made him think he was her one and only. She'd liked him okay on the first date, but only okay, just enough that she'd said yes to a second date. The second date had turned her off, though; there hadn't been anything *horrible* about Brad, just a general feeling that she didn't want to go there. As it turned out, her instinct had been right on the money, but too late where Brad was concerned, because he'd already fixated on her.

She got a similar feel about Darby, an uneasiness that made her not want to be alone with him. Stalker? Nah, she didn't think so. Asshole? Oh, yeah.

"Rodeos never appealed to me," she said flatly, which was the truth even though she was from Houston. She'd never been to one, and had no feelings about them one way or the other.

"Maybe you should give them a try, watch some real men in action."

"Don't think so. Not interested."

God, how much plainer could she get?

He moved closer, close enough that her pulse gave a huge leap of alarm. A smug smile was on his face. "Don't you get lonely, Carly? A pretty woman like you, you must need more than cooking and cleaning to satisfy you. Darby's here for you, sugar, all you have to do is say the—"

Carlin lunged to the side and grabbed the broom she'd had out earlier, got a good grip, and pointed the handle toward Darby as if it were a weapon. "Out," she snapped.

"Whoa!" he said, startled. He put on an innocent expression, and raised his hands in the air as if she held a gun on him and he was surrendering. "I didn't do anything. I was just being friendly."

"Be friendly somewhere else. Out!" she said again, more forcefully this time.

"All right, I'm going, I'm going. Jesus, you're a little nuts, you know? Anyone ever tell you that you overreact?"

"Don't try to pull that crap on me. Only someone delusional could have thought I was in any way interested." She followed him into the mudroom, her broom pointed at him the whole time. He said he'd be leaving the ranch soon, but unless he was on his way right this minute, it wouldn't be soon enough to suit her.

When he reached the door he said uneasily, "There's no need to tell the boss about our little misunderstanding."

"I didn't misunderstand anything," Carlin snapped. She didn't intend to go running to Zeke with a complaint, but she wasn't about to tell Darby that. Let him stew; it would serve him right. Would Zeke even care that one of his hands had made a crude, awkward pass at her? Probably not; after all, Darby hadn't touched her. She'd handle this herself.

"You're not allowed in this house alone with me again," she said shortly. "You don't show up for a meal early and you don't stay late. If you ignore me on this I won't say anything to Zeke, but I'll tell the entire crew, over pie or brownies. I think they'll understand why I don't want you hanging around after our *misunderstanding*."

"You're being a bitch about nothing," he grumbled as he walked through the door. "Can't blame a man for trying."

"Actually, I can." She slammed the door on him, locked it, and then stood there for a moment, trying to still her pounding heart.

She couldn't allow every jerk she ran into to send her into a panic, or make her doubt herself. This was *not* about her. She wasn't a raving beauty, she didn't wear any makeup these days, and honestly, why bother fixing her hair beyond brushing it and pulling it up into a ponytail? Being the only female on the ranch might bump her up the attractiveness scale a notch or two, but it wasn't like she was giving off signals that she was on the hunt. Some men were occasionally going to flirt, because that's the way they were built. Just her luck, this flirt happened to be the ranch hand she liked the least, and his attempt at flirting was cringe-worthy.

Should she tell anyone about the awkward moment? She'd told her friends in Houston that Brad had been a dud, and she'd told them when he'd started following her around. But none of them had witnessed anything, and Brad had been smart enough, skilled enough, to cover his tracks. In the end, it had been his word against hers, and his word had carried the most weight.

What if she found herself in that situation again? And besides, who would she tell? Zeke was the obvious choice, but Darby really hadn't done anything, other than be obnoxious. She'd never been a whiner or a snitch, anyway. Should she casually mention it to Spencer, who'd become the closest friend she had on the ranch? No, he was too much of a Galahad; if he knew Darby had made her uncomfortable he might feel obligated to defend her honor, and goodness knows he didn't need to do anything that might reinjure his shoulder when he was so close to being out of his sling.

She could take care of herself. She *would* take care of herself. If there was a next time, she wouldn't pull a broom on Darby, she'd go for one of the knives.

And she hadn't been kidding about not allowing him to be in the house alone with her again.

THE OCTOBER MARKET was over, finally, and Zeke had a chance to go over the books. Financially, it was a good year, better than he'd expected. He'd done well at market, and now he could settle into a slow winter. The weather always made every chore more difficult, but there was also a lot less to do. Finally he had a chance to catch his breath, look at plans for the following year, relax. There was always maintenance to be taken care of, and animals to be fed, but this was the resting-up phase of his year and everything was going as well for him as he could ask.

Except for Carlin.

He wasn't getting anywhere with her. Not that he'd tried real hard, because he didn't want to spook her, but she hadn't relaxed her guard at all. He'd counted on fa-

miliarity to gradually get her to unbend, and she had—
with the hands. With him, though, all the spikes and
bristles were still in place.

For his part, getting used to having her there hadn't
taken any time at all. She could cook well enough, she
kept the house and his clothes clean. The hands all liked
her, or at least they seemed to, and she got along well with
them. Whenever he drove up and saw the light on in the
kitchen, or even during the day, he could feel his pulse
quicken because he knew she was inside, and it didn't
have a damn thing to do with how well she cleaned house.

The barrier she kept between them was frustrating, especially since he knew she wouldn't keep it so prominent
if she wasn't attracted to him, too. It was evident in the
way she even avoided saying his name. She had no problem calling everyone else by name, but she never called
him anything. Not Zeke, not A.Z., not Mr. Decker, not
even boss. Hell, she didn't even say "Hey, you!" It was
like that old country song . . . she never called him by his
name, and she sure as hell didn't call him darlin'.

They'd all been so busy up until now that giving her
space had been easy; she did her job and he did his, and
except for mealtimes their paths hadn't crossed all that
often. But what the hell was he supposed to do now that
market was over and he'd be here in the house far more
often? The days were getting shorter and shorter, and
while she had her part of the house to live in and he had
his, they were bound to run into each other more fre-
quently than they had so far.

Her workload was about to become lighter, as well.
Spencer would be out of his sling soon. As soon as Bo and
Darby took off for Texas and the rodeoing they loved,
and Patrick and Eli went home for a couple of months,
there would be fewer mouths to feed. What were they
going to do? Occupy the house for hours on end without

speaking? Or did she expect him to spend his days in the barn?

They needed a truce. *He* needed a breach in that wall of hers. And he wanted her to call him . . . something.

With that in mind, he pushed back from his desk and went searching for her, not that she was hard to find. If she wasn't doing housework, she was in the kitchen, which often looked like a mad scientist had been doing experiments in there. She still had duds, but overall she was becoming a more than decent cook, and she seemed driven to prove herself in that department. Sure enough, the kitchen was where he found her. The radio was on, and she was sort of dancing as she swept, using the broom as a partner, that fine ass swinging. He'd have had to be dead not to notice, especially since he was already susceptible to her ass.

She'd been experimenting again. Something that smelled good was baking in the oven, and there seemed to have been a mini-explosion of flour. The white stuff was on the floor, on the counter, and on her face. He was pretty sure it was also in her hair.

The broom wasn't doing a great job, smearing the flour around instead of gathering it up, but as long as she kept up the dancing, he sure as hell didn't care.

She must have come to the same conclusion about the broom, because she stopped dancing and turned. As soon as she saw him, her spine stiffened.

"Carlin," he said in way of greeting, wondering if she'd answer with a curt *Zeke*.

Instead she just said. "What can I do for you?" It was an almost polite way of asking, *What the hell are you doing in my kitchen?*

He couldn't tell her the truth, that he wanted to push at her, so he said, "Something smells good."

"Never Fail White Cake." She gave him a defiant look,

then turned away and put the broom in the closet, getting out a mop instead.

Zeke grimaced. "Really?"

"I've been meaning to try the recipe again, but I've been so busy I just haven't had the time."

"I don't suppose you took Spencer's advice and started with a cake mix this time?"

"No. That would be cheating. Giving in. Letting a stupid cake get the best of me." She grinned a little, as if she were making fun of herself. "You sound almost afraid."

"Hell, yes, I'm afraid," he said bluntly. "I'm pretty sure I still haven't digested that first bite."

"This one will be better," she said confidently. "I used the right kind of flour, and I didn't overmix the batter."

"Left out the concrete this time, did you?"

"Very funny." She started to smile, then realized what she was doing and shut her expression down as if she'd flipped a light switch. Holding the mop as if it were a weapon, again she asked, "What can I do for you?"

The image that sprang to mind wasn't something he was about to tell her, but his dick swiftly responded. Damn it, if she looked down— No danger of that, though. She'd barely look him in the eye, much less the crotch.

"I smelled something good. I came to see what it was. Can't a man hang out in his own kitchen?"

"For the duration this isn't your kitchen; it's mine. You need to *hang out* elsewhere. Don't you have some cows that need your attention?"

"Not at the moment."

"A horse, then."

"Not that I know of."

"Well, I don't need your attention, either," she said, and then she literally shooed him toward the mudroom. "Go dig a hole, or something. Put a post in it and call it a fence." Because the whole point of what he was trying to do was get her to trust him, he allowed himself to be shooed. As he did, though, he noted to himself that she still hadn't called him a damn thing. At this rate, he'd settle for "asshole."

In the mudroom, he stopped to pull on a coat. When he looked down he spotted a pair of small, ugly green boots. He bent down and picked up one, turned it over to check the sole. What a piece of crap. "Please tell me these aren't your boots," he called, raising his voice so Carlin could hear him.

He heard something that sounded like a snort, then she called back sharply, "No, they belong to the *other* ranch employee who wears a woman's size seven."

Zeke headed back toward the kitchen, one size-seven boot in his hand. She'd wasted her money, because these boots wouldn't hold up to a Wyoming winter. They were good for rainy weather, at best. He knew what she needed and he'd damn well tell her: a decent pair of boots, a heavy coat, thermal socks and underwear, something to cover her head. Then he stopped. He knew why she'd bought these boots: they were cheap. She was saving every dime she could, so she could continue to hide from the psycho who had her running scared.

He returned the boot to its place and headed out the door, into a cold wind. He'd taken a few steps before he realized that Carlin had run him out of his own damn house.

CARLIN WATCHED THE faces of the hands as she placed the cake on the table. They recognized the cake, of course, and the expressions varied from wary to alarmed. She heard a muttered curse word or two, and more than one very sad sigh. It was Spencer who finally said, "Miss Carly, that cake sure is pretty, but I'm not sure I can eat another bite."

That got them going. There was a round of very polite

"I'm so full" and "I shouldn't have eaten so much" and one apologetic "I think I'm allergic to white cake."

She wasn't surprised, but she was a tad disappointed. She'd worked hard on the cake, and though the *batter* had tasted good, there was no way to tell if the finished product was any better than the first one if no one tasted it. It looked as if she'd be the sole guinea pig, and even if it was good and she told them so, they probably wouldn't believe her.

She wheeled around to return to the kitchen with the entire cake, when Zeke stood, reached across Walt for a plate and knife, and motioned for her to move closer.

Brave man. Or foolish—she wasn't sure which. Still, she couldn't help being grateful. She placed the cake in front of him, and watched as he cut a big piece. "If everyone else is too full, that just means more for me," he said without looking at her.

She turned and hurried into the kitchen for the decaf, poured a cup as Zeke sat down and eyed the huge piece of cake as if it were an obstacle he had to overcome, a task, a challenge. She scowled at him, gratitude turning to ire. He must have sensed he was dragging this out too long, because finally he dug in. He forked a big piece and carried it to his mouth. Everyone watched. Carlin didn't breathe, and she didn't think anyone else at the table did, either. Zeke chewed, swallowed, and the relief in his eyes told the story.

It was good.

She gave a whoop, and pumped her fist in the air, and everyone except for Darby burst out laughing.

Zeke washed down the big bite with a sip of coffee. "You guys are missing out on some good cake. Like I said, more for me."

Walt cut himself a piece then, and Spencer decided maybe he wasn't too full after all. One by one, the men helped themselves, laughing and joking but generally having good things to say about the dessert. Well, Darby had nothing good to say, but that wasn't unusual. Probably everyone would have fallen out of their chairs if he'd given anyone or anything a compliment. Carlin went back toward the kitchen for more coffee mugs, but she stopped in the doorway and looked toward Zeke. She caught his eye, and even though she knew it was a bad idea she mouthed the words, "Thank you."

He acknowledged her thanks with a slight nod of his head. No one else noticed the little byplay; they were all too busy eating.

Her step was a light one as she gathered more mugs. The white cake was a success! She'd taken it on, and won.

Next up?

Biscuits.

Chapter Fifteen

CARLIN SWISHED THE brush around the inside edge of the toilet bowl, then flushed. The bathroom smelled piney fresh now; the shower had been cleaned, the bathtub had been dusted—she doubted the tub had seen any water since Zeke had moved into the master bedroom—and now the john itself, in its private little room, was finished. She'd mopped the tile floors, polished the mirrors over the double vanities, polished the faucets and handles.

Maybe it was overkill, but she'd also lit scented candles in there and in the bedroom while she worked. It wasn't that the rooms stank; in fact, she liked the smell of man—of Zeke—that came from his choice of clothes, the leather boots and belts and felt hats, the flannel shirts, the jeans, the man himself. A closet full of silk suits would have smelled completely different. And could the pheromones of a diplomat ever compete with those of a man who did hard physical work? Maybe for some women, yeah, but Carlin had discovered her own cave-woman core that definitely preferred the hard-muscles/hard-work variety. So: scented candles to overpower the pheromones. That might work. Maybe. Couldn't hurt.

It was a measure of how bad her case of Zeke-itis was that she didn't mind swabbing his beard shavings out of the sink, or cleaning his toilet. Okay, it helped her feelings that she was being paid to do those chores, but even if she'd rather have her toenails pulled out than be honest with him about how she felt or even who she really was, she had to be honest with herself, and that meant admitting she *liked* being in his bedroom, *liked* doing his laundry and hanging up his clean clothes, *liked* stripping off the Zeke-scented sheets from his bed and remaking it with fresh sheets.

At least she could honestly say that, though she didn't mind cleaning his toilet, no way did she *like* it, so maybe there was still a shred of sanity left in her pheromone-drunk brain.

She hung fresh towels and washcloths on the racks, then put all her cleaning stuff in the bucket she used to cart it all from one location to another. In one arm she gathered the used towels from the floor, opened the bathroom door with her free hand, then did a quick dip to pick up the cleaning bucket. Head down, preoccupied, both arms laden, she hurried out of the bathroom and barreled straight into a solid obstacle.

The flood of adrenaline through her was like being electrified. It was akin to panic, but somehow different. Seeing someone in the grocery store who reminded her of Brad had been one thing; the terrifying realization that someone was *in the room* with her was something else entirely. She shrieked, her body reacting before thought could form, before any semblance of logic could kick in. There *was* no logic, there was only the jarring knowledge that someone was in the house, that this supposedly safe haven had been breached.

Going from *safe* to *unsafe* in a nanosecond literally jarred her out of her wits. She had a weird sensation of leaving reality, of drawing deep inside herself where she was safe even while her body reacted in a primal bid to survive. Everything was distant, blurred. She could hear herself screaming, though the sound was oddly muted; there was a deep voice, the words indistinguishable. She had a brief glimpse of bare flesh, but her instincts didn't give her time to put two and two together and come up with a logical identity for the half-naked man in the bed-room. Before her synapses could click and the name *Zeke* form in her brain, she was already moving, drop-ping everything to the floor and swinging her right fist with everything she had behind the punch.

Existing on two different planes was so disorienting she couldn't tell what she was doing until she'd already done it. Here was her body, moving, acting, and her brain was somewhere else, scrambling to make sense of what was happening. It was as if her thoughts were lip-syncing two beats behind the music, and she couldn't catch up, couldn't make the two come together. Just about the time she was beginning to think instead of sim-ply react, he ducked to the side to avoid losing a tooth or maybe getting his nose broken, then came in low, catch-ing her middle with his shoulder. The impact was solid enough to jar her; the world turned topsy-turvy, her feet off the ground, nothing making sense, then she was flat on her back on the carpet and he was holding her down, both wrists caught in one big hand and held above her head. Dazed, she stared up into green eyes gone narrow and dark with some emotion she couldn't read, didn't want to read.

"What are you doing here?" she blurted, zooming from terror to outrage at warp speed. Getting outraged at his intrusion was absurd, she fully recognized that, but again she couldn't catch her mental balance. The shock of panic, anger, sheer survival instinct—whatever it was, and in whatever mixture—had left her brain still scram-bling to catch up, not just with events, but with her mouth as well.

"I'm pretty sure I still live here," he bit out.

At least that cleared up her confusion about his emotion. He was annoyed. No, he was pissed as hell.

She blinked, caught her breath, waited for her thoughts to settle. At least they were settling now, instead of darting around like crazed squirrels. "No. I mean—what are you doing here *now*? I would say I'm sorry but—no, I am sorry, I'd *never* have tried to punch you out if I'd recognized you in time. Wait. Maybe I don't mean that. *Never* is too final. Someday I may really want to punch you out. But today I didn't mean to, so I'm sorry."

He cocked his head a little to the side as he navigated that warren of sentences, then he squeezed his eyes shut and heaved a put-upon sort of sigh. The movement of his bare chest momentarily pressing on her breasts slammed her with a sudden jolt of self-awareness, and there was an almost audible *click* in her head as her brain and body realigned in perfect sync.

Oh, damn, this wasn't good. She'd tried so hard to keep him at a safe distance, to not touch him even casually because she'd known, instinctively, that he was too attractive to her, too much of a temptation. Letting him become important to her wasn't fair to either of them, given her situation. With those boundaries in mind even a touch on her hand had been rebuffed . . . and now here he was, lying heavily on top of her, his muscled weight hot and confining and so exciting her stomach, her entire body, tightened in response.

Hunger gnawed at her, hunger that had nothing to do with food and everything to do with being a woman. Because of Brad she'd not only been prevented from forming any romantic relationships, she'd come to doubt her own instincts when it came to men. She'd held herself in emotional solitary confinement, not letting herself enjoy the normal flirtations or even casual dates, much less anything more serious.

And yet, despite all her precautions, here she was, flat

on her back on the floor, with Zeke heavy on top of her—and everything about it thrilled her. Her muscles tightened, her body seizing control and arching upward of its own volition, seeking that for which she was so starved. Desperately she caught herself, tried to turn the arch into a squirm as if she was trying to free herself.

He was too close, close enough that she could see each individual whisker on his jaw, his five o'clock shadow coming in several hours early. His face was right above hers, those green eyes going even darker. She could see her own tiny reflection in their black centers, and the striations, both dark and light, in his irises. The heat from his body, especially his bare upper torso, seared through her clothes. She could smell him, the scent of hot skin, the somewhat acrid smell of the horse he'd been riding, hay, leather, the outdoors—so many smells mixing together and forming a signature that was his alone. A pinching, aching sensation in her nipples told her they had hardened, were standing taut. *Could he feel them?* Her cheeks burned at the thought, but at the same time she was excited by the idea.

Even more exciting, as far as feeling went, she could very definitely detect the hard length growing in his jeans, pressing into the softness of her crotch. Maybe getting an erection was nothing more than an automatic reaction for a man when he was on top of a woman, but she was the woman he was on top of, and from his expression there was nothing automatic about it.

Oh, God! She wanted so much to open her legs, wrap them around him, pull him closer. She clenched her teeth against the moan of wanting that rose in her throat. She wanted to be a normal woman again, live a normal life. She wanted *him*.

But she couldn't. She didn't dare. This must *not* happen. No matter what it cost her, she had to push him away, both mentally and physically.

Mentally, she could manage—just barely. Physically, though she put her hands on his shoulders and pushed, it was a useless effort. Helplessly she clenched her fingers on the thick pads of muscle in his shoulders, delighting in the strength she could feel there, the heat and power and life. She stared up into his face, her breath coming shallow and fast, panting against his lips.

"Let me up," she managed to say, the words faint. If she'd meant them her voice would have been stronger, but if she'd meant them she'd already have shoved him away and gotten to her feet. She knew it, he knew it. There was a long pause, so long that her heartbeat leaped into double-time because his gaze had gone heavy-lidded and was focused on her mouth. He was going to kiss her. Oh, God, he was going to kiss her. And she was going to let him. Despite everything, despite all of her very good reasons for not letting anything develop between them, in that moment the temptation was so close and raw that she *knew* she wouldn't be able to stop either him or herself.

Then he planted his hands on either side of her shoulders and levered himself up, jacking to his feet with a lithe, athletic movement so easy she could almost overlook the amount of strength it required. Almost.

Reprieve. Or rejection. She couldn't decide which, but she could decide that it didn't matter; what mattered was that he'd saved her from her own stupidity.

He reached down a big, work-hardened hand, and automatically she put her right hand in it. With a quick tug he had her standing on her feet, but he didn't release her hand. Her heart leaped and once again she was certain he was going to kiss her, once again her body sent her head spinning. Instead he pulled her close, his head bent down as he glared directly into her eyes. "That's twice you've panicked," he said sharply. "The first time you tried to run. This time you managed a swing that a ten-year-old could have ducked. Considering your situation, why the hell haven't you taken some self-defense lessons?"

What he said was so far from what she'd been expecting that, for a few seconds, she scrambled for a reply. She opened her mouth, couldn't think of an answer, closed it again. Then she shook herself, literally. There *were* reasons, a couple of very good ones.

"Money. Time. And knowing how to punch someone won't protect me from a bullet."

His head jerked back, green gaze going dark again, and abruptly she realized that he hadn't been angry because she'd swung at him, he'd been angry because she'd *missed*. "The bastard has *shot* at you?" he barked.

Not at her. At Jina. But he'd thought he was shooting at Carlin, and Jina had paid with her life. She shook again, this time as the horror washed over her again, horror and grief and bone-deep regret. She didn't go into the details, simply said "Yes," because Brad had thought he was shooting at her and the outcome didn't change his intention.

Zeke's jaw set, his mouth as grim as she'd ever seen it, which was plenty grim. "You need shooting lessons."

"Why? I don't have a gun." And she couldn't buy one, either, because the background check could possibly alert Brad to her location. She didn't know enough about background checks, whether they were state or federal, or how easily accessible the data was. She could find out, using Zeke's computer, but buying a gun would still be problematic.

He gave a cold smile that in no way alleviated the grimness of his expression.

"Getting you a weapon isn't a problem."

"But the background check—"

"Doesn't apply to private sales."

"Oh." Suddenly faced with an option that a second ago had seemed impossible, all she could do was swallow. Not having a gun kept her from having to make some hard decisions, such as whether or not she would actually use one. She wasn't a violent person; Brad had forced her into a lifestyle that was so far removed from her natural inclinations that sometimes she didn't recognize herself. Or was she simply discovering facets of her personality that, under less drastic circumstances, would never have come to the fore?

"Don't worry about getting a weapon. I'll see to that. And you're also going to learn how to protect yourself. Before I'm through with you, you'll not only know how to shoot, you'll know how to fight."

Chapter Sixteen

IT WAS TURNING cold. Not just chilly, but definitely cold. Zeke and the men had just about caught up on all the maintenance that needed doing; another week, and it would be done, and he'd cut back on the number of employees for the winter. Darby and Bo would head south for the rodeo circuit, Patrick and Eli would look for work farther south to tide them over until next spring—or maybe not, he never knew for certain whether or not they'd come back, though they had for the past few years. Kenneth and Micah would be here; as married men, they stayed put, and were available if he needed them during the winter. Walt was a permanent fixture, and Spencer was almost one, though the kid would take some time off during the winter to visit his folks.

Their employment schedule was no secret from the men. Ranch work was seasonal. As they were finishing up repair on a pumping station, Darby straightened and rolled his shoulders. "This is about it, right, boss?"

"Looks like it. Another week, maybe."

"Reckon you could do without me? There's a rodeo in Tucson I'd like to hit before I move on to Texas."

"Sure, we can handle the rest of it."

"Mind if I head back to the bunkhouse early, so I can

get my shit packed up? I'm thinking I'll start out early tomorrow morning."

Zeke glanced at Walt, silently checking if Walt had something lined up that he'd need Darby's help with. Walt gave a "why not" shrug. Nothing was in the works that the rest of them couldn't handle.

"Go ahead, we're good here."

"Thanks." Darby collected his tools, loaded everything into one of the ranch pickups, and headed out. They had four trucks there, so getting everyone back wasn't a problem.

Darby had been gone about ten minutes when Zeke got an uneasy feeling. First, Darby would have had plenty of time tonight to pack; it wasn't as if he needed a moving van. Second, Carlin was there alone, and though she was still religious about keeping the door locked, this was also the time of day, when normally all the men were gone, that she would do some light cleaning in the bunkhouse, and in Walt's cabin.

Maybe it was nothing. As far as he knew, Darby had taken his first warning to heart and not bothered Carlin in any way. Nor would he necessarily know her house-cleaning schedule, unless he had happened to go back one day to fetch a needed tool, and noticed her coming or going to the bunkhouse. That was a stretch. But . . . would Darby know how fanatic she was about keeping the doors locked while she was in the house? Her edict on locks hadn't extended to the bunkhouse, because she wasn't in there all that much. She dusted, she swept, and the rest of it was left to the hands to keep their space clean.

So far as he knew, the subject of the locked doors had never come up with the men. He knew about the locks; Spencer knew about the locks. But he'd never mentioned it, and he didn't think Spencer had either, unless it was in the bunkhouse at night.

He was worrying about nothing.

On the other hand, he and everyone else had noticed a distinct coolness in the way she treated Darby, something that had been the subject of a lot of jokes at the ranch hand's expense, and which Darby hadn't taken well. He had an outsized ego, maybe from the rodeo groupies, maybe because that was just in his makeup. He'd already caused trouble with one housekeeper, though to be fair two other people had been involved, it wasn't just Darby.

But would he hold a grudge against Carlin? Oh, shit yeah.

Zeke ignored his gut feeling for another few seconds, then straightened and pulled off his gloves. "I'm going back to the house," he said abruptly. "I don't trust Darby."

Walt straightened, too, thought about it for a second. "Good call. We'll go with you."

Every last one of them loaded up in the remaining pickups. The job wouldn't get finished today, Zeke thought, but so fucking what? Making sure Carlin was okay was more important.

He kept his boot jammed on the gas pedal harder than he normally would have, the truck bouncing hard on the cold, rough ground of the pasture. The trail they normally drove would have been smoother, but he was more interested in speed than comfort, or the springs on the truck. The two other trucks followed right behind him.

Spencer, in the passenger seat, held on tight with his good arm. For once, he wasn't smiling. "I don't think Darby would *hurt* Miss Carly," he said, worry evident in his tone. "But he might mess with her some and upset her."

Zeke grunted. He wasn't prepared to take the chance with her safety, period. If he made a fool of himself by rushing to the rescue when no rescue was needed, if

Darby was in the bunkhouse packing his belongings the way he said and Carlin was in the kitchen cooking supper, he was okay with that. But the fact that even Spencer, who normally gave everyone the benefit of the doubt, thought it was possible Darby might try something with Carlin, made him drive even faster. Darby had a tenminute head start, but by cutting across the pasture like this he could make up most of that time.

THE GUYS DID a decent job of keeping the bunkhouse clean. At least they did their laundry, and mostly kept their clutter out of the common area. Carlin didn't go into their rooms, but she did go through the common area every day and do a fast neatening; overall, she spent about half an hour or forty-five minutes in the bunkhouse, and if Walt had asked her to do the same in his little cabin she'd give it a fast polishing-up, too, but that seldom took more than fifteen minutes. She didn't have to do it all at once, either. Her schedule was her own, varying according to what else she needed to be doing. She might sweep, then go back to the house and put on a load of laundry, or get the next meal started, before returning to finish the job.

She was dusting, almost finished with the bunkhouse for the day, when she heard a truck drive up. She was so attuned to the rhythm and routine of the ranch by now that she registered immediately that the truck had approached from the rear instead of coming up the road to the house, which meant it was one of the ranch trucks. The men were all doing some much needed maintenance work around the ranch, so probably Zeke had sent someone back for some tool or piece of equipment they'd discovered they needed. She continued what she was doing, not thinking anything of it though she half-listened for the sound of the truck heading back out again.

Because the door was closed against the cold weather, she didn't hear any footsteps approaching the bunkhouse door. Abruptly the door was pulled open and a muscular, stocky man was framed against the sunlight. Carlin jumped, startled; the man in the doorway went still for a moment, too, then continued on into the bunkhouse and closed the door behind him.

"Well, look who's here," Darby drawled, his gaze raking down her.

"I was just finishing," she said without inflection, moving into the kitchen area. The common space was open, kitchen, dining, and den all together. Not only did she want some furniture between her and Darby, she wanted to be closer to the block of knives that sat on the counter.

"Don't hurry on my account." He leaned a shoulder against the doorframe, watched her with hooded eyes. Resentment gleamed in those eyes, showed plainly in his reflection. "I came back to pack up my stuff. I'm leaving tomorrow."

Good riddance hovered on her tongue, but she didn't say anything, just gave a curt nod.

The gleam in his eyes changed. "You could send me on my way with a smile, you know."

A cold twist of fear tightened her stomach. She was alone here with him; before, there had been someone still outside, within hearing distance if she screamed. Today, she could scream her head off and no one would hear. But damned if she'd show how scared she was. Very deliberately, she reached out and pulled the largest knife from the block, turned the blade so it caught the light.

She didn't say anything, just stood there with the knife in her hand. Her heartbeat was thundering so hard she was surprised he couldn't hear it, but damned if she'd let him guess for even a second how scared she was. Darby wasn't particularly tall, but he was thickly muscled, and if he got his hands on her she didn't know that she'd be able to fight free. Maybe if he thought he'd suffer some damage, he'd back down. Maybe.

Instead his eyes got meaner. He took a step toward her.

"Back off," Carlin said, standing her ground and managing to keep her tone level.

"Or what?" he sneered. "You'll use that knife on me? I don't think so." He took another step.

"Think again." Swiftly she grabbed another knife from the block and held both of them poised. He could grab one of her arms and twist it to make her drop the knife, but he'd need both hands to do so and in the meanwhile she'd do whatever she had to. Darby was no more a self-defense artist than she was a fighter; she was bound to inflict some damage on him, and from the flicker in his expression, he'd come to that realization, too.

He changed tactics, holding his hands up as if he were totally innocent, smiling at her. "Hey, you don't want to do something stupid. I'm just trying to be friendly. You don't have to get all bent out of shape. All I'm suggesting is that we have a little fun before I go. I can promise you a good ride, but without the eight-second clock on me, if you know what I mean."

"Not really," she said coldly, though of course, living in Texas, she at least knew that a bull ride lasted eight seconds—if the rider stayed on that long.

He took another step. "Don't play innocent. I figure you're giving the boss all he wants every night when the lights go out. I don't mind—and he won't mind what he don't know about."

"If you take another step, I'll make damn sure he knows about it." She could feel herself start shaking and she tried to hide it. The last thing she wanted him to know was how scared she was, because that would make him bolder. Chills were running up and down her spine, dread solidifying in her stomach.

"Don't be like that, sugar. You've got a pretty mouth, you know that? We don't have to fuck. Maybe you can just go down on me. You look like you could suck the chrome off a bumper—"

The door behind him was jerked open and Darby halted, half-turning to face the newcomer. Zeke filled the doorway. Carlin felt her knees wobble and she made a rough sound in her throat at the sight of him.

Zeke glanced at Darby, then at Carlin. His gaze dropped to the two knives she held, traveled back up to her white face, then zeroed in on Darby again. There was no mistaking the import of the scene, the tension, or the reason she was standing on guard with two knives. She'd never seen him look like that, gone pale under his tan, his eyes like green ice.

"Boss, I—" Darby began, then Zeke took one long stride forward and hit him, a powerful uppercut to the chin that sent Darby crashing back into one of the recliners. It tipped over on its back, taking a table and lamp with it. The lamp broke, sending shards of ceramic flying. Zeke was on the man like a panther on its prey, grabbing him by his belt and literally tossing him toward the door. Darby managed to yelp, "Wait! Nothing—" before Zeke was on him again, this time throwing him completely out the door.

Carlin didn't move. She couldn't, not right now. She was breathing hard, and feeling as if she might faint. Tears stung her eyes; she blinked them back. Still holding tightly to the knives, she glanced out the kitchen window in time to see Zeke hold Darby up by his shirt with one hand while he pounded his other big fist into Darby's face, over and over. Blood and snot were flying.

Two men came rushing into the bunkhouse. She blinked

at them, recognized Walt and Spencer. They both skidded to a halt, staring at the knives. Carlin looked down at her hands. One of the knives was a big chef's knife; the other was a serrated bread knife. Like Zeke, they realized immediately why she was holding them.

Very carefully, she turned and slid the knives back into the appropriate slots in the wood block.

"Are you all right, Miss Carly?" Walt asked in a rumbly, cautious tone.

She took a deep breath, tried to master her voice so it would be louder than a squeak. "Yes. He didn't do anything. He was trash-talking, working himself up, but—not yet." She sounded thin, even to herself, but at least she wasn't crying.

"That's good."

She glanced out the window again. Darby had rallied and as she watched he got in a couple of punches, himself. Wincing, she turned her head. She had a vague feeling that she should do something to stop the fight—wasn't that what women always did?—but she didn't feel capable of the effort. Besides, some primitive part of her enjoyed watching Darby get pounded. She didn't like Zeke getting hit, though.

"Should . . . should we stop Zeke?" she asked.

Spencer glanced out the door, pursed his lips as he considered the scene. The sounds of fists and cursing and scuffling came through loud and clear. "Not just yet. Let the boss get in a few more licks."

Carlin pulled out a chair and sat down. Her knees were definitely wobbly, and this situation looked as if it could take a while.

She was wrong; she heard a flurry of punches, then someone—Micah, she thought—said, "That's enough, boss. He needs to be in good enough condition to drive."

She listened to a few seconds of heavy breathing, then

Zeke growled, "Good point. Get up, asshole. Get your shit packed and get out of here, and don't bother coming back in the spring."

"Like I want to work at this shit-hole end of nowhere," Darby snarled back, his voice thick. There was the sound of spitting. "I'm gonna file charges against you for assault."

"Assault, my ass," someone else said contemptuously. Eli. "I saw you trip and fall out of your own damn truck."

"Yeah. And I remember you bragging to all of us how you might stage an accident and sue the boss." That was Bo.

"You lying sons of bitches!"

"I didn't hear them say a single lie," Spencer put in from the door, his innocent face as virtuous as a nun's.

"I'll help you pack." That was Kenneth. "You just stand out here and I'll throw your shit out the door. You can pick it up. I bet you can be on the road in ten minutes."

Carlin thought she might cry. In true western fashion, these men had come to her rescue. Zeke had gotten into a fight because of her—no, not because of *her*, but because Darby was an asshole jerk. Regardless, he'd gotten into a fight on her behalf. She wanted to kiss him. She wanted to kiss all of them. And she'd try her damnedest not to cry, because that would only make the men uncomfortable.

"I wasn't going to do nothing she didn't want," Darby said sullenly, and outrage brought her surging to her feet, wobbly knees forgotten.

Walt shot her an alarmed look and wedged himself in the door, effectively blocking it. "Yeah," he said contemptuously to Darby. "That's why she had two knives in her hands, right?"

She could hear angry muttering from the other men, and something defensive from Darby, but with all the muttering she couldn't make out exactly what he was saying, which was probably for the best.

Abruptly she was very tired, and wanted nothing more than to get back to the house. She'd just as soon not ever have to see Darby again, but she wasn't going to run out the back door as if she had done something to be ashamed of. "It's okay," she said to Walt's back. "He's a jerk, but I'm okay, and I just want to go to the house and get dinner started."

Walt glanced over his shoulder, critically eyed her as if judging her state for himself, and gave a brief nod of approval. "All right, then," he said, stepping aside.

Carlin gathered her cleaning supplies and went out the door, looking each man in the eye and saying a quiet "Thank you." Two of the men stood with Zeke behind them, presumably because they weren't yet certain he wouldn't light into Darby again. She got a good look at his face, though; the damage didn't look too bad, one cheek was reddened and might swell, but that was about it. Darby hadn't come off nearly as well, but so what. She didn't give a damn what kind of shape he was in, which might say something about her as a person, but right at the moment she didn't give a damn about that, either.

Then she stopped and looked at Zeke again, eyeing him critically. What was nothing but a red place now could become an awful bruise if it wasn't iced immediately.

"You need to come to the house, too," she said briskly. "Put some ice on your face."

"His hands will need it more." Spencer fell into step beside her, taking the bucket of cleaning supplies in his good hand.

That made sense. Zeke hadn't moved, so she stopped, gave him a death stare, and lifted her eyebrows. She didn't want to say anything else in front of the men; while she got an evil enjoyment out of being a smart-ass to him when no one else could hear, in front of the men she at least acted the way a normal employee would.

"Spencer's right," Walt said. "If you don't ice your hands, they'll be too sore tomorrow for you to get any work done."

That commonsense argument worked when general bullheadedness might have kept Zeke there until Darby had packed up and left. He wasn't as pale as he had been but his jaw still looked like granite, his lips a thin grim line, and she sensed it wouldn't take much to reignite him. Icing him down was a good thing, in more ways than one.

"Come on," she said, and he followed her and Spencer to the house.

CARLIN COULDN'T SLEEP. The wind was howling, bringing colder weather with it, but it was more than the wind keeping her awake. Dinner had been strange, with an underlying tension despite Darby's absence. Their group chemistry had been upset, and even though Darby hadn't been a particular friend to any of them, they'd generally accepted his complaining and gotten along with him. No one joked around, the way they normally did. On the other hand, no one seemed to particularly miss him, so Carlin decided everyone simply needed some time to settle down.

The knuckles of both Zeke's hands were scraped and bruised, though thanks to sessions of soaking them in bowls of ice water the swelling was minimal. He could flex both hands, and make fists, so no bones were broken. His left cheekbone had some puffiness to it, but again a judicious application of ice had done wonders.

The idea that Zeke had gotten into a fight for her— *that* was what was bothering her. After Brad, she simply hadn't been tempted by any kind of relationship, but Zeke was kind of the antidote for Brad. Brad threatened her; Zeke protected her. Under those same circumstances she thought he'd have stepped up for any woman, not just for her, and that in itself made her heart hurt because it spoke to the kind of man he was.

But it wasn't just that. There was fire between them, fire that was becoming more and more difficult for her to ignore. It would be so much easier if she didn't occasionally catch him looking at her in a way that revealed too much, with a hooded intensity that took her breath. When she caught some men mentally stripping her, she felt annoyed, as if they were encroaching on her privacy even if they never said anything. When she caught Zeke doing the X-ray vision thing, it made her breathless, warm, and restless in her own skin.

Since he'd startled her in his bedroom and she'd found herself lying beneath him, wanting what she couldn't have, feeling that he wanted the same thing, the temptation had grown sharper.

She should've left this place weeks ago.

She could leave now. Tonight.

But she wouldn't. She was caught in a balancing act: this was a safe haven from Brad, she was socking away money, and damned if she didn't like what she was doing. On the other side of the seesaw was the emotional cost of staying here, and that cost was growing larger with time. There had to be a tipping point, but she could only trust that she'd know when that time came, when she sensed the cost of staying outweighed the benefits. That was when she'd move on.

But right now, she had to deal with her sleeplessness. No matter what had happened today, in the morning she still had to get up at the same friggin' ungodly hour to start breakfast. She needed to relax, settle her mind.

She threw back the covers and stepped into the warm slippers that were sitting beside her bed, then grabbed the bathrobe that hung over the footboard and headed for the door with great purpose. There was one piece of apple pie left. That and a glass of milk would help her get to sleep. And if not, well, she'd be sleepless and happy instead of sleepless and fretful. Maybe it wasn't a win-win, but it definitely rated a win.

There was a nightlight in the hallway, another in the kitchen. The house was quiet except for the sound of the buffeting wind. Zeke was an early riser, which meant he went to bed early, too; he'd probably been asleep for a couple of hours. It was unlikely that he could hear her from his upstairs bedroom, but still, she made an effort to be quiet as she raided the fridge.

She sat at the small kitchen table with the last piece of apple pie, a fork, and a small glass of milk. The simple task of gathering the midnight snack hadn't stopped her mind from spinning, and it certainly hadn't done anything to settle the wind, but still . . . apple pie would make everything better.

She didn't hear him coming, didn't have a clue, but without warning he was there, looming in the doorway between the dining room and the kitchen, filling the space and charging the air with the electricity that seemed to be part of his aura. When he entered a room, he *owned* it, somehow.

He stopped in the doorway, surprise flitting across his face. Of course he was surprised; if he'd expected her to be in the kitchen, he probably wouldn't have come down in nothing except a pair of jeans, which told her he didn't sleep in pajamas—but then, she already knew that, because she did his laundry, and there had never been even a pair of sleep pants. Whether he slept naked or in his boxers, she didn't know, and damn, she sure wished her mind hadn't gone there, because, *damn,* he looked good. No shoes, no shirt. Long and lean and hard. He hadn't worked out in a gym for those muscles, he'd gotten them the old-fashioned way, with hard labor. The bare skin on his shoulders gleamed, his arms were sinewy and thick with ropes of muscles, his big hands rough with calluses, the knuckles raw from the fight that afternoon—

This time she didn't panic; panic was the furthest thing from her mind. She looked at him and had to swallow hard, because she knew what those muscles felt like, knew how his skin smelled, how warm, how heavy he was—oh, thank God for the pie, because it gave her an excuse for swallowing again. Her mouth was literally watering.

"Sorry," he said, and then he turned to go back the way he'd come.

"Wait." She knew she shouldn't have said it. Bad idea. The smartest thing would be for him to go back to bed. Maybe she could forget what he looked like, barefoot and shirtless. Maybe she could forget how he smelled. Yeah, and maybe she'd find a magic wand under her bed and she could wave it around and all her troubles would be gone.

But this was his house, after all, and she really shouldn't run him out of his own kitchen, even if she considered it her kitchen, for the duration.

He stopped, turned. The light from his new position didn't offer as tempting a view, since he was almost entirely in shadow, which was just as well, she supposed. She swallowed another excess of saliva. "What do you need?"

He gave a short, sharp exhale, not quite a snort. "I came down for that last piece of apple pie. You beat me to it, fair and square." She heard the soft humor in his voice. There was none of the bite she often heard when he gave her a hard time.

"It's a big piece. I'm happy to share." Before he could protest she got up and fetched an extra plate from the cabinet. She grabbed another fork, too, and a knife to cut the pie in half. "Milk?" she asked. He wasn't much of a milk drinker, but there was no decaf coffee made.

"I'll get it."

He poured a glass while she returned to the table, cut the piece of pie in half, and slid the bigger half to another place—one on the other side of the table. Zeke sat, flicked an assessing look between their two slices of pie, winked at her, and then dug in. Carlin found herself playing with her pie, taking a small bite, flaking the crust with a tine of her fork. Jesus God, he'd *winked* at her. No flirting! She couldn't allow flirting.

The wind picked up, a gust howling like a wolf as it swirled around the house. "The wind is something else," she said.

"Cold front," he replied.

"I figured as much."

"Supposed to be snow by the end of the week."

Oh good lord, she was sitting in the dimly lit kitchen at midnight with a half-naked man who made her forget that she should be on the move, who made her mouth water, who drove her crazy in more ways than she could count, and they were talking about the *weather*. How pitiful was that? And even more pitiful was that she was *grateful* they were just talking about the weather.

"I've never seen much snow." Unless flurries counted—and rare flurries, at that. She still couldn't believe that she, who loved sun and beaches, was about to willingly go through a Wyoming winter.

He made a sound that might've been a half laugh. "That's about to change." His gaze lifted, hard green lasers boring into her. "You're not going to run, are you?"

How had he guessed that every day she was more and

more torn? She wanted to be here, she did, so much that she was becoming more and more afraid to stay. She tried for a nonchalant tone. "I thought you didn't want me here. Spencer will be out of his sling in a few days, and he can always—"

"Just promise me you're not going to run."

Carlin picked at her pie, took a small bite, chased it with some milk. She could feel Zeke looking at her. She could feel him waiting. "No," she finally answered. "I won't promise. But I'll do my best to stay until spring." That was as close to a promise, and a warning, as she could get.

She finished her pie and milk, took her plate and fork and glass to the sink, rinsed them out, and left them for when she ran the dishwasher after breakfast. So much for a nice, relaxing piece of pie. So much for getting to sleep anytime soon. The man she worked for had worked his way under her skin, and she liked it. Damnation.

And then he was there, moving silently on bare feet, placing his dishes in the sink beside hers. He was so close she could feel his body heat, and she could swear every little hair on her body was standing at attention. It was like electricity was running through her veins, like her insides had turned to fire and ice. She waited for him to move away, but he didn't. He just stood there, close, warm, a temptation.

She turned her head and looked up. She wasn't sure why, but she was compelled. It was like the stupid girl going down into the dark basement in the slasher movies. He was right there, that bare chest was *right there*. She could lean forward just a few inches and put her mouth on him, taste him. . . . She squirmed, but didn't move away, not even when Zeke's head moved toward hers, his focus on her mouth, his intent so clear she had plenty of time to back away, to tell him to stop . . . but she didn't.

He kissed her. *Kiss* was much too simple a word for what happened, much too small a word for the powerful connection that rocked her to her core. She felt that kiss in her toes, in the top of her head, all through her body. She felt alive, really alive, for the first time in a long while. With his mouth on hers she wasn't thinking about running, the howling wind, the coming snow, or Brad or Jina or painful regrets. She didn't *think* at all. She just felt.

He slowly lifted his mouth from hers, licked his lips as if he was still tasting her. Maybe the rough sound he muttered was a curse word; she couldn't be sure. She did know the kiss had been wonderful—more than wonderful—but it had to stop here, or she *would* have to leave. Apparently he knew it, too. He didn't move back in, didn't put his arms around her. She wanted him to, but, God, number one bad idea on her long list of bad ideas.

"Let me help you."

She shook her head, knowing exactly what he meant. "No. I won't drag you into this."

"You're not dragging me anywhere. I want to help."

"Teach me how to punch. That'll help." She managed a twisted smile. "Then maybe I won't have to grab the kitchen knives."

"And shoot," he added.

"Maybe."

He put his hand under her chin, nudged it upward. His thumb swept over the edge of her jaw. "Do you know, you never use my name?" he murmured.

"Sorry, Mr. Decker." He was right: she didn't. She couldn't say why, unless it was some instinctive—and obviously useless—attempt to keep him at a distance. She tried to keep her voice calm but it was a struggle she lost.

"Really?" His mouth curved in amusement. "Mr. Decker?"

"Just Decker, then. Or boss."

"No," he said, his voice low. "Say it, just once." His thumb rubbed her chin. "Come on, Carlin, how hard can it be?"

She should show him that it was just a name, no different from any of the others. But it was different, because it was his. Her heart pounded.

"Good night, Zeke," she said, her voice a whisper.

He smiled. "Good night, Carlin."

Chapter Seventeen

THE WEATHER HAD definitely turned. Zeke walked from the hardware store to Kat's to find the usual crowd not such a crowd. He told his cousin he'd pick up the pies Carlin had ordered on his way out of town, then left again; he still had a few errands to run. He could've asked for Kat's help with those errands, but he didn't want to do that. She'd probably make too much out of something that was just common sense, plus she couldn't exactly leave the café whenever she wanted.

Carlin and Spencer had taken care of the grocery shopping a couple of days earlier. He hadn't even asked her if she wanted to make the trip to town today with him. After that kiss, he knew spending that much time so close to her would be a bad idea; he didn't want to push too hard. It was smarter to let her settle down, work the situation over in her mind the way women did, and decide he'd just been comforting her some because of Darby. He mentally snorted. Yeah, right. Like men ever kissed women that way to comfort them. Besides, she'd probably try to stop him from doing what he knew had to be done.

He went into Tillman's, kind of annoyed with Carlin for making this errand necessary, but at the same time understanding why she held so tightly to her money. He was determined to get this done. Carlin was going to stay through the winter, and she would damn well be prepared before the first snow moved in, which could be any minute, considering how the clouds looked.

He knew Alice Tillman well, had gone to school with her boys. They'd long since moved on, leaving Battle Ridge as so many others had in the past few years. He nodded a greeting to Mrs. Tillman as he headed toward a rack of heavy coats, and she asked him how things were going. He responded with a generic "fine." If she was confused by the fact that he was headed toward the women's section of the small store, she didn't say so.

No way was he going to browse. He picked up a heavy coat that caught his eye, held it at arm's length and checked it out for size. Deciding it would do, he moved on to the selection of boots. Size seven, she'd said. He already knew what he wanted. He didn't care how pretty the boots were, didn't care if they were in style or not. What she needed was something waterproof, with good insulation and a thick sole, something that would keep her feet dry and warm when the snow reached her knees. He lifted one sample and held it in the air. "You got this in a seven?"

"Hardly looks like your style or your size," Mrs. Tillman said with more than a hint of humor.

"I think they'll work," he called after her as she headed into the back room, going along with the joke. While she was gone, he looked over the sale table where Carlin had probably found her ugly-ass green boots. A few boxes, some of them dented or missing lids, sat on that table looking sad and unwanted. It pissed him off that this was where Carlin felt compelled to shop, that she was so terrified of not having enough money to make her next escape that she automatically looked for bargains.

Mrs. Tillman placed a large, sturdy shoe box on the

front counter. "I don't suppose you'll be trying these on," she teased.

"No, ma'am." As he walked toward the counter, she looked at the coat he carried. Her smile faded, just a little. He preempted her with a rueful smile. "The coat's not for me, either."

She looked momentarily conflicted, and then she said, "I'm never one to turn away a sale, especially such a good one, but I want to make sure before I ring it up. Did you check out the price on that coat?"

"No, should I?"

"You should."

He found the tag, lifted it, and came to a stop in the middle of the aisle. "Holy—" He stopped himself in mid-exclamation. "Are the pockets lined with gold?" He had a shearling coat himself so he hadn't expected it to be cheap, but he hadn't expected a thousand-dollar price tag, either.

Mrs. Tillman explained. "It's the best garment in the store, *very* good quality, but I have to make sure you're aware of the price before I ring it up. I stock a few of these every year, in case some rich hunters come through and need a heavy coat. You'd be surprised how seldom I have to carry them over to another season."

He could afford the coat; Carlin needed something good and heavy. But, damn, he was pretty sure his first truck hadn't cost this much.

"This wouldn't by chance be for your new cook, would it? Carly, isn't that her name?" Mrs. Tillman asked as she read the expression on his face and walked past him, snagging the coat from his hand as she went by.

He mentally shrugged. Small towns. If he'd been worried about keeping this a secret, then he'd have gone to Cheyenne. "It is, on both counts."

"When she was in here a while back she looked at this

very coat. I'm sure she'd love it, but I have other coats that will be a lot more practical."

"You saw her. Did I get the right size?"

"I'd say so. I think she's about the size of my daughter-in-law." Mrs. Tillman returned the shearling coat to the rack and grabbed a dark blue parka, fluffy and thick, but about a quarter the weight of the shearling. "This will keep her warm, and it's a lot easier to take care of."

They returned to the counter, where the parka and the shoe box sat side by side. He looked at his choices so far, and sighed. They weren't enough. Carlin wasn't accustomed to Wyoming winters, and that meant she'd need hats, gloves, scarves, long underwear.

Mrs. Tillman was delighted to help him gather what was needed. He chose good-quality stuff without going for the most expensive. Soon he had all he was going to purchase piled on the front counter.

He had to draw the line somewhere. Carlin was by God going to have to buy her own underwear, long or otherwise.

SHE STARED AT the merchandise Zeke had presented to her with no fanfare at all. He'd practically shoved the bags into her arms, and then he'd left the house. A cow needed him, or something, although how he could have known that when he had just returned from town, she didn't know; some kind of psychic cow-call? It wasn't until she'd laid the things he'd bought across her bed that she realized how much all of this stuff must've cost.

She was both embarrassed and disconcerted. She hated that he'd spent all this money on her when she had the cash to buy these things for herself, but she'd made the conscious decision to do without, or make do with what she could scrounge up around the house, because she was saving every dime she could, just in case.

She was beginning to hate those words. "Just in case" had come to define her life, and it sucked.

As for "disconcerted," what was she supposed to think? It wasn't as if he'd bought her some lingerie. This was practical, unornamental, much-needed winter outdoors stuff.

When he came back in, a couple of hours after delivering pie and Wyoming-appropriate winter outerwear, she was waiting for him. She wouldn't have chosen that precise time, because she was all but covered in flour. Agitated, needing something to occupy her, she'd decided to try to make biscuits tonight—real, homemade biscuits, not the frozen or canned kind, not from a mix. Real biscuits. It was messy work. And, from her previous experience, potentially dangerous.

"What on earth were you thinking?" she asked as he came in from the mudroom.

He raised his eyebrows, acting as if he had no idea what she was talking about, but she knew he wasn't that dense. She pointed a finger at him, a finger that was coated with shortening and flour.

"That coat is much too expensive, and the boots . . . I don't even want to know how much those boots set you back."

"You needed them; I bought them. No big deal," he said flatly. He eyed the kitchen, and her floured self. "Somebody booby-trapped the flour and it exploded on you, huh?"

"Don't try to distract me." Maybe it wasn't a big deal to him, but it was to her. She didn't want to owe anyone, she wanted to stay unfettered. She was caught, though, because returning the merchandise might insult him, might hurt him—Zeke Decker, with hurt feelings?—and he was the man who had punched Darby out in her behalf. "Fine. I'll pay you back," she said, chin up in a defiant pose.

"Like hell you will," he growled.

She had to. Accepting such a gift would tie her to him, to this place, and damn it she was tied down enough as it was. "It's too much. I can't accept . . ."

"If it makes you feel better, call it a Christmas present," he barked.

"Christmas is two months away!"

"Damn it, can't you just say *thank you* like a normal woman? I don't want you to fall walking to the garage because the soles of those cheap boots are too slick. I don't want you freezing to death walking from The Pie Hole to the library. Since when do safety concerns about an employee make me the bad guy?"

"There's no need to yell," she said in a calm voice that she knew would annoy him.

"I'm not yelling!"

"Actually, you are." She sighed. "The thought was very nice, but it's not like I'm going to freeze this winter. I was just going to borrow one of your old coats when I needed to, and there are a hundred pairs of gloves and twice as many hats in this house. The boots I bought will do. I'll just be extra careful when it's slick outside. That coat . . . it's very nice, it really is, but it's too much."

"Fine," Zeke snapped. At least he was no longer yelling. "The boots and the coat come with the job. When you quit in the spring you can leave them here for the next cook, *if* that makes you feel better."

"It does, actually."

"Good." He headed toward the door, a bit of anger in his step and in his voice. "I'm going to get a shower before supper."

As he stepped into the dining room, on his way to the stairs near the front door, Carlin stopped him with a softly spoken, "Zeke?"

He stopped instantly when she spoke his name, turned slowly to face her. Her heart was racing again. What on earth had she gotten herself into? A coat and a pair of boots wouldn't hold her here, no matter how expensive they were, so she might as well face it. It wasn't the stuff. It was him. It was the deep down, undeniable sense that Zeke needed her that held her here. Not the kiss, not the physical attraction. Those things should send her running, not make her determined to stay. Zeke Decker, tough guy with a chip on his shoulder, needed her. For a while, at least.

"Thank you," she said.

"You're welcome." He turned and walked away, and while she was still within earshot he added, in a slightly raised voice. "Now really, was that so hard?"

Chapter Eighteen

CARLIN HAD SEEN snow before, kind of, but not like this. She'd seen flurries, a dusting, but mostly her experience with snow was of the television variety.

The snow began to fall, and it kept coming down. She'd looked out her bedroom window a time or two, during the night, entranced by the sight and how it made everything take on a soft glow. It came down hard, and then soft, silent and beautiful. By morning, there was at least a foot of the white stuff, probably more. As far as she could see, out that same window, was an untouched white blanket that covered everything.

She threw together a breakfast casserole and popped it into the oven. One-dish meals had become her best friend since she'd started working here. She rarely turned to them for breakfast, but this morning was different. Feeling a little bit like a child—and not minding at all— she wanted to be the first to put her mark in the snow. She wanted to see that white blanket stretching before her, unmarked and unbroken.

Instead of pulling on the new coat Zeke had bought for her, she snagged a heavy coat off the rack—one she'd never seen him wear so surely he wouldn't complain if she put it to use—and pulled it on. It was much too big, but with the sleeves folded back it would do. The new boots he'd bought her were perfect; she needed waterproof, at the moment. She also pulled on the knit hat and gloves he'd bought, bundling herself up good.

The cold wind hit her in the face the minute she stepped out on the front porch. It was crisp and clean and made her shudder, but she ignored it and kept going, stepping down the stairs, carefully, since she didn't know if the steps under that snow would be slick with ice or not. One step, then another, feeling as if she were an infant just learning how to walk. She pulled the hood of the borrowed coat up to protect her cheeks as she finally reached ground level, and measured the depth of the snow. Yes, at least a foot. Every step was an effort; she had to pick her feet straight up with every step, like someone in a marching band. The wind stilled, and abruptly the temperature was much more comfortable.

For a long minute she stood there, scanning the horizon, wondering if she had ever seen anything so beautiful in her entire life. She'd always loved the beach, and there had been a time when she'd been certain nothing could be as breathtaking as the ocean stretching endlessly before her. But now . . . this beauty was different, but just as awe inspiring.

If she didn't have to be so careful, if she didn't need to stay on the move . . . this place could be home. It had been such a long time since she'd thought of anyplace as anything more than a temporary stop along the way. Even before Brad, she'd simply been moving from one job to the next, waiting for her life to restart, waiting for a place, anyplace, to feel like home.

She was so damned tired of waiting. Battle Ridge— this ranch—they were different. And she was different here.

Like it or not, Zeke was a big part of the unexpected feeling of home.

Bad idea. Come spring she'd be on the move again. She had to keep that foremost in her mind. Until she could think of something to do about Brad, or he overplayed his hand in some other way and got caught, everything in her life was transitional. This was a temporary stop, a detour along the way. It wasn't home. Acknowledging that made her heart ache and she stared at the beauty before her to imprint it in her mind, so she wouldn't forget it. Yes, it was terribly cold, but that was a small price to pay for . . . this.

She walked toward the nearest pasture, watching the way her feet made deep tracks in the snow. Giddy was too strong a word, and she'd never let anyone see that something as simple as a good snow could make her feel this way, but right now, at this moment, she was . . . happy. Content. When she was halfway between the house and the fence line, she dropped down and grabbed a handful of snow. It was powdery, light, and as a cloud moved by and the early-morning sun shone down, it seemed to sparkle.

With the sun on the snow, the world was so bright and clean she had to squint. The next time she came out, she'd wear her sunglasses. She shook the snow out of her hand, watched it fall as she'd watched it fall during the night.

Everything was so quiet she heard the door open and close, even though it was obvious Zeke was trying to be quiet. She turned to face the house, and him. Like her, he was bundled up against the cold.

He strode straight for her—maybe *stomping* was a better word—and he wasn't smiling.

"Why aren't you wearing your new coat?"

So much for contentment. "I didn't want to get it dirty."

He sighed at that. "Coats are supposed to be worn. They're supposed to get dirty!"

"When they cost as much as that one did, they should be framed and hung on the wall for display!"

"Your new coat is . . ."

"You mean the cook's coat. It's not actually mine."

His jaw clenched, and then he said, "Fine, the damned *cook's* coat would be much warmer than that one."

"I'm fine," she responded. "Perfectly warm, in fact. I'd like to point out that I'm wearing one of *your* old coats. Why did you buy it if it isn't warm enough? *Huh?*" Satisfied that she'd won that exchange, she didn't want to look at him anymore. The man made her antsy in so many ways. He stirred her temper and she always ended up getting defensive. He knew exactly how to push her buttons—every single one of them—and he turned her on. She didn't need any of that, not on this peaceful morning, so she turned to face the mountains again. "It's beautiful, isn't it?"

"Yes." The anger was gone from Zeke's voice, in that one simple word. Did he still see it the way she did, even though he'd lived with it all his life? He walked past her, continued on toward the barn. His footsteps crunched softly in the snow, and he left marks as she had, only his footsteps were much farther apart. "This is beautiful, but don't let it fool you. Just wait until we have a big snow."

For a moment, Carlin watched him walk away, which had never been an onerous sight. Man, there was a lot to be said for cowboy butt. Then she called after him. "What do you mean *big*. This isn't big? There's at least a foot of snow!"

Zeke laughed. "Rookie."

"Tell the guys, breakfast in thirty minutes," she called.

He waved his hand to indicate he'd heard. She sighed and turned her back on him and the snow-covered pastures and mountains. "I'm nothing but a kitchen slave," she muttered, then grinned to herself as she headed back to the house.

BRAD STOOD AT attention at the new police chief's desk. Inside he seethed, but he didn't let his anger show. There was no upside to jumping over the desk and throttling his new boss.

It had been easier when the police chief of this small municipality just outside Houston had been old, lazy, and trusting. Brad had been able to talk his way out of almost anything. But the new chief was a stickler for the rules, and he didn't trust anyone.

"Officer Henderson, this is the second complaint against you I've seen in less than three months. Both cite excessive violence. Would you care to explain?"

The scumbags pissed me off. Who cares about a drugged-up thief or a skanky hooker? They had it coming. All true, but he couldn't say that and expect to keep his job. He also couldn't explain that his frustration at not being able to find Carlin had his temper simmering barely beneath the surface. He lost his temper too easily these days. If every criminal he'd given a beat down to in the past three months came forward, there would be no talking his way out of this.

"In both cases, I believed myself to be in imminent danger."

It sounded good, even if it wasn't true. The chief had a skeptical look on his face—he wasn't buying it at all. "I don't have any choice. You're on administrative leave, effective immediately, while we conduct a full investigation."

Brad didn't move, but his mind was several steps ahead. A full investigation would pull up Carlin's complaint from the previous year, as well as the Dallas police in-

quiry into a murder for which he had an alibi. An alibi
that would fall apart if anyone who knew what they were
doing got into his personal computer and found the pro-
gram that made it look as if he'd been chatting when in
fact he'd been in Dallas, killing the wrong woman. Damn
red raincoat.

The old chief had bought his explanation that Carlin
was a nutcase, that *she'd* been the one obsessed with *him*.
This one wasn't going to buy anything.

He nodded his head. "I'll cooperate in every way possible," he said stiffly, because to say anything else would
make him sound guilty. He turned in his service weapon—
not that that made any difference, because he had other
weapons, and even if he didn't, he could always buy one
on the street—and left the building, his steps long but
casual. To hurry would look bad. He couldn't run. He
pushed through the outer door and headed for his car.
The weather was a bit chilly today, smelling of fall, of a
winter that hadn't yet arrived, not that south Texas ever
had that much of a winter. Sometimes it got pretty cold,
but that was about it.

For a moment he thought about turning, going back
inside, and shooting the new chief just for chuckles, but
there were too many people around, too many cameras.
He wasn't sure when or how the investigation would
begin. He had time, he thought, but maybe not. Something was making him feel as if he didn't have any time
at all.

He'd run by the house, grab his computer and some
cash, and hit the road. He'd stop by the bank on his way
out of town and clean out his account there. He had to
get on the move before the chief put two and two together. Carlin was one matter, and he might be able to
explain that away. But Dallas . . . if the police there got
another heads-up they might look harder at him, maybe

hard enough that they pulled in a forensic computer guy . . . he had to make sure they never got their hands on his hard drive. He would dump it, but God damn it he'd put a lot of time and effort into that setup, and he didn't want to destroy it.

Brad sped toward home, his mind spinning, feeling oddly off-balance. He'd loved his job, and he figured he might as well kiss it good-bye. Even if the chief didn't dig deep enough this time around, he'd be at the top of the list to be shit-canned at the least little complaint or infraction. He knew how it worked. Once you got the label of troublemaker, they got rid of you.

This was all Carlin's fault. No police force in the country would hire him after this. If he wasn't very careful, he'd end up in jail for murdering the wrong damn woman. For a few minutes he was close to panic, his breath shallow, his heart beating too fast. He'd always been the hunter, not the hunted. He didn't like being on the wrong side of that equation.

But soon his heartbeat slowed and he breathed deep. As bad as things were, there was an upside to this new development.

He could now devote twenty-four hours a day to finding Carlin. Tracking her down was no longer a hobby . . . it had just become his life.

ZEKE HATED TO admit it, but Libby had been right. Her comment about him finding a wife, as she'd left, had been a line she'd thrown at him to put him on the defensive, and she probably hadn't thought twice about it again after making her escape.

But now and then, he remembered those words. He could hear them, the tone of her voice, the pitch. He even experienced that feeling of sheer frustration again.

He worked hard; he loved the land. If he wasn't ever going to marry and have a family, then why keep at it? So he could grow old alone, until he couldn't keep up with the work anymore and he'd have to sell off and move to an assisted-living facility somewhere? His sisters weren't interested in the ranch. They'd run far and fast and married professional men who wouldn't know one end of a horse from the other. They weren't coming back for anything more than a quick visit. His mom was the same. She'd been a good rancher's wife because she'd loved the rancher, not because she loved the place.

If the Rocking D was going to survive and thrive, he needed kids who could work beside him and love the land the way he did. Sure, maybe none of them would like ranch life, but he'd bet at least one would, son or daughter, didn't matter. He needed a wife.

Not someone like Rachel, who'd been pretty but spoiled and worthless everywhere except in the bedroom. He'd let his dick choose his first wife. Next time around, he intended to let his brain have a say.

His dick was pointing toward Carlin Hunt, even though his brain knew she wasn't going to stay. He couldn't be certain she'd be here from one morning to the next, even though she'd said she'd "do her best" to stay until spring. So why did Libby's words come back to haunt him whenever Carlin was around?

She walked into the kitchen from the mudroom, shaking off the cold. When she saw him standing by the coffeepot, she didn't hesitate the way she had in the beginning. Instead, she smiled and tilted her head toward the outdoors. "It's not so pretty anymore," she said. "Just a few hours, and it's turned from pretty white into gray mush." She wrinkled her nose and headed for him. More accurately, she headed for the coffeepot. He stepped out of the way as she reached for a mug.

"Chili for supper," she said without looking at him. "Chili and corn bread. That sounds like a perfect cold weather meal to me."

"This isn't really cold, you know."

"What?" She turned, leaned against the counter, and took a sip of her coffee. "It's freezing out there!"

"Wait until it gets twenty or thirty degrees below zero."

"You're just trying to scare me," she said, a twinkle in her eye. "I know it gets cold here, but *below* zero?"

"Damn right."

She gave this news some thought, then said, "Well, I'll just stay inside when it gets that cold. I'll cook and do laundry and sit by the fire and watch television."

"Who's supposed to do the shopping while you're warming yourself by the fire?"

"Spencer, or Walt, or—hey, here's a thought—*you!*" She was teasing him, trying to get a rise out of him. These days, that wasn't hard to do. She took another sip. "I'm pretty sure going outdoors when it's below zero isn't in my job description."

Sleeping with the boss wasn't in her job description, either, but if she stayed here until spring . . .

He had time to find a wife. Later, much later, when Carlin was just a memory.

"Maybe I should make biscuits instead of corn bread. I need the practice."

"Corn bread, please," Zeke said. "I could've pounded nails with that last batch of biscuits."

The sound she made was a sigh and a grunt rolled into one. "Well, I won't get any better if I don't keep trying. Remember the white cake."

It sounded like a battle cry, Carlin's own *Remember the Alamo.* "I'll make you a deal. You make it corn bread and save the concrete—I mean biscuits—for another day, and I'll give you your first self-defense lesson."

"Does that mean I get to hit you?"

Zeke smiled. "You can try."

Carlin had serious problems and wouldn't let him help, at least not in the way he wanted. He wanted a lot of things he wasn't going to get. But he could, by God, teach her how to protect herself.

Chapter Nineteen

ZEKE OPENED THE door into the mudroom and yelled, "Carly!"

She was in the kitchen emptying the dishwasher; if he'd stepped inside, he'd have seen her. "I'm right here," she called back. Someone must be within hearing distance, otherwise he'd have called her Carlin. He never messed up; when they were alone he said Carlin, when anyone else was around he invariably said Carly. Considering how her own mouth was sometimes two steps ahead of her brain, she had to be impressed by his precise control.

"Stop what you're doing and come out behind the barn. I've set up a target for you to do some shooting." The door shut, telling her he wasn't waiting for her.

Shooting! Real shooting? Her pulse rate shot up, and not just for one reason. She'd thought a lot about taking shooting lessons since Zeke had first mentioned it, and still couldn't make a firm decision about whether or not she wanted to go that far. Arming herself seemed like such a drastic step. On the other hand, Brad was definitely armed, and if by some nightmare she found herself face-to-face with him she never, ever wanted to be empty-handed and defenseless.

There was her answer right there, reluctantly arrived at or not.

Add in the fact that it seemed Zeke himself was going to teach her, no wonder her pulse rate was skyrocketing. Part of her, the masochistic part, had hoped Zeke would be the one who gave her lessons, because when she thought about it, learning how to shoot was a lot like learning how to play golf, with the instructor's arms around the student, demonstrating and guiding. Or maybe not; maybe that was just a movie invention. Never mind reality; she'd still hoped—which meant she was an idiot, but an excited one.

She grabbed a jacket from the line of coat hooks and pulled it on. The jacket was brown, and smelled like horses and cows. The fumes made her sinuses burn. How could she not have noticed the smell before? Oh, right— because most of Zeke's dirty clothing, which was in a laundry basket right there, smelled the same. She made a mental note to toss the jacket in the washer when she got back to the house. Smelly or not, the jacket was welcome when she stepped outside, because the air was cold and crisp. She'd have liked to have on a pair of gloves and thought about going back for her own, but wasn't certain she'd be able to shoot with them on. They weren't the sleek leather gloves assassins always wore in the movies, but thick fleece ones meant to keep her hands warm, not prevent her from leaving fingerprints behind.

Carlin rounded the back corner of the barn and skidded to a halt, taken aback by the cluster of men waiting for her arrival.

Everyone turned to look at her. Yep, they were all here: Walt, Spencer, Eli, Patrick, Micah, Bo, Kenneth, plus Zeke himself. Good Lord, what was going on?

"What's up?" she asked uneasily, edging backward. This had to be a sign that learning how to shoot was a bad idea. Humiliating herself in front of a crowd had never been her favorite pastime.

Somehow when she had envisioned shooting lessons she'd thought of it as a semiprivate endeavor, not a social event, with every hand on the Rocking D gathered to watch her failures. Had her cooking somehow gravely offended them? Was this payback for the initial Never Fail White Cake failure? She'd have expected retribution if she'd made them actually *eat* it—on the other hand, if she'd made them eat it, they would all still be sitting around the table gnawing on the culinary mystery. And hadn't she made up for it by cooking approximately two tons of potatoes for them?

"They all want to help," Zeke said. An unholy light in his eyes said he was enjoying her discomfiture. That unholy light might actually be a smile, which made her stomach turn flips. He indicated a rough worktable set up behind the barn, on which a variety of weapons were lined up.

"We thought you might want to learn about more than one kind of gun," Walt said. He held up a shotgun. "But this double-barrel right here will take care of any kind of human trouble you might run into, and most of the animal kind."

Carlin cleared her throat. She'd seen shotguns in movies, and knew the shotgun was a shotgun because it had two barrels; as far as she'd ever heard rifles had just one barrel. Shotguns kicked, didn't they? "Oh, I get it. All of you want to see me shoot that thing and get knocked on my butt, right?"

Spencer looked shocked. "We'd never do that to you, Miss Carly!" Then he hesitated, shot a look at the others. "Well, maybe." That was Spencer, honest to a fault, and completely unable to keep his mouth shut.

"No, ma'am, I wouldn't try to give you a weapon you couldn't handle," Walt said firmly. "She has a little kick to her, but not bad. My ten-year-old grandson can handle it just fine."

"I like a thirty aught-six, myself," Eli put in, lifting a rifle outfitted with a scope.

"She isn't going deer or elk hunting," Kenneth groused. He lifted a pistol, one that looked as if Wyatt Earp would have been proud to haul it around. "She needs something that's easy to carry, and easy to handle."

That was easy to carry and handle? Good lord, it was a foot long! The mental picture of herself was so ridiculous she burst out laughing as she pointed at the pistol. "If I wore that in a holster, it would reach all the way to my knee! And it sure wouldn't go in my purse."

"Get a bigger purse," Kenneth advised, which, when she thought about it, was, from a man's point of view, a completely logical solution—but then, men didn't carry purses. Neither did she, anymore. If it didn't go in the pockets of her TEC jacket, or her jeans pockets, then she didn't carry it, which brought up another issue.

"Wouldn't I have to get a permit to carry a pistol?" Anything that required a background check was off the table.

"Not in Wyoming," Zeke said. "Concealed carry is legal."

Holy cow. That changed everything. She eyed the pistol with renewed interest. On the other hand, if she could shoot the shotgun without getting knocked on her keister, how cool was that? When it came to the fear factor, a shotgun beat a measly little pistol hands down—and hitting a target with a shotgun was way easier than hitting one with a pistol.

"We'll let her try everything," Zeke said, moving to the table and picking up a set of ear protectors. "That way she can tell which one suits her best."

Evidently the men had all contributed their own favored weapons for her initial lesson. The gesture gave her a lump in her throat. Despite her sometimes less-than-stellar cooking efforts, they were showing her they cared about her well-being. Tears welled in her eyes, and she got sniffly. "This is so sweet of all of you," she choked out, and gave them all a beaming if somewhat watery smile.

There was some scuffling of boots all around, and a chorus of incoherent muttering that she took to mean something along the lines of "aw, it isn't anything much." She'd seldom been so touched. A few months ago when she'd arrived in Battle Ridge she'd felt completely alone in the world, prevented by fear from so much as calling anyone in her family. She'd been on the run, seeking a safe burrow to hide in, but always feeling as if any moment might be her last. Since the day she'd walked into The Pie Hole, she'd found friends, she'd found safety, she'd found people who cared. And she'd found Zeke—maddening, sexy, stubborn, capable, sexy . . . oh, wait, she'd already said that. And she shouldn't think along these lines, shouldn't let herself even dream that maybe someday she might be able to think of something she could do about Brad, that when she didn't have a target on her back she could come back to Battle Ridge and, if Zeke was still single—

Stop it, she sternly ordered her imagination, or her libido, or both. She couldn't plan her life around *maybes*. She had to deal with reality. And for some reason, she had to keep telling herself that.

Zeke handed her the ear protectors. She started to put them on, then stopped. There was just the one set. "What about everyone else?"

"Everyone else can stick their fingers in their ears," he replied, then took a cotton ball out of his pocket, pulled it in two, and stuffed a half into each of his ears. "We're the only two who won't be able to do that."

She looked at the men. "Don't all of you have ear protectors?"

"Fancy ones," Walt said, grinning. "The kind that kill the sound of gunfire but let you hear a deer tippy-toeing through the leaves. But why get 'em out when we can just stick our fingers in our ears, like the boss said?"

That made her feel better; she didn't want to deafen anyone, and maybe sticking their fingers in their ears was more manly than wearing the ear protector headsets. It dawned on her that the set she was holding probably belonged to Zeke.

"Go ahead and put them on," he instructed. "You'll be able to hear everything I say just fine."

She put on the headset, adjusted it so it fit better. Contrary to what he'd said, the protectors worked so well she was now effectively deaf. Then he lightly cupped her chin to hold her head still, did something to one of the ear cups, and she jumped as sound exploded in her ear. She could hear every shuffle of a boot, every word they were saying, even their *breathing,* for God's sake. No—that was Zeke's breathing, strong and steady, right beside her.

"Wow," she said, her eyes wide at all the amplified noise. "Magic earmuffs."

"Too loud?" he asked in what was probably a very low tone, and she nodded emphatically. He touched the ear cup again and the noise subsided. There was evidently a switch and volume control on the headset, and thank heaven for that. This must be the fancy kind Walt had been talking about.

Zeke touched her elbow, turned her toward the worktable. "First, we're going to show you how each weapon works."

As far as fun times went, this wasn't. Each man had to demonstrate how to load and unload his favorite weapon, then instruct her while she did it. She'd had more fun blow-drying her hair. But she kept at it, until she didn't feel as if she was all thumbs fumbling with the shells and cartridges, and working the mechanisms on the variety of rifles. There were two pistols, a revolver and an automatic; until they showed her the difference between them, she'd never thought much about it. To her, a pistol was a pistol. She'd been wrong.

The shotgun was surprisingly easy to load and handle. She'd expected it to be exceptionally heavy, but it didn't weigh much more than one of the big deer rifles with the scopes. And . . . wow. She was in awe of the weapon. It might be an ordinary shotgun and the men had been around shotguns all their lives so it wasn't anything special to them, but to someone who had never before today held any kind of firearm in her hands, this was heady stuff.

Her stomach felt jittery; she wasn't just in awe, she was a little afraid, too. Because she was afraid, she said, "I want to shoot this first," before she had time to chicken out entirely. If the shotgun *did* knock her on her keister, she'd survive; everyone would have a laugh, she'd get up and dust off her butt, and move on to the next weapon. But, boy, she hoped she could handle that baby because a shotgun would make any bad guy sit up and take notice.

No one tried to talk her out of shooting the shotgun, to her relief, because she was afraid one word of discouragement would be all she needed to change her mind. The target, a huge piece of cardboard with a big bull's-eye drawn on it, was already set up and attached to a stack of hay bales. Zeke stepped behind her and the scene in her imagination came to life. His big body cradled hers from behind, his arms surrounded her as he showed her how to fit the stock of the shotgun to her shoulder. The long muscled length of him pressed against her back, his heat burning through their clothes, making her forget about what she was doing and why—

Then he sniffed, and sniffed again. "What's that smell?"

She thudded back to earth. "It's your jacket," she replied. "It stinks."

"No argument there."

"Hey, I'm not the one who wallowed in cow manure."

He helped her steady the weapon, showed her how to aim it . . . and then he dropped his arms from around her and stepped back.

Shocked, feeling both abruptly vulnerable and disappointed because his arms weren't around her any longer, Carlin hesitated and bit her lip. Okay. She could do this. If she ever needed to shoot a shotgun in a real-life situation, Zeke wouldn't be standing there with his arms around her.

Lifting the stock to her shoulder, she settled it the way Zeke had showed her, carefully held it as steady as she could while bringing the sights in alignment . . . and she pulled the trigger.

There was very little noise; the magic earmuffs muffled what had to be a deafening *boom*. The shotgun bucked in her hands, but not nearly as much as she'd expected. There was a kick against her shoulder, but, again, not what she'd thought it would be. Smoke and the acrid but somehow pleasant smell of gunpowder filled the air.

"I did it! I did it!" she shrieked, jumping up and down in joy.

Zeke reached out and hastily snagged the shotgun from her hand. He was grinning. "You kind of did it," he said.

"No, I *did* it! I pulled the trigger! And it didn't knock me on my butt!"

The men were laughing, but because of the noise suppression the sound was muffled, which was strange because Zeke's voice was loud and clear, which told her the men were really howling. She stopped her victory dance to glare at them. "What's so funny?" she demanded, eyes narrowing.

Zeke indicated the target.

Oh, right. The target. She turned and looked at the big square of cardboard.

It was untouched.

"I'm not sure how you missed the whole target with a load of buckshot," Zeke said. She could tell he was biting the inside of his cheek to keep from laughing. "I guess you were aiming at a bird."

"Details!" She waved away the question of accuracy. "I *shot* it! Don't you see? Everything after this is a cakewalk. I was afraid to shoot the shotgun, so I did it first. If I could shoot it, then I could shoot anything. And I did."

There was a brief, unreadable flicker in his expression, then he said, "Want to shoot it again? And maybe this time hit the target?"

"Yes," she said exuberantly. "I want to shoot *everything*. This is *fun*!"

They took her at her word, and she shot round after round at the target. The second time around with the shotgun, some of the buckshot actually hit the target, and she kept at it until the cardboard was shredded and was replaced with a new piece. Then they moved on to the variety of rifles. Strange. She was way more accurate with the rifles, but she didn't like them. They weren't as much fun, the scopes were kind of awkward for her, and one of the rifles recoiled worse than the shotgun. After shooting it, she jerked it away from her shoulder and scowled. "That hurt! I don't like this one."

"Told you," Kenneth told Eli.

But when she picked up the first pistol, she felt something click inside her. As much fun as the shotgun had been, some primitive gene deep inside her sat up and took notice when her hand closed around the butt of the pistol. Oh my God. This was it. This was what suited her best. Kenneth had been exactly right.

"I like this," she murmured.

"If you could see your expression," Zeke said, his own voice low, but coming in plain through the headset. His eyes were heavy-lidded, intent.

Mentally she shook herself, took a step away from him, squared herself with the target. "Like this?" she asked, two-handing the pistol as she brought the sights on target.

"Just like that." This time he didn't step up behind her, didn't show her where to put her hands. They had already been over the loading and unloading, the safety or lack thereof, the trigger and hammer and all sorts of things. This was a revolver, the big one Kenneth had provided for her practice. She lined up the sights and pulled the trigger. The barrel kicked upward, and just as she'd been told she pulled it down, found the sights, pulled the trigger again. She shot until the pistol was empty, then they examined the target.

The good news was that she'd hit the cardboard with every shot. The bad news was that only three shots had actually been anywhere in the bull's-eye.

"You'll get better," Spencer said in encouragement, seeing her disappointment.

"Damn right I will," she said, her jaw setting. "Let me see that automatic."

By the time Zeke called an end to the session, she'd blasted away four targets, and burned through more ammunition than she wanted to think about. Reluctantly she agreed that they had to stop; the men had work to do, and so did she. But she'd found her weapon. As right as the revolver had felt when she picked it up, the automatic had been even better. It was harder to load, harder to shoot, but she'd been more accurate with it. With some more practice—a lot more practice, probably—she'd be able to hit the target at least half the time.

And she wouldn't be helpless the next time Brad caught

up with her. She didn't feel invincible, but neither did she feel so vulnerable and frightened. That could be a good thing, or a bad thing. She wasn't going to do anything reckless out of a sense of power, but it was nice to know she had some knowledge of how to protect herself.

Amazing what a gun could do for a girl.

Chapter Twenty

THANK GOD SPENCER was out of his sling and could drive the pickup, Carlin thought, though Zeke still had the young hand on light duty. She was deeply grateful, because that meant Spencer had gone into town with her today, and not Zeke. Anything that kept her away from Zeke was all to the good. It was rough on her nerves to be close to him. If he was with her in a small enclosed space like the truck cab for an extended period of time, she'd probably explode.

She felt as if she were on the edge of an explosion a lot these days.

They had just left Battle Ridge when it started snowing. "Great," Spencer muttered. "It wasn't supposed to snow until tonight."

Carlin stared out the window at the mountains, already blurred by the snowfall. The winter weather system had moved in earlier than predicted—*hours* earlier. She'd hoped to be home with the groceries unloaded and put away before the first flake fell. Remembering how enchanted she'd been by that first snow, she could only mentally roll her eyes at herself. The white stuff had fallen several times since then, but around the ranch and in town where boot after dirty boot stomped through it, it never stayed white for long. Instead it turned gray and mushy and then refroze overnight, coating everything in a sheen of slippery, dangerous ice.

And it was just November.

"We can make it back to the ranch, right?" she asked, because already the snow seemed to be getting heavier, and the shoulders of the road were turning white.

"Yeah, sure." His easy reassurance would have been, well, reassuring, if he hadn't immediately followed it with, "I hope." That was Spencer, both optimistic and honest.

But he knew how to drive in this kind of weather, and she sure as hell didn't, so she had to trust the first part of his statement.

The other times it had snowed, she'd been safely at the ranch. This was the first time she'd been on the road when the weather turned nasty, though she supposed to a seasoned Wyomingite this didn't really qualify as nasty. It was pretty much weather as usual . . . she hoped. Now she knew why Spencer had added that qualifier.

The roads seemed to be fine—at least for now—so she relaxed and watched the scenery. She never got tired of the mountains. The views still took her breath away, in all seasons and all weather. The mountaintops had stayed white for a few weeks now, but watching the snow begin to cover all the slopes was almost hypnotic. The interior of the truck was nice and warm, and the rhythmic sound of the windshield wipers made her sleepy, but in a good kind of way. Looking out at the snow and knowing how cold it was, while she was dry and warm in the truck, gave her the same kind of cozy feeling being curled up in front of the fireplace provided.

They left the paved road and for the first time they hit some ice; the tires spun a little, but Spencer held the truck steady and they regained traction. He slowed some, so he wouldn't have to use the brake as much.

Huh. That wasn't good. They were still a good distance from the ranch, and the road would only get worse as it climbed in altitude. No longer sleepy, Carlin sat up and paid attention, though there was nothing she could do to aid Spencer's driving other than silently willing the tires not to spin.

They started up an incline that had never seemed treacherously steep before, but today Spencer slowed down to almost a crawl, and still the tires spun and grabbed, every inch a victory. Carlin gripped the armrest. "Ruh roh."

Spencer grinned at her Scooby imitation, though the grin was short-lived. "We'll be okay," he said, just as the truck bounced in a rut, then slid sideways on the icy road. "Maybe."

He had to cut that out. It worried her when he cut the legs out from under his reassuring statements. "Take it easy," she said, though of course the admonition was useless. "We have precious cargo."

"We do?" he asked in surprise, blinking at her.

"Watch the road!" she yelped. "The eggs." She peered through the window at the narrow road ahead. "I've got six dozen eggs in the backseat." She couldn't seem to buy enough eggs to keep Zeke and his men happy. Eggs, bread, and milk: those were the staples she went through the fastest.

Spencer gripped the steering wheel and leaned forward, intently watching the road. He looked a little worried, a totally new expression for him. Seeing anything other than happy optimism on his face was such a departure, Carlin decided she should be concerned, too.

"Do we need to go back?"

He gave her an appalled look, and she got the feeling she'd somehow challenged his manhood. "No, we can make it. But I should've put the spikes in the truck this morning, before we left."

Vintage Spencer: optimism, honesty. "Spikes?" What did they need spikes for? She had a vision of long spearlike things to drive into the ice as they climbed sheer frozen walls, or something like that. There was a lot to this Wyoming-winter stuff that a warm-weather person like her didn't know.

"For the tires," he clarified. "Can't drive with them on dry roads, but when there's ice it makes for a good grip. Don't usually need them this early, and I figured we'd be home before the roads got bad. This looks awfully icy." The worried expression came back. "The boss is going to kill me for forgetting the spikes . . ."

"We'll get home fine," she said, borrowing his optimism, as if saying the words would make it so. But she didn't want him to think she doubted him. She *didn't* doubt him, but ice was dangerous. Snow . . . *meh*. She'd already become blasé about snow. Ice was in a different category. The inherent danger of driving on ice made every muscle in her tighten in preparation for whatever might happen.

She didn't need bad weather to make her tense, these days. She stayed on edge, wound tight, and when she felt as if she were jumping out of her skin it wasn't because she was afraid of Brad, it was because being close to Zeke had every cell in her body on alert. She wanted him. She couldn't have him. God knew she was in too deep as it was! In the beginning she'd looked at this job as a way to hide through the winter, a chance to sock away some money for the next time she ran. And now here she was with friends, and a place that felt like home, and a man who teased her and taught her to defend herself and looked at her as if he wanted the same things she did.

And Zeke was a man who went after what he wanted. Carlin hadn't needed Kat's warning to make her wary of him, because any woman with one working brain cell would have been able to tell that he wasn't someone who accepted defeat, he took a situation and shook it, mauled it around, until it suited him. Funny—Brad hadn't accepted "no" for an answer, either, and yet the two men couldn't be more different. Brad couldn't conceive of any woman not wanting him. Zeke looked beneath the surface and somehow saw her potent reaction to him. He *knew* somehow, damn it, that what she said and what she felt were two completely different things. Brad was a danger to her life. Zeke was a danger to her emotions.

The road climbed around a curve, and the tires spun again, jerking her attention back to the present. Spencer let off on the gas, let the tires do their job, and they regained their momentum again. Carlin looked around, trying to figure out where they were. She'd been this route often enough that in good weather she could look around and have a good idea how far she was from the ranch, but the snow changed everything. She didn't recognize any landmarks; one snow-covered mountain or ravine looked pretty much like the next one, and she hadn't been paying attention to the passage of time. The truck's digital clock told her they'd been on the road almost an hour. In normal weather, they'd already have been back at the ranch.

Spencer slowed down more and more as the road wound up and down through the mountains, eventually going more down than up. The weather didn't get any better, though. Visibility decreased by the moment, until they could barely see a few feet in front of the truck. Carlin found herself leaning forward, as far as the confines of the seat belt would let her, as if by going on point she could somehow extend her vision and see through the thick, wind-swirled snowfall.

The sound of the tires changed, and looking out the side window Carlin saw they were crawling across a bridge, and suddenly she knew where they were, but wished she didn't. Even in good weather, this section of the road gave her an uneasy feeling. Immediately after crossing the bridge the road took a sharp left turn, and to the right was a steep ravine, the land falling away for a long, long drop to where a pencil-thin creek wound its way down the mountain. Because the snow was so heavy she couldn't see the drop, much less the creek, but she knew it was there and her heart began racing, her right hand tightened on the armrest and her left one on the edge of the seat.

Right at the end of the bridge the tires began spinning again, and the rear end of the truck began swinging to the right, toward the ravine. Spencer reacted swiftly, taking his foot off the gas, gently steering to the right to get in front of the spin, but he didn't have a lot of room to maneuver and as they bumped off the bridge the two right tires were on the shoulder. Carlin's heart jumped into her mouth and she closed her eyes.

"We're good," Spencer said, his voice a little higher than usual. He blew out a breath as he feathered the gas and his steering, trying to ease them back onto the road.

He might have made it, if it hadn't been for the deer. It came bounding out of the snow so suddenly that one second it wasn't there and the next second it was. Instinctively Spencer hit his brakes; the deer was right *there,* in front of the truck. The brakes locked, the tires lost traction, and the truck began sliding back and to the right, toward the ravine—and then they went over.

Carlin screamed, seeing nothing but the ghostly deer as it seemed to turn in mid-bound and disappear back into the snow. Time turned into molasses, every second stretching out unbearably. She saw Spencer's ashen face, his eyes wide, and she felt a deep ache that he was going to die so young, without having the chance to get married, have kids, have a life. She saw the snow swirling, silent and beautiful. She saw the limbs of an evergreen drooping under the white weight. She saw her own hand, reaching out, as if she could claw the air and hold them in place.

Then there was an impact that jerked her forward against the seat belt, which instantly jerked back and pinned her against the seat, and the truck crashed to a stop, hood pointed in the air.

For a moment Carlin could do nothing except stare up at the silent white bombardment of snow, coming down on the windshield.

"Are you okay?" Spencer asked breathlessly, his own hands clenched around the steering wheel.

"Ah . . . yeah. You?"

"Fine." His voice cracked on the word. He was looking at the windshield, too.

Strange thought, but all of a sudden it was loud and urgent. "My eggs!" She started to turn toward the backseat, but at her movement there was a sort of groaning sound, and it came from the metal of the truck.

"Don't move, Miss Carly!" Spencer was whispering now, and if he'd been ashen before, his face was now bloodless. "We . . . we're kind of balanced."

Balanced. *Balanced?*

"How? On what?"

"A tree," he said, visibly swallowing, and she realized he hadn't been looking out the windshield, he'd been looking in the rearview mirror.

A tree. That was good. Except . . . *a* tree. Plural, trees, would have been much better. "How big a tree?"

"Um . . . not big."

She glanced out the side window, and nearly passed out from sheer terror. There was nothing there, just more white flakes, dropping down, down, down, to some resting place she couldn't see. And all that was keeping them from plummeting down with the snowflakes was a not-big tree.

"Exactly how big is not-big?"

"Just don't move."

"Not that big of a not-big tree, then."

He swallowed again. "It's holding. It's just that we're kind of off-center."

Panic tightened her chest, making it impossible to take anything other than shallow, rapid breaths. A small tree. Off-center. The least move could send them tilting off their precarious perch. The tree could snap under the weight of the truck. The roots might tear loose. They were basically suspended in midair by nothing more than unbelievable luck and angels' breath.

Slowly Spencer reached for the console and the radio there, moving only his arm, holding his torso rigidly still. He turned it on, pushed a button, and spoke into the microphone. "Boss, you there?"

Zeke's deep voice answered so quickly Carlin wondered if he'd been waiting by the radio. "Where the hell are you?" The reception wasn't great; it broke up a time or two, but it was easy enough to get what Zeke was saying, and to hear the force in his tone.

"We slid off the road," Spencer said. "We're just past the bridge on the loop road, right before you get to the turnoff."

"Is Carlin okay?" The words were hard and sharp.

Carlin, not Carly. She caught her breath at the slip, the first time he'd done that. She wondered if Spencer would notice the hard end to her name, or just write it off to bad reception.

"Miss Carly's fine. But get here fast, boss. A tree is all that's holding us, and we can't move to get out of the truck."

"I'll be right there. Just don't move, and everything will be okay."

That authoritative tone was both reassuring and maddening. He said it would be okay with all the confidence that his orders could countermand both weight and gravity; part of her was reassured simply because he was so confident, and the more sane part of her was infuriated by his arrogance.

Please, please, God, she prayed, *overlook his arrogance this once and let him be right.*

She and Spencer sat frozen in their seats. There was nothing they could do except wait—wait for Zeke or Death, whoever got there first.

Zeke spotted the bumper of the truck peeking over the shoulder of the road. The snow was coming down so hard that it had partially covered the truck; if he hadn't known almost exactly where they were, if he hadn't been looking, he might have driven on by.

The sight of the truck's position made his heart thump heavily, but he grimly pushed the surge of panic away; now wasn't the time to lose it over what might happen, but to deal with what *had* happened—and what had happened was enough to turn his blood as icy as the road. It was a miracle the pickup wasn't at the bottom of the ravine right now.

He shoved the gear lever into Park and had the door open and was out of his truck before it had rocked back on the springs. The shoulder of the road was pure ice; his boots slipped beneath him as he eased up to the edge of the road and assessed the situation. His back teeth clenched; the situation wasn't good.

Through the snow that half-covered the windshield, melting from the truck's heat, he could see Carlin and Spencer motionless in their seats, their white faces frozen and blank, as if they were afraid even to blink their eyes.

He could see the thin tree that had caught the truck's back bumper off-center, on Spencer's side of the truck, bending under the massive weight. It could break at any time, sending them to their deaths.

No, by God. *No.* Not while he had breath in his body. Carlin—

He cut the thought off before it could form, and scrambled back into the four-wheel-drive dual-axle diesel pickup he'd driven because it had a winch on the front. Walt, who had been following, drove up and stopped at a safe distance as Zeke turned the dually around so he was facing Walt. This wasn't going to be easy. In fact, he wasn't at all certain he could get the truck out.

Walt met him at the winch, surveyed the situation, and said, "Holy shit," his tone quiet so Spencer and Carlin couldn't hear him.

The rest of the hands were on the way, but Zeke estimated Micah was at least ten minutes away, and Kenneth was about five minutes behind them. He didn't dare wait for any of them.

"We'll use the snatch block," Zeke said. They had to winch the truck up from an angle, which the snatch block made possible. The road wasn't wide enough for him to line up bumper to bumper and pull the other truck up. The winch was rated for ten thousand pounds, so it would handle the weight; the treacherous footing was a problem, and the position of the other truck was a bigger one. He couldn't hook the steel cable to the bumper, because bumpers weren't secure; it would pull right off. He had to attach it to the frame or axle. The shoulder of the road was pure ice; getting down to the truck and working his way under it was going to be a bitch. If he slipped and went into the ravine, he would die. If he bumped the truck and tilted it off its delicate balance, all three of them would die.

He had to get the cable around a sturdy part of the truck, ideally the K frame of the engine cradle, as close to center as possible so the truck wouldn't tilt over on its side. If he couldn't reach the K frame, he'd go for the axle or any other part he could reach, as long as it would prevent the truck from toppling down the ravine. He didn't care if the steel cable ruined the axle. Trucks were replaceable; people weren't.

Walt eased close to the edge of the shoulder to make his own assessment; he began slipping on the ice, too, waving his arms to regain his balance. "Careful," Zeke said, grabbing the back of Walt's jacket and hauling him back to secure footing. But Walt had seen the same thing that Zeke had, and his lined face was worried. Where the truck had gone off wasn't a straight drop; they were on a sharp slope that became almost vertical a few yards behind the back bumper. Maybe there was a dip in the terrain, but for whatever reason, the front bumper was almost touching the ground. There was no way he could wiggle under from the front. He'd have to go down and work his way in from the side, *without* being able to hold to the steel cable, which he'd have to feed under the bumper first to get the hook in the correct position. Then he'd have to get under the truck and secure the cable.

And he had to do it fast, before a gust of wind blew the truck off its precarious balance, or the spindly looking tree gave out and splintered.

"I'll do it," Walt volunteered. "I'm skinnier than you."

That was true. Zeke was taller and heavier than the older man, deeper in the chest, wider in the shoulders. And Walt was as tough as shoe leather, but it wasn't a question of toughness, or even of size. "Doesn't matter," Zeke replied. "It's my job." He simply wasn't going to risk anyone else's life. He wasn't going to let Carlin's life rest in anyone else's hands.

"But boss—"

"My responsibility. My job."

Walt knew that tone of voice and didn't waste any more time arguing; instead he set about getting the snatch block ready. Zeke removed his hat and put it inside the cab, and pulled the hood of his coat up over his head. Then, free-spooling the cable, he pulled it to the edge of the shoulder of the road and got down on his stomach in the snow so he could see the best place to feed the hook and cable under the truck. The falling snow had already covered the bumper, and gently Zeke began wiping the snow away with his gloved hand, a little bit at a time, not wanting to hit the bumper. Finally he could see a gap, and he eased the hook and cable through it under the truck.

"Ready?" he called over his shoulder to Walt.

"Ready."

Zeke didn't bother getting to his feet. Still on his stomach, he slithered headfirst over the edge of the ravine, sliding on the ice but able to dig in the toes of his heavy boots enough to maintain some control. The slope was steep, littered with rocks and half-buried boulders. The rocks gave him some traction, something rough to grab on to as he clawed his way down. He didn't have far to go, maybe five or six feet, but he had to control his motion to a maddeningly slow pace or he'd gain too much momentum and go sliding off the bluff. The cold seeped through his jeans and thermal underwear, even through the thick coat he was wearing, snow and ice sticking to his garments and then melting, making him even colder.

He was on Carlin's side of the truck. He didn't dare look up, didn't want to see her stiff, terrified face looking out the window at him. He might lose his concentration, move too fast. There were already enough things that could go wrong without him adding to the list. Hell, if a bird landed on the roof of the truck that could be enough to tilt it off-balance; good thing birds weren't flying in this weather.

He was farther down the side of the truck than he wanted to be, perilously close to the edge, before there was enough space under the truck for him to slide under it. Carefully turning himself perpendicular to the truck, he eased his head under the chassis—and almost laughed in relief, quickly followed by what felt suspiciously like the burn of tears. He blinked and swallowed, then blew out a big breath. The little tree wasn't all that was holding the truck. The transmission block was caught on an underground boulder that stuck just a foot or so above the ground. The truck was solidly wedged; it wasn't going anywhere even if that tree did break, which it almost definitely would have if the rock hadn't caught most of the truck's weight.

That was the good news. The bad was that the bulk of the boulder made it more difficult for him to reach the winch cable. On the balance of things, though, he'd take having a tougher job for himself as long as the vehicle was more stable.

"The truck's caught on a boulder!" he yelled out to Walt, knowing that Spencer and Carlin would probably be able to hear him inside the truck, and wanting to relieve the stress everyone was feeling. "It's secure as long as they don't move around too much." The last thing he wanted was for them to think they could just open their doors and get out; not only was the ground so icy they might slide right off, but the truck could still be tilted off-balance, and he was still underneath it. He'd really like to avoid getting crushed.

The tight quarters meant his thick coat was now a liability he couldn't afford. Carefully he backed out from beneath the truck and quickly shucked the coat. The bitter cold immediately bit through his clothing, and snow gathered on his hair, melting and refreezing. Shit! He had to get this done in a hurry before he got hypothermia.

But hurrying was one thing he couldn't do. Every move had to be deliberate and precise.

He inched forward under the truck again, looking for the winch cable, this time angling himself toward the front of the truck because the boulder would have prevented the cable from coming any farther back. It was a tight fit, even without the bulk of his coat. Walt would have been the better choice, size-wise, and he still had the option of backing out, climbing back up to the road, and letting Walt do this—but the risk, though much diminished from what they'd originally thought, was still there, and he wouldn't willingly send any of his men in his place into a dangerous situation when he could do the job himself.

A nerve-racking minute later, he got his hand on the cable. That was the easy part. The hard part was getting it secured without jarring the truck any more than necessary. Sweat broke out on his face and froze, and the pain on his skin was bad enough he had to take a minute and wipe the ice away. He began shivering uncontrollably, so bad he didn't dare try to attach the cable while he was shaking like that. Instead he deliberately shook and shivered as hard as he could, ramping up his core temperature enough that when he stopped, his body felt warm enough that he could resume without the shivering. He had to do that once more before he had the cable secured around the frame of the engine cradle.

Just as cautiously as he had wormed his way under the truck, he wormed his way back out. God almighty, the cold was biting bone deep, like an animal with its fangs sunk into his body. As soon as he was clear he grabbed his coat and dragged it on, but the fabric was cold, the outer layer covered with snow, and there was precious little warmth he could get from it.

He clawed his way up to the icy shoulder of the road, dragged himself over the edge. Micah and Kenneth had both arrived, and were standing beside Walt, though right now there was nothing they could do.

Looking back at the truck, Zeke caught Carlin's terrified gaze and gave her a thumbs-up. Maybe she hadn't heard him yell to Walt; maybe, when you were in this situation, you weren't reassured until you were actually *out* of the situation. His own gut had been knotted with fear; how much worse had it been for her, and for Spencer?

As soon as he was on his feet and staggering out of the way, Walt pressed the button on the remote to start the winch. He had everything ready, even the hood up on the dually to protect the windshield if the cable broke, and an old jacket thrown over the cable itself to help smother any backlash. The motor whined and slowly began reeling in the cable. The line pulled taut, metal grating on rock as the pickup began to roll forward, scraping the underside along the boulder that had prevented it from plummeting down the ravine.

A few minutes later, the pickup was on the road. Walt stopped the winch and free-spooled some slack in it so the cable could be unhooked. Micah hurried forward to take care of that chore.

Spencer had opened his door and tumbled out, but Carlin still sat in the passenger seat, unmoving. Was she hurt? Urgency biting into him again, Zeke grabbed the handle and jerked it open. "Are you all right?"

She swallowed. Maybe her lips trembled a little. She said, "My legs . . ."

God almighty. Were they broken, had she suffered a spinal injury? He barked, "Your legs—"

"No! My eggs. *Eggs!* If the eggs are broken I don't know what I'll be feeding all of you for the next week, because I'll be damned if I'll go back to the grocery store until the spring thaw!"

Relief roaring through him, he reached in and unclipped her seat belt, then hauled her out of the truck. Walt and Micah were both laughing, more than a little relief in their own reactions.

Spencer wasn't laughing. He stood in the snow, his

shoulders hunched, looking miserable. Zeke already knew why. "Damn it," he growled, bits of snow stinging his face. "Where are the spikes?" If Spencer had thrown them in the back of the truck—a common precaution—he'd have put them on when they turned off the paved road, he wouldn't have slid off the shoulder, and none of this would have happened.

Spencer looked even more miserable. "I'm sorry, boss. I thought we'd be home long before this moved in."

The system had come in earlier than predicted, but weather didn't punch a time clock and they all knew it. You prepared for the worst, and that way you weren't caught without something you needed. On the other hand, there wasn't anything he could say to the kid that would be worse than hanging suspended like that, thinking they could fall the rest of the way if they so much as breathed too hard.

It was over, thank God, and no one was hurt. But he didn't know if he'd ever fully recover from those minutes of terror.

CARLIN PULLED OPEN the back door of the extended cab. Groceries had been flung everywhere, jarred by the impact of hitting the rock and the tree. The floorboard was filled with canned goods, mostly, as well as a large pack of toilet paper. She usually put the meat and anything breakable in the backseat.

Like the eggs.

The eggs gave her something to focus on, something to pull her back from the edge of terror, from the sensation of hysteria building inside her. She was not going to break down in front of the men. *Not. Going. To. Happen.* So she plastered on a pissed expression and said, "Damn it!" as she leaned in and began putting canned goods back in bags, checking the eggs—at least a dozen were broken, maybe more. Now she'd have to think of something else to cook for breakfast for at least a few days, to make the remaining eggs last longer.

"Leave it," Zeke said, gripping her arm and pulling her away from the truck. "You're riding back with me. The truck is staying here until we can get back with some spikes; I won't risk anyone driving it a foot farther on this mountain."

"I can't leave the groceries—"

"Spencer will bring them. He can ride back with one of the other men."

She looked at him, prepared to argue because arguing seemed like a good idea right now, anything to keep her going. But the words stopped when she got a good look at him. He looked like the Abominable Snowman, his clothes caked with snow and ice; even his eyebrows and lashes were icy. He'd risked his life to save theirs. Instead of arguing she ducked her head against the icy wind, leaned into him for warmth and the support he offered.

"I'm going to get you home. Spencer, get the groceries and ride back with one of the others."

"Yes sir." Spencer pressed his lips together, his expression so guilty the dictionary could have used him as the definition of the word. "Miss Carly, I—"

"I'm fine," she said, breaking into an apology that she was sure would shred every nerve she had left, which wasn't many. "You'd better worry about what you'll be getting for breakfast, though, because we're short on eggs now."

She was fine. She *was*. She would be.

Zeke helped her into the passenger seat and closed her door. She didn't utter a single word about how she wasn't helpless, how she didn't need his help. Instead she gathered her control for what she knew she needed to do now. As Zeke rounded the hood of the truck to climb into the driver's seat, she let down her window and shouted to the men, "See if you can save some of the eggs! I'm serious. If they're just cracked, save them, and I'll use them tonight!"

Kenneth and Micah and Walt all laughed, but Spencer didn't. He didn't dare.

Carlin looked out the side window as Zeke drove back to the house. She would have been content with the silence, with not having to bear the strain of conversation, but he said, "Want me to fire Spencer?"

Appalled, she snapped her head around and glared at him. "No, of course not! It wasn't his fault. A deer came out of nowhere and he swerved to miss it, lost control, and there—there we went." Wrong choice of words. It brought everything back too clearly.

Zeke's gaze was cool and deadly serious. "I like Spencer. If he hangs in with me, I'd planned on making him foreman one day. But he knew snow was coming in; he should've had those snow spikes in the truck, just in case. His carelessness could have killed you both."

"But it didn't," she replied tersely. "It was an accident. Period." Because she couldn't bear talking about the wreck any longer, she began telling him about their trip to Battle Ridge. She didn't normally have diarrhea of the mouth, but this one time she chatted her head off. She talked about seeing Kat, and about how warm her coat was—*her* coat, not the cook's coat, or the outerwear that came with the job. *Hers*. She talked a bit about how her menus for the week would have to be altered, considering what had probably been lost in the wreck, and assuming she wouldn't make it back to town for at least a couple of days—and for an even greater assumption, that she wanted to make that drive at all until the snow melted.

He parked in the garage, walked with her to the house. He unlocked the door to the mudroom and for once didn't bitch about the locked doors, and they walked into the welcome dry warmth of the house. They removed their

coats and hung them on the rack just past the door. Carlin
sat on the bench there and removed her boots. Sitting beside her, he did the same. Then they moved into the kitchen
on sock feet, and just inside the room Carlin stopped and
looked around, trying to decide what to do. She felt as if
she should do something, but her brain had locked and
she couldn't think of anything.

"What's wrong?" he asked.

She blinked up at him as a strange mixture of turbu-
lence and paralysis gripped her. *Kiss me.*

The words hovered on her lips, but by the grace of
God she managed to keep them unsaid. What was *wrong*
with her? She couldn't say something like that to Zeke,
couldn't undermine herself that way. Maybe she needed
a little comforting, but that was all. She was okay. She'd
handle it.

"Nothing," she finally said. "Just thinking about what
to cook for supper."

He grunted as he left the kitchen, headed up the stairs
no doubt for a hot shower. She should do the same, but
the men would be here soon with the groceries. They
could put everything away, but she preferred to do it herself. She wanted to keep busy. She wanted to forget the
insane words that she'd almost said aloud.

Kiss me.

Chapter Twenty-one

CARLIN STOOD IN the shower and cried. She felt like a doofus for crying—she was alive, she wasn't even hurt—but her nerves were shattered and she'd held herself together as long as she could. Finally being alone was such a relief that she almost cried from that. The men meant well, but their concern had in a way only added to the stress, because she hadn't wanted to upset them by getting teary.

The whole afternoon and evening had been a strain, first with the wreck, then the men fussing over her, asking her again and again if she was all right—well, everyone except Zeke. After that first sharp "Are you okay?" he'd let the subject lie, but every time she'd looked around she'd find him watching her with that sharp, narrow-eyed gaze of his that missed nothing. For the men—especially Spencer, so he wouldn't feel guilty—she'd put up a front, assured everyone that she was fine, not even banged up. The latter might be true, but she wasn't fine. She was so far from fine she wasn't even in the same state with it.

After getting dressed in her normal sleep attire, sweatpants and a T-shirt, she went into her sitting room and tried to watch some TV to settle her nerves. It didn't work. Maybe she should just give up on the evening and go to bed. Restlessly she hovered in the doorway between the sitting room and bedroom, staring at the bed. It was bedtime, but there wasn't any point in even going through the motions, because sleep was a long, long way from coming. Maybe if she did the normal things she would feel more normal, but she didn't think so.

Blowing out a deep breath, she shoved a hand through her hair and turned back into the sitting room and the TV. The noise grated on her nerves like fine grit against glass. She grabbed up the remote and turned the TV off, filling the space, her space, with blessed silence.

Except now she could hear the clock ticking, and it reminded her of the way time had dragged by while she and Spencer hovered over death, waiting for either the tree to snap, the truck to teeter off-balance, or Zeke to arrive. Whichever happened first would determine whether they lived or died.

Her insides hadn't stopped shaking all evening long, and she couldn't stop thinking about what would have happened if the truck had gone the rest of the way over the side of the mountain, if there hadn't been a boulder sticking up just enough to catch the truck, if that terrifyingly small tree hadn't been in the way. She still couldn't believe the spindly looking trunk had somehow been strong enough to hold the truck so precariously balanced. Okay, so the boulder had held the truck, but the tree had balanced it. And at the time she hadn't known about the boulder; she'd put all her faith in that pitiful little tree.

Sitting there waiting for Zeke, not daring to move, almost not daring to breathe lest she upset that delicate balance, had been an eternity. She didn't know if she'd ever be able to forget how it felt to teeter for so long on the razor's edge of sure death, dangling over that high, terrifying drop. Terror wasn't a stranger to her; she'd met it before—moments of it, keen and slicing—when she'd seen Brad on the street in Dallas and realized he'd followed her, again when she'd found out Jina had been murdered in the street and known Brad had mistaken Jina for her, not knowing where he was, if each step might be her last. But those had been moments, and sitting in that truck had felt like a lifetime, each second agonizingly slow, and so precious as they dripped away.

What if the tree *did* snap? What if the truck plummeted all the way to the bottom of the mountain? If it caught fire and burned, which seemed like at least a good possibility, her driver's license would burn and no one would ever know her real name, her family couldn't be notified, and they would spend the rest of their lives not knowing what had happened to her.

She didn't want to die, hiding away so no one knew who she really was. She wanted to *live*. She'd disrupted her life, turned her world upside down, torn herself away from both family and friends, spent months on the run, because she wanted to live.

But until she'd sat in the truck for those endless minutes, waiting to die, she hadn't realized that she *hadn't* been living. She'd been running. She'd been enduring. She'd been surviving. But she hadn't been *living*. Instead she'd been holding life at a distance, trying not to let herself get so close to anyone that she cared about them or they cared about her.

That wasn't living. Living was about people, about connections, about loving and being loved. It was about letting others into the warp and woof of your life, and becoming enmeshed in theirs.

What was maddening was that her long-term situation hadn't changed. No, not long term. She couldn't bear the thought of Brad, fear of Brad, controlling her life for years on end. But he was at least midterm, lingering in her future like a giant black cloud, and she had done nothing, could think of nothing she *could* do, to resolve the situation. Hope he moved his obsession on to someone else? Hope he'd get killed in a car wreck? Boy, that was taking charge of her life, wasn't it?

Since Jina's murder her emotions had gone through a number of phases, from grief and terror to numbness, then determination. She'd learned to watch her back, to stay hypervigilant, and now she'd even learned how to use various firearms—not at expert level, but at least she was less helpless than she'd been before.

To what end, though? To stay alive but stop living?

Restlessly she paced around the small sitting room, so angry she felt as if her skin would barely contain her. She'd let Brad do this to her. Oh, it wasn't her fault that he was a homicidal stalker or that he'd fixated on her, but how she'd responded was completely on her. She'd let fear define her life.

But what was she supposed to do? If she'd remained in Houston, Brad would have killed her. If she hadn't left Dallas, Brad would have killed her.

The anger mixed with a frustration so raw and powerful she wanted to scream, wanted to clench her fists, tilt her head back, and scream and scream and scream, until she didn't have a voice left. She wanted to throw a temper tantrum, wanted to break windows and smash furniture, anything to express how furious she was that she was caught in this trap, wanting to live but afraid to, afraid to form relationships—afraid, always afraid, walking a tight-rope because that *bastard* was out there.

If it weren't for Brad, she'd have kissed Zeke back in a way that would have made his head spin. She'd have acted on the sizzling attraction she felt for him, the burn-ing need to touch his bare skin and take him inside her body. It had been so long since she'd felt anything close to the power of what she felt for Zeke, so long since she'd *needed* sex, a man. Brad had put her off men, made her hesitant to trust her own judgment because even though she'd spotted his weirdness pretty fast she hadn't been fast enough. Two dates was all it had taken for him to target her. What if she hadn't gone on that second date? Would one date have been enough to trigger whatever insanity drove him? And if just one date did happen to be enough, then how could she ever let down her guard again?

She hated Brad, hated him down to the core of her being, hated him with such passion that abruptly she knew she didn't want to break windows and smash furniture, she wanted to smash Brad himself, she wanted to physically beat him to a pulp for what he'd done to her, to her life, but most of all for what he'd done to Jina.

She couldn't. He wasn't here, thank God. She was safe in this place, protected, hidden, all thanks to the man who slept upstairs while she paced restlessly down here wishing things were different, wishing she were free to go to him—

Why wasn't she?

Why did she keep letting Brad set the boundaries that kept her hemmed in?

Abruptly she was even more furious with herself than she was with Brad, because while there were some things that were out of her control, and some things she'd been pushed into, there were still other parts of her life where she didn't have to play dead and let Brad dictate what she did or didn't do.

Zeke knew the score. He knew her situation. Today she had come so close to dying, and if that had happened she would have gone without having known what it was like to cradle Zeke's powerful body with hers, without feeling the driving force of his lovemaking. She'd thought she was protecting herself, protecting him, and all she'd been doing was depriving them.

She'd be *damned* if she'd let Brad have that much control over her, over her life.

She was out the door almost before she knew it, making her way through the night-shadowed house, moving around the obstacle course of furniture with ease, because by now she knew every inch of this house, where every chair was, every table, every lamp. The kitchen was lit by the dim glow of digital clocks on the oven, the coffeemaker, the microwave, but other than that the house was dark.

Then her bare feet touched the stairs, her hand gripped the banister, and reality slapped her in the face. She faltered, but didn't stop, pushing herself upward. Was she really going to go into Zeke Decker's bedroom and invite him to have sex with her?

Oh, hell yeah.

Enough was enough. She couldn't take back control of her entire life, but right here, tonight, she could be a woman. She refused to let Brad keep that from her anymore.

The oblong of Zeke's bedroom door was just barely lighter than the surrounding darkness, telling her that it was open; why wouldn't it be, when he was the only one up here? He could be walking around naked every night and every morning, for all she knew, because she never ventured up here while he was still in the house—part of her stupid "keep Zeke at a distance" strategy.

She reached the doorway, almost breathless from the fury that had been sweeping her along. Every cell in her body wanted to keep going, to simply take a flying leap and land on him, but common sense kicked in. If she did that, considering the lightning-fast reaction she'd seen from him before, she would likely find herself tossed across the room. So she stopped, almost panting. She could see his bed, see the long bulk of his body, the faint gleam of starlight on the skin of his bare shoulder and arm. Taking a deep breath, she forced herself to knock lightly on the doorframe. "Zeke."

Her voice was strained and low, so low she didn't think he could possibly hear her even if he was awake—

He was. He did. He was out of the bed by the time the sound of his name had barely touched the air. "What's wrong? Are you all right?" he asked sharply.

He was naked. Carlin caught her breath, staring at the outline of his muscled frame. The room was too dark for her to see much, but just knowing he was naked was almost as good as seeing. Distracted, she still managed to say, "Nothing. No."

He moved toward her, darkness advancing. "Nothing's wrong, but no, you're not all right?"

She sucked in another breath, her heart beating so violently she could feel it hammering against her ribs. "I'm okay, but—I'm not all right."

He reached her, his big hands cupping her elbows, the warmth of his palms searing all the way to the bone. "Are you hurting anywhere? You got banged around—"

He was close, so close. Carlin let her head drop forward, resting it against his chest. Heat and scent swirled around her, enveloped her. Instinctively she swayed toward him, but by some desperate surge of willpower she kept her arms down, her hands to herself. Don't assume . . . yeah, most men would jump at the chance for sex, but Zeke wasn't most men. Zeke was steel where she was used to aluminum. She had to be clear, she had to knock down all the walls and let herself be exposed.

"I could have died today."

His hands tightened almost painfully, squeezing her arms. "I know."

"I don't—" She stopped, shuddering, and closed her eyes. "I don't want to die without having you." Her voice trailed away on the last word and she stood there, head resting against him, eyes closed, waiting for his reaction.

If his grip had been tight before, now his fingers felt as if they were digging down into bone. For an endless moment there was nothing other than the sounds of their breathing, and horrified embarrassment was beginning to knot her stomach when he said harshly, "I want to make sure I'm not misunderstanding anything here. You want me to fuck you?"

The hard, primitive word sent shockwaves of excitement rolling along her nerves. Carlin opened her eyes and raised her head. "No. *I* want to fuck *you*." Now that the words were said, the rest of it boiled out of her. "No relationship, no couple, no you-and-me stuff, because nothing has changed and I may have to leave at any time, without notice."

"So what do you want from me? Other than my dick?" His tone had gone from harsh to flint hard.

Boldly, desperately, she reached out and touched him, closed her hand around the thick, hard length of his penis, jutting out from his groin. He was already erect, but at her touch she felt him harden even more, getting thicker. "Just this. Just let me have this."

"Employee with benefits?"

She'd made him angry. She didn't understand it but she could feel it, and part of her was sorry because she hadn't meant to insult him, but anger was good, anger had brought her this far. "That'll do," she snapped back. "I can't risk any more, but I'll be damned if I let him steal this from me, too."

His breath blew out like an angry bull's, but in one swift motion he grasped the bottom of her T-shirt and pulled it over her head, tossed it aside. "First round is yours," he said grimly. "But, by God, the second one is mine."

The challenge barely made it through her consciousness, but it clicked. She gave a low, rough laugh. "You haven't made it through the first one yet," she said, and pushed him. He backed up a step, letting her have control. She knew he was letting her, that he could put a stop to it and have this time any way he wanted, but she didn't care. She was getting what she wanted, and anticipation burned through her veins like whiskey.

He moved his hands to her hips. "Get out of these," he said, pushing her sweatpants down. Bracing her hands on his shoulders, she stepped out of the garment. Straightening, he pulled her in tight against him.

She'd been kissed before. *He'd* kissed her before. But "before" had almost no relationship with "now," because she'd never been kissed the way he was kissing her, as if he wanted to take everything she was, his mouth so hungry on hers she forgot that she was the one who was supposed to be doing the taking and simply hung there in his arms, her toes barely touching the floor. Everywhere their skin touched, she burned: her breasts, her belly, her thighs. Deep inside she ached, empty and needing, already throbbing as her body readied itself for his invasion. No. Not *his* invasion—*hers*. Because this was her round.

He'd said this time was hers, but he was taking it instead, if she let him. She tore her mouth away, panting, and once more wrapped her hand around his erection. "I'm doing this," she said, stroking, feeling the silky hot skin move over the iron beneath.

"Yeah? Well, I'm doing this." He pushed a big hand between her legs, two hard fingers pushing up inside her.

Oh, *God*. She almost collapsed against him, a weak cry escaping her throat as she went weak from the onslaught of pleasure. She was so on edge, so close, that she didn't need foreplay, she needed only him.

"Stop, stop!" She released him, pushed against his chest again, taking them almost to the bed. "Bed. Now!"

He laughed, the sound ruthless and male. "How about

this?" he said, catching her behind the thighs and lifting
her. Instantly she knew what he was doing; she wrapped
her legs around his hips and reached for him yet again,
gripping his penis and guiding the thick bulb to the moist
opening of her body, then slowly letting herself sink
down.

The angle was too extreme and she gasped with pain,
then tightened her legs and lifted herself, repositioning.
Once again she let herself down, carefully, the pressure
of her body weight making her opening flower around
him. Slowly she took him in, the hot length searing and
stretching as she took more, and more.

He made a hissing sound through his clenched teeth.
His fingers clenched on her bottom and he fell backward
onto the bed, holding her locked to him.

The impact drove him deep into her, pulled a high,
keening cry from her chest. She almost sobbed, not because it hurt, but because until she was so completely
filled she hadn't realized how empty she was. The pleasure of it was almost blinding, almost more than she
could bear, and yet she wanted more.

Planting her hands on his chest, gripping his hips with
her knees, she slowly lifted herself off his impaling length
until only the head remained inside her, then even more
slowly she drifted back down, enveloping him. She cried
out again, almost choking because breathing was almost
impossible now, the tension in her body had it locked so
tightly. Up. Down. He cupped her breasts, holding them
for just a moment before lightly pinching her nipples, pulling them until the tension in her lower body linked to the
tension in her nipples and multiplied the electric effect.

She climaxed hard, riding him, riding the deep hard
waves until there was nothing else, rising and falling, seeing nothing, hearing from afar the guttural, almost ani-
malistic cries that she could feel tearing from her throat.

The world tilted on its axis, she felt herself being buffeted, then she realized that she was somehow on her back and he was on top of her, between her legs, still inside her and thrusting hard.

He wasn't being gentle with her, but she didn't want gentle, didn't need it. She needed life, and this was it.

Chapter Twenty-two

CARLIN FELT AS if a huge weight had been lifted off her shoulders, as if something in the universe that had been out of kilter was now finally right. After weeks—months—of having to deny herself what she wanted, she'd finally worked up the nerve to take it. It had taken a near-death experience to get her there, but she didn't regret what had happened with Zeke. She was a little sore and a *lot* relaxed.

And nothing had changed.

She'd slipped out of Zeke's bed in the middle of the night, leaving him sleeping. If she'd stayed they would've had sex again, and before that happened she had to clear the air. This morning wasn't going to be as much fun as last night had been.

No, *fun* was the wrong word for what had happened last night. After much too long a time making sure she didn't get too emotionally close to anyone, she'd made a connection with another human being. She'd allowed herself to be vulnerable, to touch and be touched in a way that went beyond the physical, for her, at least. For Zeke she was probably just another lay.

She hoped that's all it was, anyway.

Who was she fooling? What was between them was way too intense to be casual, for either of them.

But she could pretend.

She got up early, too early to start breakfast, but it was never too early to start the coffee. She'd finished a cup of coffee and was working on the second when Zeke came into the kitchen. He looked a little stone-faced. Maybe he was annoyed that she hadn't stayed, maybe he didn't want a morning-after analysis—tough shit—but under the stone was an undeniable air of satisfaction. Did he move a little differently this morning? More smoothly, more relaxed, a *tiny* bit slower? Good lord, the man was gorgeous—not pretty, but gorgeous the way a real man was supposed to be, lean and hard and easy on the eyes.

He poured his own cup of coffee, silently eyeing her all the while. Just as he lifted the cup for that important first sip, she said, "We need to talk."

He groaned, then went for the coffee. "Well, shit."

"What? I didn't even tell you what I want to talk about."

"The words 'we need to talk' are never good news for any man." He strolled to the table and sat across from her. Those eyes, those magnificent green eyes, were hooded and sexy. And piercing, as if he could see right through her. "If you're going to tell me that last night was a mistake and it'll never happen again . . ."

"I'm not," Carlin said. "It wasn't a mistake, and I suspect it will happen again." Sooner rather than later, but not right this minute . . . damn it. He was just too tempting.

She took a deep breath, wrapped her hands around the warm coffee mug. "I need to tell you some things. My real name is Carlin Reed. You know why I'm here, why I'm using a false name and don't want my social security number on the books anywhere, but . . . yesterday it struck me that if anything happened to me, if I died, my family would never know. I would just disappear from the face of the earth and they'd be left to . . ." She choked on the very idea. Not the idea that she might die—that was a given for everyone—but that Robin and Kin would never know the truth of what had happened to her. It would be cruel to leave them wondering if she was dead or alive, and never knowing for sure.

"You have family," Zeke said, his voice low.

Carlin nodded. "A brother and a sister, a brother-in-law, two nieces, and a nephew. I haven't seen them for more than a year, but I do keep in touch by email. Facebook, actually. I use the computers at the library."

Zeke took a sip of his coffee, giving her a hard look over the edge of the cup. "I have a computer in my office. You can use it any time."

She was shaking her head even before he'd finished. "No, Brad is a hacker, and I'm sorry to say he's a very good one." How good, she didn't know, but he'd found her before and she suspected he would again, if she gave him the chance. "If he ever figures out how I'm getting in touch with my family, he'll be able to trace the computer I used."

"Huh. Really?"

Strangely, Carlin found herself smiling at the man on the other side of the table. "How computer savvy are you?"

"Savvy enough to do what needs to be done. I'm no hacker, though."

Thank God.

So he'd be sure to understand, she explained further. "One of the reasons I've been so careful about not telling anyone my name is that if anyone starts checking into the situation, if they search for me on the Internet, I think it will be enough for Brad. You know, you can get alerts if anyone plugs your name into a search engine." If only she'd lived a hundred years ago, shoot, even twenty years ago! Computers had screwed things up for everyone who wanted to lie low. If only her parents had named her

Debbie or Jenny or Sue, if they'd given her a common girl's name this would be so much easier! There were millions of women with those names. How many Carlins were there? Not many, which made it that much easier for Brad.

Zeke shifted his weight, thoughtfully drank more coffee. "Exactly how bad is your situation? You said a friend died in your place. What happened?"

She sighed, and started at the beginning. "I went out on two dates with him. The first one was okay, nothing special, but okay. The second one . . . I don't know, there was just something about him that made me uneasy, so I wouldn't go out with him again. He started harassing me at work. I ended up quitting my job just to get away from him, because no one would believe a woman who'd been in town for six months over a police officer who'd lived there his whole life. When I figured out that he'd broken into my apartment while I wasn't at home, I knew I had to get out. I hoped it would be out of sight, out of mind."

"It wasn't, though."

"No. He was a creep, and yeah, I did worry that one day he was going to come into my apartment while I was sleeping, or in the shower, but I didn't really think he was dangerous. Just . . . odd, and obsessed. My job was nothing special, but it paid well enough. I was an office manager for a company that sold restaurant supplies, and I was good. Organized, efficient, never sick, no kids to wear me out or screw up my work schedule. With my references and a great recommendation from my boss I found a new job in Dallas, and I moved."

Her gaze went distant and she fiddled with her coffee cup, turning it around and around. "Brad followed me to Dallas, and he killed my friend. Jina was wearing my raincoat. He thought it was me, I just . . . I can't prove it, but I *know* it. I should've gone farther, I should've known he'd follow me. That's a mistake I can't undo. I can't go back and save her."

Zeke went very still, for a long moment. She waited for him to question her, to challenge her, to try to reason with her that she must be wrong, but instead he sat and waited, and listened.

The story spilled out of her, every detail of what had happened to Jina, how the police hadn't believed her, how Brad had manufactured an alibi and because he was a cop they'd bought it without digging deep enough to find the holes in his story. His computer showed that he'd been online when Jina had been shot—online, chatting about his garden, for God's sake. Obviously he'd either had someone else using his computer or else he'd fabricated the whole thing using his computer skills. Her word alone hadn't been enough to warrant further investigation.

She hadn't realized how much she'd needed to share her burden until she was sharing it all with Zeke. He listened, not stopping her to ask questions, not so much as uttering a word.

She finished the story with a retelling of driving into Battle Ridge with no intention of staying. He knew everything from there.

For a couple of very long minutes, he just sat in his chair and drank his coffee. She could tell his mind was spinning, that he was mentally working through everything she'd told him. Finally, he placed his cup on the table and looked her in the eye. "What's Brad's last name?"

Carlin stood so fast her chair made a sharp scraping squeal as it was pushed back across the floor, and her coffee cup shook, almost sending coffee over the rim. "No. I'm not telling you his last name. I know you too well, Zeke Decker. You want to do something, to track him down, to . . . to fix it. I won't let you. This is my problem, not yours."

He wasn't flustered by her reaction. Did anything ever

get under his skin? "I'm no hacker," he said calmly, "but I'm guessing any PI worth his salt could take Carlin Reed, Brad, Houston, and Dallas and come up with any details you omitted."

"Please don't," she whispered, her head spinning. Damn it, she was going to have to run again, to start over. To leave Zeke.

Maybe he read the thoughts on her face. Maybe he already knew her much too well. He stood, rounded the small kitchen table, and took her face in his hands. "You're safe here."

"I know. Please promise me you won't . . ." Again, she choked.

He kissed her. This kiss was softer than the ones they'd shared last night, and oh, she needed it, needed the feel of his lips on hers, the connection, the sheer physical pleasure.

He pulled his mouth from hers. "I won't do anything, not now, but you can't go on like this. You can't hide forever. Let me help. At least think about it."

"If you interfere in this, if you hire a PI or start digging into my past, I'll leave. I'll have no choice." She leaned into him. "I don't want to leave, Zeke. Not yet."

She might've said more, he might've said more, but a furious knocking at the back door interrupted the moment.

Carlin broke away and ran into the mudroom. She should've unlocked the back door by now, but she'd been distracted. Spencer stood there, shivering in the cold.

She and Spencer returned to the kitchen, where Zeke had retaken his seat at the table. As Spencer chattered away, Carlin looked Zeke in the eye.

Promise, she mouthed, not a whisper of sound escaping.

He responded the same way, with a reluctant *For now.*

It wasn't enough, but it would do. For now.

*   *   *

ZEKE TRIED TO lose himself in hard, physical labor, but nothing could distract him entirely from the matter at hand. Splitting wood was a chore one of the hands normally took care of, but today he needed to do something that would allow him to work out his aggression. Splitting firewood should do the trick.

Common sense dictated that he avoid Carlin like the plague. If everything she'd told him was true—and he believed that it was—then she was a barrel full of trouble. He didn't need to buy, borrow, or fuck trouble.

Unfortunately, it wasn't that simple. Life rarely was. And common sense had nothing to do with this situation. Carlin didn't want to leave; he didn't want her to go. He wanted more, and unless he'd completely misread her so did she. He had some condoms in his truck. They were old, but not yet expired. He didn't think for a minute that Carlin was on any kind of birth control. Neither of them had been thinking about that last night, but if they were going to continue he was going to have to think. He'd fetch what he had in his truck glove compartment and put them in his bedside table. And before long, he'd have to stop at the drugstore for a refill.

She'd been right when she accused him—and it *had* been an accusation—of wanting to fix things for her. Whether she stayed or not the idea of Carlin spending years, perhaps her entire life, running from her own boogeyman was unthinkable. She deserved better. She deserved to have a life, and if he could give her life back to her he would.

But he'd promised her. Patience wasn't his strong suit, but for Carlin he'd wait. For a while.

SHE NEVER SHOULD'VE told Zeke her real name, should've known that the information she'd given him would be enough for him to start digging into her past. A part of her was screaming *Run!* But she didn't, and she wouldn't. Zeke was a man of his word.

Telling him everything had been such an unexpected relief. She'd been bottling so much inside, keeping her secrets, protecting those around her as well as herself. But a shared burden was indeed lighter. For the moment, for the next several weeks and maybe even for a few months, she wasn't entirely alone.

She'd written Robin's contact information on a slip of paper and hidden it at the bottom of her sock drawer. Tonight she'd tell Zeke where it was, in case anything happened to her while she was here. It would be one less worry, one burden off her shoulders.

And if something happened to her after she left? Well, she wasn't going to worry about that right now. She'd gotten accustomed to living her life one day at a time, and that hadn't changed, couldn't change. Maybe she'd write out something, carry the letter with her, as . . . well, not a safety measure, but for her peace of mind, and for her family's.

Dinner that night was a big pot of homemade soup and jalapeño corn bread. If anyone was aware that things had changed between her and Zeke, they didn't let it show, but then how could anyone know anything? After breakfast, she and Zeke had spent the day apart, doing their normal things. The conversation around the dinner table was normal, too, mostly about work and the weather. Normal felt good. Belonging somewhere felt good.

After dinner, after Zeke had locked and bolted the back door and returned to the kitchen, they walked toward each other without any pretense. She wondered if he had ever pretended to be someone he was not, if he'd ever played the kinds of games men and women played.

He kissed her, and then he said, "I have condoms."

"Good." She let herself fall into his chest, resting her cheek above his heart.

"Are we going to talk about the absence of condoms last night?"

"Not now," she said. "It's . . . not likely to be a problem, timing-wise." She'd make a trip to the clinic one day soon and get herself on the pill, but that would take some time to kick in. And, crap, could she get a prescription under a fake name? Something else to worry about. Maybe they'd have to make do with condoms, until she worked that out. It was very annoying to live off the grid, to have to hide who she was and what she wanted.

Thank goodness she didn't have to hide either from the man who held her. She also didn't feel the need to pretend that she didn't want him again. One day at a time. Each and every one of those days didn't have to be lived on edge and alone.

She looked up, her arms fitting comfortably around Zeke's waist. "Your room or mine?"

Chapter Twenty-three

THE PARKA ZEKE had bought for her kept her warm, even on the coldest of days. Carlin was grateful when the cold—which wasn't going anywhere for the next few months—didn't come with any form of precipitation, whether it was snow, sleet, or ice. It was pretty from a distance, but up close it was just a pain in the ass.

Today's cold weather was dry, and the temps hadn't yet dropped into dangerous subzero territory. Those days were coming, she'd been warned. Spencer had driven her to town and was taking care of business at the hardware store. On the way out of town they'd buy groceries. For now, Carlin sat at the counter in The Pie Hole, drinking coffee and biding her time while Kat finished with the men who'd come in for a late breakfast.

She stared out the window, daydreaming. Spring was probably something to see around here. Summer, too. She'd arrived on the heels of summer, never really seeing it in its full glory. It was tempting, to stick around to see through the year, to stay in Zeke's bed awhile longer, to stay here in this place that already felt too much like home.

She wasn't pregnant, and since that first night she and Zeke had been very careful about using protection. Now and then she worried that the hands might know what

was going on, that they might see that things had changed
between their boss and the cook who lived in the house
with him. But if they suspected, they didn't let it show.
There had been no knowing glances, no nosy questions . . . at least, not while she was around.

Maybe it didn't matter. Maybe no one would care.

The customers paid and left, and Kat planted herself
in front of Carlin, the spotless counter between them.

"How goes it?"

Carlin dragged herself back to reality. "What? Oh.
Fine. Everything's fine."

"How's Zeke treating you?" Kat asked, her eyes narrowing slightly.

"Fine, really, just . . . fine."

"Oh. My. *God*." Kat pursed her lips. "That's four
fines in thirty seconds! How long have you been sleeping
with him?"

Carlin's mouth fell open. She spun around to look behind her, even though she knew—well, was pretty sure—
that there were no customers in the café at the moment.
"I don't know what you're talking about," she said de-
fensively. "That's . . . that's . . ."

"For someone who's on the run, with a false name and
her cash stashed under a mattress, you are a *terrible* liar."
Kat sighed and shook her head. "I can't believe you didn't
tell me immediately. What did I tell you about cowboys
breaking your heart? Wasn't I clear enough?"

Carlin argued silently that Zeke couldn't break her heart
because what they had was strictly physical. Her heart
was not involved. She could and would take what she
wanted—and needed—and then leave without her heart
ever entering the equation. *Uh-huh*. But one thing was for
certain: she'd definitely leave before she brought trouble
to any of the people here. Not for the world would she put
any of them in danger. "It's not like that."

"Honey, it's always like that." Kat propped her elbow

on the counter, put her chin in her hand, and leaned forward. "Of course, if you fall for Zeke you'll stay, and I'd like that just *fine*. If you have to fall for a cowboy, it might as well be him."

Carlin put on her toughest expression; it wasn't easy, because right now she wasn't feeling tough at all. She was feeling mushy and emotional, for all the good it did her. She looked directly into Kat's witchy eyes. "I'm not falling for Zeke, and I can't stay. You know that. And really, how *did* you know? Too many 'fines' in any amount of time does not, in any way, add up to sleeping with your cousin."

Kat shrugged. "I kind of suspected already."

"Why? How?" And more important, did anyone else suspect?

"You two have always had . . . sparks. On the day you met, right here in The Pie Hole . . ."

"That wasn't a spark, that was just my annoyance shining through. He called me a stray."

"You called him worse."

What was worse than a stray? "It's not serious," Carlin said, giving up on the pretense that nothing was going on but clinging to the one that she was still heart-whole. Said heart gave a hard thump in her chest. "It's just . . . a thing. Two unattached adults doing what comes naturally. Nothing more." Except . . . she cleared her throat. "There's a problem."

"Yeah? What kind?"

"A birth control kind." She cleared her throat again. "I can't get a prescription for birth control pills without showing my ID. I'm not sure what kind of databases are out there on drugstores, but the problem is, everyone here knows me as Carly Hunt—"

"Which obviously isn't the name on your ID."

"Right. And I don't want anyone curious enough to search my name online."

Kat sighed. "You do know this'll set off a minor explosion of gossip, with people wondering just who in hell I'm sleeping with."

Grateful that Kat had immediately guessed what was being asked of her, Carlin was still suddenly guilt-stricken.

"I'm sorry. It was a bad idea."

"Don't be ridiculous. I think it'll be kind of fun, because obviously I'm not sleeping with anyone. Hell, I haven't even been *out* with anyone in so long I'm not sure I remember my table manners. As for the other, I think I've become a virgin again. But the guessing game will be hilarious. And it might be good for business, because everyone will come around to see if they can pick up any clues as to who the nonexistent guy is."

"Oh, God, *thank* you."

"You're welcome," Kat said blithely. "I'll have them for you . . . well, I'll have to call the doctor and see when I can get an appointment, given I have to work around the café hours. But I'll call you when I know."

A new customer came in, the bell over the door chiming, and Kat moved away to take care of business. Feeling relieved down to her toes, Carlin slid from the stool, grabbed the purse she'd started carrying since switching from the TEC jacket to the parka, and went in search of Spencer.

Much to her relief, the call came two days later. To give herself an excuse, she ordered some pies from Kat, then had Spencer drive her in the next day to pick them up. There was always an item or two that the ranch needed from the hardware or feed store, so she sent him off and darted into The Pie Hole.

Unfortunately the place wasn't empty even though she'd timed her visit to be after lunch. Sitting at the far end of the counter, Carlin waited anxiously for the last customer in The Pie Hole to pay and leave. Finally!

"Did you get them?" she asked, her voice lowered even though they were alone. She felt as if she were on a covert operation.

Kat raised finely shaped eyebrows. "I'm fine, thank you so much for asking. How about you?"

Carlin sighed. "Sorry. How are you? Has business been good? Made any new and exciting lunch specials lately?"

Kat leaned her elbows on the counter and narrowed her eyes. "No, but I am in the middle of an illicit drug deal that could send me to jail and ruin my good reputation."

She reached beneath the counter and came up with a small, white bag.

It was all Carlin could do not to snatch the bag out of Kat's hand, even though Kat held the bag just out of reach.

"You've turned me into a criminal," Kat said. Then she sighed and passed the bag to Carlin. "But it's not like *I* need them."

Carlin peeked into the top of the bag. Birth control pills! It would be a while before they were effective, but once they were . . . no more annoying condoms. No more interrupting that very hot moment when she couldn't wait to have Zeke inside her to put the blasted things on, no more barrier between her and Zeke when they were together. Damn it, that thought alone was a pretty strong turn-on.

"Thanks," Carlin said as she put the bag in her purse and pulled out the folded bills to pay for the pills. "I just can't get a prescription under a false name."

"I get that, Miss Linoleum," Kat said wryly as she took the offered cash and stuck it in her apron pocket. "What are you going to do if you get sick and need an antibiotic? What if you get the flu?"

"I'll handle that problem if and when it happens,"

Carlin said pragmatically. Goodness knows she had enough real problems to deal with, like falling for Zeke, and trying to figure out how to end the nightmare with Brad. She'd been taking it one day at a time for so long, getting a prescription for birth control pills that would take a couple of weeks to kick in seemed like a long-term commitment.

Kat poured herself a cup of coffee and warmed up Carlin's. "Well, there is one good thing about you taking up with Zeke, even if it is contrary to my very sound advice about cowboys."

"What's that?"

Kat grinned. "It looks to me as if you'll be sticking around for *at least* the next twenty-eight days."

THANKSGIVING HAD NEVER been Zeke's favorite holiday. Usually more than half the hands wanted the day—or four—off to visit with family, which meant more work for those who remained behind. It wasn't their busiest time of the year, so it wasn't like they couldn't spare a few hands for less than a week, but eating massive amounts of food was hardly Zeke's idea of a celebration that required time off. Depending on who was cooking, at the Decker ranch there was either a feast or sandwiches and chips. Even when Libby had been working here, she'd occasionally taken a few days off and flown south to be with her daughter and grandkids. Those had been the sandwich years.

This year was different. Carlin had thrown herself wholeheartedly into preparing a traditional Thanksgiving meal; she'd been at work since long before dawn. Hell, technically she'd started work yesterday, which seemed like way too much work to him. A kitchen seeing action well before dawn wasn't all that unusual on a ranch, but today Carlin was almost giddy, as if turkey and dressing and blackberry cobbler represented something more than just a feast to remember the pilgrims.

He thought about escorting her into this kitchen for the first time, watching the horror on her face as she'd surveyed the damage he'd left behind, telling himself the whole time that she was a temporary solution and nothing more. Boy, how things had changed in the past two months!

Watching her bustle around the house, as excited as a kid, made his heart squeeze. Of course, she still insisted that there was nothing he could do to help her, and was adamant that he not interfere.

Normally he'd just plow ahead and do what he knew was right; he'd make her business his business and end this nightmare once and for all. But if he did, she'd leave. He saw that truth in her eyes every time he broached the subject. She was still clinging to the idea of leaving in the spring, because there was nothing he could do to help and anything he did would just worsen her situation.

Zeke so-the-hell didn't agree. Brad Whatever-his-last-name-was was just a man. He could be stopped; he *should* be stopped. But it was something they'd have to do together, and Carlin wouldn't even discuss the possibilities with him.

If he went behind her back, she'd never forgive him. He shouldn't care about that, given that she kept insisting that she was temporary, that what they had was a nice fling while it lasted. But, damn it, this didn't feel temporary. It felt as if Carlin was *his*.

"You look like you've done this before." He stood in the doorway between the dining room and the kitchen, watching Carlin flit back and forth between a counter covered with bowls and dishes and food, to an oven that had been in use for hours—make that days—to the sink overflowing with dirty dishes. She settled in one spot with a deep bowl and a long-handled wooden spoon. "Does your family always do a big Thanksgiving?"

She didn't pause, but continued to stir the ingredients for something in that oversized bowl. "When I was little, and Mom and Dad were still alive, we did the usual thing. Robin and Kin and I made turkey decorations and put them all over the house, Mom cooked for three days, and the food was pretty much gone in twenty minutes." She glanced over her shoulder and smiled. "My dad always took care of the cleanup. I think that's an excellent idea, by the way. The man of the house *should* chip in to do his share of the work."

"Don't look at me like that. I don't do dishes."

Carlin poured the gooey mixture she'd been working into a huge oblong pan. "Come to think of it, I do remember that." She licked the spoon and smiled. "Oh, I hope this turns out okay! I've never made corn bread dressing before." She opened the oven door and carefully slid the big pan inside.

Carlin had never been one to share much about herself, as if being on the run meant she wasn't entitled to a past, as if it meant she wasn't just hiding from a stalker, she was hiding from everyone. He was intensely interested in this little slice of her life that she was revealing. "When did they die? Your parents. How long have they been gone?"

She didn't answer right away, and he began to wonder if she'd answer at all, though he didn't see anything about the question that would alarm her. Finally she said, "It's been eight years, almost nine. After that the family kind of drifted apart, as if our parents had been the glue that held us together and we didn't know how to be a family without them. Robin had her husband and one baby, at that time, and Kin had a new career, and I . . . I wanted to start a new and exciting life. I wanted to be independent, I wanted to see different things, do different things." She looked at him again. "Stuff happens for a reason. Always. Brad knew I wasn't close to my brother and sister. When he asked about them, I should've realized something was off. But I didn't. I thought he was just making conversation, trying to get to know me. If he thought he could get to me through them, he would. Even though I don't see or talk to Robin or Kin much these days, we're closer than we've been since Mom and Dad died."

Before he could ask another question, Carlin waved the wooden spoon at him as if she meant to smack him with it. "I do *not* want to talk about him today! I refuse to let him spoil this. What about your family? Why aren't they all here for Thanksgiving?" She glanced at him. "Or why aren't you there?"

"My family visits in the summer, when travel isn't so iffy and the kids are out of school. And I don't leave the ranch for an extended time very often. There's too much to do."

She made a scoffing sound in her throat. "You have a perfectly good foreman who can handle things while you're away. You don't have to do everything yourself, you know."

"I've heard that before."

"And yet you don't quite believe that the ranch can survive without you." There was a teasing note in her voice.

"Fine." He walked toward her slowly. "I'll go visit my family for Christmas. I'll fly down and stay with my oldest sister and her crazy-ass family for a full week." It wasn't like she hadn't asked a hundred times. Carlin looked a little surprised, and then he threw in the kicker. "As long as you come with me."

Frowning, she looked down, then tossed the spoon into the sink. "You know very well the answer is no."

"Why? What could go wrong? Don't you think I can

protect you?" It was what he wanted to do more than anything: protect her. Fix all that had gone wrong in her life.

"It's not that." She turned her back to him and started fiddling with bowls and spoons, needlessly straightening her mess.

He wrapped his arms around her, pulled her back against his chest. "Okay, then. You'll meet them in the summer, when they come for a visit."

"You know I won't be here when summer rolls around." She tried to sound cool and matter-of-fact, but didn't quite pull it off.

It was some comfort that she sounded sad about that fact. Instead of arguing with her—which was, he had discovered, a waste of breath—he kissed her on the neck and then let her go. "I'll be back in less than two hours."

She watched him head for the mudroom. "Don't you dare be late! And tell the others they'd better not be late, either. Kat will be here by one, she said. I told her I didn't need any help, goodness knows she spends too much time cooking, but she said she's bringing dessert and rolls anyway. We *will* all be at the table and eating no later than two. Got that?" She sighed. "It's going to be perfect."

The meal, maybe. The day, sure. He'd had plenty of perfect days lately. But her *life* wouldn't be perfect until her fear of Brad was gone, until Brad himself was gone, and he couldn't figure out how to make that happen without breaking his word to her. He knew what he risked if he broke his promise. She might never forgive him, and everything they had would be gone.

But as much as he didn't want to let her go, he had to wonder if it wouldn't be a worthwhile sacrifice if it meant she would finally be free.

*   *   *

CARLIN WAS PLEASED with the meal, but damn, it had been a lot of work! Exactly as she remembered from her home life when she was younger, the food had disappeared quickly. They didn't have a huge bunch of people to celebrate with, but Walt and Spencer were there. Kat, too, and she kept the conversation going. Spencer's family had a big to-do planned for the weekend, and by then Kenneth and Micah would be back at work. Life on a ranch didn't stop for any holiday. The animals had to be taken care of, if nothing else. And as Walt had pointed out, anything that didn't get done today would just have to be done tomorrow.

She tried not to let her lingering horror show, as she accepted compliments on the meal, but when Zeke had mentioned taking her to meet his family, her heart had jumped into her throat and had stayed there for a while.

Maybe she was crazy about him, maybe the sex was stellar, maybe she even sometimes thought she loved him. None of that changed anything. She had to deal with reality, and while her current reality was pretty damn perfect, the bigger reality of Brad loomed out there like a huge storm.

This would be her only Thanksgiving with Zeke. Christmas was coming and it would be her only Christmas with him. She wanted to savor every moment, to make every day between now and then as perfect as it could possibly be. Spring would be here all too soon.

When she stood and reached for Walt's empty plate, Zeke reached over and covered her hand with his. "You sit. We'll get the dishes."

Kat's eyebrows shot up, but she immediately leaned back in her chair and relaxed, smiling.

Carlin's first thought was that the men couldn't possibly do the job of cleanup properly, but then she sat and relaxed. Who cared if they didn't do it the way she would have? Her feet hurt from standing all day, and she was exhausted. Without a word every man at the table had gotten busy gathering dishes and leftovers. This had been planned, and she loved them for it. Even I-don't-do-dishes Zeke had grabbed his dirty plate and taken it out. Presumably Spencer knew how to run the dishwasher, so everything would be taken care of.

Carlin stretched her legs out, watched the men scramble, and said—in a very sweet voice, "Thanks, guys. I think Kat and I will head into the den and plop ourselves down in those nice, fat recliners, and watch some football."

"I love me some football," Kat said, smiling widely, then she made big questioning eyes at Carlin and shrugged her shoulders, from which Carlin gathered that Kat *might*, just might, know the difference between baseball and football.

"We'll be right there," Walt called from the kitchen. "This won't take long."

Carlin laughed at that. She'd used every bowl and utensil in the kitchen, as well as almost every casserole dish and baking pan.

Kat leaned onto the table and lowered her voice. "Oh my God, you have got these men eating out of the palm of your hand. Way to go, girl."

For a moment Carlin listened to the men's voices, to the rattle and clank of dishes, to the occasional laughter.

Thanksgiving wasn't about food, it was about family. And for now, for today, this was hers.

Chapter Twenty-four

ZEKE LEANED HIS shoulder against the frame of the kitchen door, watching Carlin as she folded a mound of towels. "You have any sweatpants, something loose and comfortable?"

She didn't look up. "Yeah, but they're too little for you. You'll have to buy your own."

"Smart ass. Go change. We're going to fight."

"Well, hell, I can do that without changing clothes," she shot back, finally shifting her attention from the towel to him. The towel dropped to the floor. She felt as if her mouth had followed the towel.

Zeke was hot enough in jeans and boots and hat. God save her, despite Kat's opinion and warning, she thought this particular cowboy was testosterone on two feet. Her resistance to him was practically zero as it was. But now he was wearing a pair of ragged sweatpants with a hole in one knee, socks, and a T-shirt that clung to his muscled torso, and she found that this scruffy look was even worse—or better, she couldn't decide which. She just knew she liked it. It was the T-shirt's fault. All too vividly she remembered every ridge of muscle, the crisp dark hair on his chest, the thick muscle padding his shoulders and rippling down his back.

Of course, the way she liked him best was stark naked, covered in nothing except maybe sweat.

The thought almost made her drool.

"Are you going to change, or not?" he asked impatiently, making her wonder how long she'd been staring at him. Probably not long; Zeke's default setting was impatience.

Mentally she shook herself and said, "I'll be right back," picking up the towel and tossing it on top of the dryer, then running for her room.

The days had rapidly grown shorter, which drastically changed Carlin's schedule. Instead of rolling out of bed, swearing beneath her breath, at four-thirty in the morning, she could sleep until the decadent-feeling hour of five-thirty. And instead of serving dinner at nine-thirty, even ten o'clock at night, to men exhausted from fourteen-to sixteen-hour days, she was putting food on the table at five-thirty, had the kitchen cleaned up and the dishwasher running by seven at the very latest, which gave her the opportunity to—gasp!—actually read or watch TV, or take a long soak in the tub, paint her toenails, and other things generally associated with Having a Life.

Cold weather and shorter days brought their own hardships, but generally life on the ranch had slowed considerably, giving everyone, including herself, time to catch a much-needed breath.

The downside was that Zeke was spending much more time in the house. Or maybe that was the upside. She knew what she *should* do, which was avoid him, and she knew what she wanted to do, what she *was* doing, which was falling into bed with him every chance she got.

She got up every morning with her heartbeat racing in anticipation of seeing him, being with him, and spent the rest of the day mentally at war with herself. It was just sex. She couldn't let it be anything more. She had to be on constant guard, not to let it get to her when he was watching her with that intent gaze that said more than he'd ever said with words. She couldn't let the domesticity of living in the same house with him, cooking his meals, and washing his clothes undermine the wall she'd been forced to build around herself. Who would ever have thought of laundry as seduction? And yet the familiarity of it all was exactly that, almost as if they were married, a family, though without the benefits. She had become so enmeshed in the day-to-day fabric of his life, and he in hers, that the ranch had come to feel like home.

She couldn't think of anything, short of a face-to-face confrontation with Brad, that was more dangerous to her safety. Her life might depend on being ready and willing to drop everything and leave at a split second's notice, and because of Zeke, she didn't know if she still had that decisiveness.

She was in trouble—big, big trouble.

She met him in the living room within five minutes, dressed pretty much the same as he was, in a T-shirt, sweatpants, and socks. He'd shoved the living room furniture against the walls to give them as much space as possible.

Zeke was a man who made good on his promises. He'd said he'd teach her how to shoot and fight, and by damn he'd do it. She might never win any marksmanship awards, but she tried to practice with the pistol at least a couple of times a week and she was becoming a fairly decent shot. Knowing how to load and shoot an automatic pistol didn't make her feel like Superwoman, but she did like knowing she had options that she hadn't had before, and perhaps the means of catching Brad by surprise if her nightmare came true and he caught up with her again. Now, it seemed, Zeke was going to teach her how to kick a man's balls into his chest cavity.

And she was going to be practicing on him.

She skidded to a stop, frowning at him.

He caught the look, frowned in return. "What?"

"I'm fond of your balls," she said abruptly.

A wary look came into his eyes. "So am I."

"I don't *love* them, but they're endearing in a cute, wrinkly kind of way. I don't want to hurt them—you."

"Let me give you a tip, buttercup: you don't tell a man his balls are *cute*."

"You're tough enough to take it. I'd be lying if I said they were pretty."

"That's good. Balls are supposed to be manly, not pretty."

"*Manly,*" she scoffed. "That's safe to say. After all, how many women have them? Barring hermaphrodites, of course, but that's a special category."

He paused, then said in a slightly baffled tone, "Why are we having this conversation?"

"You're going to teach me how to kick a man's balls up into his chest cavity, right?"

For a split second he seemed dumbfounded, then he began laughing. Zeke wasn't a man who laughed a lot, and the sound pleased her more than she liked. She was losing her own internal fight not to love him, had maybe lost it weeks ago and just hadn't admitted it to herself yet. Was this the same as admitting it? She didn't know, and didn't want to think about it. Later, maybe, she'd deal with the fact that hearing him laugh made her feel . . . *tender*. Then again—maybe not.

To cover that disturbing softness, she said, "I don't see what's so funny."

"You can't see the bloodthirsty look on your own face. And just because I'm going to teach you the basic technique doesn't mean I'll actually let you *do* it."

"I figured I'd line up like a field-goal kicker and pretend I was kicking your balls over the goal post."

His mouth quirked again, and he reached out to give a strand of her hair a little tug. "That'd work only if your target just stood there. He'd have to either be unconscious beforehand, or you took him by surprise from behind. What are the odds you'd be in either of those scenarios? And would that be the best action even if you were?"

He was using a generic "him," but they both knew he meant Brad. She started to say she'd take any chance she had to kick Brad in the balls, then paused, thinking it over. Was that what Zeke wanted her to do, to think . . . what was the word . . . *tactically*? Mentally put herself in those possible situations and figure out what would be the smartest thing to do?

She'd been on the defensive for so long, she longed to be the one in control of the situation. The danger was that she let that longing pull her into something she couldn't handle. So . . . if somehow she'd knocked Brad out, what should she do then? Kicking him in the balls would be satisfying, but it wouldn't be the smartest thing to do. What if he recovered faster than anticipated? What if he was only faking it, to lure her within arm's reach so he could grab her?

"I could run while I had the chance," she said, working through the possibilities. "Or I could kill him."

The bottom dropped out of her stomach when she said those words, and she stared at him in dismay. For months she'd gone over and over nightmare scenarios, imagining what would happen if Brad found her again, wondering if he'd simply kill her as he had Jina, or if he'd kidnap her and take her to some isolated spot where he'd rape, torture, and *then* kill her. Of the two horrible choices, she'd much prefer being killed outright, but if Brad was in control there was no telling what he'd do. She couldn't assume he'd simply go for the kill because that was what he'd done to Jina. He'd had time to think since then, to plan, to get more and more angry. He might want to work that anger out on her.

And yet—she didn't think she had it in her to shoot an

unconscious man. From behind, maybe, depending on the circumstances, but she couldn't come up with a situation that would fit. If she were free to move around, and had a weapon, why would Brad turn his back on her? If he didn't know she was there and she came up behind him . . . but if he didn't know she was there, then all she had to do was simply leave, sneak away. She wanted Brad to pay for what he'd done to Jina, but she wanted the *law* to work and put him away for the rest of his life. She didn't see herself as an executioner, and that was what Zeke wanted her to work through. If she couldn't do something, then she shouldn't waste time planning how she would do it; she should move on to what she *could* do.

"I couldn't shoot him from behind or if he was unconscious," she said slowly, still feeling her way through her own thoughts. "Maybe I'm stupid, or weak, but I just couldn't. I'm not saying I couldn't shoot him if I had to, just that I couldn't do it under those circumstances."

Zeke didn't argue with her, just nodded. "Knowing your own limits doesn't make you stupid or weak, it makes you smart. He's a cop, which means he's done strength training, he had to pass firearms testing, and he's been trained to fight. You aren't going to get the better of him in a straight-up fight. But forget about him specifically; let's work on some basic stuff so you won't panic if you're caught by surprise."

Not panicking was a good start, as far as she was concerned. When Zeke had startled her that day in the bedroom, she'd been so frightened she'd actually disconnected from herself, and that hadn't been a good feeling at all. If that had been Brad instead of Zeke, the ending would have been bad, because she'd been totally ineffective. Anything Zeke could teach her, no matter how small, could be enormously important.

"Have you had any training?" she asked as she hitched her sweatpants up on her hips. They were a little loose in the waist because they were old and the elastic was weak, and they kept sliding down.

"You mean martial arts, stuff like that?" He shrugged. "No. I was a hell-raiser when I was a kid and got into a lot of fights, plus my dad taught me some things. And when we graduated from high school, one of my cousins went into law enforcement, so of course he had to show me all the stuff he learned. The main thing is to forget about fighting by the rules. You can't hesitate. If you get cornered, you have to fight hard, and you have to fight dirty."

"So show me how to fight dirty." Her initial eagerness had faded, to be replaced by determination.

So, for almost two hours, he did. The first thing he got out of the way was how to kick a man in the balls—not with her foot, and not at a distance. Instead she was supposed to grab the guy by the shirt and haul him in close, which was usually the last thing the guy was expecting and knocked him off balance, then *hold him there* while she repeatedly hammered his crotch with her knee. She was careful not to actually hammer him, and he was extra careful not to get hammered, but she got the idea. Grabbing a guy instead of trying to get away was a twist she hadn't expected, so she could see how the move would work.

He taught her how to gouge an eye (thumb) and hit the larynx (knuckles or the edge of her hand). The thought of gouging someone in the eye grossed her out, until she imagined it was Brad's eye, and that took care of any squeamishness. Zeke didn't think she'd be able to crush anyone's larynx except by accident, but she could still make her target choke, which would let her get away.

He also taught her that her legs were her strongest muscles, and how to use them if she got knocked down, how to lie on her side and kick for the knees and groin. The whole idea of everything he showed her was to disable

her attacker enough to let her get away. She wasn't strong
enough or expert enough to take on anyone in a physical
fight and expect to win, so simply running was the best
outcome for her.

There were a few holds he showed her how to break,
and if someone caught her from behind how to bend
down, grab the guy's ankle, and jerk upward so the attacker landed on his ass. The physical exercise was more
demanding than she'd expected, and soon they were both
sweating. At first she paid rapt attention through the dem-
onstrations and practice repetitions, but the physical reality of such tutoring was a lot of touching, of feeling Zeke's
arms around her in his mock attacks, and the hard, muscled length of his body against her. The soft fabric of his
pants didn't do anything to hide the thickening erection
that pushed against her bottom, or her crotch, depending
on the position of the move he was showing her.

Concentrating became harder and harder, right along
with his penis, and finally she stopped even trying. Leaning back against him, she gripped his thick wrists and
closed her eyes. "I think I've lost my motivation."

"Is that so?" His tone was low and rough. His arms
tightened around her, pulling her more snugly against
him, and one big hand slid under the edge of her T-shirt
to flatten on the smooth flesh of her stomach. He rested
it there a moment, rubbing his fingertips lightly on her
skin, then slicked his hand downward, sliding it under
her loose waistband. His thumb circled her navel, then
with two deliberate moves he had her pants sliding down
her legs to pool around her knees. "Looks like your motivation isn't all you're losing."

He bent his head and his mouth moved slow and hot
over the side of her neck, and just like that she was ready
for him, her heartbeat thundering, her breath panting
out fast and deep. She lifted one arm and curved it back,
resting her hand on the back of his neck, feeling the heat

pouring off his body, the hard pads of muscle even there. Her posture offered up her breasts and he took them, covering them with his rough palms, catching her upright nipples between his fingers and gently, at first, pulling them even tighter. Then his fingers tightened and the pulling wasn't quite so gentle, and she didn't care. Hot prickles of sensation speared from her nipples straight to her vagina, to her entire body. Every muscle in her tightened, clamping down, and she gave a hoarse cry at her emptiness.

Either her cry was a signal or he'd zoomed from zero to a hundred the same way she had. Swiftly he turned her, clamped his hands on her waist, and boosted her over his shoulder. Dizzily she clung to him as he took the stairs up to his bedroom and deposited her on the bed. He stripped her pants and underwear the rest of the way off, tugged her shirt over her head and tossed it aside. While he was doing that she was fighting his clothes, trying to get his shirt up and off, his pants down and off, or at least enough that she could get her hands on him.

He didn't give her a chance, sliding between her legs and reaching down between them to guide his penis into place at her opening. Carlin took a deep breath and stilled, her eyes almost shut, holding herself ready for that hot, penetrating slide of flesh into her. It came, not slow as he sometimes did, but deep and a little rough. There it was, the magic of feeling him enter her, the stretching of her body around him, the heat and clinging and something else, something *more*, something exciting and precious and terrifying.

And afterward, when she was limp from coming, when every muscle was shaking with fatigue and all she wanted to do was curl up in his arms and not move again until she had to get up and cook breakfast, she had to force herself to crawl out of his arms, out of the warm, tangled covers, and search for her clothes.

"Sleep here tonight," he said, the iron in his tone telling her he didn't like it one bit that she refused to spend the night with him, and that he wasn't getting resigned to sleeping alone.

"No, I can't," she said, though she could have cried from the depth of her longing to do just what he wanted. "It's too dangerous." Then she hurried out of the room before she began crying, and he realized she wasn't talking about the danger of some of the hands maybe seeing them together. She'd checked that the doors were locked so that wasn't going to happen. The real danger was to herself, and she was way, way too late to stop it.

THE DAYS TICKED past. All in all, Carlin felt ridiculously content. She was happy to stay indoors when it was so cold simply breathing was dangerous. Chili was simmering in the slow cooker, and the hot ham and cheese sandwiches that would accompany it wouldn't take any time at all to throw together. She'd thought about trying a recipe for chocolate cobbler, but decided to stick with something she knew would be a success: cookies. Zeke was a sucker for homemade chocolate chip cookies.

And she was a sucker for him. Now and then she tried to talk herself out of getting too deeply involved, but it was much too late for that. She was crazy about him. The sex was great, but there was more. That human connection she'd been searching for, and had found, tied her to him in a way she hadn't expected.

And it was . . . nice.

Carlin heard the crackle of the radio from Zeke's office, where he'd been at work for a couple of hours. She couldn't tell what was being said, but it could be anything: cows being moved, a fence down, a truck or some other kind of equipment broken down. She'd even heard the question "What's for supper?" crackling over that two-way radio a time or twelve.

Minutes later, Zeke all but ran though the kitchen, a rifle in his hand. She'd never seen him armed, beyond their shooting lessons, and immediately her heart jumped into her throat and stayed there.

She followed him into the mudroom. "What's wrong?"

He handed her the rifle, and she held it as he pulled on boots. "Wolves." He continued to prepare himself to leave, with a heavy coat, hat, and gloves.

Carlin swallowed before repeating his single, alarming word. "Wolves? Shouldn't you stay inside if there are *wolves* out there?"

He smiled at her, leaned down, and planted a quick and familiar kiss on her mouth. "City girl," he said.

"Insane man!" she countered as he took the rifle from her. "Who goes out looking for wolves?"

"They killed a cow. We have to take care of this now." He glanced over his shoulder as he headed out the door. "Lock it behind me. Spencer and Walt are going with me, and there's no reason for anyone else to head this way before it's time for supper."

After he was gone, she flipped the deadbolt with a vengeance, and pursed her mouth as she watched Zeke cross the space between the house and the bunkhouse in long, easy strides. Weren't there wolf exterminators in this part of the country? Why did Zeke have to be the one riding out looking for hairy, fanged predators? Walt could do it, or Spencer . . . no, Spencer would probably want to adopt any furry animals he ran across, even if they threatened to eat him alive. She stood there for a few minutes, worried about all three of them, before she returned to the kitchen. Zeke did it because he was the boss, because it was his land and his responsibility, and he took care of what was his.

Carlin wondered if they'd take an all-terrain vehicle or horses. She wondered what would happen if one of the men got thrown, if a wolf might spook one of the horses and cause an accident. In her mind she could see Zeke going toe to toe . . . well, toe to paw . . . with a wolf. In her mind, a series of things went wrong. The rifle didn't fire, the wolf leaped, claws and fangs flashing, and Zeke ended up on the ground, bloody and torn. What if there was more than one wolf that attacked? What if Spencer and Walt weren't fast enough to save him?

Oh, shit. She needed to get one of the guns and go help, just to guard him.

Except they were already gone.

She finally sat at the kitchen table and forced herself to stop acting nuts. Zeke was perfectly capable, more capable than any man she'd ever known. His rifle was going to work just fine. He'd probably done this a hundred times . . . she just hadn't been here to wait and worry.

While she was waiting she might as well do something, so she made two batches of cookies: the chocolate chip Zeke liked and oatmeal-raisin because that was what she preferred. Sitting was impossible, and cooking kept her hands and her mind busy . . . most of the time. Possible disastrous scenarios ran through her mind, though she did try to keep her mind on what she was doing and not on what they might or might not be doing.

It had been a very long time since she'd had anyone in her life to worry about on a daily basis.

Finally she heard them drive up, and a little while later she heard his footsteps. Before he could unlock the door she was there, opening the door, checking out the little bit of exposed skin she could see for scratches, scrapes, blood. He looked fine. More than fine, he looked great— and annoyed.

"Didn't find 'em, huh?" she said, being very careful not to give too much of herself away. It wouldn't do for

Zeke to know that she'd been half-wild with worry for him.

"No." He handed her the rifle and began to peel off his outerwear. "We'll head back out early tomorrow. We have a good idea of where they'll be, we just ran out of daylight."

Great. She'd worry all over again! Not that she could let him see her concern. Their relationship was supposed to be employee to employer . . . and sex. No worrying, no taking on each other's problems.

If she took on his, then he'd probably feel obligated to take hers on, as well.

She walked into the kitchen, still holding the rifle. Instead of handing the weapon back to Zeke she propped it in the corner—carefully—then turned to face him. Her arms snaked around his neck. His arms went around her.

"I missed you," she whispered.

His eyebrows raised slightly. "We weren't gone all that long."

Long enough. Too long. "I made cookies."

He smiled. "I smell 'em. Maybe you should miss me more often."

He lifted her; she wrapped her legs around his waist.

"The guys will be in soon for supper," Zeke said, nuzzling her neck and sounding almost angry at the timing.

"This is true." She kissed him on the side of the neck.

"Maybe I should just deadbolt the door and let them fend for themselves. One night won't hurt 'em. I think there's some tuna in the bunkhouse pantry. Crackers, too. Now, there's a balanced meal."

Zeke's suggestion was tempting, even if he was kidding. At least, she thought he was kidding.

"You get a quick shower," Carlin said as he reluctantly placed her on her feet. "We'll get everyone fed and out the door in no time."

And once they were alone again they wouldn't talk about wolves or Brad or the rapidly approaching spring.

MAYBE BECAUSE THEY spent a few energetic hours before Carlin slipped out of his bed to go back to her own room—and, damn it, he wished to hell she'd quit doing that—the next morning didn't start quite as it normally did.

Zeke knew something was wrong before he reached the kitchen. The lights weren't on, there was no scent of freshly brewed coffee to draw him in that direction, and all was quiet. Well, shit.

Either Carlin had overslept or she'd bolted in the night. He didn't think she'd leave, not now, or at least not without saying something. But . . . damn, what if she had? He'd been so tired last night after she'd gone to her own bedroom that he'd slept like a dead man until the alarm went off.

No, he wouldn't let himself think that. For one thing, since the accident she'd been extremely leery—and with good reason—about driving on icy roads. If there was any moisture on the roads, they froze over every night. If she were going to leave, she'd do it at high noon, after the ice had melted on the roads.

He headed down the hallway to her rooms. Her door was closed, which wasn't a surprise. He knocked, called out. "Carlin!" No response.

Hell, *had* she left in the middle of the night, despite the ice? His own blood felt like ice as he tried the doorknob. Locked. That wasn't a surprise, given her fondness for deadbolts. Relief flooded through him, because unless she'd gone out the window, that meant she was in there.

He pounded on the door and called her name, louder this time. He finally heard her on the other side of the door, and started grinning. Not that he could make out every word, but there were several "Oh, shits," followed by a slightly frantic, "Coming!"

The door opened, and Carlin darted past him, a rumpled, wild-haired frenzy in a blue bathrobe.

"I overslept!" she yelped without looking back. "Oh, shit! Shit, shit, shit!"

He followed her at a slower pace, relieved that she was still here, strangely attracted by her fresh-out-of-bed messiness. He stood in the kitchen doorway and watched her blast around like a crazed hummingbird—a very sexy hummingbird, with sleep-flushed cheeks, blond hair falling this way and that, and those pajamas clinging to her ass and boobs as she moved around. Her robe didn't do much to conceal, well, anything. The hem flipped and danced as she got to work.

No woman in this particular state should make him hard, but Carlin did. She wasn't just rumpled, she was flustered, and still amazingly efficient. In less than a minute she had the coffeepot going and a carton of eggs out of the fridge. There wasn't much time before the hands would start showing up for breakfast. It wouldn't be a day for pancakes or omelets. He suspected this would be a scrambled egg day. She'd fix something else, too, because she knew they all needed plenty of calories, especially in this cold, but she didn't have a lot of time.

She glanced over her shoulder. "I'm so sorry," she said. "I must've turned off the alarm in my sleep. I never do that! Well, I guess I do. *Normally* I never do that. Coffee will be ready in a minute."

In an easy and practiced motion, Carlin reached into the freezer and came out with a bag of frozen biscuits. She turned on the oven, grabbed a cookie sheet out of a cabinet, and in the same smooth move she opened the fridge and grabbed a package of ham.

God, forget the biscuits, he thought. He wanted to eat *her*. Fresh from the bed, heavy-lidded and mussed and sexy as hell . . . he wanted to take that bathrobe off of her, kiss her neck, then peel off those pajamas and fuck her on the kitchen table. And if he didn't get his mind off that picture right now, the men would know as soon as they came into the kitchen because he'd have a hard-on that would tear out his zipper.

When the first knock sounded at the door, Carlin cinched the sash of her bathrobe tight and ran a hand through her hair. It didn't help much.

He went to unlock the door. "Guess who overslept," he said as the men tromped in. There was no doubt who the someone was, given he was showered and shaved and dressed, and she looked as if she'd been chased around the kitchen by the Hounds of the Baskervilles. But she had scrambled eggs, ham, and biscuits on the table in record time, and they all laughed when she heaved a big "Whoo!" as she set the plates down.

"I feel as if I've run a marathon," she announced. "I need coffee. If any of you somehow break every bone in your body and need me to spoon-feed you, yell out, but otherwise I'm going to sit in the kitchen and suck down some caffeine."

"Just don't go to sleep again," Walt said, grinning.

"Hah. As if I could."

Zeke watched her go. She didn't know she was gorgeous, didn't realize how tempting she was. If she checked, she'd definitely see how tempting she was to him. Thank God he was sitting down now, because no way could he hide his physical reaction to her. And, damn, did she have to use the word "suck"? He could barely focus on eating.

When Walt—the last to finish—left by way of the mudroom, Zeke followed him to the door, told his foreman he had a little paperwork to take care of, and once Walt was out of earshot, locked the door.

He returned to the kitchen and—again—just watched Carlin as she piled dirty dishes in the sink. When she saw him, she smiled. "What a way to start the morning! My heart is still pounding. Now that it's over, I think I'll have some more coffee before I—" She registered his expression and stopped in mid-sentence. Her smile changed, her eyes growing heavy-lidded. "I'm not going to get that cup of coffee just yet, am I?"

Zeke shook his head and walked toward her.

She tried to argue with him. "I need a shower, and some makeup, and a hairbrush . . ."

"You don't need a thing. Except maybe me." He kissed her neck, her mouth, and while he kissed he untied the bathrobe sash and slipped his hands inside the robe. She was warm and soft, yielding and . . . his.

She sighed as he kissed her neck, reached between them to put her hand over his erection. "Who knew that frazzled and unkempt was such a turn-on for you?" she murmured.

He slid his hand inside the waistband of her pajama bottoms and pushed them down.

"Zeke!" She ruined the protest with a laugh. She was already breathing hard, her nipples peaking under the thin cotton of her pajama top.

He stopped both the protest and the laugh with a hand between her legs. He found her soft opening and pushed, slipping a finger inside her, then another. She was wet and hot, ready for him, clinging to him and gasping.

"Here?" she whispered, and to answer her own question she unfastened and unzipped his jeans and pushed them down.

He lifted her and she kicked her pajama bottoms aside, wrapped her legs around his waist. He turned and pinned her to the nearest wall, held her while she guided his penis into her hot body, slick and tight and as ready for him as he was for her. She rode him, slow at first, eyes closed and head back as if she savored every stroke. Heart pounding, he gripped her ass and moved her faster, up and down, going into her deeper and harder.

She climaxed, a cry tearing out of her throat, and her hot inner muscles clamped down on him like a soft fist, milked him as he came with her, fast and hard, and damn, at that moment life was good.

Life was good because he had Carlin in his kitchen, most nights in his bed, and right now wrapped around his body. And, shit, he hadn't even made it as far as the kitchen table.

Chapter Twenty-five

"LIBBY'S COMING TO visit," Zeke announced one morning in January. "I just got off the phone with her."

Carlin kept her expression calm, but panic squeezed her stomach. Libby! The famous, perfect Libby—here. In what was now Carlin's domain. She couldn't have been more terrified if the ranch were being invaded by the Huns.

"That's nice," she managed to say. "When?"

"Next week. I'll pick her up at the bus stop in town."

Men. "Exactly when, next week? Monday? Thursday? I need to plan the meals, so I'll have to time the grocery shopping." That sounded reasonable, didn't it? "And how long is she staying?"

"A week, tops," he replied, answering her second question first. "And she'll be here on Tuesday."

Today was Thursday. She had five days to prepare. Suddenly, five *weeks* didn't sound like enough time for all she had to do. The place had to be perfectly clean—good luck with that, considering she had to deal with Zeke the Laundry-Making Monster—and, please God, don't let her burn anything when she was cooking!

The days passed in a frenzy of preparations. She went over menus, new dishes, and finally rejected everything new because now was certainly not the time to be experimenting! She was as nervous about meeting Libby as she would've been if she was meeting Zeke's family. He'd said his mom and sisters and their families usually came for a visit in the summer, so she didn't worry about them; she'd be gone by then, and because she wouldn't be around for much longer she really shouldn't be worried about meeting Libby. What did it matter if Libby liked her or not?

Because it mattered to Zeke, that was what.

Because it mattered to him, it mattered to her. Never mind that if she stuck with her plan, she'd be gone in two months.

"If?" When had it become "if"?

She had to stop thinking that way. She still didn't know where she'd go, but it didn't really matter, did it? What mattered was that whenever she tried to think about her next step, she faltered. She didn't want to leave—not in the spring, not ever.

Falling in love with Zeke hadn't been part of the plan. Some nights she had to bite her lip to keep from saying the words.

The winter had gone by too fast. She tried to hold on to the good times, had tried to make Christmas and even New Year's Eve as special as possible so she—and maybe even Zeke—would have something to remember when days were not so bright. They'd laughed together, they'd spent hours making love in his big warm bed upstairs, they'd spent other hours snuggled in front of the fireplace just enjoying each other's company. The men felt like family. This felt like home.

Now it was January, the weather was as ungodly cold as they'd warned her it would be, and spring was too damn close.

When she'd given herself a deadline for leaving, she hadn't specified *late* spring or *early* spring, and from all she'd heard could she really leave Zeke in the middle of the very busy calving season? He'd need her then, even if he did work from before dawn until well after dark and she didn't get to see him nearly as often as she'd like. She was talking herself into staying, and that scared the hell out of her because she didn't have to put a whole lot of effort into it.

But now Libby was coming to visit, and Carlin was beginning to wish she'd left yesterday, spring or no spring.

Tuesday came way too fast. Zeke went into town to meet Libby's bus. Carlin stayed behind to prepare a big dinner: roast and potatoes, green bean casserole, corn pudding, soft rolls, and white cake for dessert. With the crew down to winter level and the married men eating their evening meals at their own homes, she'd been cooking for a smaller crowd lately. There were usually seven for breakfast and lunch instead of ten, since Patrick had returned earlier than expected, but it would be eight while Libby was visiting. Dinner would now be for six, instead of five. It was amazing what a difference the absence of three men made when it came to cooking and grocery shopping!

With the cake finished and everything else in the slow cooker or the oven, Carlin ran back to her rooms— Libby's old rooms—to freshen up a bit. She could say all she wanted that she didn't care what Libby thought of her, but the woman was important to Zeke, so like it or not she *did* care. She brushed her hair, put on a touch of pale lipstick, and changed into a blouse that didn't have a single food stain on it. She almost always wore an apron when she cooked, but she was a messy cook and no apron covered everything.

What she really needed was a smock, like the ones chefs wore on the cooking channels she'd been watching since coming here. Since she'd learned to cook maybe her next job would be in the kitchen, too. At least she'd expanded her capabilities.

Her next job. It was a concept so vague she couldn't hold it in her head for more than a few seconds.

She was back in the kitchen when she heard the key in the lock, followed by a bewildered female voice saying, "Why on earth have you started locking the door in the middle of the day?"

They'd decided not to tell Libby any details about Carlin's situation. Only Zeke and Kat knew the truth, and it was better that way.

She couldn't hear Zeke's explanation, which was delivered in a lowered voice that didn't carry from the mudroom.

Libby walked into the kitchen, took a long, deep breath, smiled at Carlin and said, "Something smells good."

The perfect Libby was short, plump, had dyed dark brown hair, and a wide beaming smile that didn't disguise the shrewdness of her gaze. She might be smiling, but she was reserving judgment.

Zeke was right behind her, two suitcases—one large, one small—in his hands. "Libby, this is Carly Hunt."

Libby's smile remained firmly in place, just as her assessing look didn't change at all. "Glad to meet you. Zeke told me all about you," she said, leaving Carlin to wonder whether Libby thought what she'd heard was good or bad. "Of course, I've heard a lot about you already, from some of my old friends around here."

Oh, no. That couldn't be good! Could it? What had she heard, and from whom had she heard it? She and Zeke had tried so hard not to let anyone realize that their relationship had changed. Kat had seen it, but she didn't think anyone else was the wiser. She instinctively didn't like that people in Battle Ridge had been talking about her, though thank God she'd covered for herself by not using her real name. Everything should be okay.

Zeke carried the bags through the dining room. "Libby, I'm going to put your bags in my old bedroom, if that suits you." His old bedroom was on the first floor.

"That's perfect," she answered. "I can still handle the stairs, but my knees don't like it much these days."

"If you want your old rooms while you're visiting, I can take the other bedroom," Carlin offered. She didn't have that many clothes or toiletries to move. It would be a pain, but she was willing.

"That's okay, I'm fine with Zeke's old room," Libby replied. "I'll just be here for a week, or two. No need to run you out of your quarters."

Or two? What the hell? Zeke had said Libby would be here a week, tops. "There are fresh sheets on the bed in Zeke's old room," Carlin said.

Libby's smile said that she certainly hoped so, that anything else was unacceptably sloppy. Carlin felt put in her place, even though Libby hadn't said a word of criticism. Dang, that was an art she needed to cultivate, herself.

"Fresh towels, soap, and shampoo, are in the downstairs bath. Is there anything else you need?"

"No." Libby's gaze moved to Carlin's hair, and the line between her brows deepened as she squinted. She pursed her lips. "I've been thinking about going blond," she said, changing the subject without warning. "This brown is way too dark, but I'm not ready to go back to red yet. I love the color of your hair. What shade do you use?"

"Uh, this is my natural color," Carlin said as Libby leaned closer.

"Really. Hmm. I change my hair color a lot. I get bored with seeing the same thing every time I look in a mirror— not that changing color takes any of the weight off my butt," Libby said, and laughed. "But I've gone back and forth between brown and red so many times I'm tired of it."

Okay, that laugh had been genuine. Carlin relaxed a

little. Maybe this wouldn't be too bad. "Dinner will be ready in twenty minutes. If you'd like to settle in before we eat . . ."

"No, I'm fine." Libby walked around the big kitchen, peeking in the slow cooker, turning on the light in the oven and peering inside. She even checked out the silverware drawer, and the junk drawer where Zeke threw odds and ends. Carlin kept expecting the woman to pull out a white glove and check the top of the fridge.

"I spent years in this kitchen," she said softly, more to herself than to Carlin. "It's mostly the same way it was, but it's different, too. It isn't mine, now."

Zeke returned to the kitchen. Hands now empty, he crossed his arms and leaned against the doorjamb between the kitchen and the dining room. And he smiled. He did that a lot, these days. He smiled at *her*.

And she'd wondered if anyone else knew about them. If they saw him looking at her this way they'd most definitely know something was going on.

But for right now, he was smiling at the both of them.

LIBBY SAT AT the dining room table and watched the men around her. Being here was both familiar and strange, because she knew these men almost as well as she knew herself. They had been in her care for years—well, except for Spencer, who wasn't that long from his mother's care. Once the round of enthusiastic greetings and hugs had subsided, the hands she'd fed for so long settled down to eat what was, she admitted, a tasty and healthy meal. She'd always had such a hard time getting the men to eat vegetables, but they dug into what was served, even the green beans.

She'd heard through the Battle Ridge grapevine that Zeke had been getting chummy with the new cook and housekeeper. It wasn't like she hadn't been meaning to visit, anyway, but the news had spurred her on. What if Carly Hunt was a gold digger, out to take Zeke for all he was worth? What if she was using him?

Her brain said that Zeke Decker could take care of himself, that he was too sharp to let himself be fooled by a pretty face again after his experience with his ex-wife, but the fact was Zeke was a man, and more than one smart man had been blinded by sex. So despite what her brain had told her, her heart had insisted she check out this new housekeeper.

Right now, Libby was reserving judgment. You couldn't see the truth of someone right off the bat, but so far she hadn't seen anything bad. Carly had done more work in the past hour than Libby had seen Rachel do in the months she'd been here, but her work ethic could be a part of a scam. She might be trying to make herself appear to be the perfect candidate for ranch wife, and then as soon as the ring was on her finger she'd change her tune.

Of course, exactly what would she gain? Zeke's lifestyle was far from extravagant. There was money in a ranch this size, if it was properly managed, which Zeke's was. But how would Carly necessarily know this? Unless she had experience with ranches, which from what everyone said she definitely didn't, she'd think Zeke was getting by. And even then—a con would mean grab the money and run, not sign on for what Libby knew was months of a lot of hard work.

The hands at the table all seemed to like Carly, and the way Zeke looked at her—well, all she could say was, Libby genuinely hoped Carly Hunt wasn't a scam artist, wasn't a gold digger. If she was genuine, if she truly cared about him the way he obviously cared about her, then she was just what the doctor ordered.

Carly left the table to fetch dessert, and returned with a tall white layer cake with fluffy white icing. Libby eyed it with hidden misgiving. What was Carly thinking? After all this time, didn't she know these men preferred chocolate, in any form, any day of the week? Were they just being polite when they acted as if they couldn't wait for a slice of that cake?

Carly placed the cake before Zeke, who started to cut it while she returned to the kitchen for decaf. Walt said something about the "Never Fail White Cake" and Patrick laughed.

Dear God, was that *the* Never Fail White Cake? Libby's eyed widened. "Oh my God!" she blurted, then clapped a hand over her mouth. She'd tried the recipe once—*once*—but thank God she'd been smart enough to do a taste test before serving it. Okay, it had simply looked good, she'd been hungry, so she'd cut herself a slice to tide her over until dinner. The cake had been like rubber and she'd tossed it in the garbage before anyone had seen. She'd never tried that recipe again. Maybe she should've scribbled a warning note in the margins of that page.

Carly paused, alarm on her face. "What?"

There was nothing to do now but explain. "I tried that recipe once. The cake was like *rubber*! It was awful. I threw the cake in the garbage and never mentioned it to anyone."

Everyone burst out laughing. Carly's mouth fell open in astonishment. "That's exactly what it was like the first time I made it!"

"You mean you *kept* making it?"

"I'd never made a cake before, so I thought it was something I'd done wrong. All of my cooking is an experiment in progress." Carly shrugged. "I just keep at it until I come up with something that's edible."

The men were grinning. Plates laden with large slices of cake were passed around the table. Libby accepted a plate, staring at the thick, fluffy white cake. She waited until she had a cup of coffee sitting in front of her before she took a bite of the cake, because she wanted something handy to wash it down, if needed. She took a small bite.

Everyone was openly watching her. The cake melted in her mouth. Her eyes rounded. "Holy crap, this is good," she blurted. "You have to show me what you did."

She took a bigger bite of the cake, and looked up just as Carly and Zeke shared a quick glance that was obviously not meant to be observed. Zeke's gaze was warm, and Carly's was . . . did she know she got that soft look in her eyes when she looked at him?

Okay, maybe she was genuine. Maybe she truly cared about Zeke. Libby wasn't completely convinced, but she had to take into account that the men here weren't fools, and they all seemed to really like the girl, and she appeared to like them as well. Maybe Zeke Decker had once again somehow twisted and mauled circumstances until they gave him exactly what he wanted.

Chapter Twenty-six

IT WAS TIME. It was past time. Zeke had held off on taking this step for weeks, even though he knew he didn't have any choice. If he kept his promise to Carlin, if he didn't try to help her, she'd move on in a few weeks and be no better off than she'd been when she'd arrived in Battle Ridge. If he could convince her to stay it would be a different matter. He'd do everything he could to protect her, but damn it all to hell and back, he couldn't protect her if she wasn't fucking *here*.

If he could help her she'd hate him—but she'd be safe, and that was the most important thing.

A second trip to town in as many days was unusual, but he didn't want Carlin or Libby or anyone else on his heels when he walked into the sheriff's auxiliary office, a sterile, boxy, newish building not far from the grocery store. He was in luck. Billy Nelson was working the Battle Ridge office today. He and Billy had gone to school together, and the deputy could be trusted to keep his word—and to keep his mouth shut, if that was asked of him.

Zeke asked for privacy, and they went into a small room and closed the door. If the receptionist at the front desk thought it was strange, she didn't let it show. She had her hands full with paperwork of some sort, files and folders and an ancient-looking computer.

He and Billy sat in matching uncomfortable chairs, and after asking for discretion—which Billy promised—Zeke told everything he knew about Carlin's past: Brad, Jina, Dallas, a nameless small town on the outskirts of Houston. He mentioned that Brad was a hacker as well as a cop, and apparently a very talented one, and asked Billy to keep any inquiries to the telephone or snail mail.

Zeke hadn't been sure what kind of reception he'd get, but Billy took the news seriously enough.

"I'll be hampered by not using the computer, but I'll see what I can do. Until then . . ." Billy reached into his pocket and pulled out a business card. "I have a cousin in Cheyenne who's a private investigator. Maybe he'll be able to do things I can't."

"Such as?" Zeke asked as he watched Billy scrawl a name and phone number on the back of his own card.

"There's not a lot I can do if you don't file a report, and a report will have to be official. If this guy is a cop, and a hacker to boot, I don't see how we could keep it a secret from him. Battle Ridge is a small town. He wouldn't have any trouble finding Carly. I'd be surprised if there are three people on main street who wouldn't recognize her picture."

Zeke took the card, wondering if he was doing the right thing, knowing that he had to do something. He'd call the PI from his cell. Even if Brad somehow found out that a private investigator in Cheyenne was looking into him—and Carlin—investigations originating in the larger city wouldn't lead him straight to the Decker Ranch. Zeke decided, before he called, to warn the PI and also to make sure there was no personal information stored on that end that might lead Brad to Battle Ridge.

He hated to lie to Carlin, hated it more than he'd

thought he would, but he knew if he told her what he'd done she'd be gone by morning. She'd saved plenty of money in her time working for him and Kat, so she had the means to just pick up and go.

Because he didn't want her to go, he'd keep his latest actions a secret, for now. With any luck, he'd find out that Brad was dead or in jail, no longer a danger to Carlin or anyone else. But until he got lucky, he'd have to lie to her—lying by omission, but still, she'd consider it a lie and so would he, if the tables were turned.

His promise, though, had come with a qualifier: *for now*. That time had passed and he knew in his gut that he couldn't wait any longer. She likely wouldn't think that was sufficient reason for him to make a move without consulting her, but he damn sure did.

A part of him wanted to call Brad himself, to hunt the bastard down and issue a challenge—*Come and get her, motherfucker, try to get through me*. But this wasn't the Old West and, unfortunately, "He needed killin'" was no longer an acceptable defense.

At the very least, he could see the son of a bitch in jail. Somehow, some way, there was evidence that would convict him of killing Carlin's friend in Dallas. But if no one was looking, nothing would ever change. It was time to look, and look hard.

LIBBY HAD SPENT much of the past three days trying to hold back her impulse to celebrate Zeke's find in Carly. It never hurt to be cautious. If there was something off about the girl, either in the way she did her job, or in the way she treated Zeke or the hands, Libby wanted to keep an open mind so she could spot it. After three days, she hadn't spotted a damn thing wrong.

Maybe it was time she stopped looking for flaws.

Maybe, in spite of her initial reservations, Carly was perfect for Zeke. She was funny. She was energetic. She was sassy, and she didn't take any guff from Zeke, which was a big plus in Libby's book. That was one thing that had been wrong with Rachel; she hadn't known how to go toe-to-toe with him, so she'd shown her unhappiness in other ways. Carly gave him as good as she got, and sometimes more. The truly funny thing was that Zeke seemed to enjoy when she shot some smart-ass comment at him.

"Good morning," Carly said cheerfully when Libby entered the kitchen. It was almost dawn, which made for an early start to the day for anyone, but Carly looked freshly scrubbed and bright-eyed. Coffee was made, something was baking and it smelled wonderful and cinnamony. As she did every morning, the next question was, "What can I get for you?"

Libby said the same thing she did every morning as she headed toward the coffeepot. "Nothing, hon. You have enough to do for these men, without waiting on me, too."

Carly nodded and got back to work.

Libby sat at the kitchen table and sipped at the coffee, content with everything she'd seen so far. Carly was exactly who she appeared to be, nothing more, nothing less: a good, hardworking woman who had landed right where she needed to be. And, just maybe, the good, hardworking woman Zeke needed by his side.

"What smells so good?" she asked.

"Cinnamon rolls." Carly rolled her eyes. "I don't know why my biscuits just don't turn out right, but the cinnamon rolls always behave just fine."

"*Homemade* cinnamon rolls?"

"Of course." Carly didn't look Libby's way, but she gave a wry smile. "A few months ago I could barely heat up a can of soup. Now I'm not afraid to try anything, as long as I have a recipe to go by. Well, more accurately, I may have doubts but why not try anyway?" At that, she did turn to look at Libby. "There is one thing I haven't dared to try."

"What's that?"

"Your chocolate cake. Everyone says it was just wonderful, and I'm afraid anything I did would suck in comparison. Oh—I don't make pies, either. Same reason, different cook."

"Kat," Libby said.

Carly nodded. "I don't suppose you would make that cake while you're here so I could see how you do it? I know Zeke—and the others, too—would fall over in fits of gratitude if I could make a chocolate cake half as good as yours."

Libby tried not to feel flattered. She didn't try hard, because it was nice to know an old dog still had a few tricks she could teach to the youngster.

Zeke came striding into the kitchen, his gaze landing on Carly and lingering. If they'd been alone in the kitchen, Libby figured Carly would have been kissed until she didn't know which way was up. It was as if there was a magnetic charge between them. Carly even took a step toward him, then stopped and moved back.

Zeke grabbed a half cup of coffee, downed it, and headed for the mudroom.

"Half an hour before breakfast," Carly said. "Don't let it get cold."

"We'll be here." He stopped in the middle of the kitchen, took a long, deep breath, and grinned. "Cinnamon rolls."

Carly smiled. "Yep."

He went on into the mudroom and after a second or two, Carly followed. "Oh, I almost forgot," she said, to explain why she was following. Soon they were out of sight.

Libby slowly stood up, a sneaky smile creasing her face.

Who did they think they were fooling? She tiptoed to the mudroom door on quiet, slippered feet, and stopped when she was close enough to hear. They weren't talking, so they were probably enjoying the kiss they'd both wanted but had denied themselves, thanks to her.

The kiss didn't last a horribly long time. Carly said, in a lowered voice. "Pull that hat down over your ears. I don't want you getting frostbite."

"I think I know how to stay warm." Heavens, when was the last time she'd heard Zeke sound so . . . relaxed?

"I know you do." Libby wondered if Carly was straightening Zeke's coat and hat, making sure he was well-bundled up. "And don't think you won't have to eat any eggs for breakfast just because there are cinnamon rolls. You need some protein or else you'll crash long before lunchtime."

"Yes ma'am."

"And one more thing," Carly said in a lowered voice Libby could barely hear from her position. "Kiss me one more time before you go."

At that, Libby returned to her seat. When Carly came back into the kitchen a few moments later, her cheeks were a little flushed, but she likely didn't realize that she looked so well kissed.

"Would you like a warmup?" Carly asked, headed for the coffeepot.

"Sure. Thank you."

Carly walked to the kitchen table with the carafe in her hand. As she was pouring coffee into the cup, Libby said, "You know, I'd be happy to teach you how to make my chocolate cake."

CARLIN PEEKED OUT the mudroom window. Yes, Libby was headed for the bunkhouse. Apparently she was going to inspect the hands' home just as she'd inspected this one.

Assured that Libby would be occupied for a few minutes, Carlin walked toward Zeke's office. Okay, she ran, just a little. Having another person in the house was a pain in the ass, even though she liked Libby, which surprised her. When Libby had first arrived it had been obvious she'd had her reservations, but Carlin had figured there wasn't anything she could do about that except be herself, and if their positions had been reversed she'd have been just as suspicious. Libby was down to earth, she liked a bawdy joke, and she was full of laughter and chatter. Carlin could see why Zeke cared about the woman who had once been his housekeeper and surrogate mother. Still, her own time here was precious, and she wanted to be alone with Zeke when she could.

He glanced up when she walked into his office, and his eyes smiled. His mouth did, too, but it was the smile in his eyes that got her every time. Carlin leaned against the doorjamb and returned it, with interest. She shouldn't love him, but there was no reason she couldn't love his smile. There was no reason she couldn't love the way he looked at her, as if he wanted to eat her up. Kat said they had "sparks." Looking at him right now, the air certainly seemed to be electrically charged. She could hardly stay in her own skin.

"Libby's visiting the bunkhouse. I think she's holding another inspection."

He shot out of his chair, rounding the desk and reaching for her. "You mean we're alone?"

Carlin nodded.

"For how long?"

"I don't know." Not long enough, she suspected, but she'd take what she could get.

He kissed her as if he were as hungry for the connection as she was. It was a good kiss, deep and stirring and unbroken, even when he dragged her out of the doorway and farther into the room. The office was all brown leather and dark wood, a man's domain, and it smelled the way a man's domain should. There had never been a single flower or scented candle in this room, she suspected, just sweat and paper and more leather.

He propped her against the desk, spread her legs and fit himself between them. So close, and yet not close enough. He was hard; his length pressed into her.

"Missed me?" she asked hoarsely when he broke the kiss and unzipped her jeans.

His eyes were hooded when he answered, "More than I should."

"I've missed you." Just a few days, and she was caught on the razor's edge of blind need after one kiss.

"How much?" Zeke pushed her jeans down and thrust his hand inside her underwear. She wiggled, scooting the jeans down, spreading her thighs to make this work.

"See for yourself, cowboy," she whispered. She was wet, pulsing, all from a kiss and the scent of his body, from the warmth and hardness she'd become accustomed to calling hers. She closed her eyes when his fingers moved deeper, parting her folds and slipping inside her.

He stroked her, brought his mouth back to hers and kissed her while he plunged his fingers inside her. She came, lightning fast and hard, her tongue thrusting into his mouth, his tongue dancing with hers.

She melted against him, heart pounding and body rubbery with satisfaction. Swiftly he unzipped his own jeans, guided his erection to her, and thrust inside. She made a small guttural sound of excitement. She'd just climaxed, but it wasn't enough. She wanted more. She wanted him.

He began thrusting fast, his face taut, as hungry after these days of deprivation as she'd been. His bedroom was, inconveniently, directly above the room where Libby was staying. Both of them had tried to hold back while Libby was here, but the frenzied need she felt in him told her that wasn't going to hold.

His powerful body bowed into hers. He ground his teeth together to hold back any sound, and began coming. His thrusts were hard now, jarring her, going as deep as he could get.

Panting, he leaned over her, spent. She felt as if she could barely move, either, but Libby would be coming back any minute. "Hurry," she whispered. He pulled out of her, and she ran for the bathroom. She had to wash, and change her underwear. She fully expected Libby to have returned by the time she was finished, but no, they still had the house to themselves.

What could Libby be doing in the bunkhouse, for this length of time?

The answer was as obvious as the blush that suddenly burned her face. Giving them time together, that was what she was doing. No one was in the bunkhouse, the men were all out doing chores, so it wasn't as if she was enjoying a chat with any of them.

This was ridiculous. Time was flying by, and she wouldn't have Zeke for much longer. Libby shouldn't have to banish herself to the bunkhouse to give them time alone.

She went to Zeke's office door again. He'd cleaned up, too, and was once more sitting at his desk, though she didn't know exactly how much attention he was paying to the paperwork in front of him. His eyes had that sleepy, sated look she adored.

"Enough's enough. My room, tonight," she said. "You'll know when Libby's asleep because she snores loud enough for the sound to make it to the kitchen."

"I don't care if she knows we're sleeping together." He

leaned back in his chair and looped his hands behind his head. "She's not an idiot, she's probably already figured it out."

"That doesn't mean I want her listening in. My room is farther away."

The back door slammed. From the kitchen, Libby's voice rang out in what was obviously a warning. "Carly, where's the lemon-scented cleaner? We need to make a run through the bunkhouse. I swear, those boys would live in filth if it was allowed."

Zeke ignored Libby's call and gave Carlin a sober look. "If a few days is like this, what's it going to be like when you're gone?"

She tried a shrug. "Out of sight, out of mind." She hoped, and she didn't hope. She'd miss him so much she already ached, and it was awful of her but she wanted him to miss her the same way.

He shook his head. "I don't think so."

LIBBY WAS SURPRISED to find that she liked the cold. She'd missed it. If she stayed here much longer she'd probably change her tune, but for now she enjoyed walking down Battle Ridge's main street bundled up from head to toe, the wind on her face as she thought about a cup of hot coffee and a slice of Kat's pie.

It was almost time for her to leave. She'd come here to check out Carly Hunt and she had. Zeke was wild about the girl, and the girl was wild about him. Maybe they were in love, maybe it was all pheromones and hormones and it wouldn't last. But Carly was just who she appeared to be, and Zeke was fine. Libby's curiosity had been satisfied, and she felt certain she was leaving the man who had been like a son to her in good hands.

Carly was good in the kitchen and she kept the house

clean. She took care of Zeke without taking any shit. She was a strong woman, and that was exactly what Zeke needed.

Libby heard a familiar voice call her name. Turning, she watched Carly wave and step into the street, and she stopped to wait for her. The girl must love to read; she went to the library every time she came to town, and always brought home at least two books, sometimes more.

Neither of them saw the truck until it was too late. Just as Carly stepped out from between two parked cars, a red pickup with a teenager behind the wheel took the corner too fast and swerved onto the main street. The inexperienced kid lost control and skidded right into Carly. She tried to jump back, and the driver tried to steer the big vehicle away from her, but he clipped her with his bumper.

There was a thud, followed by a curse. Carly hit the ground on the other side of the truck. Her purse and the books she'd been carrying flew out of her hands and skidded away, landing under the nearest parked vehicle.

Her heart in her mouth, Libby ran. She forgot her knees, forgot everything in her rush to get to Carly. If she was seriously hurt, or, oh God, she might die, and what would Zeke do—

Other people were running toward the scene. Kat came flying out of the café, screaming Carly's name. Libby skidded around the vehicle that hid Carly from view, and almost passed out from relief. Carly was half-sprawled, half-sitting on the asphalt, dazed but apparently unbroken. Best of all, she looked pissed.

"Don't move!" Kat ordered when Carly tried to stand. She turned her attention to another bystander, and immediately contradicted herself. "You, help me get her up. She needs to be checked out at the clinic." Then she was on her knees beside Carly. "Is anything broken? No, don't move!"

"I have to move if you're going to get me up," Carly said testily. "I'm fine. Really. I think. At any rate, I don't think anything's broken." She held her hands out and Kat caught one, while the man Kat had dragooned gripped the other one and together they got her to her feet. When she reeled back, Kat was there to catch and steady her.

"You might have a concussion," Kat said.

"I don't, I'm fine—"

"You're going to the clinic, and I'm going with you." Kat looked up and spotted a friend. "Mary, would you watch the café for me for a while?"

"I'm just shaken up, honest."

"Carly, you go on," Libby said firmly. "Kat's right. I'll take care of everything here. Wasn't that the Collins boy?" she demanded angrily of someone.

"Yeah, that was him. Here he comes back, thank God. He'd have been in a world of trouble if he'd kept going."

Carly did seem to be a bit out of it; she didn't even look toward the truck that had hit her. Young Collins climbed out of the truck, his face white. "Is she okay?"

"No thanks to you, dumb ass!" Libby barked. "You know better than to be speeding in town." Libby allowed Kat to help Carly to the clinic, while she handled the more mundane chores, such as tearing a strip off the Collins kid's hide. She also rounded up Carly's purse and the books she'd checked out, then waited around until a deputy arrived to take her statement.

When that was taken care of, Libby walked down to the clinic. There were a woman and child in the waiting room, but no sign of Carly and Kat, so they must've been taken in to see the doctor.

Libby knew the receptionist, because there was just this one clinic in town and she'd come here herself for years.

Evelyn Fortier had lived in Battle Ridge forever. She'd worked for three different doctors in this same clinic.

"Hi, Evelyn," Libby said as she walked up to the desk. "How on earth are you?"

They talked a moment, catching up. They hadn't been great friends, but they had always been friendly acquaintances. Finally Libby asked, "Any word on Carly? I hope she's not seriously hurt."

Evelyn's eyebrows shot up. "Well, of course you're here with Carly. I should've realized that right away." She tsked. "You don't know if she has any insurance, do you?"

"No, but Zeke will take care of all the bills, if she doesn't."

"Oh, I know he will. We will need some identification of some kind for our records, before she leaves. Kat just hustled her on back and I didn't even get to make a copy of her driver's license."

"I have her purse. Let me check."

Good heavens, Carly's purse was so neat and organized! A place for everything and everything in its place. The canister of pepper spray was a little startling, but not unusual. Maybe she should get some herself. Libby pulled out Carly's wallet, all the while considering the pepper spray and noting the brand name, and opened it. There was plenty of cash, more than she'd expected to find, but not a single credit card. No driver's license or insurance card, either.

"Well, I don't see one."

The phone rang, and Evelyn answered. Libby walked away, still shuffling through the wallet. Carly had driven one of Zeke's work trucks to town, so surely she had a license and had it with her. The contents of the wallet were off, somehow. It was just *odd*. Libby's own wallet contained two credit cards, an AARP card, an AAA card, and two grocery store rewards cards, as well as a driver's

license and her insurance cards. And pictures, of course—
all of her grandkids, but still . . . there was nothing in
Carly's wallet to identify the owner. Nothing.

She started searching for hidden pockets, and found
one. There, shoved into a side pocket low and tight, was
a card. Libby managed to wrangle the card to the surface.

She looked down at it, immediately recognizing Carly's
photo. Then the name hit her between the eyes and her
heart sank. She held in her hand a Texas driver's license
with an unsmiling photo of Carly staring back at her. The
name on the license wasn't Carly Hunt, it was Carlin
Reed. Carlin Jane Reed, to be precise. She could see Carly
being a nickname, but Reed? Why was her last name different?

That, along with the lack of any other personal information, made the hairs on the back of her neck stand up.
She'd been so worried about Carly scamming Zeke, she
hadn't even considered that the girl would be so good
that she herself could be scammed, as well.

Why would she use a false name? Was she wanted by
the police? On the FBI most wanted list? Then Libby
mentally smacked herself in the forehead. Duh. The most
logical reason for a different last name was marriage. Was
Carly a married woman? Oh my God. That would break
Zeke's heart.

What on earth was she supposed to do now?

"Any luck?" Evelyn called.

Libby shoved Carly's driver's license back in the hidden pocket. Until she decided what to do, there was no
reason to share what she'd found. "No, I'm sorry. Carly
must've left her license at home."

It was tempting to tell everyone what she'd found, to
shout *fraud* at the top of her lungs when Carly—*Carlin*—
returned, battered and unsettled, some bandages on her
scraped hands but essentially whole. But maybe subtlety

was called for. Before she started throwing accusations around, accusations the fraud probably had ready answers for, she was going to do a little digging on her own.

She wasn't leaving until she knew what the hell was going on.

Chapter Twenty-seven

LIBBY WAITED UNTIL Carly had her hands full with laundry before she sneaked into Zeke's office and sat at the desk chair. Zeke wouldn't be back for at least another hour, maybe two. She had plenty of time as far as he was concerned, and if Carly came in she'd just say she was emailing her daughter.

If she simply asked why Carly was using a false name, the girl would probably have a good answer, one that Zeke would buy without question because he was blinded by testosterone. She needed to know what she was up against before she confronted Carlin Reed. Maybe she'd find a marriage announcement out of some Texas newspaper. Were divorce announcements posted anywhere? She didn't think so, but it wouldn't hurt to look.

Libby plugged Carly's real name—including the Jane—into Google and hit "enter." If she was wanted by the police, if there was an article about her online, if there were pictures of a wedding, maybe Google would provide proof. A lot of Jane Reeds came up, but after shuffling through several possibilities Libby searched again using just Carlin Reed.

Nothing. At least, no one by that name who could be Carly. How could anyone not be on the Internet somewhere? There were links to places where she could pay to see public records, and she might have to resort to that later, but for right now that seemed a little drastic.

Libby pushed away from the desk. Now what? The simple explanation was that Carly was married—or recently divorced and now using her maiden name. But just because it was the simple explanation, that didn't mean it was the right one. The lack of credit cards and other paraphernalia hinted at something more.

But what?

BRAD WAS LYING back on the hotel bed, hands behind his head and watching some shit on the cheap-ass TV, when his computer dinged, alerting him that a message had come in. He didn't rush to the desk to check out whatever it was; usually the alerts were nothing.

In a couple of days, maybe three, he'd be in Cheyenne and he'd find out if the PI who'd searched his name was in any way related to Carlin. He'd tried to hack in, but the PI had impressive firewalls. Who else but Carlin would've hired a PI to check him out? Maybe she thought he'd given up on her. Maybe she thought she was safe, the stupid bitch.

She made him wild. Everything that had happened to him was all her fault. How could she not see how perfect they were together? And yet, after the way she'd acted, he'd have to be stupid himself to want her. His emotions warred within him, hate and love and fury so mixed together he didn't even try to sort them out. He loved her. She'd thrown that love back at him, she'd filed stupid charges against him, and eventually caused him to lose his job. Every mistake he'd ever made was because of her. She *deserved* to be eliminated—not just killed, though he'd settle for that if necessary, but *punished* for everything she'd done. And then—then, he'd release himself by killing her. Then he could start fresh.

But look at where he was now, all because of her, and he didn't like it. He'd never imagined he'd find himself driving into Wyoming in January. It was too fucking cold this far north, too alien. He was used to flat land and hot temperatures, the ocean, but here he was surrounded by mountains so fucking enormous they didn't seem real, and weather so cold it bit into his lungs like a wild animal.

He hadn't come up here unprepared, though. He'd done some research, gathered the things he'd need. He had chains for his tires in the truck, in case it snowed and he needed them. He kept blankets, candles, water, and power bars in the truck, too. He'd had to stop in Colorado to buy a new heavy coat to keep himself from freezing to death. Why couldn't she have hired a PI in Florida, or maybe Southern California? This was ridiculous. She'd pay, when he found her.

But when he got up and finally read the message waiting for him, Brad forgot the cold and the expense and the sorry-ass TV, and everything else. *Carlin Jane Reed.* There was no mistaking who that search had been for. He'd had false leads before, searches for and by other Carlin Reeds—though there weren't many—but this one, it had to be her. Forgetting the PI, forgetting everything, his fingers flew over the keyboard.

Maybe he wouldn't be going to Cheyenne after all.

CARLIN SMILED AT Libby as the woman walked into the kitchen. Her clothes were put away, and a load of towels was in the dryer. The roast she'd put in the slow cooker that morning was filling the kitchen with a mouthwatering aroma, and the corn bread was ready to go in the oven. Her hip was a little sore, thanks to the minor accident that afternoon, but aside from that ache and a small headache, all was well. It could've been a lot worse. Privately she admitted that she'd have liked to curl up in a recliner and not do anything for the rest of the day, but if she'd given in to that urge all hell would have broken loose around her and she'd have found herself carted off to a hospital, willy-nilly, so she kept going.

Libby didn't return the smile. Instead the look she gave Carlin was distinctly somber, and immediately a spike of adrenaline sent her heart racing. "What's wrong? Zeke! Has something happened to Zeke?"

"He's fine, as far as I know," Libby said. She stared hard at Carlin. "As for whether or not something's wrong, I was hoping you'd tell me, *Ms. Reed.*"

Her knees went weak. Carlin grabbed the kitchen counter behind her for balance as her vision swam. Everything seemed to close in on her, the world closing down to a narrow tunnel and everything around it turning gray. It was an effort to remain on her feet.

The shock was sickening. She'd known this would happen, she'd known she'd be found out eventually, but Libby using her real name had come without warning, and Carlin felt like someone had swiped her legs out from under her.

She'd been found, she was no longer safe . . . oh, God, she was going to have to leave Zeke.

Carlin came to her senses enough to realize that Libby had noticed her reaction and was staring at her with a mixture of alarm and puzzlement. "How did you . . . what . . ."

"This afternoon Evelyn asked for your driver's license. I had to dig for it, but . . ."

But she'd found it, tucked into a side pocket. Carlin turned and ran toward her rooms to pack, to collect her fairly substantial stash of cash and go. The receptionist at the clinic would've innocently plugged her real name into the computer. Brad would know. He was probably already on his way to Battle Ridge . . .

Libby's voice was distant, even though it was right behind her. She dimly heard *Carly, Carly,* over and over again, and then finally a sharp, "Carlin Jane!" for all the world like a frustrated mother. "I didn't give Evelyn the license, if that's what has you in such a state," Libby said sharply. "Good heavens, what's wrong? Why does it matter?"

Relief washed through her, as strong and unbalancing as the fear had been. Carlin stopped in the hallway and slumped against the wall.

Libby placed fisted hands on her generous hips. "Do you want to explain to me what's going on? You're not married, are you? It would break Zeke's heart . . ."

"No," Carlin answered, her voice not as steady as it should've been. "I'm not married. Never have been."

"Then why the name Hunt instead of Reed?"

Because I spotted a bottle of ketchup as I was talking to Kat . . .

Zeke knew the story. Kat knew, too. Would one more person being in on the secret really matter all that much? *Yes.* With every person who knew her secret, there was a bigger chance that someone would spill the beans. Then more people would know, and more, and the next thing you know Brad is showing up at Zeke's front door.

But what choice did she have? She either told Libby everything and begged her to keep the secret, or else she left this place without looking back. And she wasn't ready to leave.

"Can we sit down for this conversation?" Carlin asked. "I could use a cup of hot tea."

"Honey, you're pale as a ghost," Libby said, as much concern in her voice as curiosity.

She'd understand why, soon enough.

They sat at the kitchen table, two cups of steaming tea

between them, and Carlin told Libby everything. The stalking, the fear, Jina, landing in Battle Ridge completely by chance.

Libby didn't say much, but her posture and expression changed as Carlin told her story. She was sympathetic and angry, and when Carlin finished she placed both of her hands over one of Carlin's.

Her gaze was fierce and direct. "You do know you can't run from that son of a bitch forever, don't you?"

Carlin nodded.

"And you do know you're not alone."

Tears burned her eyes at that simple statement. She'd been alone in this until she'd come to Battle Ridge, but now she had Zeke, and Kat, and Spencer and Walt . . . and a town full of friends who would stand up for her if it was necessary.

Libby did have one question, and she asked it straight out. "Do you love Zeke?"

"Yes." Simple answer to a complicated question. She shouldn't, she really couldn't, but there it was, the truth in all its unadorned, unreasoning splendor.

"I've seen it since I came here, that's why I was so upset when I found that driver's license and thought maybe you were married."

The back door opened and closed. Carlin listened as Zeke removed his outerwear, shucked off his boots, and kicked them under the bench. He walked into the kitchen in his sock feet, looking tired and dirty and wonderful. He glanced from her to Libby and back again, and his expression changed.

"What's up?"

"Libby found my driver's license while I was seeing the doctor this afternoon," Carlin explained. "She knows . . . everything."

Libby gave Zeke a stern glare. "What are you going to do about this, A.Z.?"

Carlin managed a small smile. Libby called upon the same tone of voice she'd used when calling her Carlin Jane.

Zeke sat beside her, took her hand in his under the table, and squeezed. "Not much I can do. Carlin doesn't want me to do anything, period."

Carlin nodded once. She wouldn't bring her troubles to Zeke's door, wouldn't put him in danger.

"But—"

That single word made her head snap around. He didn't look the least bit guilty, damn him, just determined. She'd seen this before, when he refused to let Walt risk his life by getting under the truck to hook up the winch, when he'd insisted on doing it himself even though the risk was greater for him because he was so much bigger than Walt. Zeke did what he thought was best, period. She glared up at him. "*But?* But what?"

Zeke squeezed her hand. "I haven't taken any drastic steps, so you can wipe that look off your face. I went hunting for some information, but I was careful how I did it. I hired a private investigator a few days ago to find out what he could about Brad Henderson. And I asked a deputy friend of mine to find out where Brad is, right now." Carlin tried to jerk her hand from his, but he tightened his grip around her fingers. "I talked to the PI this afternoon. Brad lost his job a couple of months ago. So far no one's been able to find where he might've gone to work, so . . . we don't know where he is."

Carlin jerked her hand from his and stood, her heart and her head pounding again. "Why did you do that?" she demanded, her voice sharp with panic. "He'll know, he always knows. Did you send an email to this private investigator? Did the PI run an online search on Brad? How much did you tell this investigator?" She was going to have to leave, after all.

"It's okay." Zeke stood and wrapped his arms around her.

"I told you, Brad is a hacker, and a damn good one. If your PI entered my name or his into a search engine, Brad will know. He'll track that search to its origin and . . . and . . . you need to warn your PI. Brad will kill him to find out where I am."

"I know, I know," Zeke said in a voice she supposed was meant to be soothing. "I warned him, and we've done all our business over the phone. Carlin, he has the Dallas police looking at Brad again. This could all be over—"

"Oh, no." Libby's soft voice, full of dismay, broke through the panic.

Carlin looked down at the seated woman. Libby had gone white.

"I didn't know," she said, pressing her hands to her lips. "Oh my God, I'm so sorry. I thought maybe you were a married woman and . . . and I just wanted to protect Zeke."

Zeke asked, his voice calm, "What did you do?"

"I did a search for Carlin Jane Reed on your office computer, just an hour or so ago."

It was a good thing that Zeke was holding her, because Carlin's legs went weak again. She clung to him, knowing this was it, knowing she had to leave. Tonight.

But Zeke was calm when he used his finger to grab her chin and tip her face toward his. His eyes were dangerous, but calm, that damned determination obvious in his expression. "You think he's coming here?"

Carlin couldn't speak; she could only nod her head as she tried to figure out how to say good-bye to this man she loved.

But Zeke gave a smile that chilled her blood, a smile that had nothing humorous in it and a whole lot that seemed as cold and deadly as when he'd beat the snot out of Darby. He said one word. "Good."

ZEKE STOOD IN the doorway and watched Carlin pack. After a few minutes of studying her as she ran back and forth between the closet and the bed where a suitcase lay open, he walked to the bed and started unpacking her things, taking them out of the suitcase as fast as she could throw them in.

"You're not going anywhere," he said calmly.

"I have to," she said frenziedly. "I don't want to go, but I won't bring my problems down on you."

"If you're right about his skills as a hacker, the damage has been done and he's on his way. Let's take the opportunity to end it now."

"End it how?" Her tone was bitter, her cry heartfelt. "What are you going to do, shoot him? As far as the law is concerned, Brad hasn't done anything illegal. There's nothing you can do. Trust me, I tried. I really did try."

Since the PI hadn't been able to track Brad, the bastard could be anywhere. He could show up here in a day, a week, a month. Maybe he'd moved on to another victim and wouldn't show up at all.

More than anything, Zeke wanted Brad to show up; he wanted to end this nightmare for Carlin, once and for all.

"I have to go," Carlin said, her hands shaking as she repacked a sweater he'd removed from her suitcase. "You don't need this, I never meant to bring my grief to your door—"

Zeke placed his hands on Carlin's shoulders and turned her around. She had never seemed more fragile than she did at this moment, and he would do anything—*anything*—to protect her. And to keep her, once and for all.

"I'm tired of being alone," he said firmly. "I want a wife and kids, I want this ranch to be more than a business."

"Any woman in the world would be happy to—"

"I don't want *any* woman. I want you."

He kissed her, because he could, because he needed it, because she needed it. When the kiss was finished, Carlin fell into him and sighed. He stroked her hair, held her close.

"Libby is leaving on the Saturday bus. She feels bad, Carlin, she really does."

"I know," she whispered. "I don't blame her. She doesn't have to leave on my account. She was trying to protect you, she wanted to make sure I wasn't going to hurt you. And that's all I've done is hurt you. You would've been better off if I'd never come here, if we'd never—"

"Not true. The past two months have been the best of my life. I wouldn't trade them for anything."

Carlin slipped her arms around his waist, and he felt her relax. "I love you," she whispered.

"Love you, too." The words came easy.

"And you're right that Brad's coming here whether I stay or not. We can't undo what's been done." She lifted her head and looked him in the eye. "I won't leave you here to face him alone."

Zeke smiled. He saw the truth in her eyes, and he also saw how much courage it took for her to say those words. "That's my girl."

Chapter Twenty-eight

WHAT KIND OF a shit-hole town all but shut down just because it was Sunday? Brad parked on the almost deserted main street, walked past business after business. They were all dark, the doors locked.

He'd lucked out, considering where he was. The temperature had skyrocketed all the way into the upper thirties in the past couple of days. As he walked he ducked his head against the cold wind. He hadn't needed his snow chains, and while he was colder than he'd like to be, he didn't feel like he was putting his life in danger just by being outside. It was definitely too cold for a leisurely stroll, though.

Maybe the downtown shops were closed, but the gas station he'd passed heading into town had been open. Someone would be there, maybe someone who would recognize Carlin's photograph. With everything else closed, the gas station would have more people around than usual, so that was the place to go.

He knew where the search had originated, and it was a good distance from town. A couple of things stopped him from heading directly to the site of the search. One, just because someone there had searched Carlin's name didn't mean she was there. She'd slipped up, and someone had found out her name. It made sense that she was close by, and Battle Ridge was the closest town—if you could call this dead-end bump in the road a town.

Two, he hadn't made it this far by underestimating Carlin. She knew what he could do with a computer. For all he knew she'd purposely plugged her name into the search engine in order to draw him into the open. The PI who'd been looking into Brad could be a part of the same plan. Maybe Carlin was as tired of running as he was of chasing her. If he headed out to the house where the search had originated, would she be waiting for him? Maybe she wouldn't be alone. Maybe she'd have a weapon.

Maybe she wanted this to end as much as he did. It was going to end, all right, but not the way she planned. He thought about that possibility for a minute, that she'd deliberately pulled him here, but it didn't feel right. From the beginning, she'd run. She hadn't tried to mend things with him, she'd simply run. That was what she did. But she didn't know he was here, so he was in control now. And Carlin was so close he could almost smell her.

TROUBLE WAS COMING, one way or another. Zeke called the hands together in the bunkhouse and laid it all on the line. They deserved to know, they deserved to be given the chance to walk away. When he was finished, he waited for the accusations and questions to start, but the men all just nodded and asked what they could do to help.

He'd realized they were all good men, and still he was surprised that to a man they were ready to defend Carlin.

In addition to those chores which couldn't wait—those that were animal-related—the men would be watching the house, as well as the main road, until Brad showed up or they learned he'd been detained elsewhere. If Carlin was right about the man, they shouldn't have long to wait: a few days, probably, since he'd need to drive from wherever his search had taken him. They would all be armed, each man choosing his own weapon.

Spencer walked back to the house with Zeke, where they'd grab coffee and sandwiches before heading out to the pasture. He'd volunteered to take the first watch, but Zeke needed Spencer's expertise with the bull this afternoon. As soon as Patrick took care of a few things, he'd be patrolling the house.

Halfway there, Zeke said, "You weren't surprised to hear what was going on with Carlin."

"Nope. I'm not stupid, boss," Spencer said. "I knew right away that something was going on with Miss Carly. At first she was more skittish than she should've been, and nothing personal, but why would a pretty woman like that be content to live on a ranch in the middle of nowhere? She never asked nobody to take her to the mall in Cheyenne, she wasn't texting girlfriends all the time, and she never complained about not going to the movies. I have sisters. I know what women are like." He shook his head. "But I figured she had a good reason for being here so I didn't say anything. And I also figured God had a good reason for sending her to us."

When Zeke didn't reply, Spencer added, "Don't you worry, boss. We'll take good care of her."

BRAD PULLED UP to the curb and parked his truck near a plain mailbox with the name "Bailey" on it. The man at the gas station had recognized Carlin's photo, and had bought Brad's story about a long-lost aunt and a substantial inheritance. Lucky for him most people were so gullible, the stupid fucks. He'd never have fallen for a story like that.

The house was on a quiet road. There were neighbors, closer than he liked, maybe a couple of hundred yards between houses—maybe too far to hear a scream, but definitely close enough to hear a shot. Even a scream might be audible, if anyone was outside. He couldn't see anyone, but that didn't mean anything.

The woman who lived in this small house was apparently not only a friend of Carlin's, she was cousin to the man, Zeke Decker, that Carlin was working for as a cook and housekeeper. A cook! He distinctly remembered Carlin saying she could barely boil water. Either that had been one of her lies, or the people here weren't very particular about their food.

Not that it mattered much now. She'd had her chance, and she'd blown it. He couldn't bear knowing she was in the world, happy without him, living her own life when she was supposed to be his.

If she wasn't his, no one would have her.

Brad left the truck, watching the windows at the front of the Bailey house for movement, a sign that the woman inside might be watching. The drapes were closed tight, and nothing fluttered as he proceeded up the walk to her front porch. Four steps, and he was at her front door. That door was solid, painted a dark green, and there was also a storm door to keep out the wind. He imagined both were locked, though normally locks on a storm door like this one were flimsy.

Since he was certain Kat Bailey hadn't been watching his approach, he could spin a tale for her—if necessary.

He knocked firmly on the door, and listened to the footsteps approaching. Sure enough, instead of the door opening a woman's voice called out. "Who is it?"

Brad smiled, then looked down to the porch to the right of his boots. He leaned in that direction, too, and shook his shoulder as if struggling to hold on to something that was trying to get away. Odds were the woman in the house was watching him through the peephole in her door, and he had to sell this. "Is this your dog? I almost hit him right in front of your house, and I hate to just drive on and leave him out there."

His smile remained nonthreatening and impassive as he heard a deadbolt in the door click.

GREAT. IT WAS probably Shelly Kane's dog that had gotten loose and was running the roads again. He was a sweet dog, but he was a pain in the ass. Kat unbolted and opened the door to confirm her suspicions and give the man who'd stopped directions to Shelly's house.

In an instant, she immediately noticed everything that was wrong, but it was too late. No dog, no smile, and the man yanked her storm door open, breaking the lock without much effort and rushing at her. He was big, dark-haired, all muscle and determination as he slammed the door behind him. He grabbed her arm, but she jerked it away and ran for the kitchen and the back door. Her heart was pounding wildly, frenzied thoughts darting through her mind. Home invasion! Robbery? Rape? Murder? *God, help me!* She knew how to hit, she'd taken some self-defense classes, but this guy was too freakin' big and she knew her limitations. There was a time to fight and a time to run. It was time to run.

He caught her before she reached the kitchen, grabbing her hair and then her shoulder, throwing her hard to the floor. The breath was knocked out of her, and her vision swam. He stared down at her, and when she struggled to rise he placed one large, booted foot on her midsection.

"Where is she?" he asked, and in a blinding flash Kat knew who he was. This was Brad, the man who'd made Carlin change her name and run. "Where's Carlin?"

Kat shook her head and gasped for breath. His foot was pressing down hard, cutting off her air. "I don't know what you're talking about."

He kicked her hard in the side. Sharp pain radiated down her side, and nausea made her gag. For a long moment, Kat couldn't breathe.

"Does she live at the ranch where she works?" He leaned closer. "Yeah, I know that much." He kicked her again and she screamed.

He came down on his knees beside her, his hand clamped over her mouth. "No screaming. We don't want to alarm your neighbors, do we?"

He removed his hand from her mouth. "If you don't want me to scream, don't break another rib." She wanted to sound tough, but she was breathless and scared and angry. Even if she screamed, would anyone hear? No one was really close by, it would have to be a freak of atmospherics or sheer chance—

"You have nice eyes, Kat Bailey. Very . . . pretty." He cocked his head to one side, as if considering them. "Tell me what I want to know, or you might lose one of them."

The thought made her sick to her stomach, but she had to focus. No matter what she told him, eventually he was going to kill her. He'd have to, if he expected to get away with whatever he had planned. How could she protect Carlin and stay alive? How could she get both of them out of this? Her mind was spinning, but it finally settled on one fact.

Zeke would know what to do. Zeke would be prepared for this.

"She's at the ranch. I can . . . give you directions."

He scoffed. "She wouldn't be alone there, would she? Let's see. There's the ranch owner, and his family. I guess there's a family. Or is he some old-fart bachelor who thinks he's died and gone to heaven because he's got a pretty girl there to clean his pipes? And let's not forget the ranch hands, too. How many?"

"Not many on a Sunday," she said, trying to sound

helpful. "Maybe . . . one or two." Five, minimum. Brad wouldn't get far once he stepped onto Decker land. It made her feel a tiny slice of hope that he didn't know anything about Zeke. If he did, he'd never have used the words "old-fart bachelor."

Brad glanced around the small living room. "No, I think I want Carlin to come to me. It'll be safer that way." He looked down and smiled again; it was not the innocuous smile he'd put on for her when he'd been standing on her front porch. It was evil, his eyes shining. "You're going to call and ask her to come over. Tell her you need a little girl time, tell her to come alone."

They'd both be dead, that way. Kat gathered all her courage and said "No."

He hit her in the face. There wasn't a lot of power behind the blow, given her position on the floor and his, kneeling; maybe he pulled the punch a little, not wanting to knock her out, but it was enough to make her see stars.

"Did that change your mind?" he whispered.

Kat shook her head. She closed her eyes and waited for another blow. Instead he laughed. She opened her eyes just in time to see him stand and move away from her. Her brain screamed *Run!* but her body didn't respond. She could barely move, much less actually run.

But if he moved far enough away, if he thought she was down for the count—

But he didn't go far. He saw her purse sitting on an end table, picked it up, and pawed through it, smiling as his hand came out with her cellphone. He began to punch buttons, stopping his search and smiling when he found what he was looking for.

"Zeke home," he read aloud from her Contacts list. He came back and stood over her, one booted foot on her aching midsection, as he hit one more button.

* * *

CARLIN JUMPED WHEN the phone rang. Damn Brad for doing this to her all over again! She was alone in the house. Zeke was working—the ranch didn't shut down for Sunday, or any other day of the year. Patrick was at the back door, just in case, occasionally walking the perimeter and making sure all was well. Another hand—she didn't know which one—was watching the road in. They both had radios. She didn't think Brad would show up so soon, even if he had been monitoring Google searches for her. He wouldn't fly, because traveling that way would leave a paper trail and Brad was nothing if not careful. She figured it would be several days before she had to worry about the possibility that he might actually show up.

She'd need to warn Kat to be on the lookout for strangers in town. If he didn't come straight to the ranch, he'd go to The Pie Hole. Just about everyone in town knew she used to work there. Maybe Kat should come here and stay, just close the café until this was over.

She didn't answer the phone. It was never for her, and whoever was calling Zeke could leave a message on his voice mail. The ringing stopped; just a few seconds later it started all over again.

Well, this could get annoying if it went on and on. Carlin grabbed the kitchen phone off the cradle and looked at the CID. Kat! Talk about coincidences. Strange that she'd just been thinking about calling Kat, and Kat had decided at the same moment to call her. She thumbed the "On" button and lifted the phone to her ear.

"Hi!" she answered brightly. "Sorry I didn't answer the first time." She waited for Kat to say something, but for a long moment all was silent. "Hello?"

She'd begun to think Kat's cell had dropped the call when she heard the breath, the sigh. *That wasn't Kat.* The fine hairs on her arms stood up. Even before he spoke, Carlin knew who was on the other end of the line.

"Hello, Carlin." Brad sounded so happy, so smug and content. "I'm at your friend's house. Come join us and come alone or things will get very ugly for Miss Bailey. No police, no ranchers, just the three of us. Understand?"

Her knees gave way. Carlin sank down to the floor, phone in hand. What she'd been so terrified of happening was actually happening . . . again. A friend was in mortal danger because of this crazy dickhead, and— She stopped herself. She had to think. "Is Kat okay? Did you—" *Hurt her, kill her, oh God not again . . .*

"She's alive, for now. Whether or not she stays that way is entirely up to you."

Carlin could feel her heart beating, too hard, too fast. She reached deep inside for some control. She couldn't allow Brad to steal her reason, her ability to function. He'd stolen far too much from her already.

"I'm not going anywhere until I know Kat's all right. Put her on the phone. Now."

Instead of handing the phone to Kat, there was a pause, then a muted thump followed by a scream. His smug, vicious voice came back on the phone. "Do you really think I'm going to let the two of you cook something up on the phone? You heard her. She's alive, for now. Now get your ass over here and maybe she'll stay that way."

It was Brad who ended the call, leaving Carlin sitting on the floor with the phone in her hand.

She wasn't going to be responsible for another friend's death. No matter what, she had to save Kat.

Carlin went to her room. Zeke had given her a pistol for Christmas and she kept it there, close by her pillow when she wasn't with him. There were several things she had to do, other than get the pistol. She would have to leave by way of a window, and the window in her room would allow her to slip away without Patrick seeing her.

She'd check to make sure he was at the back door, before slipping out, and not walking around the house—and maybe right past her window at the same time she was crawling out. There was nothing to be done about whoever was watching the road, but she'd be on her way by then, and with luck they'd think one of the other hands was headed to town.

She bundled up, dressing warmly and thanking her lucky stars that there was no ice on the road today.

Yeah, lucky stars. She was real lucky.

She unlocked and opened her window, letting in a rush of cold air. The window was close enough to the ground and she slipped out—one leg, then the other. A quick glance to either side assured her she was alone. She tried to close the window, but now that she was on the ground it was too high for her to reach. She didn't waste time with the window, just headed for the garage with her head down against the wind. A part of her wanted to run toward Zeke, not away. A part of her wanted to believe that she was no longer alone in this. But she couldn't take a chance with Kat's life, not even for Zeke—not even for the chance to say good-bye.

Chapter Twenty-nine

ZEKE WAS ALREADY distracted when the radio clipped to his belt crackled with a puzzled sounding, "Who's headed to town?"

Zeke snatched up the radio and spoke. "No one."

Micah responded. "Sorry, boss, but someone's headed toward the main road like a bat out of hell."

"Which vehicle?" He had a bad feeling about this. He was already wheeling his truck around, back toward the house.

"The old blue pickup."

That was the one Carlin occasionally drove to town.

He was there in minutes. He pushed past Patrick, who was still posted at the back door. The time it took to take out the key and slide it into the lock seemed to be minutes wasted, when in fact it was only seconds—but seconds that might count.

"What's wrong?" Patrick asked.

"Tell me you didn't let Carlin get away."

"I thought I was here to keep some man out, not keep Miss Carly in?" Patrick's voice was touched with horror.

Zeke called her name. Once, twice. Nothing. He headed down the hallway into her bedroom, and stopped dead one step into the room.

The window was open, and Carlin was gone.

His first thought was that she'd bolted. She would change her name, get another job that paid cash, and he'd never find her.

Then common sense kicked in. He knew her; she wasn't a coward. If she made up her mind to leave, she'd do it straight up, so he wouldn't worry. She wouldn't run away, not without talking to him first. And she would have taken her Subaru, not one of his ranch trucks.

By the time he returned to the kitchen, Patrick and Spencer were there, waiting. They looked as scared as he felt.

He couldn't just take off, not knowing where she was headed, or why. He couldn't just stand there, either.

And then he spotted the cordless phone, not sitting in the cradle charging, as it should've been, but lying on the floor beneath the table. He grabbed it and immediately checked the last calls recorded on the CID.

Two calls from Kat's cell. One missed, one a couple of minutes long. He checked the time—there were less than five minutes from the time the call had ended until Micah had seen Carlin headed for town like a bat out of hell.

Sunday. Kat would be at home.

He started to hit redial, then stopped, thought. He said to Patrick, "Let me see your cellphone."

Patrick handed it over. Sometimes service was spotty, but the phone showed two bars. Not great, but good enough. He called Kat's cellphone. After a couple of seconds he heard the call go through; it rang and rang, then went to Kat's voice mail.

CARLIN GRIPPED THE steering wheel and pushed the pedal to the floorboard, testing the limits of the old truck. She hadn't had a chance to save Jina. She'd never really had a confrontation with Brad at all. He'd scared her; she'd run. If she'd stayed, if she'd fought him instead of going to Dallas, Jina would still be alive. She'd likely be dead herself; she'd known all along that Brad was dangerous, but this time—

This time she would *not* let that happen. She'd save Kat, somehow. Even if it meant she died, even if it meant her life was over, she would not lose another friend to the man who'd stolen her life from her.

Carlin kept her eyes on the road, willing the miles to pass more quickly, wondering if Brad had hurt Kat again after their call had ended.

It was true that Brad had stolen her life from her, but that was her old life; she'd found a new one here, with Zeke and Kat and Spencer and all the guys—it was new, and damn it, it was good. It was a better life than the one she'd left behind. Not that she'd ever thank Brad for putting her on the run, but he'd been a big part of giving her something worth fighting for.

Her pistol lay on the passenger seat, fully loaded, one in the chamber. Thanks to Zeke, she knew how to use it. And she would, by God, fight for her life and the lives of everyone she loved. Brad knew her as a woman who would run rather than fight. He knew her as an easily frightened, manipulatable, scared mouse.

That wasn't who she was anymore. She'd changed— and she was more than willing to fight for what was hers.

THE PSYCHO WASN'T taking any chances. Kat could barely move, but he'd insisted on moving her into a kitchen chair and tying her to it, using a length of rope out of her own kitchen and her own damned duct tape. He placed that chair in the middle of the living room where she'd have a front-row seat for what was to come.

Brad was almost giddy. He acted like a child on Christmas Eve, too excited to settle down. He'd checked his weapon, an automatic pistol, three times already, though she didn't think he planned to shoot Carlin the moment she walked through the door. That would be too neat for him, too quick.

Good. If he delayed, there was a chance she and Carlin might come out of this alive.

She knew Zeke had taught Carlin how to shoot a gun and how to fight dirty. The question was: would she panic and come here unprepared? Would she forget everything she'd learned and put herself at Brad's nonexistent mercy, or would she have a plan?

Brad was getting antsy. She'd told him it was a long drive from the ranch, but apparently he wasn't good at waiting. The antsier he was, the more likely he was to make a rash move when Carlin arrived. As much as Kat wanted to fade into the background and hope the fuckwad would forget about her, she didn't want his impatience to make him act too soon.

She lifted her chin, took a deep breath that hurt, and asked, "Why her?"

Brad spun around, looked down at Kat, and cocked his head. "What do you mean?"

"Why Carlin?" She would have shrugged, even tied up the way she was, but with her ribs injured shrugging wasn't something she wanted to tackle. "You know the saying, fish in the sea and all that. I mean, she's cute and all, but there are lots of prettier women in the world. Isn't there a Miss Texas out there somewhere who would incite this kind of devotion?" She chose the word "devotion" over "obsession" or "psychotic break" because she didn't want to get hit again.

A creepy smile bloomed on his face. "Jealous?"

Oh, hell no. "Just curious."

Brad didn't answer for a few minutes. He checked his gun again, looked at the front door as if willing Carlin to walk through it. Finally he said, "She needed me. I saw that the first time I looked into her eyes, the first time she smiled. She was so . . . fragile. I wanted to take care of her, to shelter her from the world and . . . keep her."

Yeah, in a jar.

"That's actually kind of sweet." *Gag.* "Have you ever told her that? Have you explained how you feel? I know how guys can be. They bottle up their feelings and sometimes a girl just doesn't understand." And if this nut thought he had a chance with Carlin, maybe he wouldn't blow her away the minute she walked into the house.

"She didn't give me the chance to explain anything." Brad sounded kind of sad, as if he were feeling sorry for himself. "I took her flowers, left them on her bed so she'd be surprised when she got home from work. I re-arranged her closet for her, put her prettiest things, the ones I liked best, in the center and separated from the rest. I called her at night, just to hear her voice and make sure she was okay. I watched her to make sure she was safe." He shook his head. "She didn't appreciate any of it."

"You need to tell her, you need to *explain*." And maybe, while he was trying to explain, Carlin could blow the psycho's head off.

Creep. God, how sick was it to break into her apartment and rearrange her closet? Carlin must have freaked; Kat knew she would have.

She heard the truck pull up outside. Carlin must've driven like hell from the ranch to get here so quickly! Surely Zeke was with her. She could have stopped down the road and let Zeke out, so he could approach on foot.

Brad heard the arriving truck, too, and stepped to the front window to pull back the curtain.

"Carlin," he said softly. And then he turned to look at Kat. "You're lucky, Miss Bailey. She came alone, as instructed."

You hope, you stupid shit.

Chapter Thirty

Because the call had come from Kat's cellphone, Zeke couldn't be sure that she'd called from home. It made sense to him that she'd be there, but it wasn't a given. She might've called from The Pie Hole, or from some other place in town. Common sense narrowed the possibilities to those two places, though. He and Spencer were headed toward Kat's house; Micah and Patrick were going to check out The Pie Hole. Kenneth and Walt were at the ranch, just in case Carlin returned there, alone or not.

He was tempted to dial 911 and get every sheriff's deputy to Kat's house right now, but more than the fact that he wasn't sure where Carlin had headed stopped him. If he was right and Brad had Kat—and would soon have Kat *and* Carlin—blaring sirens and flashing lights and more guns weren't going to help matters at all.

Carlin had been so sure Brad would show up at the ranch. So had he, and that had been a mistake—the worst kind, because now two people he loved were in danger.

Spencer, who usually talked nonstop when they were driving anywhere, had been ominously quiet. They were more than halfway to town, maybe fifteen minutes behind Carlin, before he spoke. "Boss, do we have a plan?"

"Can't make a plan until I know what we're going to

find." Fifteen minutes. *Anything* could happen in fifteen minutes. He did his best to make up some of that time, but he knew Carlin hadn't driven at a leisurely pace. Still, his truck had a more powerful engine than the old one Carlin had taken. That would help—it sure as hell wouldn't hurt.

When had Carlin become so important to him that he couldn't imagine life without her? He'd gotten along just fine on his own for years, and now after just a few months he was in a near panic at the thought of losing her.

"I'm a good shot, you know," Spencer said, his tone serious. "Never shot a person before, never wanted to shoot a person before, but if it comes to that I'll do what has to be done."

"Same here," Zeke said, though that wasn't strictly true. He wasn't going into that now; it was ancient history.

Fifteen minutes was a lifetime.

CARLIN SLIPPED THE pistol into her waistband at the small of her back, concealed beneath her parka and a long sweater, then turned off the ignition and got out of the truck. She didn't recognize the pickup she'd parked behind, but it had to be Brad's. It wasn't the car he'd been driving when she'd met him. Like her, he'd made changes. Living on the road would do that to anyone, she imagined, even Brad.

She'd only been to Kat's house once before, one Sunday afternoon a while back. The house was a neat one-story house on a quiet road of similar houses just outside of town. She had neighbors, but no one really close. On a normal day, she probably had no more than a fifteen-minute drive to the café. When it was icy, though, she stayed in the upstairs room where Carlin had once lived and saved herself the trip. If it had been icy today, would

Kat be safe? Would Brad have found her at The Pie Hole or would he be on his way to the ranch, without a hostage, and walking straight into the buzz saw that was Zeke Decker?

It didn't matter. Kat was here; Brad was here. And now Carlin was here, too. The gun pressed into her spine, cold and hard. She knew how to use it, but she wasn't a quick-draw artist. Her advantage was that Brad wouldn't expect her to be armed. He saw her as weak, always had, otherwise he would never have fixated on her.

She saw the curtain in the front window move. Up and down the road, all was quiet. It was too cold for kids to be out playing on their lawns, too cold for folks to be barbecuing or washing their cars. She was effectively alone. Once bullets started flying, that would probably change . . .

Halfway between Zeke's truck and Kat's front door, Carlin stopped. If she just walked through the front door, she and Kat would both be dead. Inside that house, Brad would be the one in control. Kat would have served her purpose, and he'd have Carlin right where he wanted her. Maybe she'd die today and maybe she wouldn't, but she would *not* sacrifice Kat.

She didn't say anything, didn't have to. The front door to Kat's neat little house opened, and there he was, the man of her nightmares. Brad was still big, but oddly enough not as big as she remembered. Her imagination had made him more than he was, had made him a boogeyman when in fact he was just a man, and a sorry one at that.

The storm door hung crooked. He pushed it open, and it squealed. No, it *shrieked,* as if warning her to go no closer. "Come on in, darlin' Carlin," Brad said calmly, using the sickening cutesy name he'd called her before.

She took a deep breath. Her feet were planted a couple of feet apart; she was as steady as possible, given the circumstances. "No. Not until you send Kat out, not until I see that she's alive and well."

He glanced back, for a moment, then looked at Carlin again. "She's alive. If you want her to stay that way—"

"I'm not walking into that house until Kat walks out," Carlin snapped. "You sick bastard."

Even from the distance of thirty feet, she saw the anger flash in his eyes. "You're not running this show."

"Until Kat comes out, I am."

Brad drew his gun and pointed it at Carlin. "If you run, I'll shoot you."

"I know." The way he'd shot Jina, the way he'd shoot Kat if he got the chance. But she wasn't running; she was standing her ground.

If he'd just wanted to shoot her, he could've done it the minute she'd stepped out of the truck. He could've lurked around town until she showed up and shot her in the back. No, he wanted her to suffer. That was her advantage, at the moment. If he wanted to really hurt her, she had to be in the house. She wasn't going into the house until Kat came out.

Brad left his position in the doorway; without him holding it open, the storm door swung drunkenly shut. He was back less than a full minute later, hauling Kat behind him. He pushed open the storm door again, shoved Kat onto the porch. Her hands were bound behind her back; her face was swollen and already turning blue. She limped, almost fell as she tried to run to Carlin. She stumbled, and Carlin caught her.

"I'm so sorry," Carlin whispered. She wanted to cry, but tears would have to wait.

"Come on, Carlin," Brad called. "Get inside." Over Kat's shoulder she saw him take aim. "If you make me shoot, Miss Bailey gets it first. Then you."

"I'll be right there."

"You packing?" Kat whispered. She lifted her head

enough that Carlin could see the pure fire and hatred burning in her eyes.

Carlin nodded.

"Good. Blow his brains out for me, will you?"

Again Carlin nodded, then she looked Kat in the eye. "If everything goes wrong and I don't make it—"

"Don't even say that!" Kat snapped, her voice surprisingly strong.

"Tell Zeke I love him." Carlin spun around so her back was to Brad, rather than allowing Kat's back to present a clear and tempting target.

"Tell him yourself," Kat whispered.

Before Kat could say anything else Carlin released her hold and turned again to face Brad. She stepped toward him; he lowered his gun—slightly—and smiled at her.

When she was not much more than a yard from the door he whispered, "I've missed you."

ZEKE TURNED ONTO Kat's road, and there it was, straight ahead—his blue truck, parked at the curb. A vehicle he didn't recognize—another truck, this one white—was parked in front of it. He caught a too-quick glimpse of fair blond hair at the door to Kat's house, and by his truck a brunette bent over in what—even from this distance—appeared to be pain.

It was Kat, wearing jeans and a long-sleeved T-shirt and no coat. Hands held awkwardly behind her back, she lurched away from the truck and into the road, as if struggling to cross to another house. She was going for help.

He wanted to rush in, wanted to drive his truck into Kat's front yard and storm the house, but one last shred of common sense made Zeke take a deep breath and pull to the side, where Brad couldn't see him. There was no need to let him know that anyone was here. Let him think, for now, that Carlin was on her own. But how long would he wait, knowing that Kat would obviously go for help? Not long. Maybe he'd tie Carlin's hands behind her and come out the door any second now, taking her to his truck.

Kat stopped in the middle of the road, looked his way, turned, and attempted to run toward him. Spencer was out of the truck in a heartbeat, running to meet Kat as he slipped off his heavy coat. He'd take care of her, do what he could. Knowing Kat was in good hands, Zeke headed for the house. He was so angry he was seeing red, could barely think. Damn it, he had to do something, *now.* A sense of urgency gnawed at him.

"Zeke, stop," Kat said weakly as she and Spencer met in the road. Spencer pulled a knife from his pocket and quickly cut the duct tape that bound her hands. Then he wrapped his coat around her and offered her a shoulder to lean on—literally. Zeke stopped, getting a good look at her. Oh, God, Kat's face, and the way she held her body, as if standing was a real effort. That son of a bitch had done a real number on her. But she said, "If you go barging in and surprise him, he'll just shoot her."

"He's got a gun," Zeke said, to clarify.

"Yeah." Kat winced as she put her weight on her right foot. "But so does Carlin." She looked at him, square on. She was hurt badly, but she still had her wits about her and she was no wimp, not even now. "She traded herself for me, even though she knows damn good and well Brad doesn't intend for either of them to leave that house alive." She turned gingerly and glanced back. "If he did, he never would've let me go."

She was right. She'd seen something Zeke hadn't seen. Brad wasn't taking Carlin anywhere, he intended to die there with her.

Time was short, too short.

Storming the house would get Carlin killed. Standing here and doing nothing would get Carlin killed.

"I think the back door is unlocked. The kitchen door," Kat said.

"You *think*?"

"I'd just taken out a sack of garbage when he knocked at the door, and . . . I just don't remember. Sometimes I lock the door immediately when I come back in, out of habit, but sometimes I forget."

Women and their locked doors.

It was his best shot. Zeke turned to Spencer. "Get her in the truck and warmed up, and call the sheriff's department. Tell them to head this way, no lights and no sirens. Talk to Billy, if you can. He knows what's going on."

With that, Zeke slanted across a neighbor's yard with the intention of cutting along the back side of the houses until he got to Kat's kitchen door. He could only pray that she wasn't as paranoid about locking her doors as Carlin was.

CARLIN STEPPED INTO the house, her head high. She'd be a fool to pretend she wasn't afraid, but in the months she'd been running from Brad she'd changed. She wasn't going to run, wasn't going to hide, not ever again. Zeke was worth fighting for. No, her *life* was worth fighting for.

"You didn't have to rough Kat up," she said, allowing her anger to show.

"If she's hurting it's her own fault," Brad explained in a calm voice. "She wouldn't tell me where you were."

"Well, here I am." She held her arms out to the sides, all but offering herself up to him.

"Take off the coat." He gestured with his gun. "I want to see you."

"You can see me just fine with the coat on." She wondered if the bulge of the pistol showed through her sweater; it would, almost certainly. If he made her turn around after she removed the parka, if he suspected she was armed . . . she would never get the chance to fight back.

Brad took a step closer. "Take the coat off. Now."

Carlin didn't move back. She actually wished he'd move even closer. Zeke had taught her to defend herself, and though she'd never actually put the proper force into those moves, she knew she could if it came to that. If she went for her gun now he'd get his shot off before she had a chance to even aim in his direction. The object wasn't just to disarm, capture, or kill Brad; it was to survive.

She wanted to survive to see another day; she wanted to wake up in Zeke's bed, again and again. She wanted to see spring and summer in Wyoming.

She slipped her parka off and tossed it onto the closest chair. "Fine. No more coat."

She couldn't outdraw him, not on a good day and definitely not with his gun already out and aimed in her direction. She couldn't beat him in a fair fight. What she could do, what she needed to do, was catch him off guard—and fight dirty.

"Do you love me?" She tilted her head, took a step toward him.

"What?" He seemed surprised. Whether it was the question or her willingly coming closer to him, she didn't know.

"I can't think of any other reason you'd come after me this way. After all this time, all the miles I tried to put between us . . . here you are. It must be love." She almost choked on the word. She knew what love was, now, and it wasn't this. It wasn't anything like *this*.

"Of course I . . ." Brad choked himself, unable to say the word. His eyes darkened. "You're mine."

"Do you think you own me, is that it?" She moved

another step closer, her heart thudding, the blood rushing in her ears.

"Yes." She'd manage to confuse Brad, at least. He'd expected terror or hysterical confrontation or both. Instead she spoke to him of love and moved gradually and steadily closer.

His gun shifted slightly, no longer pointed directly at her. If he were to fire now a bullet might get her in the side, or the shoulder. His head cocked to the side. Carlin prayed no sirens—police or ambulance—broke the spell. Not yet. She needed one more minute, maybe two.

"I don't like running," she said. "I don't want to run anymore. Please, Brad, let me stop."

"Why did you leave?" he asked, and the gun lowered a few more inches.

She reached out, touched his chest. She saw the surprise in his eyes, the sudden leap of sick lust, the insane smugness, as if he'd known all along that she really wanted him. She moved closer, put her other hand on his chest, too. Then she gripped his shirt hard in both fists and pulled him toward her. If she hadn't already been moving his way he might've been alarmed by the move, but instead he opened his freakin' mouth as if he intended to *kiss* her.

She held him close and rammed her knee into his groin. *His* nuts she didn't care about at all, so she gave it everything she had. Once, twice, pumping her knee back and forth like a jackhammer. The first blow took him so by surprise he didn't react, and the second blow made him howl in pain. The gun swung toward her again, but without releasing his shirt she threw up her elbow and blocked his arm. The third knee to the nuts sent him to the floor; he dropped to his knees, cussing a blue streak. She released his shirt and kicked at his arm, hitting it hard enough to knock the gun out of his hand, sending it clattering across the floor.

Swiftly she backed up and pulled the pistol from her waistband, held it firmly in both hands, and aimed at Brad's head.

She couldn't do it. She couldn't pull the trigger. As she had suspected all along, she couldn't shoot an unarmed man, not even Brad. She fought to keep him from reading it in her face. All she had to do was hold him here until Zeke and the guys and the sheriff arrived. A few minutes; surely no more than that. Kat had already had time to make phone calls. Was Zeke already on his way? Had whoever was watching the road away from the ranch realized she was the one headed to town?

Gagging, cupping his balls, Brad struggled to his knees. Tears of pain filled his eyes, and his voice didn't shake or quiver as he said, "Shoot me. Pull the trigger."

Carlin backed toward the front door. One step, then another. She didn't want to be any closer to Brad than she had to be.

"Maybe you think I won't. Do you think I haven't prepared for this? This is *my* pistol, and I've shot a hell of a lot of rounds through it, thinking about the day I'd be aiming it at you." If he knew she didn't intend to pull the trigger he might go for his own pistol again. She didn't want that. She didn't want to shoot, period, but she especially didn't want to be forced into trying to shoot a moving target. She knew her limitations.

Of course, if he went for his gun, she'd have no choice but to shoot. Her squeamishness had its limits.

"I'd rather be dead than go to prison. Do you know what it's like for a cop in prison? Do you have any idea?" He sounded infuriated, as if he'd been unjustly accused of something.

"I don't care. I hope you rot in jail." Carlin couldn't find an ounce of pity in her. He'd stolen months of her life. He'd murdered Jina, a woman whose only crime had been to be a friend and borrow a raincoat—oh, yeah, for Jina she wanted Brad to suffer. The miserable son of a bitch, she wanted him to suffer and *then* die.

Brad smiled. "That's what I thought." The smile changed to a smirk. "You're not going to shoot me. If you were, you'd have done it by now." He pushed himself forward and up, reaching for his gun. The son of a bitch was doing it!

Carlin let out a curse word and aimed, praying wildly, bracing herself, hoping she at least hit him somewhere because he was moving and she'd never practiced that—

And then she heard the back door open.

Brad heard it, too. The door squealed and a floorboard creaked as someone took a step into the house. He dove the rest of the way for the gun, grabbed it, rolled, and aimed for the door between the living room and the kitchen.

It could be anyone. Zeke, Kat, a deputy, a neighbor Kat had sent to help. She couldn't let any of them be harmed.

She dug deep inside herself, took aim, and fired. He grunted and fell back, blood blooming on his side. From his position on the floor he turned and looked at her, surprised, then sat up as he swung the gun toward her once more. "You bitch, you shot me!"

The blood distracted her. There was a lot of it, and it was darker than she'd expected, and shooting a person wasn't at all like shooting a target. Then Zeke came through the door, low and fast, weapon in his hand. Carlin barely had time to recognize him, but she saw Brad jerk his head around at this new threat, saw him settle and decide and bring his pistol back around toward her, his finger tightening on the trigger. Zeke fired, and the side of Brad's head blew out in a red mist of blood and brain matter.

Carlin stood frozen for a moment, completely incapable of doing anything. Somehow she held on to the pistol, didn't let it drop; when she had some command of her body again she carefully, very carefully, put it on an end table and backed away. Zeke was right there, closing his arms around her, sheltering her head against his shoulder.

She held on tight, because she could. Because she needed it.

"It's over," he said gently. "It's done."

She wanted to tell Zeke that she loved him, that he'd given her something worth fighting for. But not now, with the scent of blood in the air. Later, when they were alone and she'd washed the stench of Brad off of her, and off of Zeke. Later, when her heart wasn't beating so hard that the drumming drowned out everything else.

And for the first time in a long while, she knew without a doubt that they would have a *later*.

Chapter Thirty-one

It HAD TAKEN some time for Zeke to convince Carlin that neither of them would face charges for shooting Brad; their actions had been clear-cut self-defense. Even if they hadn't been able to document Brad's violent behavior and finally tie him to the murder in Dallas, there was also Kat's testimony, and her injuries. It turned out two of her ribs were cracked, so she was in for some painful days.

The sheriff had known Kat—and Zeke—forever and a day, and he was a big fan of Kat's cherry pie. No charges would be filed. Maybe "he needed killin'" wasn't an acceptable excuse now, but add on son of a bitch, as in "the son of a bitch needed killin'," and it came close. Regardless, there were no repercussions.

It had been a few long damn days, but the worst was behind them. Kat was healing, Brad was gone for good, and Carlin was still here. She didn't *have* to stay now; she didn't *have* to squirrel away cash, watch every penny she spent, so that meant every day she was there was a day she wanted to be there. She'd called her brother and sister, on his house phone, at his insistence, and talked to them for hours. He didn't give a damn what the final bill would be; her joy at actually talking to them, at being *free*, was worth every penny.

He woke with her in his arms. Snow had been falling all night, and the temperature was predicted to drop well below zero for the next few days, and God only knew what the windchill would be. They'd have their hands full, protecting the animals and the machinery. Carlin would make chili or soup, or maybe even the Mexican shepherd's pie if the guys wanted something really substantial, but at any rate it would be something hot to warm them all from the inside out, and at night she'd be here, in his bed. The only question that remained was: would she stay?

After what she'd been through, he figured the best thing he could do was not push her, let her decide for herself what she wanted to do, where she wanted to be. He wanted her here, he wanted her to stay, but the best way to show her that he loved her was to be willing to let her go, if that's what she wanted. But, damn, it wasn't easy to back off when every instinct he had made him want to hold her close.

She fit against his side as if she'd been born to be there. She snuggled in tight and warm. In a few minutes they had to get up and start the day, but for now . . . it was nice and warm, and felt as if this was the way the world was supposed to be.

"I'm going to see Kat today," she finally said around a yawn. "And I plan to take her a *real* get-well present— flowers, or a coffee mug filled with candy."

"WD-40 *is* a real get-well present when your back door squeals like a son of a bitch," Zeke argued.

She tried, unsuccessfully, to smother a smile. "Well, it did make her laugh," she conceded.

Even if laughing still hurt.

He rubbed his hand over her bare shoulder. "Just a couple of months until spring," he said, keeping his voice casual. "March will be here before you know it."

She shifted, the movement rubbing her body against

his. "That's true. Have you put out an ad for a grumpy old man to take my place?"

"Not yet." He tilted his head to look down at her. "Should I?"

She was quiet for a long moment. Then she rose up, leaned over him so they were chest to chest and eye to eye. "I've been wondering what spring and summer would be like here. I'd like to watch everything turn green, and maybe see a calf born and learn how to ride a horse, and you know what you need, Zeke? You need a dog. Make that two or three dogs. I would kind of . . . like to have a dog."

"A dog," he repeated. He'd had dogs before, would have them again, but he'd hardly expected that would be a reason Carlin might want to stay.

"And besides," she said, turning her head slightly so she was no longer looking him directly in the eye. "I think I love you, and I'd like to see where we go when there's no crisis between us."

She'd said it before, without the qualifier, but this felt like the first time because before had been, well, *before*.

"You *think* you love me."

She slanted a look up at him. "Fine, I love you. I didn't face down Brad just to save Kat, though that was reason enough. I took him on so I'd be free to stay here, to see what we're like—"

He rolled her over and fitted himself between her legs. "What kind of dog do you want?"

She wrapped her legs around him and laughed. "That's all you have to say? I tell you I love you and you want to know what kind of *dog* I want?"

"Well, I've already told you I love you. Isn't once enough?" he asked, teasing her. Then he said, "Stay," and interrupted her laughter. "I want you here. No one else, Carlin. You. Be my wife. Let's have kids to go with those dogs." So much for taking it slow.

"Not wasting any time, are you?"

"I'm tired of wasting time."

Her hands skimmed down his sides. "Boys or girls?"

"Are we talking about the dogs or the kids?"

She laughed, and he liked it. He loved it. "The kids."

"Both, though I don't think we get to actually place an order for gender."

"Married to a cowboy," Carlin said, her voice dreamy. "I must really be a glutton for punishment. Kat warned me about cowboys, but did I listen? Oh, nooooo. I had to fall hard for one."

"I love you," Zeke said. "Cautious, Carly, Carlin . . . whoever you are today, whoever you're going to be tomorrow, I love you."

She heaved a big, contented sigh. "That's perfectly wonderful. Now . . . how about a ride?"

"Yes ma'am," he said, and did as commanded.

RECIPES

Mexican Shepherd's Pie

1 pound ground beef
1 onion, minced
1 pack taco seasoning
1 can Mexicorn, undrained
1 can pinto beans
1 pack instant potatoes, or a pack of hash browns with
    peppers and onions
2 cups shredded cheddar cheese
Salt to taste

Preheat oven to 350°F.

Brown the beef and onion together; drain, add the taco seasoning. Then mix with the corn and pinto beans, heat, and pour into a casserole dish. Make the instant potatoes, and spread over the top of the beef mixture, making sure entire surface is covered. Make extra potatoes if you have to. Bake for 30 minutes. Remove from oven, spread the shredded cheese over the entire surface, and return to oven for 5 minutes, just until the cheese is melted.

Serve either as a stand-alone dish, or use it as a hearty dip, with tortilla chips.

I made this often for the construction crew when we were building a house. I cooked for them a lot—scones, muffins, homemade ice cream, biscuits, and salmon patties, but I think the Mexican shepherd's pie was their favorite. The guys told me that this was the only time they'd GAINED weight on a job. —Linda Howard

Snow Cream

Milk
Sugar
Vanilla flavoring
Snow

Mix the first three together until you like the way it tastes. (Hint: try a fairly small batch at first, so maybe 1½ or 2 cups of milk, then sugar and flavoring to taste.) It takes more sugar than you'd expect. Then fold in the snow until it reaches an un-runny consistency. I don't know if "un-runny" is a word, but it's certainly a description.

Eat.

If you make too much, you can freeze it. The consistency is different after that, but the taste is still there. Are Southerners the only ones who make snow cream? Surely not, though I admit a lot of people make faces at the idea of eating snow. Of course, they're from places where the snow is yellow, or gray, or any other unappetizing color. Here in the South, and out in the rural areas, the snow is as white as . . . well, you know what it's as white as. And we eat it. —Linda Howard

Biscuits

2 cups White Lily self-rising flour
$^1/_3$ cup Crisco (yep, the solidified kind)
$^1/_4$ teaspoon salt (I add salt because real Southern bis-
    cuits have a very faint salty taste)
Buttermilk—just enough so the dough forms a ball, but
    1 cup is about right. You might have to add another
    tablespoon or so. I don't even measure it, I just keep
    stirring until that ball forms and there's no dry flour in
    the bottom of the bowl.
$^1/_2$ stick (4 tablespoons) butter, melted

Preheat oven to 425°F.

Using your hand, squeeze together the flour, Crisco,
and salt; it's easier than it sounds, and a lot faster than
using a pastry blender or fork. Stir in the buttermilk
until the dough forms a ball in the bowl; I use nonfat
buttermilk, and it works just fine.

Grease a cookie sheet or biscuit pan, but a cookie sheet
is about the right size. I use butter-flavored Pam to spray
the pan. For that matter, I cover the baking pan with
aluminum foil and spray the foil, because I hate washing
baking pans! Anything to make cleaning up easier :-).

Dump the dough onto a floured surface, and sift a very
light covering of flour over the top of the ball. DO NOT
KNEAD THE DOUGH AT ALL. If you do, it'll make
the biscuits tough. The tenderness of biscuits depends
on the amount of oxygen in the dough, and kneading
works the oxygen out. Use a rolling pin, the smallest,
lightest one you can find, to very gently roll out the
dough until it's about ½ inch thick. Using a medium-
sized biscuit cutter, cut out the biscuits and place them on
the baking pan so they're touching each other; this forces

them to rise since they don't have room to spread out. This should make about 8 biscuits.

Don't roll the leftover pieces together to try to make another biscuit or two. Just take the dough tidbits and arrange them on the baking pan with the biscuits. They're odd sizes and shapes, of course, but you'd be surprised how this will turn out.

Bake in the oven for 8 to 9 minutes. These biscuits won't be brown on top; if you want a brown top crust, turn on the broiler for a minute, but watch them very closely. While the biscuits are baking, melt the half stick of butter, and as soon as you take the biscuits out of the oven brush the melted butter on top of them, including the odd biscuit tidbits. Tip: Even if you're using salted butter, which I recommend, you may want to add a dash of salt to the melted butter anyway. The difference to the finished product is amazing. If you follow this recipe, guaranteed you'll have fat, pretty, incredibly tender biscuits—and kids will love the biscuit tidbits. For that matter, a lot of the adults in my family prefer the tidbits over the actual biscuits. Go figure.

If you have any biscuits left over from the meal, put them in a Ziploc bag. To reheat, wrap them in a damp paper towel and microwave 15 to 30 seconds, depending on how hot you want them. The damp paper towel restores the tenderness.

I've made it my mission to teach as many people as possible to make biscuits, because it's a dying art. The most important things to remember about biscuit-making are: don't mess with the dough, and make sure the biscuits are touching each other in the pan. If you feel an awful urge to knead the dough, then use it to make something else, because the biscuits will be heavy and tough. —Linda Howard

LJ's Corn Bread

3 boxes Jiffy corn muffin mix
2 sticks of butter, soft
16 ounces sour cream
16-ounce can creamed corn
16-ounce can whole-kernel corn, drained
4 eggs

Preheat oven to 350°F.

Mix all the ingredients together, pour into an 11 × 15-inch pan, and bake for 45 minutes, until good and browned.

This makes a HUGE amount. I'm sure it can be cut down by half, or even a third, but I don't have those measurements. I can't figure out how to come up with ⅓ or ⅔ of 4 eggs. Go ahead and make the whole batch, and forget the math. This is as good as any cake. —Linda Jones

Never Fail White Cake

2 cups sugar
3 cups flour
²/₃ cup shortening
¹/₄ teaspoon salt
2 teaspoons baking powder
1 cup water
4 egg whites
1 teaspoon baking powder
1 teaspoon vanilla

Preheat oven to 375°F.

Cream first six ingredients in a large bowl, about 2 minutes with an electric mixer. Beat egg whites until frothy. Add baking powder and beat until stiff. Fold the vanilla and beaten egg whites into flour mixture. Pour into greased and floured pans—two 9-inch pans or three 8-inch pans, depending on whether you want thin layers or thick. Bake for 25 to 30 minutes.

I made this cake when I was seventeen and living at home. My sister broke a plastic fork in it, trying to cut a bite-sized piece. It failed miserably. I never figured out why. This gives a whole new meaning to "write what you know." Proceed at your own risk. —Linda Jones

Tuna Casserole

2 cups cooked rice
1 to 1½ cups vegetables of choice (mixed vegetables, corn, green beans—whatever strikes your fancy), drained
1 can cream of mushroom soup
2 cans tuna, drained
½ cup milk
8 ounces shredded cheese (cheddar, pepper jack, or monterey jack)
Salt and pepper to taste

Preheat oven to 350°F.

Mix together the rice, vegetables, mushroom soup, tuna, milk, half of the cheese, and salt and pepper to taste. Bake for 35 minutes, then sprinkle remaining cheese on top and return to oven until slightly browned.

When Linda H. said I needed to provide a recipe for the tuna casserole, I was momentarily dumbfounded. A recipe? For tuna casserole? You put together what's in the cupboard, cover it with cheese, cross your fingers, and bake. We had tuna casserole so often growing up, our mealtime prayer began "Give us this day our daily tuna." You can use noodles instead of rice, cream of celery soup instead of mushroom, and if you have any other leftover veggies, throw them in. It doesn't ever have to be the same meal twice! —Linda Jones

Read on for an exciting preview
of Linda Howard's

SHADOW WOMAN

Available now from Ballantine Books

Prologue

SAN FRANCISCO, FOUR YEARS EARLIER

ELEVEN P.M. THE president and first lady, Eli and Natalie Thorndike, had retired to their hotel suite for the evening. It had been a long day, beginning with the president's cross-country flight, then going straight into a flurry of campaign speeches—supposedly *not* campaign speeches, but all of them really were—then culminating in a huge fund-raiser dinner where each plate was ten thousand dollars. The first lady had been by his side the entire time, so she had not only logged the same number of hours, she'd done it wearing three-inch heels.

Laurel Rose, an eleven-year veteran currently assigned to the first lady's detail, was so tired she could barely see straight, but at last her shift was over. She hadn't been wearing heels, but her feet were killing her anyway. She tried her best not to limp as she made her way to the room assigned to her, down the hall but on the same floor as the president's suite so she would be swiftly available if needed. The on-duty agents were in a room directly across from the suite. She didn't envy them the graveyard shift, but at least now, with POTUS and FLOTUS in for the night, they could relax somewhat.

Three entire floors of the hotel had been secured, with the president and first lady in the middle floor. Guests who lived in the hotel had been relocated to other rooms, the stairways and elevators were secured, the hotel staff had been investigated and cleared, the buildings across the street had been secured, all known risks in the area had been contacted to let them know the Secret Service knew about them and was watching, though most of them had been judged incapable of carrying through on their threats. The first couple was as safe as the Service could make them.

That didn't mean nothing could go wrong. It just meant they had made it as difficult as possible for anything to happen. There was always an uneasy feeling deep inside Laurel's gut that reminded her anything *could* happen, keeping some small part of herself perpetually on edge.

"You're limping," observed her fellow agent, Tyrone Ebert, as he fell in beside her on his way to his own room. So much for hiding how much her feet hurt, she thought wryly. She didn't bother denying it, because he'd just look down at her with one of those see-through-you-like-glass looks of his. Tyrone had been with the Service for seven years; there was something a bit spooky about him, his dark eyes seeing everything while he himself revealed nothing, but Laurel trusted his razor-sharp instincts. So far he wasn't showing any signs of burnout, something she deeply appreciated, because she herself was hanging on by a thread.

"Yeah, it's been a long day."

Nothing was new about that. The days were all long. Since the Service had been moved from Treasury to Homeland Security, in her opinion things had pretty much gone to shit. They hadn't been great, anyway—Secret Service management was an oxymoron; *mis*management was more like it. But now the long hours were longer, morale was in the crapper, their equipment was shit, and on another subject entirely, her mother, who lived in Indianapolis, was getting older and less able to do things for herself. Laurel had put in for a transfer to the Indianapolis area, but in the perversion that passed for the norm in managing such things, she had little hope in getting transferred even though there was a position open. That wasn't the way things worked; unless you had some juice and knew someone who could pull strings, you weren't likely to get the transfer.

Laurel didn't have the needed juice. She hated office politics, so she'd never played the games, and now she was seeing far too clearly that her career with the Secret Service was nearing an end. That was another big problem with the Secret Service: they couldn't keep good people because of their asinine policies. And, damn it, Laurel knew she was a good agent, despite the underfunding, understaffing, outdated weaponry, and increasingly long hours. She just couldn't take it any longer. Well, for not much longer, anyway. She hadn't quite brought herself to the quitting point.

It was such a cool job, in some ways. Not great pay, but cool. She loved what they did, and was able to compartmentalize her emotions so it didn't matter who sat in the Oval Office: the job was what mattered. She didn't have to like the first lady; she just had to protect her. The job would have been easier if the Thorndikes had been more personable, but they weren't; at least they weren't as horrendous as some of the previous presidents she'd heard tales about. Natalie Thorndike wasn't rude, or a lush, or hateful. It was more as if she didn't see the agents protecting her as people; she was proud and cool and remote. Sometimes Laurel wished Mrs. Thorndike *was* a lush, which would at least have made for more interesting detail work.

The president was pretty much the same way, cool

and remote, disconnected from everything except politics. On camera, or in campaign mode, he exuded warmth and likability, but he was a superb actor. In private, he was calculating and manipulative—not that Mrs. Thorndike seemed to care. Occasionally they were on the outs with each other; the agents could always tell because the typical coolness would become downright glacial, but other than that there was no outward sign of discord, no loud arguments, no verbal sniping, no slamming doors. For the most part, though, the political power couple marched in lockstep. Their unity had already gotten them to the White House, where they planned on spending another term. With the president's ruthless instincts and the first lady's powerful family behind them, they would be part of the nation's inner political circle for years to come, amassing wealth and power, even after he was no longer in office.

On the other hand, the detail charged with protecting the couple's son, thirty-one-year-old Carter Eli Thorndike, had their hands full. The spoiled only child of capitol elite, on his mother's side, and the down-and-dirty politician that was his father, had supposedly never heard the word "no." He drank, he partied, he hired prostitutes, he did drugs—hell, he *sold* drugs—he tried his best to ditch his detail, and he whined to his parents every time the Secret Service tried to keep him out of trouble. He'd gotten his way every time, until he roughed up one of his prostitutes and wound up in the back of a squad car, his sneering expression captured by ever-present cellphones. Purportedly it had taken the president's damage-control team a lot of effort and cost a lot of money to make those photos and videos forever disappear, and since then Carter had been buttoned down tight, his detail practically sitting on him to prevent a recurrence of a potentially explosive scandal that might cost the president a second term.

Laurel would take protecting a cold fish like Natalie Thorndike, instead of her son, any day of the week.

"See you in the morning," Tyrone said as they reached his room.

"Good night," she said automatically, a little surprised he'd said as much as he had. He wasn't much on small talk, or on socializing. She actually knew very little about him, other than that he performed his duties impeccably. She'd worked beside him for two years now, since he'd come on the first lady's detail, and—come to think of it—she still didn't even know if he was married or not. He didn't wear a ring, but that wasn't necessarily indicative of anything. If he *was* married, or involved with anyone, he never mentioned it. On the other hand, he never hit on her either, or on any of the other female agents. Tyrone was . . . solitary.

As Laurel continued to her room, two down from his and on the opposite side of the hall, she realized for the first time that something about him gave her a little thrill in her stomach. She'd blocked it out because of the job, but now that she'd admitted to herself that she probably wouldn't be here much longer, it was as if she'd given her subconscious permission to bring the attraction to her attention.

She liked him. He wasn't a pretty boy, but he was damn striking, in a take-no-prisoners, dangerous kind of way. Tyrone would never blend into a crowd. He was tall and muscled, and moved with the kind of graceful power one saw in professional athletes or trained special forces soldiers. Physically, he did it for her. She liked being around him, even though he wasn't much of a talker. And she trusted him, which was big.

She slid her key card into the slot and turned the handle when the green light came on, stepping into the coolness of her room. The bedside lamp and the bathroom light were on, just the way she'd left them. She still took a moment to check her room, because double-checking was what she did. Everything was normal.

Wincing, she toed off her shoes, then groaned with relief as she rotated each ankle in turn, arching her feet, stretching the ligaments. The soles of her feet still burned, though, and nothing would help that other than getting off them for the next few hours, which she planned to do as fast as possible.

She stripped off her jacket and dropped it on the bed, and was starting to shrug out of her shoulder holster when she heard a faint *pop-pop-pop*. She didn't have to stop and listen, didn't have to think; she *knew* what the sound was. Adrenaline seared her veins in a huge rush. She wasn't aware of leaping for the door, only of surging into the hall and seeing Tyrone right ahead of her, doing the same thing, his weapon in his hand as he charged full speed down the hall toward the president's suite. They weren't the only ones. The night shift had erupted from the room they occupied, and the head of the president's detail, Charlie Dankins, was kicking in the double door.

Oh my God. The shots had come from *inside* the suite.

The doors and locks were sturdy; it took Charlie several attempts, and by that time Laurel and Tyrone and a swarm of other agents had reached them. Tyrone positioned himself beside Charlie and said, "Now," and they kicked together, the combined force finally crashing the doors inward. The agents went in high and low, weapons ready, rapidly sweeping the parlor for the threat.

The room was empty. She couldn't hear anything, which was even more horrifying, but her heartbeat was thundering in her ears so maybe it was drowning out any sounds. To the right, the door to the first lady's bedroom stood open, but Laurel controlled her instinct to rush toward it. Right now, their priority was the president, which meant Charlie was in charge.

The door to the president's bedroom, on the left, was closed. Charlie rapidly assessed the situation; until they knew where the president was, they could assume nothing. He pointed at Laurel and Tyrone and the rest of the first lady's detail, indicating they should check her half of the suite, while he and the others swept the president's quarters.

His tactics were sound. The detail moved toward the first lady's bedroom in an endlessly rehearsed procedure.

The lamps had been turned off in the bedroom, but light from the open bathroom door streamed across the polished marble floor and plush oriental rug. They rushed the room in precision, halting when they spotted Natalie Thorndike standing motionless on the other side of the sofa, her left side turned toward them.

Laurel had taken the left-hand position as they moved into the room, with Adam Heyes, the detail leader, to her right, and Tyrone to Adam's right. Adam said sharply, "Ma'am, are you—"

Then they saw that someone was lying on the floor in front of the first lady, someone with thick dark hair that had gone mostly gray: the president.

The next couple of seconds came in lightning-fast slices, as if time had become a strobe light.

Flash.

Mrs. Thorndike swung around, and that's when they saw the weapon in her hand.

Flash.

Laurel had a split-second, a frozen instant, to register the horrible blankness of the first lady's expression, then light flashed from the muzzle of the weapon and what had been only a "pop" from a distance was an endless blast of noise in the confines of the hotel room as the first lady fired and kept firing, her finger jerking on the trigger.

Flash.

A huge force slammed into Laurel, knocking her backward to the floor. On some distant level she knew she'd been shot, even recognized that she was dying.

Flash.

She had another of those split seconds of sharp awareness: Adam was down, too, sprawled beside her. Her dimming vision caught Tyrone's expression, set and grim, as he fired his own weapon.

Doing what he had to do.

Dear God, Laurel thought.

Maybe it was a prayer, maybe an expression of the horror she couldn't fully realize. There were no more flashes. She gave a small exhalation and quietly died.

THE ASSASSINATION OF the president by his own wife, and her subsequent death at the hands of the Secret Service when she opened fire on them, killing one of the agents in her own protective detail and wounding another, was almost too massive a blow for the national psyche to take in. The country as a whole was in shock, but the mechanism of government automatically kept moving. On the other side of the country, the vice-president, William Berry, was sworn into office almost before the news of the president's death hit the wire services. The military went on high alert, in case this was the beginning of a bigger attack, but gradually the pieces were put together to form a sordid picture.

The picture was literally a photograph, found in the first lady's luggage, of the president engaged in intimate relations with her own sister. Whitney Porter Leighton, four years younger than the first lady and a power in Washington in her own right, immediately went into seclusion. Her husband, Senator David Leighton, had no comment other than, "The president's death is a tragedy for the nation." He didn't file for divorce, but then no one in the know in the capital expected him to; regardless of the situation, his wife was still a member of the powerful Porter family, and he wasn't about to cut his political throat because the president had been banging his wife.

A few people wondered what had made the first lady snap, because the liaison wasn't exactly a secret and she had to have known about it for some time, but in the end it was decided that no one would ever know for certain.

Secret Service agent Laurel Rose was buried with honor, and her name immortalized among those others who had given their lives in the performance of their duties. Adam Heyes was severely wounded, his recovery taking months, and had to retire from the Service. After several months, the agent who had shot and killed the first lady, Tyrone Ebert, quietly resigned from the Service.

And the government ticked on, the wheels turning, the papers being shuffled, the computers humming.

Chapter One

IT WAS A normal morning. Lizette Henry—Liz to her co-workers, Liz or Lizzie to her friends, and once upon a time Zette-the-Jet to her family and childhood friends—rolled out of bed at her usual time of 5:59 A.M., one minute before her alarm was set to go off. In the kitchen, the automatic timer on the coffeemaker would have just started the brewing process. Yawning, Lizette went into her bathroom, turned on the water in the shower, then while the water was heating she took a desperately needed pee. By the time she was finished, the water in the shower was just right.

She liked starting her mornings off with a nice relaxing shower. She didn't sing, she didn't plan her day, she didn't worry about politics or the economy or anything else. While she was in the shower, she simply chilled—or more aptly, warmed.

On this particular June morning, her routine so honed and finely tuned she didn't need to look at a clock to know what time it was at any point during that routine, she showered for almost precisely how long it would take the coffeemaker to finish its brewing process, then wrapped a towel around her wet hair and dried herself with a second towel.

Though the open door of the bathroom, the wonderful aroma of the coffee called to her. The bathroom mirror was fogged over with steam, but it would be clear by the time she fetched her first cup of the morning. Wrapping herself in her knee-length terry-cloth robe, she went barefoot into the kitchen and grabbed one of the mugs from the cabinet. She liked her coffee sweet and light, so she added sugar and milk first, then poured the hot coffee into the mixture. It was like having a dessert first thing in the morning, which in her book was a nice way to start off any day.

She took the coffee with her into the bathroom, to sip while she blow-dried her hair and put on the small amount of makeup she wore to work.

Setting the cup on the vanity, she unwound the towel from her head and bent over from the waist, vigorously rubbing her shoulder-length dark brown hair. Then she straightened, tossing her hair back, and turned to the mirror—

—and stared into the face of a stranger.

The damp towel slid from her suddenly nerveless fingers, puddling on the floor at her feet.

Who was that woman?

It wasn't her. Lizette knew what she looked like, and this wasn't her reflection. She whirled wildly around, looking for the woman reflected in the mirror, ready to duck, ready to run, ready to fight for her life, but no one was there. She was alone in the bathroom, alone in the house, alone—

Alone.

The word whispered through her mind, a ghost of a sound, barely registering. Turning back to the mirror, she fought through confusion and terror, studying this new person as though she were an adversary rather than . . . rather than what? Or, *who*?

This didn't make sense. Her breathing came in swift,

shallow gulps, the sound distant and panicked. What the hell was going on? She didn't have amnesia. She knew who she was, where she was, remembered her childhood, her friends, what clothes were in her closet, and what she'd planned to wear today. She remembered what she'd had for dinner the night before. She remembered everything, it seemed—except that face.

It wasn't hers.

Her own features, what she saw in her mind, were softer, rounder, maybe even prettier, though the face she was looking at was attractive, if more angular. The eyes were the same: blue, the same distance apart, maybe a little more deeper set. How was that possible? How could her eyes have gotten more deep set?

What else was the same? She leaned closer to the mirror, looking for the faint freckle on the left side of her chin. Yes, there it was, where it had always been; darker when she'd been younger, almost invisible now, but still there.

Everything else was . . . wrong. This nose was thinner and more aquiline; her cheekbones more prominent, higher than they should have been; her jawline was more square, her chin more defined.

She was so completely befuddled and frightened that she stood there, paralyzed, incapable of any action even if one had occurred to her. She kept staring into the mirror, her thoughts darting around in search of any reasonable explanation.

There wasn't one. What could account for this? If she'd been in an accident and required massive facial restructuring, while she might not remember the accident itself, surely she'd remember afterward, know if she'd been in a hospital and undergone multiple surgeries, remembered the rehab; someone would have *told* her about everything, even if she'd been in a coma during her recovery. But she hadn't been in a coma. Ever.

She *remembered* her life. There hadn't been any accident, except for the one when she was eighteen that had killed her parents and turned her world completely upside down, but she hadn't been in the car; she'd dealt with the aftermath, with the crushing grief, the sense of floating untethered in the black space of her life with all of her former security gone in the space of a heartbeat.

She had that same feeling now, of such unfathomable *wrongness* that she didn't know what to do, couldn't take in all the meanings at once, couldn't grasp how fully this affected everything she knew.

Maybe she was crazy. Maybe she'd had a stroke during the night. Yes. A stroke; that would make sense, because it could screw with her memory. To test herself, she smiled, and in the mirror watched both sides of her mouth turn up evenly. In turn, she winked each eye. Then she held both arms up. They both worked, though after showering and washing her hair she thought she'd have already noticed if one of them hadn't.

"Ten, twelve, one, forty-two, eighteen," she whispered. Then she waited thirty seconds and said them again. "Ten, twelve, one, forty-two, eighteen." She was certain she'd said the same numbers, in the same sequence, though if she'd had a stroke would she be in any shape to judge?

Brain and body both appeared to be in working order, so that likely ruled out a stroke.

Now what?

Call someone. Who?

Diana. Of course. Her best friend would know, though Lizette wasn't certain how she could possibly phrase the question. *Hey, Di; when I get to work this morning, look at me and let me know if I have the same face today that I had yesterday, okay?*

The idea was ludicrous, but the need was compelling.

Lizette was already on her way to the phone when sudden panic froze her in midstep.

No.

She couldn't call anyone.

If she did, *they* would know.

They? Who was "*they*?"